DREXEL

THE OMEGA GROUP SERIES

DREXEL

The Omega Group Series

Eric P. Bishop

BruNoe Media Publishing

eBook ISBN-979-8-9917666-5-4

Paperback ISBN-979-8-9917666-6-1

Hardcover ISBN-979-8-9917666-7-8

Library of Congress Cataloging-in-Publication Identifiers: LCCN: 2025926523

Author Photo by Bruce Bishop Photos

Book Cover by Momir Borocki

Book Formatting by Atticus

First Edition January 2026

Printed in The United States of America

10 9 8 7 6 5 4 3 2 1

PRAISE FOR WORKS BY ERIC P. BISHOP

"Congratulations on the publication of THE BODY MAN! Looking forward to my signed copy."

--Jack Carr, #1 New York Times Bestselling Author

"In a crowded field of today's political thrillers, THE BODY MAN will keep you guessing until the final page."

--Don Bentley, New York Times Bestselling Author of Tom Clancy and Vince Flynn Series

"I loved THE BODY MAN! A taut, torn-from-the-pages thriller that takes readers into the world of secrets and power...packed with compelling characters who are so authentic I feel I've met them."

--Adam Hamdy, Sunday Times Bestselling Author

"THE BODY MAN is a spectacular political thriller!"

--Kashif Hussain, Best Thriller Books

"In a world of tired cliches, Eric has crafted the rip-roaring world with RAN-SOMED DAUGHTER. This novella is a pure shot of intellectual adrenaline!"

--John Guarnieri, Security Director, Former USSS

"With a keen eye for details and unmatched research, Eric P. Bishop is a rising star in the thriller genre!"

--Dr. Jason Piccolo, Author, Veteran, and Retired Federal Agent

"BABYLON WILL RISE is a gripping, fast-paced thriller!

--Fred Burton, NY Times Bestselling Author and Former Special Agent

"Bishop's writing is like watching a Netflix thriller!"

--F.X. Regan, Retired FBI Agent and Author

"His best work yet. Bishop knocks it out of the park! A proven leader in the thriller genre."

--Michael Carlson, Veteran and Author

DEDICATION

For all those who responded to the terrorist acts on 9/11
and the days that followed. True heroes.

Zechariah 14:12

Now this will be the plague with which the Lord
will strike all the people who have gone to war
against Jerusalem; their flesh will rot while they
stand on their feet, and their eyes will rot
in their sockets, and their tongue will rot in their mouth.

PROLOGUE

Philadelphia, Pennsylvania

April 8, 1994

A bead of sweat formed on Tony Mariano's temple and followed a deep wrinkle along his brow before it descended towards his square jawline. With brown eyes and a full head of dark hair, albeit with some graying at the temples, Tony's ethnicity was easy to trace from his facial features.

Behind Tony, in the booth seat of the sleeper cab, Special Agent in Charge Mark Cummings looked straight ahead. His eyes darted back and forth from the road to the structures that lined the pavement. Observance of details set Mark apart from ninety-nine percent of the general population. A trait perfectly suited for his chosen line of work. With his eyes ahead, he watched as the tiny bead of water made the trek down the side of Tony's face.

"You ok, Tony?" Mark asked.

Tony hesitated and replied with a slight stutter in his voice. "Um, yeah, of course."

Mark's response indicated he didn't believe him. "You look anxious," he replied.

"Nah, I'm good," Tony said. "Just another load. No worries."

The man riding in the passenger seat couldn't keep his mouth shut any longer.

"Don't let this paisano's facade fool you, Agent Cummings. He gets pretty worked up when we deliver these loads, and in fact, he popped four Imodium before we left DC."

"Luigi. Shut the big pie-hole you call a mouth," Tony said as his eyes narrowed and he shot a perturbed glance at his closest friend.

Mark smiled. The constant banter started soon after loading up at the Hoover building and never let up. These two could give Abbott and Costello a run for their money.

Luigi DiDomenico responded by sticking his middle finger in the air towards Tony.

"How have you two not killed each other so far?" Mark asked.

Tony grunted, "Trust me, the thought has crossed my mind once or twice. Off the record, of course, and I know you feds don't encourage that type of behavior."

"Hey. I didn't hear a thing," said Mark. "Hear no evil, see no evil, speak no evil."

A familiar voice in Mark's earpiece broke the banter. He cupped a hand over his right ear and listened to the instructions that followed. "Two miles ahead, we take exit 22," Mark stated as he removed his hand from his ear.

"Got it," Tony said as his fingers gripped the wheel tighter and his eyes focused on the road in front of him with a renewed purpose.

⋯⋯⋯◆⋯⋯⋯

The convoy took the Independence Hall off-ramp. Sixty seconds till visual. Muhammad Jarah heard the words in his earpiece. "Copy that," Muhammad replied as he lay prone on the rooftop of a building at 5th and Market. He wore all black and blended into the shadows. Above, the full moon shone without a cloud in the night sky. It was 2:45 am, and the crisp air revealed a hint of fall. A welcome relief after several humid nights.

From his vantage point atop the eleventh story, Muhammad had an unobstructed view down the length of 6th Street. As he peered through the Leica

Duovid binoculars, he stared intently for his mark and waited for the motorcade to come into view. "It's time," he said. The comm unit broadcast his command to the others on his team.

A moment later, Muhammad watched as the lead Suburban emerged into his line of sight and proceeded down 6th Street. His pulse quickened as the grip on the binoculars tightened, and his eyes remained fixated on the second vehicle, the tractor-trailer.

The convoy of vehicles approached Race Street in a single line evenly spaced.

"Youssef," Muhammad said into the microphone clasped to the collar of his shirt.

"Yes," came the reply in his earpiece.

"Proceed on my mark."

"Understood," Youssef replied.

Time slowed as the five vehicles made their way down 6th Street. Muhammad's eyes narrowed as his mind ran through scenarios one after the other. He knew the hastily organized plan would be challenging to pull off, but not impossible. After all, his years fighting in the arid climate of the desert taught him nothing was impossible, and victory only came to the warriors who persevered.

◆◇◆

Tony let off the gas to give more space between his rig and the lead Suburban ahead of him. As they approached the Arch Street intersection, Luigi reached over, tapped him on the arm, and pointed towards the left side of the road up ahead.

"Yo, Tony, that's the Liberty Bell Center where they keep the actual bell."

Tony's lips curled. "Yeah, so? Everybody knows the bell is here."

"Well, you ever seen it?" Luigi asked.

"Nah. I've passed by Philly a bunch but never came downtown. Maybe we should stick around for a few days. You know, play tourists. We can tell the wives we got held up. Course, if we do, we're gonna have to decide between Geno's or Pat's."

"I'm game for that," Luigi said before he turned around in his seat. "You ever been to Philly, Agent Cummings?"

Mark nodded. "Yes, many times." His eyes scanned the area, looking for any threats or things out of the ordinary. He was in the zone, fully alert while also cognizant of the conversation going on.

"Worth a visit?" Luigi asked.

"Absolutely," Mark nodded. "And for what it's worth, forget Geno's or Pats. They're nothing more than tourist traps. If you want a real authentic Philly cheesesteak, go to Sonny's."

"Well, now you're making me hungry," Luigi said.

"You're always ready to eat, fat ass," Tony replied.

Mark pointed straight ahead. "We're approaching Chestnut and 6th. One more block to Sansom and then make a right."

Tony nodded, "Gotcha."

The distance between the tractor-trailer and the lead support vehicle grew as they proceeded down 6th Street, with the space between them and the lead vehicle more than Mark would have liked. He pointed forward. "Speed up, Tony, close the gap, please."

⚓

"Go now." Muhammad gave the command from his perch overlooking Independence National Historic Park. The NODS he wore gave him a grainy picture of the sprawling park below.

Those two words set not only the dump truck in motion but also a garbage truck and six armored SUVs. Most of his team had snuck into the country over the past weeks from various Middle Eastern countries. As expected, the United States border proved porous, with immigration and customs at some national airports no better than a joke. With very little coaching, his team entered with ease.

Over a dozen of the men entered on student visas, while a few already lived in the United States as part of sleeper cells in place for several years. Muhammad recruited the men from wherever he could find them to complete the mission. With more advance notice, he would've gathered more men, better equipped for such a task. Given his druthers, he would have preferred to bring over his own trusted fighters who were engaged in jihad on multiple continents, but there just wasn't enough time.

Muhammad's body tensed as adrenaline and norepinephrine surged through his bloodstream. His heart raced, and he felt the rhythmic beat as it pulsated against the flat rooftop. Recognizing the hormonal change, he worked to control his breathing and lower not only his heart rate but also his blood pressure. With several slow, deep gulps of cool air, he felt his tension decrease. Also, his body responded to the increase in stress by releasing cortisol, which aided in lowering his anxiety.

He shifted the optics back and forth from the convoy to the intersection where the strike would take place. The seconds seemed like minutes as he ran through scenarios, much like a chess player orchestrating future moves around the board in search of the elusive checkmate.

"Allahu Akbar," the last words slipped off his tongue as a solemn prayer to Allah and motivation for his men. Many of whom sped to their imminent demise.

⚬

Mark knew from years of experience there were two ways to protect the contents inside the semi.

Bigger is better or *lighter and tighter*.

After months of planning, the powers that be chose the latter.

Anyway, rolling up with dozens of vehicles screamed, *Look at me*. And the FBI preferred discretion, or, when possible, invisibility.

The convoy comprised a lead vehicle, the tractor-trailer, and three support vehicles, including a Special Reaction Team (SRT) vehicle. A Bell 407 helicopter from the FBI Tactical Helicopter Unit hovered above and provided air support for their movements while staying in constant contact with the command center in DC.

As the lead Suburban passed through the intersection at 6th and Chestnut, Tony's semi still lagged.

Mark noticed the garbage truck parked on the right side of the street, just past the intersection.

His mind screamed, *Warning, warning*, just as the vehicle suddenly moved forward and pulled out, cutting them off from the lead vehicle while blocking the roadway.

Tony saw the movement ahead and slammed hard on the brakes to keep from hitting the garbage truck.

Inside the cab, the three men lurched forward as the semi shuddered violently, struggling to slow. Brake pads ground into the rotors and screeched as the rig came to a stop with a final jerk. The cab made it through the intersection and just missed the garbage truck by a few feet as the trailer stuck out and blocked the intersection. A burning stench from the red-hot brakes made its way inside the cab, which aggravated their throats.

Tony yelled out in frustration and threw his arms into the air.

"What the hell is this assho…"

Stopped in mid-word, a round pierced the windshield with a pop and split Tony's forehead open. The contents of his head blew out of the gaping hole created as the bullet mushroomed and exited the back of his skull with the velocity of a bolt of lightning.

Luigi turned his head just in time to watch the bullet impact. He screamed, but as the shrill sound left his mouth, a second round punctured the glass and silenced him alongside his best friend.

Special Agent in Charge Cummings, now splattered with bone fragments, brain matter, and blood from both men, reacted without hesitation.

He dove for cover on the floor behind Tony's seat while yelling into his comms, "Shots fired, I repeat, shots fired."

A third round passed through the window and struck the booth seat where Mark sat a second before. Pressed as close to the ground as he could, Mark's mind raced. *What the hell is going on?*

An instant later, the dump truck loaded down with tons of gravel barreled through the intersection. It struck the trailer broadside with a screeching sound as metal struck metal. The impact of the crash ripped the trailer from the cab and tore open the metal trailer frame like a can opener slicing through a piece of flimsy aluminum.

The cab dislodged from the trailer with a violent shudder as it went airborne, and the three bodies inside the rig flew into the air like rag dolls thrust into zero gravity.

For Special Agent in Charge Mark Cummings, it all went black as his head smacked against a hard surface with a dull thud.

The rig rolled over several times and came to a stop atop the red brick pavers in front of Independence Hall.

⚬

Muhammad watched the dump truck strike the semi broadside at almost forty miles an hour as the front of the vehicle crumpled when it came in contact with two state-of-the-art Mosler safes. The impact killed the driver while the momentum from the crash caused the two safes to careen through the opposite side of the trailer. The safe closest to the rear of the trailer somersaulted through the thin metal, slicing through it like a sharp blade. After turning over several times, it came to rest upside down, leaning against the brick wall and black wrought-iron fence that led to the Liberty Bell Center.

Taking the brunt of the strike, the other safe, positioned in the middle of the trailer, careened out and rolled down Chestnut Street. Flipping end over end, the enormous safe pulverized the bricks beneath each time it somersaulted. With a loud crash, it came to rest upright, several feet short of the George Washington statue before Independence Hall.

Muhammad watched as six armored SUVs arrived within seconds. During the proceeding days, Muhammad reiterated to his men that time was against them and they must hurry. Delays and poor execution would cause failure. He made it clear establishing a perimeter was essential to breach the safes and remove the contents before reinforcements arrived.

He turned his attention to the lead FBI Suburban which came to a halt at 6th and Sansom. Muhammad watched with a touch of amusement as the steel panel on the side of the garbage truck slid open, revealing the M134 minigun. The FBI agents, unaware of their impending doom, jumped out of the vehicle with weapons raised. They moved in a tight formation towards the chaotic scene of mangled debris that littered the crash site.

The sight of the mini gun stopped them in their tracks, but it was too late. Exposed in the center of the street with no cover, the six men in kevlar with assault rifles stood no chance against six thousand rounds per minute of searing hot lead. Within seconds, the minigun mowed down the agents with its deadly barrage.

A second minigun positioned on the other side of the garbage truck intended to fire on the trailing vehicles. However, an axel from the destroyed trailer rested against the side of the vehicle and blocked the door from sliding open.

One team down, three more to go, Muhammad muttered to himself as he watched the bloodbath below. So far, everything progressed mostly as planned. The thirty men under his direction arrived and climbed out of the SUV's, and took up defensive positions around the two safes while using their vehicles as cover.

Muhammad made a career of fighting alongside his men in some of the most god-forsaken places on earth. Rarely did his new recruits last long on the battle-fields, but as the men formed a perimeter, he found himself impressed with how well they followed instructions. Not having the second minigun left them at a tactical disadvantage, but he knew complications would arise.

The Bell 407 helicopter circled high above, its rotor wash picked up fine granules of dirt from the roof, which blew into his eyes. Once the helicopter maintained a steady altitude, the side doors opened on both sides as two snipers took up offensive positions.

They could pick off his men with ease, but Muhammad couldn't let that happen.

He pulled off his optics and moved a few feet to his right. The metal box had three latches, which he opened in a few seconds. He hoisted the thirty-three-and-a-half-pound cylindrical tube atop his shoulders and flipped the sights in place. It took less than a minute from the time he moved until he had the helicopter zeroed in. He activated his S&A switch and waited until he had good tone before he pulled back on the trigger. The launcher jerked enough to make him shuffle his feet to keep steady. The missile left the tube and streaked through the air at two and a half times the speed of sound as it tracked towards the helicopter and the four FBI agents inside.

The poor bastards never stood a chance.

⸻◆⸻

Rapid gunfire erupted all around like a cacophony of terror as Mark regained consciousness with a shudder. His head felt like two oversized hands belonging to Andre the Giant encircled his skull and squeezed it like a vice. Warm, thick blood oozed from a large gash on his temple and flowed down the bridge of his nose, finding its way into his agape mouth. He tried to open his eyes, but they felt sewn shut. A deafening explosion from above jostled him, and for a moment it felt like he was once again a nineteen-year-old member of the 1st Marine Division fighting in Huế during the Tet offensive.

He summoned the strength and finally after a few seconds that felt more like minutes, his eyes reluctantly opened. With several rapid-fire blinks, his eyes squinted allowing him to focus.

Carnage greeted Mark all around.

As he strained his neck looking up and to his left, he saw bodies wrapped in black tactical uniforms with the letters *F.B.I.* littered down 6th Street towards

Sansom. It was clear from their grotesque positions and missing limbs the men from the lead Suburban were all dead.

Next, he turned his head to the right. Less than one-hundred feet away, the mangled fuselage of the FBI Tactical Helicopter looked like a bonfire as it lay ablaze with smoke billowing from the wreckage.

As he looked around he realized the cab came to rest upside down. Between the bright moon above and the well-positioned street lights, he could clearly see the men surrounding the two exposed safes. Other men approached with what looked like wands in their hands. A moment later reddish and orange colored flames spat out of the end as sparks bounced off the red pavers in an endless display of dazzling lights.

They're gonna try and burn through the hinges. Blinking several times, he rubbed his forearm over his brow to keep the blood from flowing in his eyes.

The earpiece in his right ear came alive as several of his men frantically called out for help. With his tactical team in trouble, his pulse raced and his eyes narrowed. In a low voice to avoid unwanted attention, he replied using his own comm unit. After several failed attempts at reaching the men, it became clear the microphone was inoperable.

Dammit. I need to reach my guys. He had a problem though. Mark knew he was trapped.

Spread out before him were twenty men launching a coordinated attack against his men. Some of them moved in a choppy, novice manners while others displayed confidence and experience as they took cover and returned fire when fired upon.

Mark needed a way to reach his men. As his eyes darted back and forth, his brain formulated a plan. His Colt M4 carbine lay just out of reach, but with a quick glance, he could see its muzzle was bent. With an inoperable barrel, the weapon was nothing more than an overpriced stick.

As he reached towards his hip the reassuring bulge of his Glock 23 brought him some measure of comfort. He wrapped his large hands around the butt of the pistol as he drew it from the holster. His thumb pushed the mag release dropping it into his left hand. Racking the slide, he ejected the chambered round and inspected his weapon. Confident the weapon was serviceable he placed the round back into the mag and slid it back. With two more mags on his hip, Mark knew he had 45 rounds at his disposal.

That was it. Not enough to take on the vast array of men before him, but hopefully enough to make an escape from the cab.

With the relentless automatic fire, it would be risky exposing himself and abandoning the cover but he also knew staying put would offer no help to his team. Plus, someone may see him sooner rather than later and then his ass would be grass anyway.

With few good options, he made the only logical move. Taking a deep breath, he lunged out of the mangled cab with his weapon drawn looking for targets. His knees burned and ached as glass embedded in his skin during the crash tore deeper into his flesh with each long stride.

⸎

Muhammad abandoned his rooftop perch as soon as the chopper went down and descended the northeast staircase to the main level and exit. Once outside, he stayed low to the ground and reduced his profile as much as possible. As he moved around the east side of the Liberty Bell Center, he made his way toward 6th and Chestnut keeping close to the brick wall using it as cover. With his NODS flipped down, he saw the surroundings clearly. The relief in downing the helicopter was short lived with the mission success far from guaranteed. Running a few minutes behind he needed to push his team and provide extra motivation.

A sudden movement to his left caught his attention. A figure darted from the overturned semi-rig. The dark silhouette moved fast, and Muhammad only made out the white letters on the person's back as they ran down 6th Street. Raising his assault rifle, he knew he must stop whoever was fleeing the crash site. Suddenly, a volley of bullets sprayed around him, striking the bricks just above his head.

The mysterious figure saw him first.

Dropping to the ground, Muhammad low-crawled ten feet to a retaining wall, which provided limited cover. Rolling onto his back, he counted to five and twisted his body as he raised himself to his elbows to return fire.

He steadied himself and pulled back on the trigger, sending a steady stream of bullets towards the target. The person in the FBI jacket disappeared into the darkened recesses further down 6th Street before any of the rounds found their mark. Muhammad slammed his clenched fist into the ground, knowing whoever it was had just escaped.

Mark didn't wait to see if his rounds hit the darkened figure. Running at full speed, he reached Sansom Street and took a hard right as several bullets struck the wall eight feet to his left.

Damn, that was close. It killed him as he ran by the bodies of his fallen brothers without stopping. However, he knew failure to meet up with the rest of his men would cause more deaths. He needed to get into the fight, stay in the fight, and see the mission through to the end.

In a flat-out sprint, he reached the intersection of Sansom Street and took a right on 7th heading north. He knew crossing back over Chestnut would be perilous, but he had no choice if he wanted to connect with his team. Without pause, he dug deep and gained speed as he crossed Chestnut. With long, powerful strides he made it across the street, relieved to find no bullets tear into his flesh. In fact, the constant barrage of automatic weapon fire appeared to have abated slightly once he left 6th Street.

In his early 50's Mark was in better shape than most twenty-five-year-olds. Still, he rarely ran with such fervor and never for his life or the lives of his men. As he approached Ranstead Street, he knew there were only two more right turns.

With his comms down, he knew sneaking up on his tactical team would have dire results for himself. Pulling out his flashlight, he slowed slightly and rounded the corner of Ranstead and 6th Street, using the beam of light to signal his approach.

Will Jacobs was the first of his men to see the beams of light and know they were from a friendly. Once Mark got close enough, Will pulled him towards his cover spot behind a thick wall on the west side of the Liberty Bell Center.

"You okay, SAC?" Will asked as he looked hard at Mark. "Thought you were a goner when they lit up that rig."

"Me too," Mark replied as he shook his head, fully out of breath.

"These bastards mowed down the lead team."

"I know," Mark said between gasps of air.

"Glad you made it," Will replied.

"Who the hell are these guys?"

Will shrugged his shoulders. "Not sure, but they're operating at high speed, low drag. These guys are pretty damn good and well-armed. They've got enough firepower to fight off a small army."

"Well, let's send them to hell where they belong. I need an assault rifle, NODS, and a new comm unit. Mine got busted up in the crash." Mark spat a gob of phlegm onto the ground.

Will passed a spare H&K MP5 and four fresh mags.

"Cocked, locked, and ready to rock, boss." Next, Will removed and reached into the backpack he wore, pulling out a spare NODS and comm unit.

Mark slipped on the night vision goggles and watched his men, their positions, and how they moved. The lack of movement by his team troubled him. Pinned down, his men appeared immobile.

Not good, not good at all.

His men were the best in the business, to be sure, but he quickly ascertained their fatal flaw. They were playing defense, and he knew that to turn the tide they needed to go on the offensive.

And fast.

"Thanks," Mark said as he patted Will on the shoulder. He clicked the safety off and verified a round was chambered. "Let's end this."

"What do you need me to do?" Will asked.

"Find Higgins. We need him sniping from on top of the Liberty Bell Center. I'll give him further instructions when he's in place."

Will nodded. "Copy that." Then he scurried off to his left, leaving Mark to hastily map out their next move.

⸺◆⸺

Muhammad found himself pinned down. Apparently, his movements caught several FBI agent's attention, and they took turns taking pot shots at him as he dove for cover which slowed his pace tremendously. However, his many years of fighting overseas taught him several tricks of the trade.

Standing up quickly, he fell just as fast a mere second before a round ripped through the sky close enough for him to feel the ripple as the bullet buzzed past his head. Landing behind a large stone planter, he played dead like a possum. Apparently, the ploy worked, and the agents believed they scored a kill and moved on. He waited a few minutes before he continued towards his team working on the safe against the brick wall that led to the Liberty Bell Center.

As he arrived and assessed the progress, it appeared they would cut through the massive hinges within three to four minutes. Their progress, while delayed, was impressive given how many men they lost. Casualties were mounting faster than Muhammad would have liked, but there was nothing he could do about that now. The mission would either succeed or fail.

With the team closest to him working frantically, he moved on to link up with the second team working on the other safe near Independence Hall. The other safe was about seventy-five feet away, and again he moved methodically. There was too little cover as he plodded his way to the other safe. The firefight picked up, and he dodged bullets all the way. One bullet ricocheted off the stone paver before him and nicked his thigh. Reaching for the wound, he found the bullet passed through and through, but it still hurt like hell.

Two minutes later he arrived at the other safe. The team fell behind and experienced mechanical issues with several of the torches. Screaming commands at a rapid-fire pace, he put the fear of Allah in the men, and they quickly got back on track.

Then it happened.

Even as far away as he was the intense heat from the explosion made his face feel flushed as the moisture evaporated from his skin in an instant. It appeared a sharpshooter hit both tanks within less than a second, amplifying the explosion and killing more men than he could spare. Reinforcements were running thin, but he knew they had to try. Muhammad's employer would not settle for failure, and he didn't intend to find out what consequences anything less than success might produce.

Moving away from the second safe, he needed to rally his few remaining men to the first safe and finish the task. Time was slipping through his fingertips, and if he didn't crack open the safes in the next few minutes, the FBI tactical unit would have the upper hand. He couldn't allow that.

Staying low, he moved away from the second safe. Suddenly, twenty feet down Chestnut Street, it happened again, and another explosion occurred behind him. The shock wave sent him somersaulting through the air until he landed on his back, staring up into the sky. His ears rang, and the hair on the back of his head was singed from the fireball that ensued. The force of the blast tore apart every man near the second safe.

Muhammad gasped for air, and his lungs breathed in a mixture of smoke laced with toxic chemicals. His head swirled as he realized he was down to his last few men. The reality of failure hung over him like a thick fog. His mind worked logically, unlike many of his brethren, who acted like die-hard zealots and gave every last drop of blood even for a losing cause.

Muhammad was no coward, as he would give his life for the right reason. But this wasn't one of them. He knew the safes that his team failed to crack weren't worth his slaughter. Besides, he had a plan worked out in case this contingency arose. Plans always required contingencies, and his attention to detail saved his ass more times than he could count over the course of his lifetime.

———◄O►———

Mark watched as the men working on the second safe blew apart. Higgins followed his instructions perfectly and hit the fuel sources that powered the exothermic torches. He knew his tactical team had the upper hand and they could finish it within a matter of minutes. The sporadic gunfire revealed several fighters remained alive, and Mark figured his men would change that with one last offensive push.

Using a pre-determined word, Mark yelled, "Geronimo, Geronimo, Geronimo," in rapid succession. His men knew what that meant and abandoned their cover while converging on the remaining fighters gathered at the base of the four steps that led to Independence Hall.

Mark joined his men with Will at his side as they sprinted down 6th Street toward Chestnut. With weapons raised, they fired at anything that moved, delivering fatal blows to the few fighters who remained.

Mark emptied the first mag, released it and slammed another one into the carbine as he scanned for another target.

———◄O►———

Muhammad scurried past the bodies of his men that littered the paver stones along Chestnut. Suddenly, a hand grabbed his ankle, almost tripping him. As Muhammad looked down, his eyes connected with a man covered in crimson blood.

"Muhammad." The word from the dying man uttered as a gurgle of blood oozed from his mouth. Fear was evident in his eyes. "Help me," he pleaded.

"Assalamu alaykum." Muhammad spoke the two words in a tone devoid of emotion.

He pointed his weapon and fired a single round from his 45-caliber pistol into the man's forehead.

Muhammad made his way along the front of Independence Hall without being detected. Taking a right onto South 5th Street, he traveled one block to Library Street, where earlier he left an old silver BWM 5 Series. Once inside the safety of the German vehicle, he allowed himself to take a deep breath before he pulled out a shiny, metallic device from the glove box.

As he turned the ignition, and the car left the scene, he pressed the red button in his right hand without a second thought.

Muhammad would live to fight another day.

As he should.

———◇———

Bullets flew past Mark and his team as they rushed the remaining gunmen. The four badly injured fighters stood huddled behind two armored SUVs in front of Independence Hall, with each man taking potshots at the approaching tactical team.

It all happened in slow motion. Mark could almost see their attack from above as if he were having an out-of-body experience. Each footfall echoed from the paver stones, while each breath seemed exaggerated and drawn out. The last twenty feet seemed to take minutes when in fact only seconds passed.

Mark and his fellow FBI agents laid down a relentless barrage of bullets that riddled the quarter panel of the SUV's leaving pockmarks along the armored plating.

Mark had never felt so alive than he did at that exact moment. Adrenaline pumped through his veins like a drug.

We got em'. The thought as he and his men reached the rear of the vehicle proved to be his last.

The intense heat from the shock wave blew the rear windows out first, splintering the glass, which flew in thousands of jagged pieces into the night sky in every direction. Next, the heavy, armor-plated rear doors flew open as the force of the explosion ripped them off their hinges and propelled them into the air. The rear of the vehicle disintegrated as the deadly RDX ignited releasing nitrogen and carbon dioxide into the atmosphere at 26,550 feet per second.

It all happened in a millisecond.

Mark's brain registered the heat, his body yanked off the ground by the shock wave and into the air. His mind didn't even have time to question what was happening. Before he could react, the concussive force tore his body apart and an intense darkness enveloped his sight while a sudden silence filled his ears.

Forty-five minutes later, the director of the FBI walked through the scene of the carnage with his deputy director to the right of him.

Already yellow-numbered plastic evidence a-frame indicators littered the brick pavers in every direction. With the stench of death in the air, the Director covered his mouth with a white handkerchief. He carefully stepped around countless body parts and pools of blood.

As they moved forward, two forklifts righted one safe.

"Any idea who did this?" The director looked at his deputy. A look of frustration mixed with anger clearly displayed across his wrinkled, aged face.

"We can't be sure, but initial indications point to Islamic terrorists."

The director shook his head. None of it made any sense. "This entire operation was classified above Top Secret. So how the hell did they know about the safes?"

"It would appear we have a leak, sir," the deputy director replied in a measured tone.

The director shook his head in disgust. "How many men did we lose?"

"Twenty-three confirmed dead. Plus, several in critical condition."

"What about the safes?" The director asked. "This location is clearly compromised."

"I agree. We'll bring them back to the Hoover Building for the time being."

"Security detail?"

The deputy director nodded. "Every agent we have available will be part of the escort back to DC."

"And then what?"

"We need the contents housed in a new secure location as soon as possible, sir."

The director raised his eyebrows. "Suggestions?"

"You know the site I originally recommended," the deputy director replied.

"The one the president ultimately decided against?"

"Yes, that's the one."

"Well, I agreed with the president at the time. Plus, I thought having the contents here in Philly seemed poetic."

"I still think the other site was a better choice, sir."

"Even after the attack last year?" The director asked.

"Actually, it's because of the attack last year that I recommended that location. The fourteen-acre plot is now one of the most secure pieces of land in our nation. I advise you bring the location back up with the president."

"But what if there's another attack?"

"Please," the deputy director shook his head, "That's impossible."

CHAPTER ONE

DREXEL, IDAHO

7 YEARS LATER, SEPTEMBER 2001

Troy Evans felt the steady rhythm of his heartbeat as he paused mid-stride. A distinct scratching sound seized his attention as he stood still and listened. The sound faded, and he strained his ears for several minutes, hoping to hear the sound again.

The scratching noise didn't return, and only the constant chirping of crickets filled the void. Troy continued the trek and only came to a stop when he reached the bottom of a ladder. It took five minutes at a steady pace from where the trailhead split off the main dirt road to where he stopped. Besides the crickets and the mysterious sound, he heard his own footfalls on the trail as the brittle leaves crumbled beneath his well-worn boots.

Darkness engulfed him as dawn was still thirty minutes away. As he paused at the base of the ladder and looked around in every direction. Certain he was alone, he slung the rifle over his shoulder and pulled it tight to his body. He reached up to the fifth ladder rung and lifted himself up. The faded green-colored metal made an audible groan with his full weight bearing upon it.

Each rung was a foot apart, with fifteen in total from the ground to the weathered platform high above. Troy's muscular arms allowed him to climb the ladder with ease. As he reached the top, he grabbed the bar above and pulled himself onto the platform in one smooth motion.

Next, he adjusted the old, soiled, FBI cap, which rarely left his head, and covered his thick, unkempt dark hair. With a tug, he pulled it low around his eyebrows. His hand brushed against the Colt 1911 .45 caliber pistol that hung on his right hip, and he drew in a deep breath of crisp air. The wooden planks that made up the platform floor creaked as he took a step towards the tree trunk and the mounted stool.

Troy looked out at the moonlit field that stretched out from the edge of the trees. Surrounded by thick grand fir trees, a babbling brook ran from east to west and split the rectangular-shaped field in half. Shadows covered much of the expanse in long, thin strips like fingers as the towering trees blocked the light from the almost full moon that hung low in the night sky.

With a quick, experienced motion, Troy pulled the bolt back and then forward on his Remington .308 rifle. The round glided effortlessly into the well-oiled chamber. With the weapon hot, he set the safety to the "on" position and placed the barrel of the weapon on the steel padded bar that served as a brace. He pulled the butt of the rifle close to his shoulder and held it taut.

His right eye focused on the lens of the scope, and with his left hand, he adjusted the power selector ring to achieve the correct magnification. A large rock in the center of the field near the brook served as his sight line. From his vantage point high in the stand, he could see even the slightest movements on the field below.

Troy glanced down at his watch.

Any minute now.

Without a doubt, the target was coming, and when he did, Troy would be ready. Time passed quickly as his head methodically moved from left to right while his eyes scanned the field and surrounding tree line.

Troy recognized the subtle signs of dawn as the moon faded away into the vast sky above, overshadowed by the sun as it stretched across the sky in magnificent beams of crimson. On the horizon, the outline of mountains materialized.

He slowed down his breathing and made sure not to move unless absolutely necessary. Any sound he made would give away his position.

Noises caught Troy's attention as dawn approached. Birds swooped and glided from one tree branch to another as nature began its daily dance and retreated once more from another night of slumber. Squirrels rustled and scurried through the tree branches as warm sun rays spread throughout the forest.

After several minutes, Troy recognized the sound that brought him out into the chilly morning air. The hair on the back of his neck rose ever so slightly. Troy's ears focused on that one sound and blocked out all others. His pulse rose, and his focus narrowed.

Movements on the right side of the field drew his attention. Several tense seconds passed as a head emerged from the thick brush that served as a perfect concealment. With cautious steps, one leg moved before the other as the target emerged from the safety of the woods.

A set of big brown eyes looked out towards the wide field. With intentional movements, the creature crept slowly out of the safety provided by the woods and towards the flowing brook.

Seventy-five yards away, Troy watched the delicate dance unfold. The magnified crosshairs never left her neck as the doe proceeded into the open.

Troy waited and watched. His finger pointed straight ahead on the cool steel; the oils of his skin rubbed off the finish from that spot years back from constant use.

Come on, baby. Where's your man?

Halfway to the brook, the doe came to a sudden stop. In a slow manner, she turned her head towards the tree line.

Troy watched her eyes and maneuvered his weapon to the right. He saw it and sighed.

Wrong man.

A small, delicate fawn emerged from the forest canopy. With unsteady movements, the fawn made its way across the field and towards its mother. The barrel of Troy's rifle didn't follow. Instead, he kept the scope dialed to where the doe and fawn emerged.

The doe waited for the fawn as both proceeded to the brook and lapped up the icy mountain water. After several minutes, the doe led the fawn over to the thick clusters of oats that covered the ground. The doe gave constant glances towards the tree line. Troy knew it was only a matter of time.

Time slowed as Troy noticed several branches tremble. A dark shadow lurked within the recesses of the forest. In one smooth motion, Troy's index finger moved from its forward position and gripped the trigger while his left hand reached up and switched the safety indicator to the off position.

Troy waited as the buck emerged from its concealment afforded by the forest.

The buck moved with guarded steps, placing one hoof forward. After a pause, he stepped once more. Troy placed the crosshairs squarely on the neck and turned his attention to the rack on the buck's head. His heart rate increased as he counted the fourteen points and guessed the spread was at least twenty-four inches.

Pops is gonna be pissed he missed this hunt.

He focused on controlling his breath and calming himself as his father taught him since he was a boy.

As the buck took several more steps into the wide-open field, he paused and looked towards the doe and fawn.

Troy's opportunity arrived.

With the crosshairs locked on the thick neck, Troy exhaled all the breath in his lungs and pulled back on the trigger slowly but in a firm manner. With a forceful recoil, the gun snapped back into his shoulder as the firing pin struck the shell. Before the buck could react to the cracking sound of the weapon's discharge, his neck exploded as a mist of red sprayed into the crisp morning air.

The beast teetered for a split second and then dropped to the ground. The precise shot severed the spinal cord, and death came instantaneously. A rare feat even for an experienced marksman like Troy. Without hesitation, he chambered another round.

As soon as the buck landed on the ground, Troy spun around on the stool towards his left where the doe and fawn rapidly fled.

Within a second Troy had the racing doe in his crosshairs, but instead of firing he removed his finger from the trigger and watched as both the doe and fawn took the last few strides through the open field. An instant later, the doe and fawn disappeared into the forest within seconds.

Could have had her too.

A few seconds passed, and Troy leaned back against the bark of the tree.

Shivers ran through his body as he came down from the adrenaline rush. He sat for a moment and considered the shot. It played back in his mind like a movie in slow motion. After a couple minutes, he stood up, slung his rifle over his shoulder and climbed down the ladder.

He reached the ground and crossed the field toward the buck. A euphoric feeling filled his mind as he took each step into the wide-open space.

As Troy stood over his kill, he leaned over the exquisite creature, reached down and gently patted it. Next, he closed his eyes and gave thanks for the food the buck would provide during the coming winter. With a full freezer and a nice rack, most men couldn't ask for much more. He couldn't wait to get back to the house and call Pops.

Troy's father Matt, whom he lovingly called Pops, taught him everything he knew about guns and hunting.

We eat what we shoot and vow to treat the animals we kill with the utmost care and respect, his father told him when he gave Troy his first gun at seven. Troy never forgot his father's words.

Most days they hunted together, but an early morning conference call with headquarters on the east coast kept Matt from joining Troy today.

Troy moved the buck to the tree line, used the rope he carried and hanged the animal to get it off the ground. Next, he followed the trail leading back to the road. Troy arrived at his four-wheeler and started the engine. In the distance, a new sound caught his attention. The knocking sound of an engine headed in his direction drowned out the low idle of the ATV.

A minute later his mom's powder blue Ford F-150 pickup truck raced around the bend of the dirt road. The vehicle came to a hard stop next to him, causing a cloud of dust to fill the air with small particles.

Troy turned his head briefly and waved his hand to keep the cloud out of his face.

As he looked back a distressed look covered his mother Amy's face as she rolled down the window.

"Get in the truck, Troy."

Troy approached the driver's side door and placed his hand on the doorframe. His mother's tone concerned him. "What is it?" He asked.

"You need to come home right now. Something has happened."

Troy's stomach tightened as he thought of the only thing that could strike fear in his mom's eyes. "Is it Pops?"

She shook her head, but her eyes betrayed her words as they revealed deep within that something horrific had occurred. "Your father's fine."

Considering his father's line of work, Troy never knew if the day would come when or if they would get, *The call*.

Troy ran around the front of the truck and to the passenger door. He pulled it open and jumped inside.

His mom put the truck in gear and backed it up.

"If Pops is okay, then what's going on? What's do you look so freaked out, Mom?"

Her mouth opened, but she paused, and no words came out for several seconds. When she found her voice, the tone rose an octave and slightly cracked.

"Troy. My love, our country is under attack," she said as a stream of tears rolled down her pinkish-hued cheeks.

Chapter Two

London, England

Waleed bin Abdulah was born in Saudi Arabia to the House of Saud. From birth, he lived a life of privilege and extreme wealth, knowing nothing of hardships or struggles. While some enter life with a silver spoon firmly implanted in their mouths, Waleed's was made of pure gold. Educated at the finest schools money could buy, he completed both his undergraduate and MBA at Harvard University. Unlike most graduates who struggle with their next steps, Waleed faced no such hardship. He received seed money totaling fifty million dollars provided to him by Prince Rajhi bin Abdulah, his father. Waleed used the money and formed his own corporation, aptly named Abdulah Worldwide Incorporated (AWI) the summer he graduated from Harvard.

The business flourished from the first day his posh office opened on Brompton Road in London, and like many other Saudi businessmen, Waleed possessed the Midas touch. His lucrative business interests spanned investment services, commercial real estate, and even media companies. But his bread and butter came from the world's largest global freight business. His cargo ships traversed the globe day and night, transporting goods through the busiest ports.

Part of the one percent elite, Waleed's net worth reached into the billions before he turned thirty. The wealth he amassed afforded him conveniences most people only dreamed of, including several private jets and over a dozen residences worldwide. His primary home, in the exclusive Knightsbridge area of London, was on South Carriage Drive at Hyde Park. The home, built in the early twentieth century, started as a six-story apartment building until Waleed bought the property in the late 1980's and gutted the entire building. He turned all six stories into a luxurious home valued at over one-hundred-million USD dollars.

By all outward appearances, Waleed appeared content with his extravagant, over-the-top life. But there was much more to Waleed than on the surface. A darker side lay just below the personable façade, and few outside his inner circle truly knew him.

Waleed's life served as a contradiction. He lived a lifestyle surrounded by un-thinkable wealth, yet those closest to him believed he was a deeply devout Muslim who railed against the arrogance, decadence, and superficiality of the West. Ironic to say the least considering his business ties to the United States and one of his four wives was an American by birth. On rare occasions, Waleed would open up to those closest to him. The words changed slightly, but the context always remained the same.

As long as the United States remains the world's only superpower, an imbalance will continue steering the world down a perilous path. We need to restore the global balance at any cost.

⸺◆⸺

The bright sun and a stiff breeze greeted Waleed as he stepped out of his ornate front door. It was early afternoon on September 11th, and he demanded Bridgette be ready for his departure. Bridgette was not a woman but his silver Bentley Azure Mark I. He named all his cars after women and asked for them only by name.

Waleed loved to travel in style, even if it was a quick jaunt to central London for a business meeting. He viewed his fleet of exotic cars as a way to express himself. Ferrari kept him on a short list to offer their newest model each year, and he never turned them down. Rumors swirled that he kept a cargo plane on retainer to shuttle his favorite vehicles between his many residences worldwide. A rumor that proved to be fact when the Wall Street Journal ran a piece on him several years ago.

Dressed in white pants, a navy-blue shirt, and brown Salvatore Ferragamo shoes, he bounded down the steps with his trademark smile. His boundless energy betrayed the fact that he turned fifty-six the month before. As he stopped at the end of the brick sidewalk that led from the road to his house, he took in a long drag of the fresh air, held it, and breathed out through his nose.

He paused and glanced down at his Patek Philippe watch before approaching Bridgette. It was 2:00 PM in London. Right on time as he expected. As his driver opened the rear passenger door his house manager, Ahmad Manzoor, hurried down the front steps and approached the car.

Waleed heard the loud footsteps and heavy breaths of Ahmad behind him. He turned around in an irritated fashion.

"What is it, Ahmad? I'm going to be late for my meeting."

Ahmad, out of shape, and overweight, took several large gulps of air before he spoke.

"Spit it out," Waleed said as he tapped on his watch.

"I'm sorry, but an incident occurred in New York City. The BBC is showing live images from lower Manhattan."

Waleed's eyebrows arched upward. "What type of incident?"

"It appears a commercial airliner crashed into the North Tower of the World Trade Center."

Silence followed the statement for a moment before Waleed responded to himself but in an audible voice. "It's finally begun..." he muttered as a smirk formed at the corner of his mouth.

"What's begun?" Ahmad asked.

No response came as Waleed walked away from the car at a hurried pace and towards the front door. "Call the office and cancel my 2:30 meeting. I'll need to be home the rest of the day."

"Of course," Ahmad replied.

The smile that spread across Waleed's face was unmistakable.

Minutes later, Waleed sat transfixed before a television, and he watched, like millions worldwide, as the second plane struck the South Tower in real time. With the second building hit, he felt sure that Sheikh Osama bin Muhammad bin Awad bin Laden committed the acts in lower Manhattan.

The rumors and gossip he heard appeared true. Tapping his fingers nervously on the mahogany table next to his Herman Miller chair he considered the images flooding across the screen.

Could it be actually happening?

Waleed met bin Laden several times, but those brief exchanges took place in Saudi Arabia at official House of Saud functions. Sympathetic to the Sheikh's cause, Waleed didn't have current ties to the man or his al-Qaeda organization. However, from time-to-time he allowed Osama's organization to use his freight shipping services at reduced rates. Those transactions stayed mostly off the books, processed through untraceable accounts involving offshore shell companies with no ties to him or bin Laden.

Several close friends and associates gathered at his home within thirty minutes as the events unfolded. When the South Tower collapsed at 2:59 PM London time, the mood within Waleed's home turned to gleeful jubilation. Most of those present believed America brought the events upon itself with its arrogance, sense of entitlement, and constant meddling in other countries's affairs.

Catered food arrived from one of Waleed's favorite restaurants, and before the evening concluded, over 75 guests descended upon the house. His mood remained festive throughout the afternoon and evening.

Most people left by 9 PM, while his closest friends and associates remained. At 10:20 PM, the BBC showed live images of World Trade Center (WTC) 7. Completely evacuated hours before the 47-story building collapsed, the destruction resulted in no loss of life or injuries.

Waleed perked up as he saw the building fall. His mind reeled at the turn of events.

Fate smiles upon me as *Allah works in mysterious ways.*

"What a waste, a 47-story building comes down and they suffer no loss of life!" Kadir Bashara exclaimed.

Waleed ignored the statement

Kadir not only worked for Waleed but served as his closest advisor. Their relationship was complicated. Waleed knew he could count on Kadir and trusted him implicitly, not the type of faith he gave on many people, including a few of his wives.

For his part, Kadir viewed Waleed as not only a mentor but very much as a father figure. A role embraced by Waleed while at the same time one he used to his advantage when the need arose.

Waleed stared at the television as it showed WTC 7 building collapse several more times in slow motion

Kadir watched Waleed transfixed on the images. His eyes narrowed.

"What is it? What are you thinking?"

Quiet for a moment Waleed paused and considered his response with great care. "Kadir, do you know the tenants of World Trade Center 7?"

Kadir knew nothing about the building.

"No, should I?"

Waleed stroked his chin. "Yes, I believe so."

"Well, I don't. So, I guess you'll have to enlighten me."

"Several important United States government agencies leased office space on various floors," Waleed said.

"Considering the location, I can't say I'm surprised. So what?"

"The collapse of WTC 7 is what really matters today."

"Are you serious? What about the two towers?"

"The destruction of the North and South Towers may have been spectacular, but I doubt it was even expected by the Sheikh himself. Besides, their collapse won't cause any serious long-term damage to the United States. In fact, it may awaken a sleeping giant."

Kadir shook his head. What Waleed said made no sense. "I don't understand. You're saying the attack wasn't a success?"

"No, I'm not saying that at all. What I'm saying is it might be a moral victory, but not one that results in the desired consequences. The events of today will not cripple the United States. In fact, it will enrage them. The government will strike out, mobilize its forces, and go after those they deem responsible for today's acts. This wicked president's cabinet is filled with warmongers. The vice president and the secretary of defense have made fortunes waging perpetual wars. They will take this attack as an impetus to start another war, a large one at that. But, WTC 7 coming down, that is the crown jewel of the day. At least, in my humble opinion."

Kadir stared at him, a look of bewilderment visible on his face. He believed Waleed must know more than he let on. "It's just an empty office building, and the collapse won't accomplish anything. The news even reported that nobody perished inside the building. Even if there were government agencies housed within the building, what makes the destruction of this one structure so special?"

Waleed glared at Kadir a moment before answering. "You don't have all the facts and can't possibly understand the significance of what occurred. At least, not yet. And that's okay. An opportunity has presented itself, and I've surely found favor with Allah. First, I need to make several phone calls to New York City, and then I will explain more."

Waleed hesitated lost in thought before he continued.

"Besides, it's not the building itself that interests me but what it held. Therein lies my opportunity."

CHAPTER THREE

DREXEL

Troy watched as the horror unfolded in lower Manhattan. His emotions fluctuated by the minute and ranged from shock to disgust before finally settling on pure rage. Troy tried to call his father, but it went straight to voicemail. He needed to hear his father's reassuring voice. Just to know he was alright.

Twenty minutes passed, and his cell phone rang. The caller ID simply read *Pops*.

"Where've you been?" Troy asked in an anxious tone.

Matt Evans was the Special Agent in Charge of the Salt Lake City FBI office, but he spent most of his time in the smaller resident agency office in Boise to be closer to his family in Drexel.

"I'm still in Boise," Matt said.

Troy's tone softened. "Good."

"Are you and your mom okay?"

"We're fine. Better now that you called."

"Sorry, it's taken so long to call you back, son. As expected, things are pretty intense around here. The Bureau is taking the lead on the investigation."

"I still can't believe this is happening, Pops. Seems like it's out of a movie or something."

"Trust me, I feel the same way. Look, Troy, I don't have long, but I wanted to let you both know I'm ok. I'll be here for a while. We're still trying to figure out who's responsible for these cowardly acts."

"News is saying they think it may have been Islamic terrorists."

"I can't say what I know, but I'm sure the news has excellent sources," Matt said.

"I'm pissed. These attacks…" Rage filled Troy's voice as he struggled to come up with the right words.

"I know."

"We've gotta fight back."

Matt could hear the anger in his son's words. "Trust me, Troy. I hear you and feel that anger. Believe me, we will hunt down whoever did this and make them pay."

"I'm going to help defend our country, Pops."

"You're not the only one that feels that way, but right now you need to keep your mom safe. We'll discuss defending our nation when I'm back home."

"Yes, sir," Troy let out an elongated breath. He realized his dad was subtly telling him to *stand down*.

"Will you have to head back east?" Troy asked.

"No, or at least not yet. For now, they've told us to stay put. I'll probably have to go to Salt Lake City soon, but for now, I'll be here in Boise. The entire country is on a heightened state of alert. Hard to separate fact from fiction with all the reports floating around. We don't know whether there will be any other attacks. Airports, railways, ports, everything is being locked down. The government is mobilizing everyone they have to help ensure we don't get hit again."

"I'm sure."

"I have to go jump on a call with headquarters in less than five. Give your mom a hug for me. Ok?"

"Yes, sir."

"Any luck hunting?"

The buck seemed like a distant memory to Troy after what occurred. "Jeez, I almost forgot with all that's going on. I bagged a big one. In fact, he's still out in the field. Mom came and got me as I was getting the ATV to load him up."

"Ten or twelve points?" Matt asked.

"Please … a twelve pointer is your biggest."

"How big?"

Troy paused for effect. "Fourteen."

"My man. Wow! I'm impressed. Nice shooting. I only wish I could have been there with you."

"Me too."

"I can't wait to hear more about it later. I love you, Troy. I'll call when I can."

"Love you too, Pops."

The call ended, and Troy turned back to the coverage on the television.

Chapter Four

Boise, Idaho

Cate Downey stepped out of the shower, and into a cloud of steam that enveloped the bathroom. It was rare she took that long of a shower, but with her roommate gone she had the two-bedroom, one-bath college dorm suite to herself.

Standing there with the water dripping down the smooth curves of her body and onto the bathmat, she looked up at the smiley face clock on the bathroom wall. The oversized neon yellow clock was a gag gift from Troy on their third date. Even a year later, every time she looked at it, an enormous grin formed on her face.

She used a towel to wrap her hair as large beads of water traveled down the small of her smooth back and followed the contours of her silky skin. Cate grabbed a bottle of lotion from the top drawer of the vanity and rubbed it over her dry skin. As she turned off the bathroom fan, she heard her phone ringing in the other room. Quickly, she pulled the towel off the hook on the back of the door, wrapped it around her naked body before she opened the door and dashed into the common room. It took her a few seconds until she found where she left her purse.

Cate located the phone just in time to see Troy's name on the caller ID. Her pulse quickened. She knew he should be in a tree stand at that moment and not calling her. She immediately thought something must be wrong. "Are you okay?" she asked as the line connected. "You're supposed to be hunting."

"I'm fine, turn on the television."

"Why?"

"Just do it, Cate," Troy said.

She picked up on the edge in his voice.

Cate grabbed the remote from the coffee table and turned one of the local Boise channels. The images on the screen caused her body to tense. A knot formed in her stomach as the video of the South Tower's collapse played. People ran screaming as a cloud of dust and particles barreled down the street and enveloped them all. A banner across the bottom of the screen said, *The World Trade Center Destroyed. Pentagon In Flames. Thousands Feared Dead.*

Troy was silent on the other end of the phone line.

For a few minutes, she said nothing. Cate's mind absorbed the images, and she listened as the news anchor recounted the morning's events. "This can't be happening," she finally said in a dull, monotone voice.

"I've been trying to call you for the past thirty minutes," Troy said.

"Have the room to myself today, so I took a long hot shower and never heard the phone ring."

They were silent as the reporter spoke in the background. Both lost in their own thoughts as they wrestled with a flood of emotions.

As the images continued on the television screen she said, "I can't stay here and watch this alone."

"The radio said classes have been canceled, so come to my parents' house."

Cate cleared her throat, which got dry as she watched with her mouth agape at the images on the television. "Okay," she replied.

"Can you make the drive? I can come get you if you'd prefer that."

"Thanks, but I can drive myself."

"Sure thing."

"I need to call my mom and dad."

"They'll wanna hear from you. I talked to your mom ten minutes ago, and everyone is fine in Coeur d'Alene. She tried calling you already."

"Thanks for checking in on them."

"Of course. They'd rather you be home but know it's way too long of a drive from Boise."

"Let me throw some clothes into a bag. I'll call them on the way to your parents."

"And Cate," Troy said.

"Yes?"

"Drive safe. I love you, babe."

"Love you, too."

Chapter Five

Drexel

As Cate pulled her eight-year-old red Honda Accord into the driveway, Troy came out to meet her. They embraced each other for several moments. Her tender embrace assured him in some small way that even though his country was in disarray, things would be okay. The touch of her skin and the smell of her hair aroused his senses. Cate had a way of easing his fears and instilling stability inside him when it was lacking.

Troy's mother, Amy, joined them outside. She treated Cate as a member of the family. The daughter she never had but always desperately wanted. "Cate, it's good to see you, dear. We're happy you made it here safe and sound. Make sure you call your folks and tell them you've arrived."

"Thanks, I called them when I pulled into the driveway. The roads were empty. It's weird driving down state highways and not seeing any other cars for long stretches. I think everyone's glued to their televisions today, and few people are venturing out."

"I'm sure 9/11 will be a day all of us will remember where we were the moment we found out about the attacks," Amy said. "Just like previous generations who experienced Pearl Harbor, the JFK assassination, and the Space Shuttle Challenger disaster."

"You're right," Cate said as her smile turned to a frown.

As the hours passed, others made their way to the Evans house to witness history unfold. Some were friends and teachers who worked with Amy at the school. Even the sheriff of Drexel, Roy Barnett, who was a close friend of Matt, stopped by to check in on the family.

An hour after the sheriff stopped by, Paul Brighton, Troy's best friend, came over. The two boys were inseparable during high school. Paul had spent so much time at the Evans house during those years he almost had his own bedroom.

Paul grew up in relative poverty and didn't have the opportunities others in town experienced. His father left when he was young, and his mom worked three jobs to provide for Paul and his four siblings. Troy's parents treated him like a member of their own family. He didn't have the money to attend college even though Matt and Amy offered to help with tuition.

After graduation, Paul landed a job at Siberdrive, a Drexel-based technology company. Thrilled to get his foot in the door, Paul started in an entry-level information technology position. He mastered computers in his teens, and even though he didn't have a degree, Siberdrive hired him on the spot. It hadn't hurt that Matt Evans called the company's owner to vouch for Paul.

Siberdrive landed an exclusive contract with the Department of Defense in the early 90's. The company was one of the primary providers of software and hardware components used in the United States military Predator drones. This included the primary control modules, internal navigation systems, and the weapons control software. Siberdrive designed, manufactured, and maintained the 'guts' within the unmanned aerial vehicles (UAV's).

⸺◦⸺

Troy, Cate, and Paul sat around the living room and watched the coverage for several hours. When the president spoke from the Oval Office, everyone hung on his every word. Troy took note as the president said he had "directed the full resources of our intelligence and law enforcement communities to find those responsible and bring them to justice." Troy's thoughts turned to the FBI and his dad. He wondered what part his father would play in the investigation, if any.

As the brief speech continued, a fire ignited in Troy. One he had not felt before. After the speech ended, Troy had enough. He stood up. "I'm done sitting around. I have a mule deer to collect. Sure, as hell, didn't make that shot this morning to let the buzzards get their fill this evening," exclaimed Troy.

"Can I join you?" Paul asked.

"Sure. I could use a powerful set of legs and arms."

Paul had a grin from ear to ear. "Cool. I'll get to observe the master at work with his knife."

"Me too," Cate said as she popped up off the couch.

"You got the stomach for skinning and butchering Miss Downey?" Paul asked with a devilish grin on his face.

Cate frowned. "I'm no city girl, Paul. I can spit and chew and hang with those that do."

Troy shook his head in admiration. "Cate's the real deal, dude. Hot as hell, and tough as nails. She may look like an angel, but don't be deceived. You wouldn't want to meet this angelic being in a back alley with ill intentions. I guarantee only one person would walk out, and it would be that fox right there." Troy cocked his head towards Cate.

Cate beamed at the compliment. "Aww, don't you say the sweetest things about me."

CHAPTER SIX

NEW YORK CITY

Aaron Ryker could taste the bile in his mouth. The stress of the day took its toll, and no matter what, his stomach and esophagus took the brunt of how his body reacted.

He glanced out the window and considered how the city, his city, changed in the blink of an eye. Located at 26 Federal Plaza, the New York City field office for the FBI was less than ten blocks from the World Trade Center complex. Aaron felt both the North and South Towers collapse, and there wasn't a goddamn thing he could do about it.

He had no time to contemplate the horror that engulfed the city. Rumors circulated faster than anyone could discount them. One call after another passed through the FBI command center that afternoon. Some calls focused on suspicious individuals, while others described mysterious packages found in the five boroughs of New York City. FBI agents ran ragged, returning every call and doing their best to protect the citizens of the greatest city in the world. Aaron fielded hundreds of calls and directed available agents to countless locations all over the city.

As late afternoon arrived, Aaron sat at his desk with his head in his hands. The emotional and physical stress of the day took its toll. Mentally spent, all Aaron wanted to do was crawl under his desk and rock back and forth. It was hard to see how the day could get any worse when his cell phone rang. *Here we go again*, he thought to himself. As he leaned over and looked at the caller ID, the screen read 'Unknown'.

With an audible sigh, Aaron answered in a monotone voice, "Special Agent Ryker."

"Aaron, I'm relieved to hear your voice."

"Waleed?" Ryker asked in a perplexed tone.

"Yes, my friend. I would ask how you are but based on what I've been watching on the television, I'm aware many Americans are not well. For this, I'm deeply sorry."

Of all the calls he had received, this one was the most unexpected. Waleed acted like he cared, even repeated the word friend. But there was no love lost between the two men. Their relationship revolved around business.

"I'm surprised you would call on this day?" Aaron asked.

Waleed feigned a surprised response. "I'm concerned about you, Aaron."

"I'm fine," Aaron answered with a touch of sarcasm. He had many interactions with Waleed over the years, most of them unpleasant. Aaron wasn't proud of the things he'd done on behalf of Waleed. Especially since one thing was certain, Waleed cared for only one person, himself.

"I'm relieved," Waleed said.

Aaron bristled as a wave of exhaustion caused a shudder. "You realize they're saying bin Laden's responsible for these attacks?"

"Yes, I'm aware, the BBC reported that a little while ago."

"Well, he's Saudi and a friend of yours, isn't he?"

"Aaron!" Waleed exclaimed. "You've had a rough day, emotions are clearly running high, and for good reason. But, to answer the question no, Osama is no friend of mine. The bin Laden family lives in Saudi Arabia, and the family is very large. They have many interactions with the House of Saud considering they own one of the largest construction companies in the kingdom. I've only met Osama a few times and had no contact with the man once he left my country years ago to wage his ridiculous jihad. In fact, I believe he even aligned with the American government in Afghanistan when the Russians occupied the country, if I recall correctly."

A pause occurred, and Aaron did his best to control his tongue. However, his rage got the best of him for a moment. "Would you denounce these audacious acts?" Ryker asked in a stern response.

"Most certainly," Waleed answered emphatically.

"Good, you damn well better!" Ryker raised his voice louder than he should have at the office. "Now that you know I'm safe, and since you only called to offer your unwavering support for the United States, let's cut the bullshit and tell me why you really called."

Although Aaron wasn't aware, Waleed smiled at the outburst. "I'll answer your question with one of my own, Aaron. Are you familiar with the government agencies that leased space in WTC 7?"

"Building 7?" asked Aaron in a surprised tone. "Who the hell cares about Building 7? It's the North and South Towers that mattered."

"I take it the answer is, no?"

"It's my business to keep track of any government agency within Manhattan, Waleed." Even though his anger intensified, he took several deep breaths and after a few seconds answered the question. "The Agency had limited personnel as did the Department of Defense (DOD), IRS, and Secret Service. And of course, the New York City Office of Emergency Management had their command center on the 23rd floor," Ryker paused for a moment then added, "Why do you care?"

Waleed ignored the question, "And what about the FBI facility? Why did you leave that out?"

Perplexed by the question, Ryker answered, "You're mistaken, Waleed. The Bureau has no presence at Building 7. You know where our office is located. You've sat here across from me at my desk before. What game are you playing?"

"Game? This is no game, Aaron. Surely a man of your stature in the Bureau knew of the secret facility?"

"What do you mean? What facility?" Ryker asked, "I don't have a clue what you're talking about."

Surprised by the response, Waleed replied, "The FBI maintained a secret facility on basement level three."

Silence passed over the line for a few seconds. "That's not possible," Ryker said. "I would have known about it. One of your government sources must have provided you faulty intel."

"No, my friend, you're the one who's mistaken," Waleed said. "The FBI maintained a top-secret location under Building 7."

Aaron didn't believe him but was growing tired of the back and forth. He acquiesced and played along. "And what purpose did this secret facility serve exactly?" Ryker had his curiosity piqued, but his voice projected an air of sarcasm mixed with doubt.

"What else do you do at a secret location but keep secrets, silly."

"Nonsense," Aaron said. "There wasn't a secret FBI facility under World Trade Center 7.

Waleed continued, "I'm very surprised you did not know, Aaron. The FBI maintained a classified documents repository onsite since the mid 90's. Inside it housed various classified documents that the FBI kept for almost a century. Until today, there had been four such facilities nationwide. The New York City location was the largest and stored the most sensitive information. The three remaining locations are in Dallas, Chicago, and Denver."

"Waleed, I've been with the Bureau for almost 20 years, and I've never heard a lick of what you're suggesting. If I didn't know about it, how did you?"

"We've worked together for a while, Aaron. You're aware all too well, I have many sources and connections at the highest levels. Trust me, the place exists."

"Okay, for argument's sake, let's say it exists. So, what? Why would a place like that interest you?"

"I live and breathe the world of information, Aaron. It's my lifeblood and the reason I've been successful. That repository housed many items that I may find to be important."

"I guess that's too bad since Building 7 is a pile of smoldering rubble now. It will be months before they even comb through what's left."

"See, we found something to agree on after all," Waleed said.

"I don't get it."

"You will."

"Can we get to the point, Waleed? I'm very busy and growing tired of this conversation."

"Well, Aaron, the FBI is nothing if not predictable. They will seal off the site and go through the debris piece by piece, looking for anything deemed to hold sensitive or classified material. No stone left unturned in their attempt to protect the government's secrets at all costs."

"And this has to do with me how?" Ryker's frustration intensified.

"I'll need you to be on the recovery team when the Bureau forms one."

"Excuse me?"

"You heard me, Aaron. I'll need you to be assigned to the team. I'm sure discussions will begin immediately about forming a recovery and assessment team."

"Why would they assign me to the team?"

In a matter-of-fact way, Waleed said, "Because I need you on it."

"How do you propose I make that happen? And for what purpose?"

"I'll take care of the how. As for what, we'll leave that for another conversation. I'll be coming to NYC soon once the president lifts the airline ban and will set up a time for us to meet. There's a fabulous restaurant in the SoHo district I've been meaning to try on one of my visits."

The gall of this man, Aaron thought. *Here we've lost countless lives, and all he can do is think of himself. What a selfish prick. I wish I never did business with him.*

"And what if I decide to skip dinner?"

"You'll be able to squeeze in dinner, Aaron. For old times' sake. Besides, I'll contribute generously to your retirement fund in the Caymans, which will make your previous compensation look paltry. We'll meet soon and answer your questions face-to-face."

Aaron didn't have time to respond. With that, the line disconnected. He placed the phone down, stood up and walked over to the window, which provided a view of lower Manhattan. He looked out towards where the towers had been earlier that day and shook his head. A severe headache started halfway through the conversation and turned into a full-blown migraine by the end of the call. *Dammit*, he thought, *What the hell has he pulled me into this time?*

Chapter Seven

London

Waleed reached behind, grabbed the lower part of his neck, just above his shoulders, and squeezed repeatedly to relieve some of the stress his body felt. Exhausted, he leaned forward in his plush leather lounge chair and let out a long breath.

Dawn arrived in London as the crimson sky pushed away the darkness of the night. Waleed spent many hours after he turned off the television coverage and made discreet phone calls to various power players scattered around Washington, D.C., and New York City. Some of these people were difficult to connect with, but Waleed persisted and successfully reached all 20 of the names he jotted onto a piece of paper as he watched the events happen in lower Manhattan.

Kadir sat in the room and listened the entire time he spoke, only hearing one side of phone conversations. Waleed figured the calls likely made Kadir more confused than enlightened.

As he looked over at Kadir, his piercing eyes softened slightly. "It's been a long day, but I'm cautiously optimistic based on what I've learned."

"Forgive me, Waleed," Kadir spoke in a measured tone. "But I don't understand your endgame."

Waleed smiled. "That's because you only know part of the story."

"Please enlighten me."

"Kadir, the Bureau has several centralized processing and storage centers for its mundane items. Literally, they have warehouses filled from floor to ceiling with data in many forms. However, the secretive stuff, the things they don't want people to discover, are housed in classified document repositories. These are the crown jewels of their intelligence. Items they don't want anyone to see the light of day."

"And under World Trade Center 7 was one of these facilities?"

"Correct."

"But wouldn't the classified documents in that location be gone? I mean, if the fire burned hot enough to collapse a 47-story office tower, don't you think it would destroy everything inside as well?"

Waleed knew it was a fair question. "I have no doubt the repository suffered severe damage. Were items destroyed? Most certainly. But will everything be destroyed? No, some items will remain. The FBI will recover, examine, and transport them to a new location. I know for a fact they housed the most secretive and sensitive items in individual boxes that were damn near impenetrable. I'm hopeful those sensitive documents survived."

"Okay, say some items aren't destroyed, and let's say Aaron is on this team and gets his hands on these classified files. Then what?"

"He will intercept the items I request and hand them over to me," Waleed said in a matter-of-fact way.

Kadir looked at his mentor with an incredulous look on his face. "And why would he do that?"

"Because I'll tell him to do so."

Kadir scoffed, "You've manipulated him occasionally, but Ryker strikes me as a patriot at heart. I don't see him handing over classified information because you ask for it, and especially not if any information damages the United States."

Waleed smiled and shook his head. "Aaron has been an excellent source for me in the past, and you're right; he wouldn't willingly betray his country on a matter of national security. However, as you're aware firsthand, Kadir, I can be very persuasive." His face contorted and his countenance changed as he finished the statement.

Kadir gulped hard. He had seen how persuasive his boss could be on more than one occasion. Anyone who required Waleed to use such tactics met a horrific end. "But can you trust him?"

"Ryker? Of course not. You can never trust the devil inside all mankind."

"But what if he betrays you? Or tells his superiors you're trying to manipulate him?"

"Fair questions to which I don't have any concrete answers yet. My conversation with him next week in New York will be telling. I'll get through to him and make my intentions clear."

"Your true intentions?"

"What I need him to know. That's all. I can sell sugar to a diabetic if need be. Salesmanship is not a weakness I embody in my arsenal of skills."

Kadir nodded. "I'm still not sure what you hope to recover amongst those documents?"

A few seconds passed. Waleed considered the question and struggled with what to say. He decided Kadir needed to hear the truth. "There's something remarkable I haven't told you. Until now, the timing wasn't right. In fact, what I am telling you no living soul has heard."

"I'm humbled you'd share something like that with me. What is it?"

"I had a vision several months ago."

Kadir looked perplexed. "You mean a dream?"

"No, a vision. I was very much awake when it occurred. It occurred during a visit to Ko Pha Ngan."

"And what happened during this vision?" Kadir asked. His inflection sounded skeptical.

"I stood in the middle of a wide road. It was a dense metropolis, large buildings and concrete surrounding me on all sides. Then it happened. I saw two enormous towers fall from the sky directly in front of where I stood. The sound of them striking the earth was deafening. The ground shook, and the impact knocked me off my feet as I fell hard to the ground. A great cloud arose and blackened the daylight. Shortly after the cloud disappeared, I witnessed a smaller tower fall."

"So, you had a premonition of the World Trade Center attack? A vision from Allah?"

"I can't be certain where it came from, but I vividly remember what happened next. There, amongst the rubble of the third tower, two hands emerged. One hand held a scorched piece of parchment. While the other hand held something else. The hand slowly opened and displayed an emblem."

Kadir, now on the edge of his seat, asked. "Who was it? The person who emerged from the debris."

"I'm not sure," replied Waleed. "Only the hands pierced the debris."

"What about the parchment? Were you able to read what it said?"

"I only made out a few words. The vision occurred quickly; the images flickered like fast-moving objects. The vision proved to be fleeting. For now, I will keep the words I read to myself."

"And the emblem in the other hand?"

Waleed smiled broadly. "It was a golden badge with blue letters. A symbol I know very well. It was an FBI badge."

"Then what happened?" Kadir asked. He sat on the edge of his chair, mesmerized by the words flowing from Waleed.

Waleed closed his eyes, as if he were reliving the vision. "Next, a voice spoke."

"A voice? From where? The rubble?"

"No, the voice came from above."

"What did it say?"

"The voice said the information buried deep within that cryptic parchment would give me the location of a device which I could use to once and for all destroy the great Satan. The destruction of the United States will hasten the return of the Twelfth Imam and fulfill the mission to bring peace and justice to all mankind."

Kadir was at a loss for words. After a few moments passed, he asked, "And you have told no one of this vision?"

"No, you are the only person who knows. I thought it best to keep it to myself."

"I'm humbled you've shared what occurred with me."

Waleed smiled. "You'll be joining me on this quest. After watching the events unfold in New York, I knew the vision was coming true. Clearly, the attack has set wheels in motion. That's how I'm certain documents survived the inferno. Plus,

I'm convinced Ryker was the agent who held the parchment and the badge. He will give it over to me whether or not he wants to. What he provides me will lead us to the device needed to fulfill the vision. In 1994, I discovered the FBI kept secret files in a secure location, and I made a play to steal them. That attempt failed, and the documents were moved elsewhere. Little did I know the significance of what the files contained until I had the vision recently. Now I know Allah has put the steps in motion for me to complete what I started in 1994 in Philadelphia."

"So, what do we do next?" Kadir asked as a confused look spread across his face.

"We travel to New York City," Waleed said. "But we must not force events to occur. We wait patiently for the revelation of our destiny to occur. Remember, Kadir, the Quran tells us that *surely Allah is with those who are patient*."

Chapter Eight

New York City

Aaron Ryker walked into the priciest French restaurant in New York City. Modeled after the Palace of Versailles, the restaurant comprised rooms patterned after the famous palace. As he stepped into the ornate lobby, his shoes squeaked on the polychromatic marble. The room was a reproduction of the royal chapel, including imposing colonnades on either wall. An ornate rug led to the maître d' desk, shaped like an altar complete with gold inlay. Aaron shook his head as he looked around, unsure if he could afford the cost of checking his coat, let alone ordering anything from such a posh establishment.

Why am I here? He thought, *I should turn around and walk away while I still can.* But he knew he couldn't just walk away; it's never that simple. Waleed had him by the short and curlies. And he knew firsthand the man had no qualms about giving them a tug.

Ryker's past with Waleed was complicated and something he grew to loathe over the years. Their interaction started innocently enough. Waleed witnessed an assault on an elected official while in NYC and met Aaron during the FBI investigation of the incident. That event sparked a communication line, and Waleed called Ryker from time to time. Eventually, the occasional favor crossed a line. Once the money changed hands, and not a small sum, Aaron knew things had gone too far. Unfortunately, Waleed had made it clear there was no going back, and if Ryker refused to help him going forward, the favors would come to light. Aaron knew his career would certainly be over while criminal prosecution would follow. He couldn't bear to see the shame in his wife's eyes if that occurred. That's why he continued working for a man he came to despise.

His pride got the best of him, and as the good book says, "Pride goes before a fall."

—◆—

Aaron gave his name to the tall, raven-haired maître d' in a black, form-fitting dress that appeared painted on her curved, exquisite body. She responded with a warm smile. "Right this way, Mr. Ryker. Your party is expecting you." Turning away, her hips swayed suggestively as she moved in long strides through the restaurant.

Aaron followed her, struggling not to stare hard, as she brought him to the back of the dining area modeled after the historic hall of mirrors. A large crescent-shaped table sat in the corner of the room.

Waleed rose and greeted him with a firm clasp of the hand as he spoke. "Aaron, kind of you to join us." He gestured with his other hand. "You remember my business associate Kadir Bashar, right?"

Aaron nodded. "Of course." He shook Kadir's hand as well. "Good to see you again," he said through clenched teeth. He despised being in the presence of either man.

"Likewise, Mr. Ryker," Kadir said. Not surprisingly, he didn't enjoy seeing Ryker any more than Ryker enjoyed seeing him.

"What a fabulous room. Don't you agree?" Waleed asked.

Aaron looked around. The room was impressive. Never had he seen such opulence. "Looks like the pictures I've seen of the actual palace."

Waleed appeared taken aback. "You've never been to Versailles?"

He shook his head. "No, never."

"Well, Aaron, you simply must go. Your wife, Sally, would fall in love with the beautiful gardens and the splendor of the palace."

"Maybe one day," Aaron said.

"I can arrange a trip if you'd like."

Aaron shook his head. "That won't be necessary, but thank you for the kind offer."

"It's a standing offer if you change your mind." Waleed pointed toward the seats. "Please, let's get comfortable. We have much to discuss."

As the three men sat down, the waiter arrived to take their drink orders.

"You like cab, don't you, Aaron?" asked Waleed.

"Yes," Aaron said in a firm tone.

"I think the Chileans do a wonderful cabernet." Waleed pointed at the menu and indicated which bottle he wanted from the extensive wine list.

The waiter left after a slight bow.

"Ironic, isn't it?" Aaron asked.

"What is?"

"We're at a French restaurant and we didn't even order their wine," Aaron said.

Waleed simply smiled but didn't respond.

"You should know by now he does as he pleases," Kadir spoke in a sharp tone as he stared at the FBI agent with a piercing glare.

"Is it wise for us to be meeting in such a public place?" Aaron asked as he ignored the stern look from Kadir and glanced around the restaurant with a questioning glance.

"Nonsense." Waleed displayed an unconcerned look on his face. "I always have my meetings out in the open. It typically causes far fewer questions, if you ask me. Besides, no one from the bureau or any other government agencies could afford to walk through the doors of this restaurant, yourself included," he added with a slight dig. "Tonight's conversation is far from any curious ears, Aaron."

"If you say so," Aaron answered warily.

For the first 45 minutes, and the initial two courses, the conversation mainly focused on New York City, the aftermath of 9/11, and how the city was coping with such an unthinkable attack. As the third course arrived, or as the French call it the 'Le Plat Principal', the conversation veered to the reason Waleed summoned him. Up to that point in the evening, Waleed had been very polite. In fact, he seemed downright enthralled with most things Ryker stated.

Taking a bite of his succulent duck and dabbing at the corners of his mouth with a napkin, Waleed finally got down to brass tacks. "So tell me, Aaron, how's the project coming? I take it you have already met with the others that will be part of the recovery at WTC 7?"

Aaron wanted nothing more than to clam up and say nothing, but he knew that would only enrage Waleed, who was not one to upset. He finished chewing his veal, which he could have cut with a baby spoon it was so tender, and responded honestly. "We had our second meeting just yesterday; although I have a feeling you knew that already." He glanced at Waleed, but all he got in response was a slight nod of the head. He continued, "It will still be weeks or possibly months before we begin Operation Core Recoup in earnest. Crews have begun the process to remove the debris from the 47 floors that comprised WTC 7. Once the excavation of the basement and substructure begins, our job will begin."

"It might be sooner than you think," Waleed said. "My sources tell me that by mid-October at the latest the excavation will begin on the substructure."

Aaron shrugged. "I have my doubts that there will be anything left when they get to that point. Between the fires, flooding, and the pancaking of the 47 stories, I can't imagine much of anything survived. Which brings us back to my central question. What is it you expect to find, Waleed?"

"I honestly don't know Aaron," Waleed replied in a very matter-of-fact tone, while lying as if it was second nature. And for him, it truly was.

"I don't believe you," Aaron answered bluntly. "A man of your stature doesn't walk into a situation unless he has pretty much complete control of what is going to happen. You've not made your billions on gambles; you've done so by cold, calculating analysis of the facts."

"That's an astute observation, Aaron, but I really don't know what's in these Core secret files. I doubt few actually do, but I can venture some guesses."

"You don't seriously believe I will hand anything over to you containing information that could be used to further harm my country, do you?"

"Aaron!" Waleed threw his arms up in mock surprise. "I am offended that you would even state such a thing. I assure you I have no such intention of harming the United States. As you know, I went to school here and even met one of my wives while I lived in this beautiful country. I adore the United States and look forward to its continued prosperity. You are misreading my intentions if that is what you think. I simply feel that some of the information within those classified documents may aid me in other ways." Waleed cracked the slightest smile as he spoke the last few words.

"Such as?" Aaron asked.

Waleed smile grew. It was a warm, inviting smile. "They might assist in my business dealings. We both know I use information to my advantage. You've played a part in that in the past. Something in those files may give me a leg up in my professional life or how do you American's phrase it, 'Allow me to hold it over someone's head'. I'm not looking for anything that could be used against US interests in any nefarious way. I can assure you, it's just business."

Aaron didn't believe him. Not for one damn second. However, he also knew that arguing the point at this stage was lunacy. So, he played along. "Okay, let's say you are right, and some files survived. How am I supposed to let you know what I find? Even harder, if I was even willing to do so, how would I get any of those files out of the secured facility? They're building their own version of Fort Knox at the former landfill, and I can assure you they'll be letting us just walk out with anything in our possession. In fact, they'll run us through the ringer every time we leave the facility each day."

"Of course, I understand your concerns," Waleed said. "We have some time to work out the details. In fact, Kadir will meet with you again in the next few weeks. He will have some fancy items to show you and go over how they work. For now, we just take it one step at a time." He paused as he saw the team of waiters approach. "Ah yes, look here comes our fourth course. Let's enjoy what the chef has brought us, and we can talk about business again later. Bon appetite gentlemen."

Chapter Nine

Washington D.C.

September 24, 2001

Another long day ended on the Hill as Senator Preston Wilcox III, who represented the citizens of the great state of Idaho, walked into his office at the Russell Senate Office Building. His right foot lagged behind the left, the normal spring in his step not present after a long day walking the halls of Capitol Hill. He passed his secretary Loretta, said hello with a wink and warm smile, and headed straight into his office. Once inside his sanctuary, he sat in his old-worn leather chair, put his feet up and let out a long slow breath. Preston realized he was getting too old for this line of work.

As he pushed the button on his digital phone, he asked Loretta to bring him a stiff drink. Within two minutes she delivered the cold, amber-colored liquid. He cradled the scotch on the rocks, spun it around inside the thick glass, and leaned back in his chair. The sight of the Macallan 30 brought a smile to his aging face.

The senator enjoyed exactly three slow sips before his silence ended as the annoying intercom on his phone disturbed the moment. "Yes, Loretta," he quipped in a tone that revealed he wasn't pleased.

"Sorry to disturb you, sir, but Senator Finkel just walked into the office and wondered if he could have a word with you?"

Preston shook his head slightly from side to side and muttered to himself, *Hot damn, that didn't take long for loose lips to get wind.*

"I'm sorry, what was that, Senator?" Loretta asked.

"Nothing. Send him in, Loretta," he said reluctantly.

A few seconds later, the door opened, and in walked Norman Finkel, the senior senator from his neighboring state of Utah.

Preston did not even attempt to stand but gestured to the seat in front of his desk. "Have a seat, Norm."

"I just heard about the Senate Committee on Armed Services meeting on the nuclear threat. Unbelievable, isn't it?"

"Jesus, Norm, I literally just walked into my office from the meeting. Which was supposedly classified and certainly a closed-door affair. How the hell did you hear about it already?"

"You know what happens on the Hill, Preston," Norm said as he let out a cackle. "Word travels faster here than the gossip pages of the supermarket magazines. You should know better than that."

"That still doesn't excuse the info leaking out this quickly."

"But is it true? Did they really discover some nuclear material on a barge coming into the Port of New Orleans?"

Preston shook his head in disgust. If someone like Norm Finkel spewed forth this info, the national media would know it within the hour. If not already. Preston bit his lip to keep from saying what he really thought. Instead, he shook his head from side to side. "No, Norm, whoever is running their mouth when they should have just shut it, is providing false information."

"Enlighten me," Senator Finkel leaned back in the chair. "Which part is bullshit?"

Preston decided to reveal the truth. "Well, they got the Port of New Orleans detail right, but the rest of what you said is flat-out wrong. It was a container ship, not a barge to start with."

"Spare me the sarcasm Preston, what I really want to know about is the nuclear material. After 9/11, you know everyone is on edge wondering if we're going to get hit again. A nuclear strike is one of the primary concerns people have right now."

Preston enjoyed yanking Norm's chain. It became a game he enjoyed more over the years. "Yes, I know Norm, and I am aware what is keeping people on edge. I've been in so many damn intelligence meetings the last few weeks, it's making my head spin. There's a lot of misinformation floating around right now, and people are getting worked into a frenzy about all of it. Hell, if they knew some of the genuine threats, most citizens wouldn't leave their homes."

"You're not answering my question, Preston. What about the nuclear material?"

"I'm getting there, Norm, you impatient old prick!"

Norm just stared at him and raised his eyebrows. "Well, we both know I'm a prick, but to be fair not much older than you. Don't make me beg."

Taking a deep breath, Senator Wilcox began, "New Orleans Port security boarded a large cargo ship while it was still in the harbor. It was just another routine search of a ship entering the port. While going through the ship, one of the security personnel picked up an unusual reading on his Geiger counter. As is the practice, anytime something suspicious occurs, he called it up the chain of command, and more people boarded the ship. After an intense search, they located the container emanating the radioactive readings. Within minutes, the Coast Guard arrived and denied the ship entry to the port while a nut to bolts search of the entire cargo vessel began."

Preston fell silent.

"And?" an anxious Senator Finkel inquired as he sat on the edge of his seat.

"Only one container set off the Geiger counter. They stripped the container bare but located nothing nuclear. In fact, it only contained a single 4x6x2 wooden crate, which was empty other than wood chips and miscellaneous fragments on the bottom."

Norm looked confused. "That's it? Why would the Geiger counters go off if no nuclear material was present?"

"It wasn't present at the time, but something radioactive must have been in that crate at some point," Preston said as he stroked his chin.

"Well, what does that mean? Where did it go?"

"That's the 64-million-dollar question. Not sure if someone unloaded the material before it crossed the ocean, while in transit, or even when it was closer to the US coast. Lots of men and women are looking into that even as we speak."

"So where did the container ship come from?"

"Yemen."

"Like the Middle East, Yemen?"

"I only know of one," responded Preston.

"And aren't you worried about this?" Norm nervously tapped on his knee.

"You see, I'm drinking scotch, Norm, not water on the rocks. Of course, I'm concerned, but there's no way of knowing if we have reason to hit the panic button yet. We met for almost three hours this afternoon, and to be honest, this was not the only threat discussed. The world is a very dangerous place and has been for some time. There have been threats against us since long before I joined the senate, and I don't think that's going to change anytime soon. The difference is that now regular Americans are pulling their heads out of the sand and taking note."

"What do we do in the meantime?" Norm asked.

"Rely on our intelligence, our partners, and our resolve. Investigate each threat as it comes and take decisive action when the time is right."

The next five minutes comprised random chit-chat

Norm, who got what he wanted out of the visit, looked at his watch and stood up in mid-sentence. Using the excuse, he was late for another meeting. No doubt to run off and tell everything he had just learned to whoever would listen.

Preston found himself alone once more. After a few minutes with his mind racing and second drink flowing through his bloodstream, Preston's memory flipped back almost 39 years. He pondered the day when his appointment to fill the vacated seat in the United States Senate took place after the untimely death of his predecessor.

Soon his thoughts turned toward the one project that would define his life. The project that no one still living knew anything about.

He wondered if the truth of what took place all those years in the past would ever come to light. Preston took comfort in knowing that when he died, so would the truth. Only one document existed that hinted at its existence, and he knew for a fact it remained buried deep in a classified FBI vault.

Lost to time.

His only prayer was that it stayed that way for eternity.

Chapter Ten

Drexel

September 29, 2001

Like many other towns out west, Drexel, Idaho, started as a boom town when a prospector discovered gold in the 1860's. However, unlike many of the towns that disappeared after gold became scarce, Drexel endured. The town remained relatively small, with a population hovering around thirty-five hundred. Nestled in the mountains, Drexel bordered the Boise National Forest and was about 45 minutes north of Boise. Gold mines continued to be the primary source of income for the town for over one hundred years after its founding.

The Harding family owned much of the town's land and started mining during the gold rush. The generations of Harding's that followed never left, and their influence only grew as time crept along. Control of the mine stayed within the family, but Jack Harding, the seventy-year-old fourth-generation patriarch of the family, diversified the family business interests during the 1980's. He made a hefty gamble and got into the up-and-coming technology business. The company he founded, Siberdrive, landed several large government contracts that proved quite lucrative for the family.

By 2001, Siberdrive was by far the largest employer in Drexel. The family's gold mining business shuttered in the mid-90's and many mine shafts were sealed off. Gold mining became a thing of the past.

Locals still swore there was gold in the hills, but the Harding family owned much of the land, and they moved on and embraced technology.

A modest river flowed through Drexel, and in 1963 a large government works project began. A medium-sized concrete dam, which created Lake Drexel, took two and a half years to build. The lake, popular in the summer, caused the population to swell between Memorial Day and Labor Day as tourists flocked to the quaint, postcard-looking town.

Matt Evan's father was one of those men who came to Drexel to build the dam in 1963. Unlike most of the workers, he and his wife fell in love with the area and never left. Matt was seven years old when his parents moved, and from that day, Drexel became home. When tragedy struck and his parents died in a car accident when Matt was in his twenties, he inherited the ranch his father worked so hard to purchase. It was all he ever knew, and he intended to one day leave that beautiful plot of land to his only son, Troy.

⊷◆⊶

Matt arrived home about 2 A.M. from his latest trip to Washington. His endless energy took a hit over the past several weeks as the Bureau demanded most of his waking hours. With dark rings under his eyes, he dropped his duffel bag on the floor and let out a loud sigh. He looked exhausted.

After a tender embrace with his wife, Amy, he climbed into bed and almost immediately fell asleep.

Amy prepared a hearty meal for Matt when he awoke. Extra crispy bacon, sausage and cheese omelet, fresh fruit, and a Belgium waffle adorned the plate. In his favorite green coffee mug, with the phrase *De Oppresso Liber* adorned in bold letters on the side, his black coffee had a steady flow of steam rising from the top.

"This looks wonderful, honey," Matt said as he took his seat. "Thanks so much."

Amy reached out and rubbed the top of his hand. "Glad to have you home, sugar."

As they sat on their rear deck overlooking the glorious mountains, Matt told her what little he knew about the mysterious project. Within ten minutes, the sound of a vehicle pulling down the gravel driveway interrupted Matt in mid-sentence.

"Sounds like the prodigal son returneth, huh?" he said with a smile towards Amy.

"You know our boy; I think he comes home on the weekends to load up on as much food as he can to get him through the coming week at school."

"Yup, that sounds about right. I don't think he'll ever come off the payroll at this rate. Cate with him?"

"Of course, those two are joined at the hip. They'll typically eat a big lunch and then go out to that training course the two of you concocted for a few hours before they head off to the firing range. After they work up enormous appetites, I get to cook a hearty dinner for them," Amy rolled her eyes.

Matt shrugged. "I offered to buy you a dachshund instead. But one day he'll move away, and we'll wish he was back eating our food and using up our laundry detergent."

"Don't remind me," Amy replied with a frown on her face. "I like things just as they are, thank you very much."

⚬

Troy climbed out of the car and looked to his left as he saw Delmar, the family bison, as he trotted from the center of the pasture close to the fence that bordered the driveway. Troy jogged over and stroked Delmar's horns plus the fur under his enormous mouth. Delmar was a gift to Troy from his parents on his eighth birthday. More pet than wild animal, Delmar brought a smile to Troy's face every time he saw him, even when he ventured into the pasture and stepped in his buffalo chips or meadow muffins as some folks call them.

Cate joined Troy and petted Delmar as well. She looked at Troy, gave him a bit of a hip bump and then stroked his arm. "He's so cute. You know you're the only guy I know who has a buffalo as a pet."

"Hey Pops!" Troy yelled as he pulled a few bags from the car.

Cate jogged up the six steps that led to the front door and gave Matt a big hug. "Hey Mr. Evans, glad to have you back safe and sound where you belong."

"Sheesh, Cate, how many times do I have to tell you Mr. Evans was my dad. My name is Matt, call me that. Hell, call me dad if you want," he said with a sly grin.

Cate returned the smile. "No, I can't do that yet. Maybe one day though." She winked as she turned her head slightly and looked back at Troy. "Can't call you Matt either."

"Well, you're not going to call me Mr. Evans either. You better come up with something one of these days."

Amy leaned over and hugged Cate first, then Troy. "Glad you two are home again." She looked down at the duffel bag of laundry her son brought. "I think it's time I taught you how to do laundry, son," she said with raised eyebrows.

⸺◆⸺

They spent the afternoon at the obstacle course Matt built for his son.

Troy expressed an intense desire to follow in his father's footsteps since childhood, and Matt had taken the interest to heart and poured all he had into Troy. Physically, Matt knew what demands Troy would face as he grew up. The obstacle course he designed would serve specific purposes with the goal of preparing Troy's body for the challenges on the career path he chose.

During those formative years, Matt's knowledge became Troy's. He imparted everything possible to his only son. What surprised Matt was that, at an early age, Troy exceeded his wildest expectations. In fact, the abilities Troy displayed far exceeded Matt's.

⸺◆⸺

As the sun began its descent into the distant horizon, they both practiced Troy's favorite exercise on the silhouetted targets in the shape of a man. Troy simply called it "two-in-one," which stood for two to the chest, one to the head. It was a mantra he shot by, and before long, Cate was an ardent believer in the drill as well.

Two in the chest, one in the head. Make sure that son of a bitch is dead. Troy didn't intend it to be crass or callous, but he wanted Cate to know what his father taught him. Matt's voice still rang in his ears all those years later. *If the need arises to shoot someone, make sure you put em' down and put em' down for good. If they can't get up, they can't hurt you or anyone else.*

Troy complimented Cate on her shooting prowess after she fired her last shot and put the safety on her firearm. "Damn, girl. That's some good shooting," he said with a wide grin.

Cate smiled, "My teacher ain't bad."

After packing up their gear, they headed to the house. Cate helped Amy make dinner while Troy and his father were in the dining room setting the table. Their conversation turned to what had occurred while Matt was in Washington that week. Never one to withhold

"Pretty vague on specifics, pops," Troy said.

Matt nodded. "I know. They are staying tight-lipped about this, at least so far."

"The rotating basis is peculiar, don't you think?"

"Yes, it is."

"What do you make of it?"

"Not sure. Clearly, we'll be working long hours, and whatever we'll be doing will be a twenty-four-seven operation until it's completed."

Troy tapped his foot on the floor. "Think it's dangerous work?"

"Nah," Matt said with a shake of his head.

"Just promise me you'll be safe, pops."

"You know me," Matt said. "I'm not much of a risk taker like you. I should know more when I go to Washington next week. In fact, I thought that maybe once the trips begin regularly, you could join me. We could spend a day or two in Washington, and then you could come to New York City for a few days. You could fly home from there. Cate could come as well. You would only have to miss a day or two of classes if we time it right."

"That sounds cool. I'd love to. Course I don't know if Miss Brainiac there would skip a class. She prides herself on her perfect attendance and all," Troy said with a smile. "I don't think she has missed one since preschool."

From the next room, he got the expected response, "I heard that, smartass. Just to disprove that goody, goody image you have of me, I'll join you two Evans boys on a cross-country trip," Cate said.

CHAPTER ELEVEN

OAK RIDGE, TENNESSEE

It was a brisk day in the mountains of eastern Tennessee as Pat O'Shea stepped onto his front porch. The bright rays of the sun beat down on his face as a piping hot cup of coffee warmed his hand. He'd been home for less than 24 hours, and the jet lag finally took its toll. The nine-hour time zone change threw his sleep pattern for a spin, and he woke up several times in the middle of the night. His body ached, and his head felt like he attended a hard rock concert the night before. A constant *thump* echoed in the void between his two ears. In short, Pat felt his age.

I'm getting too old for this shit, Pat said to himself as he considered the past few days. The week started with a frenzied call from his boss. People high up the food chain became worried, and his job was to assuage those fears. As a result, he and several members of his team boarded a private government jet flying halfway around the world. After several intense days, their investigation yielded no concrete evidence. After a less than desired outcome, they headed back to the United States.

Standing on the front porch, he saw his office building at the Y-12 National Security Complex. Few Americans knew about the secretive facility, and those who heard of it didn't normally hold it in high regard. Made famous as part of the Manhattan Project in the early 1940's; the facility enriched uranium used for the very first atomic bomb.

Pat worked for the National Nuclear Security Administration (NNSA), part of the United States Department of Energy. Since formed in the year 2000, the NNSA has worked closely with the military and other government entities to ensure the protection, transportation, and emergency response regarding all nuclear material for the entire nation. Pat joined in late 2000 as executive director for the Office of Counterterrorism and Counter-Proliferation. The role allowed Pat to work alongside members of the Department of Defense, FBI, NSA, CIA, as well as various other government entities with the shared goal of preventing and detecting any nuclear-related incident against American interests, both domestic and foreign.

When his phone rang the previous Saturday morning, Pat and his team rushed to the Port of New Orleans to investigate the radioactive-laced container. With no nuclear material located, his team flew to Yemen, where the ship originated. There, along with other US government agencies, a thorough search of the Port of Aden took place. Leaving empty-handed, they flew back to Washington to deliver the unfortunate news.

Behind closed doors, he and his team met with the National Security team at the White House, the Senate Committee on Armed Services, and finally the FBI. None of the meetings went well considering they found no trace of the nuclear material. They assured the various agencies that the search would continue until they located the source of the radioactive material. Pat and the others knew that, based on the limited amount of information uncovered, they were looking for a needle in a haystack.

While meeting at the FBI headquarters about the nuclear findings, Pat sat next to Matt Evans. Once their meeting concluded, the two men struck up a conversation and quickly discovered they both shared a common love of the outdoors.

Born in Boston to second-generation Irish immigrants, his parents moved the entire family across the country to Bend, Oregon, when he was four years old. Growing up amidst such natural beauty fostered an appreciation of the outdoors. After completing six years in the Navy, he attended college at the University of

North Carolina, Chapel Hill. After graduating, Pat took a job with the Department of Defense. He and his wife moved to Washington, D.C., where they had three children: two girls and one boy.

Pat had no desire for his family to grow up in the rat race of Northern Virginia. When the opportunity presented itself to take the role with the NNSA and move to eastern Tennessee, he and his wife jumped at the opportunity to escape the beltway.

The silence of his Sunday morning ended as his cell phone rang. He looked at the caller ID and recognized his deputy director's number.

"Hello Steve, how are you on this fine, crisp morning?" Pat asked.

"Doing well, boss, and don't you sound chipper this morning."

"It's a lie. I feel like crap. That's just the caffeine doing the talking."

"Well, I'm sorry to bother you. I know it's a Sunday and you've barely been home a day."

"Nonsense," Pat replied, "I told you to provide me any updates. What do you have?"

"Just wanted to let you know we completed our questioning of the cargo ship's captain in New Orleans."

"And?"

"Every indication is that he's telling us the truth. There is no evidence that the ship made any stops after leaving the port in Yemen. The investigative team concluded there is no plausible way nuclear material was moved off the ship during the transatlantic crossing."

"No way another ship could have met them and unloaded the material during transit?" Pat asked.

"No, we went through the digital logs and at no time did the ship slow down enough to tender with another ship. It never deviated from the course once it left the port. We confirmed that the container in question was sealed prior to departure in Yemen and that the seal remained intact until the port authority personnel broke it and entered the container in New Orleans. The crew all passed the polygraphs we administered. Besides finding a guy on the crew who failed to pay child support, nothing came up on anybody's background check. They're all clean. Nobody on that ship knew about the contents of that container, from what we've determined."

"So where does that leave us? The radiation signature proves the material was in that container at some point."

"I agree; the Geiger counter doesn't lie. We'll keep investigating, but so far, we've got dick."

"Yeah, the fellas in D.C. didn't like when I reported as much yesterday."

"I bet."

"Everybody's gearing up for a cover your ass party if we get hit again," Pat said in a solemn tone.

"As usual, the old Potomac two-step, boss."

"I don't give a damn about their politics, never have. Sure, I can play the game if the circumstances dictate I must. But my primary concern is always that no nuclear material makes its way into the United States. Our job is to protect the interests of the United States and its allies."

"Everyone on the team feels the same way."

"Thanks for all the hard work on this, Steve. Keep digging."

"Will do, Pat. I'll let you know as soon as something turns up."

With that, the phone call ended. Pat took a sip of his now lukewarm coffee, grimaced as the liquid swished around in his mouth. He dumped the remaining coffee over the porch railing before heading back inside to pour a fresh cup.

Chapter Twelve

London

October 2001

Waleed bin Abdulah stared out the bay window of his study, which afforded him an unparalleled view of Hyde Park. A weathered oak and a rounded beech tree that resembled an oversized green mushroom caught his attention. Several members of his staff packed his suitcase upstairs as he prepared to depart for New York City for his second trip stateside in two weeks.

Kadir found him in the study, "It's almost time for us to leave."

Waleed nodded but said nothing for a moment. It was clear his mind was elsewhere. "The trees are beautiful this time of year. Don't you agree?" Waleed asked.

"They are," Kadir answered as he glared intently at his boss, trying to read his thoughts. As usual, this proved difficult.

Waleed was a master at concealing his emotions; even those closest to him had difficulty gauging what went on behind his dark brown eyes. For another minute he looked out the window. Then he turned back and met Kadir's intense gaze. "I see you have a question for me, yes?"

"The teams will start recovery efforts in two days, correct?"

"Yes, I've been told they are very close to the rubble from the third sub-basement. The first truckloads should leave lower Manhattan for the secure site in two days."

"And your sources are sure about the final destination?"

Waleed nodded. "I know that for the past few weeks I've kept you busy on other tasks, but we have much to discuss on the flight. All the debris from the World

Trade Center site is being transported to a landfill named Fresh Kills on Staten Island. However, the FBI knows the sensitive nature of the information contained within many of the containers housed within the secret document repository, so they have erected their own secured facility at Fresh Kills. All material from the Building 7 subfloors will be transported via secure trucks and sorted at their private facility."

"I'm still in awe that you got Aaron on the team."

Waleed smiled from ear to ear. "The House of Saud has friends in prominent places within the United States government. Ryker has a flawless record with the FBI, so getting him assigned to the team was not difficult. His name was on the short list even before I became involved. Like I've told you before, he's the perfect mole. I know you don't trust him, and neither do I, but he knows nothing of my true intentions. Aaron believes at worst I'm a crooked businessman looking for a leg up on my competitors."

Kadir nodded, even though he did not agree with his boss. He also knew it was not his place to question him. "Tell me again about your vision. You said this document will lead you to a device that will be used to bring the United States to its knees. What kind of device is it?"

Waleed rubbed his chin for a moment and ignored the question. "Are you familiar with the Cold War?"

Kadir's gaze narrowed. "Of course."

"Then you've heard of mutually assured destruction?" Waleed asked.

"Yes," Kadi replied., "The mutually assured destruction (MAD) military strategy was based on deterrence. Most people believed that if the United States launched missiles at the Soviets, they would launch their own missiles and both nations would be annihilated. The hope was that MAD would deter any nuclear strikes by either side."

"Excellent, Kadir, you have always been my best student." Waleed patted him on the shoulder. "The United States knew where all the Soviet nukes were, and the Soviets knew where the US ones were located as both nations spied heavily on each other. Honestly, there really was very little chance that a nuclear strike would actually occur."

"That is my understanding as well," Kadir said. "The fact that all sites were known by both sides was likely a stabilizing force that prevented an actual nuclear holocaust."

"Ah...but what if an unknown site existed? Let's say a nuclear weapon was hidden by the Americans from everyone, even the highest-ranking members of the military or government."

"Impossible," Kadir said. "No secret like that could have existed."

Waleed shook his pointer finger back and forth. "Don't be so hasty in that assessment."

"You really believe there was some secret, hidden nuclear weapon in the United States?" Kadir's face revealed his doubt as he continued, "I've heard no such rumors."

Waleed changed the subject. "Do you know the books of the Bible?"

"You know the answer to that; you have instructed me to study the Bible along with the Koran daily for many years."

"Go grab the Bible from the shelf over there," Waleed pointed to the shelf behind Kadir. "Turn to the Old Testament."

"Which book?" Kadir asked.

"Zechariah!" Waleed exclaimed. "Read Chapter 14 verse 12 several times to yourself."

Kadir did as instructed. He read the verse and then re-read it three more times. "What does it mean?" he asked.

"Many scholars differ on what the plague may be," Waleed said.

"And what do you think it means?" Kadir asked.

"It doesn't matter what I believe. What others believed at one time, now that greatly interests me."

"Sorry, but I don't follow," Kadir said as he looked at him with a puzzled look.

"What men have inferred from that passage is complicated and varied. I'm privy to things known too few others, and if rumors I hear are true, this particular verse started a classified project that many people believe never occurred."

"And what project was that?"

"The Zechariah Option," Waleed said.

Chapter Thirteen

Washington D.C.

Inside the secure conference room at the Hoover Building, the tension was palpable. Reeking of sweat and the smell of stale coffee, there was enough testosterone crammed into six hundred square feet to power a nuclear reactor. It would be fair to say that most of the men in the room were alpha males, and even the few women present could hold their own against their male counterparts.

Assembled that day were the FBI team members that made up Operation Core Recoup. Two conference room tables accommodated the thirty-two men and women present. At the head of one table sat the Director of the FBI, and at the other, the deputy director.

The director stood up, and everyone stopped talking. "As you have all been made aware, the FBI had a highly classified document repository beneath World Trade Center Building 7. The facility, known to very few agents, safeguarded our nation's most critical secrets. It was the fourth location we maintained in the nation and by far the largest. The attacks of 9/11 might have destroyed the building, but we feel confident that many of those secrets survived the fire and water damage that occurred in the substructure. Within the next few days, the first shipment of material will make its way to a facility constructed at the Fresh Kills location. That's why we are here today."

He looked around the room briefly before continuing, "You'll be working in five-person teams on 12-hour rotations. Once this mission starts, it will run 24/7 until we have retrieved every single file held within the repository. Make no mistake, the workdays will be intense and the pressure unrelenting, ladies and gentlemen. One supervisor and four special agents on sight per shift and various support personnel. As the material is brought in, the team will work together to categorize, analyze, and properly handle any recovered documents. Some of the material may be damaged, but it's your job to find any items that are salvageable. Documents found in satisfactory condition will be sealed in new containers, locked in safes, and then shipped nightly via air transport back to Washington. Any document severely damaged by water or fire will be incinerated on site. When in doubt, you'll keep the file, and it will be examined further by the team here at the Hoover Building."

"There were three categories of material stored below Building 7. All the files were contained within metallic color-coded boxes. Material categorized as *Secret* were held in green boxes. Items with the designation *Top Secret* were in yellow boxes. Finally, items labeled *Core Secret*, our most sensitive and classified status, were held in red containers. While all three classifications are critical to the national interests the Core Secret items concern us the most. If the red containers are intact, they should not be opened under any circumstances. Those will be immediately loaded into the designated secure safes for transportation back to Washington. However, if the red containers appear to have been damaged or the contents are exposed, a visual inspection of the contents is necessary to check the status of the material found within."

"All of you were selected based on your impeccable standing within the Bureau. Obviously, the content of the material you will handle is for our eyes only; no word of what you handle can be uttered outside that building. That includes discussing amongst yourselves, or with fellow agents when you return to your regular jobs." He paused as he looked slowly around the room and made eye contact with many of the agents. "You get the drift. Each team member will pass through a security checkpoint as they enter and then later as they exit the facility each day. Many foreign interests, governments, intelligence agencies, and other groups would love to get their hands on the classified material. We won't allow that. During your rotation or between shifts, if you observe any suspicious activity or are contacted by anyone out of the ordinary, report it to the special agent in charge of your shift immediately. We are treating Operation Core Recoup as one of the greatest intelligence retrieval missions the Bureau has ever faced and need all of you to do likewise."

⸺◆⸺

As the Director spoke, Aaron Ryker felt for a moment that the Director looked straight at him. *Could he have known of his contact with Waleed?* It was unlikely, but stranger things had happened. Ryker also wondered how Waleed had found out about the facility. Waleed's sources within the government must be even higher and more powerful than he suspected.

A powerful wave of guilt washed over him as the director continued. Ryker's mind contemplated how he could get out of the situation with Waleed. Unfortunately, he saw no way out. Waleed had too much dirt on him, and Aaron felt deep down the bribes he had accepted in the past would come back to haunt him one day. He did his best to push the thoughts out of his mind and focus on the director.

⸺◆⸺

The director continued to speak in a curt tone for several more minutes before the assignment of the six teams took place.

Aaron Ryker's team comprised Ken Flemming from the Milwaukee field office, David Woods from Richmond, and Marco Santiago from Orlando. The special agent in charge was Matt Evans from Idaho.

The five-member teams split up and spent several minutes getting to know one another. Matt Evans was a natural leader, which was clear from the moment he opened his mouth to address his team. As was usually the case, Matt spoke very little about his accomplishments within the Bureau and spent more of his time talking about his only son, Troy.

After ten minutes, the teams re-assembled at the two tables to hear the director's parting words.

"Our mission is clear, ladies and gentlemen. It is vital that we conduct ourselves in absolute secrecy. I know all of you will perform flawlessly. You have all been given a packet of information to review in the coming days. On the last page of the packet, you'll find my personal cell phone and office line. You can contact me with questions or concerns you have, night or day. We don't know how long the effort will take, but we will see it through. I thank you in advance for the time and effort you will spend as this mission is an invaluable effort on behalf of the United States of America."

With that, the meeting ended.

—◦◦◦—

Ninety minutes later, Aaron Ryker sat alone at the United Airlines A21 terminal in Dulles International. With a slight bump in the middle of the black seat cushion, his ass ached. Looking around the boarding area there were no empty seats. *Another full bus flying through the damn sky*, he thought. Moving to another seat really wasn't an option, so he adjusted as best he could to find a more comfortable position. The bump still annoyed the hell out of him no matter how he moved.

His mind turned to his family. He hated that he missed his son's soccer practice. The flight to JFK would get in around 9PM, much too late to say goodnight to his kids, or even his wife.

A bead of sweat formed on his brow as he thought about the day. Pissed at himself for getting into the predicament with Waleed, his mind raced for a way out. For the thousandth time, nothing seemed to provide him with the out he needed. Aaron knew better and should have walked away when he had the chance. Shakespeare's *Merchant of Venice* and the pound of flesh analogy came to mind as he considered his dilemma.

His throat tightened, and he reached into his pocket to grab a breath mint. Retrieving the contents, he found not only the Certs mint but also the business card Matt Evans handed him. He flipped it over through his fingers several times as he considered the man whose name adorned the plain white card stock with black letters. Then he popped the mint into his mouth.

Aaron had never met him before, but by reputation, Matt was a rock star in the Bureau. Before leaving for D.C., Aaron's boss told him that if he was lucky, he'd be placed on Matt's team. *Maybe my boss knew what was going to happen and gave me a little insider information?* For the briefest of seconds, he wondered if he should share with his boss or even Matt about how Waleed approached him. Immediately, those thoughts fled his mind as he saw himself being dragged away in shackles if he admitted to any collusion. *There's got to be another way out of this shit,* he thought to himself as the boarding gate came alive and the peppy female voice announced they were now beginning pre-boarding for his flight. Aaron sucked on the mint, shook his head, and let out a long sigh of wintergreen breath.

Chapter Fourteen

Washington D.C.

When the all-day meeting ended around 6:30 PM, Matt checked his cell phone and saw four new voicemails. A smile formed on his face as he played the first one from his wife. Just checking in with him, her message said she missed him and loved him. Matt knew how fortunate he was to have a partner like Amy. He missed her immensely when they were apart. The next message from his assistant back in the Boise office filled him in on the events of the past few days but didn't include any issues he had to deal with at the moment.

When he played the third message, he let out an audible laugh. The distinguished senior senator from his home state of Idaho asked in a baritone voice if he wanted to go out for drinks while he was in Washington. Matt had known Senator Preston Wilcox III for over 20 years. Their paths crossed years ago while they were both involved with a racketeering (RICO) scandal involving the then governor of the state. The political fallout was ugly, but during the investigation, the two men became fast friends. Over the years they had grown close, and Senator Wilcox had become like a grandfather to Troy. Matt's dad died before Troy's birth, and Amy's dad passed away while she attended college. Before checking the fourth message, Matt called the senator, and they agreed to meet for drinks plus dinner at The Capital Grille on Pennsylvania Ave. Matt figured it would probably be the highlight of the trip.

The fourth message from Pat O'Shea, the director at the NNSA he met recently. Said he was in town until Saturday and wondered if they could meet. Matt didn't want to pass up an opportunity to talk with Pat again, so he called the senator back, who readily agreed to invite Pat to dinner as well.

Pat walked into The Capital Grille and up to the hostess, who greeted him with a warm smile. He gave the attractive young lady his name.

She replied, "The gentlemen have already arrived and are waiting for you. Right this way, sir." The hostess led him through the restaurant to the Fabric Room.

He walked through the heavy doors into the elegant room. Two men deep in conversation stopped talking and stood as he entered.

Matt shook his hand first. "Pat, it's nice to see you again. I'm glad you called. Let me introduce you to my very own senator from Idaho, and also a dear friend, the distinguished Preston Wilcox," Matt spoke the words with a warm smile.

"Knock that distinguished malarkey off, Matthew," the senator said as he gave Pat a firm handshake and slap on the shoulder. "Good to meet you, Pat. Take a seat and get comfortable. Pick your poison, son," he said as he handed him the drink list.

"It's an honor, Senator Wilcox. You have quite the reputation around D.C.," Pat said as he glanced down at the extensive drink menu.

"Is that good or bad?" Preston asked with a wink and a crooked grin.

"You have an extremely positive reputation, senator," Pat said.

"Well good, but please call me Preston. All the senator formality can get old. Tonight, we can break bread as friends and enjoy this beautiful setting for a meal."

Pat dipped his head. "That sounds like a great idea."

"So, Matt tells me you work for the NNSA. What's your role with them if you don't mind my asking?"

"Not at all, I'm the Executive Director of the Office of Counterterrorism and Counter Proliferation."

A waiter knocked, disturbing the conversation, then entered as instructed. He took their orders for drinks and dinner.

After the waiter left, Preston continued the conversation. "Ah yes, of course, I am very familiar with the NNSA and that role in particular."

Pat smiled. "That's nice to hear since most folks I talk to on Capitol Hill have never even heard of us."

"Yes, well, I've been on the Senate Committee on Armed Services for a long, long time and have had the privilege of serving as the chairperson as well. I'm also a member of the Energy and Natural Resources Committee and was instrumental in the formation of the NNSA in 2000."

"I take it I have you to thank for having a job," Pat said with a wide smile.

"Hardly," Preston said. "But I think that forming the NNSA and putting all our nuclear resources under one roof was a wise idea, especially based on the grave threats we face these days."

"I agree," Pat nodded. "It's a pretty screwed up world."

"You enjoy the role?" Matt asked. "Don't miss the rat race up here in D.C., do you? You're in Tennessee, right?"

"Yes, I love my job. I moved my family down there last year when I accepted the role. Nestled in the mountains, it really feels like we're in God's country. My family and I don't miss the beltway in the least. No offense, Preston," he said as he looked towards the senator.

"None taken, I'm an Idaho boy at heart," Preston said as he looked back and forth between the men across the table from him. "I'll tell you boys the God's honest truth. Most people come to D.C. to do good. Really, they do. But the politics, special interests and overall wrangling that take place really beat the average person down. Before long, they bend their morals and overall principles and fall in line with what the members of their particular party, or powerful lobbyists who may have gotten them elected, tell them to do. There are very few Mr. Smiths in Washington anymore."

"You as well?" Matt asked, with eyebrows slightly raised and a broad grin.

"We have had this conversation many times my boy," Preston stared at Matt. "I've fared better than most but yes to some extent you must give in when you come to Washington. Holding your ground and sticking to your guns in every instance just means you lose ground. The system will abandon you quickly. Washington is very much a city about adapting. I feel that I've stuck to my core principles, but to get things accomplished, compromise is necessary. But enough about me, I'm an old man after all. I would much rather hear about the two of you."

"I hear you will spend a lot of time in the New York City area in the coming months," Pat said. "There's some sort of big FBI operation going on, and your name was in the mix from what I heard."

"Really?" Matt replied in somewhat a surprised tone. "I'm disappointed the word leaked out so quickly. What have you heard?"

"You're in Washington, my boy," Preston chimed in. "Secrets here last about as long a funnel cake at the county fair."

"Good point," Matt said with a frown.

"I've heard very little, to be honest," Pat said truthfully. "Just inter-agency chatter, of course. No one really knows what the FBI is up to, but the rumor is it is something involving the World Trade Center site. That is about all I have heard."

"Interesting," Matt said.

"I take it you can't say much about what is going on, can you?" Pat asked.

With a cheeky grin Matt said, "I'd have to kill you, Pat."

They all chuckled.

"All joking aside, I'm sworn to secrecy on this one. Although it may not be as interesting as The Drudge Report might concoct about what we're doing."

"I hear ya. The NNSA is filled with many secrets. I'm good at keeping my lips shut, but it can be hard with a wife and young kids. Makes it tough to disappear for a week or two and not tell your family a single thing that happened, or where you even went," Pat said.

"I know exactly what you mean," Matt replied.

"Any stories like that, Preston?" Pat asked as he looked toward the senator.

"Me? No, of course not. I am merely a humble United States Senator, gentlemen," Preston replied with a smile. "Nothing interesting to report on my end."

"Don't let that grin fool you, Pat," Matt replied. "I know for a fact Preston here spent some time during 1947, while in the Air Force, at a little-known place called Roswell, New Mexico."

"Did you now?" Pat asked. He had a genuinely shocked expression on his face.

Preston glanced back at both men, smirked and then replied, "I can neither confirm nor deny the events of July 8, 1947."

Waiters arrived as he finished the statement, and the conversation shifted.

As Preston cut into his lamb chops, "Tell me, Pat. In the wake of 9/11 and the horrific events not just in New York City, but also here in Washington, what do you feel is our gravest threat?"

Pat stroked his chin. "Without a doubt, the threat of a nuclear or biological attack. Not a day has gone by since 9/11 that the NNSA has not received credible threats and information from the NSA and CIA about intentions that various terrorists or rogue nations have expressed."

"But how likely are they to get the material to strike us?" Matt asked.

"That's the million-dollar question right now," Pat said. "Not sure what the answer is either. There are plenty of nations out there with nuclear capabilities that would like nothing more than to see the utterly annihilation of the United States. And while getting material out of some nations and smuggling it safely into the States would be difficult, it wouldn't be impossible. Our border is porous, and we have thousands of miles of coastline to safeguard as well. There would be any number of ways to get either nuclear or biological material here."

"It's an extremely serious issue. I've seen some of the same intelligence," Preston said as he shook his head in agreement.

"We also have to consider the material we have right here in the United States," Pat added. "While I feel extremely confident it's secure, don't doubt for a second that terrorists aren't trying to acquire and use it against us. I'd like to think that wasn't possible. However, if you asked me a few months ago if they could have hijacked four planes and coordinated attacks in Washington and New York City, I would have scoffed at any such notion. I would have thought it to be lunacy. And here we sit."

Matt nodded in agreement but said nothing in response.

For the next fifteen minutes, he and Pat went down a rabbit hole discussing nuclear threats and how close the nation might be to facing an imminent attack. Preston sat back with arms folded and nodded occasionally.

It was imperceptible, but the senator perked up when Pat discussed specifics on the nuclear material that was housed throughout the United States. He knew something neither man at the table knew, and he hoped to God that the deep dark secret stayed right where it was, a distant memory of days passed.

—◆—

Later that evening, long after the wonderful dinner ended, Senator Wilcox sat alone in his study on the second floor. His townhouse in Georgetown on O Street between 33rd and 34th was his sanctuary while in the nation's capital. He had purchased the three-story Victorian-designed building in the late 1960's when Georgetown was hardly as trendy as it had become. His wife, Sarah, had passed away three years prior from breast cancer, and Preston now lived alone. It was far too large of a house just for him, but he had owned it for so long he just would not part with it. He had other ideas about what should happen to the property one day after he passed.

He poured himself a second glass of scotch and opened the humidor that sat next to his desk, which was an exquisite reproduction of the Resolute Desk that resided in the Oval Office. Preston removed a La Flor Dominicana Double Ligero Chisel cigar. Sipping at the smooth scotch and sucking in a draw from the potent cigar, his mind went back to October 1962 when life as he knew it changed in an instant.

Chapter Fifteen

Washington, D.C.

October 1, 1962

Three-term Congressman Preston Wilcox III from District One in Idaho appeared shocked as he placed the phone back in its cradle. He sat for several minutes lost in his thoughts at his office in the Cannon House Office Building. The caller had informed him that US Senator Charles Hall, the senior senator from his home state of Idaho, passed away less than an hour ago after a sudden illness. The Wilcox and Hall families had been closely tied in Idaho politics over the years, and it was unthinkable he suddenly lost his mentor. But more than that, he lost a dear friend.

The rest of the day was a blur for the congressman. Many of his fellow House of Representatives members and even some from the Senate came by his office to offer their sincere condolences. They all knew how very close he had been to Charles. Of course, this was Washington, and it didn't take long before whispers spread around the Capitol complex about who would be selected to fill Senator Hall's remaining term.

The next day he received a call. It was brief and to the point since the person who placed the call never minced words and did not like to have long drawn-out conversations. Governor James Owing of Idaho expressed his deepest sympathies to Preston, but then promptly informed the congressman of his intention to appoint him to the vacated seat in the United States Senate.

The governor allowed time for the senator's burial and waited until October 13th before holding a press conference announcing that Congressman Preston Wilcox III would fill the vacancy and finish out the remaining 2 years of Senator Hall's term.

The next day, Congressman Wilcox took the Senate oath of office, which was administered by the President of the Senate, and officially became Senator Preston Wilcox III. It was a title he would hold for 39 years.

Immediately the transition of his office and staff from the Cannon House Office Building to the Russell Senate Office Building began. Boxes were still being packed within his predecessor's office when he walked in for the first time. Senator Wilcox was seated at his new desk when the world, as he knew it, changed in an instant.

As the new senator sat at his desk for the first time, a U-2 spy plane being piloted by Major Richard Heyser took 928 photographs while flying over western Cuba. Some photos showed the construction of an SS-4 ballistic missile site.

It took about a day before the CIA's National Photographic Interpretation Center realized what those images showed. Late on the evening of October 15th, the President's National Security Advisor McGeorge Bundy was notified of the finding. He waited until the next morning before informing the president about the grave find.

Word spread like wildfire on the Hill, and within less than 60 minutes, Preston knew about the impending crisis as well. The Cuban Missile Crisis had begun, and the United States was about to be as close as it ever would be to having an all-out nuclear war with the Soviet Union.

—◦—

Another major development on October 16th, at least for Senator Wilcox, occurred when he was informed he would take the spot vacated by Senator Hall on the Senate Committee on Armed Services. This was quite a surprise for many folks on the Hill. The Senate Committee on Armed Services was one of the most powerful and sought-after committee posts a senator could achieve. More than a few heads shook disapprovingly, and many verbal arrows were uttered in Senator Wilcox's direction after the announcement.

With the dire situation taking place in Cuba, Preston walked nervously into room 228 at the Russell Senate Building. As he took his assigned seat, a warm hand landed on his shoulder and a friendly voice with a deep Southern drawl greeted him. "Preston, we're glad to have someone of your caliber joining our committee."

Preston looked back and saw the unmistakable smile of Senator Richard Griffith from the state of Georgia. "Senator Griffith, good to see you. It is an honor to be selected for the committee, sir."

"It seemed the right thing to do," Richard said. "Charlie Hall was a valuable member of this committee for many years, and we all recognize the fact that he was your mentor."

"That he was senator."

"Please Preston, we are colleagues now, call me Dick, everyone else does. Although I am sure some of them say it in a very disparaging way," Senator Griffith followed the statement with a belly laugh.

"I'll try to remember that, sir," Preston said.

"No, Preston, not sir either, Dick will do just fine," he said with a kind smile. "You're sure joining us in the middle of one big tinderbox now, aren't you?"

"Appears to be that way, Sena ... uh ... Dick. I think many people are afraid we may be closer to nuclear war with the Soviets than ever before."

"Mutually assured destruction, Preston, is the only thing keeping us from all-out nuclear war with those dirty Reds I fear," Richard said as he bit at his lower lip. "I just hope it's enough, and that's my prayer to the good Lord right now."

The committee meeting came to order, and the next two hours were a blur to Preston.

Over the next several days, the committee would meet countless times as the two most powerful nations on earth slid closer to all-out nuclear war. During those tense days, Senator Griffith took the newly appointed senator from Idaho under his wing and guided him through how the Senate really worked.

The two men complemented each other well and became fast friends even though the senator from Georgia was almost 20 years older. Dick's sweet southern drawl could turn into a razor-sharp viper tongue if the need arose. He was brilliant but struggled with the ability to talk to people at their level. People recoiled since they felt he was talking down to those around him. That's where Preston's panache counterbalanced him so well. The junior senator from Idaho might not be the most knowledgeable man on the Hill, but he surely did not lack confidence. Preston had a way of talking to people that would sway them towards his position and eventually lead most of them to do exactly what it was he wanted.

Fortunately, the Cuban Missile Crisis abated by late October. Even though the potential end of civilization was averted, there were scars that remained. During the subsequent weeks and months that followed, the junior senator from Idaho and senior senator from Georgia spoke regularly, even in private discussions, about the threat of all-out nuclear war.

One Monday evening while out for dinner, their discussions became intense. As usual, Dick drove the conversation that night.

"Let's just say I'm right, Preston, and one day the Reds launch their nuclear weapons, what then?"

"Well, for starters," Preston replied. "We will nuke them back. So, in essence, we'll all be dead."

"Do you know for a fact we will all be dead?" Richard asked.

"Of course not. I don't know who would live and who would die, only God knows that. But I am confident that most of our civilization would be destroyed. Those that live through the initial detonations won't stand much of a chance at long-term survival, at least not if they stay in what is left of the United States. The nuclear winter that follows will probably kill many that don't starve to death."

Richard changed the subject as he asked, "I know you are a man of faith, Preston. So tell me, what does the Bible say about the United States in the end times?"

Thinking for a moment, Preston replied, "As far as I know, we aren't mentioned."

"Precisely," Richard said.

"What do you think that means?" Preston asked.

"Lots of intelligent men have all sorts of theories about that. Unfortunately, they are all guesses. I disagree with you and think that there will be countless souls that survive a nuclear war with the Soviets."

"And? Preston asked.

"Those poor bastards will be left with a nation in shambles. Their way of life, and most major cities, annihilated. Citizens will have been vaporized, and the nuclear arsenal we have built so meticulously these last 20 years will be gone forever."

"Sounds like a horrific ending to the United States, Dick."

"I concur, and that's why I want to change it."

"How so? Do you have a way to make sure a nuclear war never occurs between our two nations?" Preston asked incredulously.

"Well, I'd love to, but I can't necessarily prevent that. What I can do though is to protect those that remain when or if a horrific event like that actually occurs."

"I'm all ears," responded Preston.

Richard smiled; it was a toothy grin. "I'm not that easy. First things first. When you go home tonight and lay down next to that pretty little wife of yours, pull out the good book. Read something for me."

"Sure. Which book?"

"Zechariah!"

"The Old Testament prophet?"

"Yes, the one and only."

"The entire book?"

"Yes, but closely study chapter 14, verse 12."

"To what end?"

"Just read it, Preston, humor an old man," he said with a warm smile. "When we meet again next week for dinner, I will lay out my plan to you."

"And what plan is that?" Preston asked.

"Why, the Zechariah Option, of course," Dick winked as he took another sip of the scotch he held in his right hand.

Chapter Sixteen

Fresh Kills, NY

It was a sunny but cool fall day in New York as Matt Evans pulled into the Fresh Kills landfill, which housed the debris from the World Trade Center site. The landfill was quite large, and the security presence remarkable. Even though his team was not scheduled to start their rotation for 10 more days, Matt wanted to watch the process unfold the first day so he and his men would be better equipped when their shift started. It spoke to Matt's meticulous nature.

After Matt presented his credentials at the main gate, the checkpoint officer directed him to the FBI building on the western side of the property. The structure was constructed quickly but securely designed. With entry into the facility strictly monitored 24 hours a day, four guards were posted at the gate leading into the facility. Each semi that brought debris from World Trade Center 7 had to pass through this single-entry point.

Matt Evans shook hands with his counterpart, Mike Rodgers, who oversaw the first team. Matt sipped his fresh, steaming coffee as the first truckload of debris pulled up to the facility. He had worked with Mike many times over the years, and they had a great rapport.

"How's the process work?" Matt asked.

Mike pointed to the big rig. "Semi's get loaded in lower Manhattan at the Building 7 site. Once ready, an armed convoy escorts the semi to this facility, and that's where we take over. Our job is to unload the contents and start examining the files."

Matt nodded. "How many trucks a day?"

"As many as the teams can process. It's our job, yours and mine, to radio the command center and tell them we are ready for another load."

Mike cocked his head. "Follow me." He led Matt inside the building and took him to the very center of the structure. The area that the teams would analyze the debris was forty feet by sixty feet. At the very center of the space were two steel rectangular tables measuring eight feet by four feet where the teams would work. Above each table was a surgical light to aid in inspection. Matt looked around as he observed the room and saw numerous cameras pointed at the two tables.

Even though Matt sat through a dozen briefings and read all the paperwork, and knew the answers, he asked Mike direct questions as if he didn't know the entire process. He knew it would be an excellent exercise for both men to go through. "What happens next?"

As the two senior agents spoke, the team in place worked efficiently and processed the first files unloaded from the semi's.

Mike motioned to an agent, who opened the first secure container. "After the document is analyzed and indexed, it is then secured in one of those ten ISM Super Platinum safes that line the northern wall." Mike pointed towards the safes.

"How long do the files stay on site?"

"Each day at 8 P.M. sharp, a chopper lands on the helipad outside. The team working that shift empties the contents of the safes into those specialized carts and gets them loaded. The chopper goes directly to headquarters in D.C., where the files will be secured until a new location is determined."

Matt watched the process for a while and was impressed by how smoothly it ran, especially since it had been developed in such a short amount of time.

"What about the files that are unreadable and too damaged to keep?"

Mike smirked, and even though he knew Matt knew all the answers, he continued to play along. He pointed to the incinerator in the far corner of the room. "They get disposed of in there. They plan to keep that thing running all day, every day."

"Good thing they got AC pumping cool air in here," Matt said.

Matt stayed on site most of the day and observed the process with a keen eye. He asked Mike questions occasionally and even provided his feedback when it was requested. It was an eventful day, and he learned a lot. Around 3 P.M. he decided he had seen enough and made flight arrangements to head back to Boise. He left the complex, grabbed some dinner and sat at the JFK International Airport terminal by 7 PM. He had the last flight out, which would get him home around 1 in the morning.

As he was waiting for his flight in the first-class lounge, his cell phone rang. He looked down at the number and recognized the NYC area code.

"This is Matt," he answered.

"Hey it's Aaron Ryker."

Matt let out a sigh. He had totally forgotten Aaron's request that he call after his visit to the facility. "Aaron, I'm so sorry I forgot to call." He stepped inside a noise-reducing booth in the lounge so he could continue his conversation in private.

"No problem. I'm sure there was a lot to take in. So how was it?" Aaron asked.

Matt spent the next 15 minutes explaining the process. "I will say they have that place locked down like Fort Knox."

"Can't say I'm surprised," Aaron answered. "Especially based on the sensitive nature of what we'll be handling."

"When you leave at the end of your shift, they run you through a metal detector and give you a complimentary pat down."

"Do they offer you a smoke after the frisking ends?" Aaron asked with a laugh.

"Nope," Matt chuckled.

The sound of his flight getting ready to board interrupted the next few words.

"Sounds like you have a flight to catch," Aaron said.

"Yes, still have a few more things to fill you and the others in on. I'll set up a conference call for the five of us when I'm back in Boise."

"Talk to you then, have a safe flight."

"Thanks, Aaron, good night."

———◆———

Aaron Ryker hung up the phone and thought about the security Matt described. He then dwelled on his meeting with Waleed. Even if he was willing to get a document out of the facility, getting it past security would prove damn near impossible. After a few minutes of mulling over the conversation, he decided he should call Waleed in the morning and fill him in on what he learned from Matt Evans.

CHAPTER SEVENTEEN

BOISE

Every Tuesday night, Troy's two roommates at Boise State both had classes until 9 P.M. meaning he had the place for himself. Cate had two roommates as well and rarely had the dorm room to herself. Typically, Troy and Cate met for dinner at their favorite sushi restaurant at six sharp and then headed back to his room.

Much to her surprise, Troy was a no-show at the sushi restaurant.

Six came and went with no sign of Troy.

Cate couldn't recall a time he didn't show up or at least call.

She waited for twenty minutes in the booth and even tried his cell phone several times. No response.

As she made her way to Keiser Hall, she got nervous. Being late was a pet peeve that irritated Troy to no end.

Cate knocked twice without an answer. Leaning over, she put her ear up to the door and heard noises coming from inside. It sounded like she heard muffled yelling. After another knock and no response, she reached into her purse and fumbled around for the key to Troy's dorm room. He gave her a spare key at the start of the semester, but she never thought she would need it in this situation.

With the lock disengaged, she twisted the knob and pushed the door open with a firm shove. It struck the doorstopper on the wall with a dull thud.

Startled by the sound of the door hitting the stopper, Troy looked up and away from the television to see Cate take several long strides as she entered the room.

"What's up, babe?" Troy asked with a stern expression. He looked upset, even frustrated. Not a typical glance he ever threw her way.

"Umm, did you forget about dinner?" Cate asked.

Troy looked at her with a dumbfounded look and then down at his watch.

"Jeez, is it really six-thirty?"

Cate pursed her lips. "Yes, it is."

"Babe, I'm so sorry I totally spaced."

She shook her head. "What have you been doing all this time?"

Troy met her gaze and then looked back at the television. "Started watching this program about Bin laden on cable news after my class got out."

Cate saw the images on the screen and then her gaze settled back on Troy. "I can see that."

Across the screen rapid-fire images of war scenes flashed one after another. Troy looked at the screen and the tension in his body became palpable. The sense of frustration spread across his face.

"Settle down there, big guy," Cate said as she got closer and grabbed his shoulder.

Troy shook his head. "I can't. This stuff gets me worked up."

Cate tried to massage his tense muscles. "I know. You've been watching all this ever since 9/11 and especially since we invaded Afghanistan."

"I want to do something, Cate. Make a difference."

"You are doing something," she said.

"Yeah, I'm sitting in classes twiddling my thumbs, listening to meaningless lectures, and taking stupid tests."

Cate took a step back. "Yeah, so you can finish your degree and do what you were born to do."

"But in the meantime," his voice trailed off as his gaze focused on the television screen.

"Look at me." Cate stepped closer and turned his face away from the screen towards her.

He looked into her eyes. Those icy blue eyes made his knees buckle and his heart melt. Every single time without fail. "I see you babe, you're gorgeous, by the way." He moved his hand to the small of her back and gave it a gentle rub.

"Yeah, you're always the charmer, aren't you?"

Troy smiled and pulled her in for a long kiss.

She gave in for almost a minute before she pulled back.

Troy had a confused look on his face. "What did I do?"

"You dissed me and left me sitting in an empty booth by myself."

"And?" Troy asked.

"I'm hungry. You know better than to let a woman get famished. Or at least you better know better by now."

"Why didn't you let another guy buy you dinner? I'm sure you had to beat them off with a stick."

"I only have eyes for you, Troy Matthew Evans," Cate said as she mocked fanning herself.

Troy smirked at the sarcastic gesture. "Aww, does that mean I'm out of the penalty box?"

Cate rolled her eyes. "No, it means you get to turn off the television, get off your ass, and buy me dinner."

"What about some dessert? I'd love a cherry on top."

"Don't push your luck," Cate said as she walked towards the dorm room door.

Chapter Eighteen

London

Waleed took the last bite of poached egg a moment before his cell phone chirped. He recognized Ryker's number displayed on his Nokia 8310. He clicked the green answer button and raised the phone to the side of his head. "Aaron, it's very early in New York, why are you calling at such an hour?"

"We have a problem," Ryker said.

Waleed cleared his throat. "I'm listening."

Their call lasted nearly twenty minutes, and after it concluded, Waleed sat in his study alone and thought about what he had been told. Nothing about the facilities or security measures the FBI implemented surprised him. In fact, he thought they might be more extreme given the sensitive nature of the material. Some modifications to a few of their processes would most certainly be needed, but that shouldn't prove difficult in the nine days before Aaron's first shift started.

The troubling part of the call was the fear he sensed within Ryker's voice.

Waleed prided himself on being able to read people very well and knew he could bring extreme pressure down on Ryker to do his bidding. Ryker must have known this as well, but ultimately Waleed needed more leverage.

He felt quite confident that the document would be found as the vision had foretold, but many possibilities for complications existed. Ryker could still report to his superiors what Waleed had requested. It was also a genuine possibility that he might get caught stealing the document. What concerned Waleed more than anything else was whether Ryker found the document but refused to hand it over. That option was simply unacceptable.

Somehow, he needed to be sure Ryker would stick with his end of the bargain. Waleed mulled over the dilemma for quite some time. After what seemed like hours, a plan came to him. He called Kadir into his study and told him he needed to contact someone from his past. This person was hard to track down, yet less than twenty minutes later Kadir returned with a phone number. Waleed looked at the number and dialed it. On the second ring, a voice answered.

"What do you want?" A voice questioned in an exasperated tone.

"How are you, Muhammad?" Waleed asked.

"It's been a very long time, and I very much doubt this is a courtesy call to discuss how things have been. You clearly want something, Waleed. Since it is not one of your people calling, it must be important."

"The years have not dulled your charm, Muhammad. Yes, I have something important to discuss. Where are you now?"

Muhammad Jarah answered truthfully. "Jalalabad."

"Afghanistan? Really? Even with the US invasion occurring there?" Waleed did not hide his surprise.

"Of course, with the great Satan in the country, there is plenty of work for men in my profession."

"I'm afraid I will need you to leave immediately," Waleed answered.

"Excuse me?" Muhammad asked.

Waleed spent the next five minutes giving very few specifics. It was enough to let Muhammad know he was needed in the United States, and that it was important. He mentioned, "an FBI agent." in the discussion but no names. Waleed knew better.

"So how will I help persuade this FBI agent to do your bidding?" Muhammad asked.

"You will of course use your witty personality and forms of persuasion."

"On him?"

"No, he is not to be touched."

"Then how?" Muhammad asked.

"He has a wife and two young children. The family lives in Queens, so I need you to be there to learn their routine and come up with some contingency plans in case we must apply some pressure."

"Why me?" Muhammad asked in a curt tone. "Why now? We have not spoken in years."

"No, not since 1994," Waleed replied.

"Ah, so my failure to secure those files for you back then is coming back to haunt me. You have finally called in the marker."

"Not at all," Waleed said." This is about redemption, not retribution. You will have the opportunity to retrieve what slipped through your grasp on that fateful day."

"You know that mission was a long shot from the start, right? The fact we almost pulled it off was a miracle in itself," Muhammad said forcefully.

"I knew it would be difficult, and surely it was brief notice, but I had faith in you and your men. Like I said, this is a story about redemption. You will help finish what was started all those years ago."

Suddenly, the sound of an enormous explosion could be heard in the background.

"What was that?" Waleed asked.

"Your friends, the Americans, are bombing the Taliban training sites and air defense systems here in Jalalabad. Sounded like that strike was probably ten miles away." explained Muhammad.

"Are you safe?"

"Waleed, in my line of work one is never truly safe," he responded.

"Is the airport still open?"

"Yes, at least for now," Muhammad said. "I don't believe the Americans will shut it down immediately."

"Okay, pack your things. I'll have a jet there shortly to pick you up. It will take you to London, where we can meet and discuss more specifics. Then within thirty-six hours I want you in Queens getting to work."

"You're not asking, are you?"

"Muhammad, you knew the minute you answered your phone I would ask nothing. Fear not, you will be glad that redemption found you. The circle will be closed when you are done."

"The marker will be settled?"

"Precisely," Waleed said. "The ledger will be clean. Plus, I'll reward you handsomely, you can name your price."

There was silence for a few seconds before Muhammad replied. "When does my plane arrive?"

"My associate Kadir will be in touch within the next hour. Just stay safe and make it to the airport in one piece."

"I'm not that easy to kill," Muhammad replied as the line clicked off.

◆

As he stood up, Waleed stretched his back, reached down, and touched his toes several times. Kadir walked back into the room, and Waleed informed him of what was said.

"Is including Muhammad wise?" Kadir asked.

"Yes, why?"

"He is wanted by the United States for many crimes, including terrorism."

"Muhammad's crimes are his problem, and the Americans have little chance of catching him, even if he walks in plain sight down Madison Ave."

"And his failure on your behalf in the past?"

"Like I said on the call, this is his chance for redemption," Waleed said.

Kadir looked unconvinced, but replied, "As you say ..."

"Anyway, if something goes wrong, we can pin the whole thing on Muhammad. He would be a perfect scapegoat. Trust me, he will not fail me this time. It's in his nature to learn and adapt. He has learned much in the last seven years. His overseas fighting has made him an asset to have."

"Can he be controlled though?"

Waleed raised his eyebrows. "Live by the bullet, die by the bullet, say the Americans. Control can be easily achieved with a nine-gram slug."

Chapter Nineteen

Queens, NY

As he looked down at his watch, the man pulled his New York Yankees ball cap low and made a note of the time. As he watched, a woman and her two young children crossed the street before him and climbed into a blue Saab.

A few minutes later, Sally Ryker took a right-hand turn from Broadway and onto Steinway St headed towards her home on 25th Ave.

Three car lengths behind Muhammad Jarah followed in a tan Honda Accord. He had arrived in New York City two nights prior and had followed the Ryker family ever since. The youngest child, Lacy, was six years old in the first grade. Her older brother Alex was eight and in third grade. Both children attended the same school on Broadway in Queens. One school made things simpler for Muhammad.

Sally pulled into a narrow driveway while Muhammad drove past the house before he made a U-turn. He found a spot to park along the curb about fifty feet from Ryker's house. He watched as Sally and the kids climbed out of the car and headed into the house and made a note of the time in his journal.

In just three days, he had already figured out the normal daily routine. Week-days, Sally dropped the kids off at school and headed to her job at an accounting firm on 36th Ave. Muhammad took the opportunity when nobody was home to enter the Ryker's home.

Muhammad was sure not to stay in the home any longer than necessary. While there, he mapped out a floor plan, which included where everyone slept. He also placed several listening devices and surveillance cameras in discreet locations.

Only a highly skilled person would notice them, as Muhammad covered his tracks well.

After getting back into his car, he flipped open his laptop and made sure that his devices were functioning properly. Next, he made his way to 26 Federal Plaza in Manhattan, where Aaron worked. He wanted to be familiar with the area, and for the next hour he simply drove around lower Manhattan. He found a parking spot near the FBI field office and parked.

Close by was an internet café. He made his way inside, ordered a coffee so as not to look suspicious, and turned on his laptop. After he paid for his internet connection, he sipped his coffee and pulled up the program that showed the tracking devices. He had placed both identical pieces of equipment on Aaron and Sally's vehicle the day he had arrived in Queens. Aaron's vehicle was parked at Federal Plaza, while Sally's vehicle was at the accounting firm in Queens.

Pleased with his progress, Muhammad headed back to his safe house in the Astoria area of Queens. He had a few hours to update the large map that hung on the wall of the living room in the apartment. It showed the locations the Ryker's frequented as well as the routes they normally took around Queens.

Just then, his cell phone rang. Muhammad looked at the number, it was Kadir.

For the next 30 minutes, Muhammad provided all the details he felt necessary. The only request Kadir relayed was that Waleed wanted the surveillance data that was being collected from the Ryker's home to be fed directly into the secure server. Muhammad acknowledged the request, and within forty-five minutes the process was complete. The data was accessible to Waleed in London.

Chapter Twenty

Boise

Both Troy and Cate's excitement was palpable as they sat in the Boise Airport terminal. The flight to Dulles International Airport would have a brief layover in Minneapolis. Cate had never been to D.C. while Troy lost count how many times he had flown to the nation's capital.

With their zone called, they walked hand in hand onto the plane and took their seats in the middle section of the fuselage. Troy, to be gallant, asked Cate if she wanted the window seat. She readily accepted and gave his backside a gentle tap, subtly acknowledging his chivalrous act. Once they were airborne and reached 30,000 feet, they cuddled up next to each other and chatted.

"Favorite place in DC?" Cate beamed as she stared into his eyes.

"Please," he said in a drawn-out fashion. "The Hoover Building, of course."

"Of course," Cate remarked. "And remind me how many times you've been there?"

"Lost count. When I was a teenager, my dad would take me on lots of trips to D.C. with him. He had to go several times a month back then."

"And what did you do while your dad worked?"

"Sometimes I chilled at the hotel, and other times I roamed around downtown. Spent a lot of time at the Smithsonian when I was about 15 or 16. Stayed with Sarah a lot, especially if homework was due when I got back home."

"Senator Wilcox and his wife, Sarah, really made you feel like part of the family, huh?"

Troy nodded.

Cate smiled. "Tell me more about working at the Capitol."

"Preston had asked me to intern in his Senate office between my junior and senior year of high school. Now that was cool. I could see parts of the Capitol few experience, and it was amazing to see how things work up there from the inside looking out. They even turned their spare room in Georgetown into a bedroom for me. Made me feel right at home, plus Sarah sure could cook."

"Rubbing elbows with a United States senator," Cate said. "I bet you did some important stuff that summer."

"Ya right! More like I made photocopies and ran errands all around the Capitol complex. Not too glamorous."

"Still cool," Cate said.

"Absolutely, I can't complain. I met a lot of politicians and celebrities that summer, and I ended up going to a bunch of political parties with Preston. That wasn't long before Sarah got sick and passed away suddenly, things changed quickly." Troy turned somber, "She was an amazing lady, and I really miss her."

Cate brought him back. Her blue eyes had a way of doing that. "I think it's wonderful that your family stayed close to the senator."

"I've known him practically my whole life, and he always treated us like we were part of the family. In a city filled with crooks and selfish people, he really is a good soul."

"So, he really brought you to the White House and introduced you to the president that summer?"

"He did," Troy leaned over and kissed Cate's forehead. "Preston took me to a state dinner that summer. Now that was an awesome experience. One in a lifetime opportunity."

"But you didn't get to see the Oval Office?"

Troy shook his head back. "No, even though I mustered the courage and asked the president personally. He said 'absolutely' and I could have my own personal tour. See not just the Oval but a full tour of the White House, including the secret underground bunker. Unfortunately, some terrorist incident took place the day of my visit, and all the scheduled events got re-arranged. I lost my chance since the summer internship ended the next week, and I headed back to Drexel. The Oval is the one place I really want to see with my own eyes."

Cate looked out the window towards the billowing clouds on the horizon. "You will one day."

"Hopefully so," Troy replied.

"Maybe it will happen before you jump out of a plane," she said with a playful nudge.

Troy shook his head emphatically, "I'm not jumping out of a perfectly good plane. Why would I?"

"To live a little," Cate said. "It's much more fun than you think. The free fall alone will take your breath away, literally!"

Troy rolled his eyes. "I'll take your word for it."

"Real men jump out of planes," Cate popped his ribs with her elbow.

"Yah, REAL idiotic ones!" Troy exclaimed. "Not gonna happen, babe."

Cate changed the subject. "So tell me, Mr. coast to coast frequent traveler, what is one place you haven't traveled to in the lower 48 states that you are dying to see?"

Without hesitation, Troy responded, "Yosemite."

Cate laughed, "I've been barely anywhere, but even I have been there!"

"Just rub it in," Troy said. "Pops and I were supposed to go a few years back. Some intense wildfires started the week before the trip, and it got canceled. We never made it back. Eventually I'll make it."

"I bet you'll take me there one day." Cate said in a sweet tone.

"Deal!" Troy said with a warm smile as he squeezed her tightly close to him.

Before long, Cate dozed. Troy could never sleep on planes. In fact, as often as he flew, the thrill and excitement of being in the air never left him. With Cate asleep, he looked over and watched her rhythmic breaths. Her chest rose and fell with each draw of air as an ever so slight smile formed on the corner of her lips. He hoped she was dreaming of them, and their future.

———— ◄O► ————

As Cate slept, his mind went back a year before, during the first day of classes at the start of his sophomore year. That was the day when a life-changing event occurred.

Troy had settled into class and had his head down with his nose buried in the syllabus. That fateful class was Psychology of Law, a prerequisite for his degree. He failed to notice the person who entered and sat in the chair to his right. As the professor handed out more paperwork, the young lady in that chair next to him handed the packet to Troy. He looked up and over towards her as he grabbed the syllabus. As they made eye contact, the young lady smiled, and Troy looked back dumbfounded. He stared at her as if in a daze, not even able to return her smile. She was simply the most beautiful woman he had ever seen with his bare eyes.

The girl next to him was strikingly beautiful, by anyone standards. She was five feet nine inches with long blond hair pulled back into a ponytail kept together with a black scrunchie. Her cute nose, high cheekbones, and icy blue eyes made Troy think she belonged on the cover of some glamor magazine, not a student at a university. Add to it her athletic build, toned legs, and curves in all the right places. Troy stared at the woman mesmerized.

The young lady extended her hand in his direction and said, "Hi, I'm Cate Downey!"

Her firm grip surprised him. He immediately deduced she could fend for herself, something he found attractive. Troy kept shaking her hand and stared at Cate for a few awkward seconds. His synapse fired a mile a minute, but they weren't going anywhere. Finally, after what must have seemed like an eternity for Cate, the awkwardness ended as he muttered. "Troy." Somehow, he managed a slight smile as he withdrew his hand.

"Nice to meet you, Troy," Cate replied, with a pause. Unsure if this strapping young man struggled with shyness or if the elevator just didn't make it all the way to the top floor.

He said, "You too."

After a few seconds of silence, with Troy staring, she said, "You don't say much do you?"

A moment later his brain connected with his mouth, and he uttered the only thought that bounced back and forth inside his head like a ricocheting bullet. "You're the most beautiful woman I have ever seen."

Not missing a beat, Cate's smile grew as she said with a raised eyebrow, "Really? Is that the best you can come up with?"

"Uh... ya..." Troy replied as he realized in an instant he must sound like a complete and total moron.

"Well, all righty then," Cate said as she shook her head from left to right. "I guess I've heard worse pickup lines than that, but I've also heard much better."

He shook off the cobwebs that had engulfed his mind as he responded, "I believe in the truth, Cate, and speak it as often as possible. What I said was the truth, plain and simple."

Cate blushed ever so slightly. His assertive tone differed greatly from the first few awkward one-word answers he gave. Now she got somewhere with this boy. She turned away from Troy and back towards the front of the class as she bit her lip with her top teeth. Her one-word reply was, "Interesting."

That's how it began; extremely awkward, to say the least, when Troy played it back in his mind. Yet, that fateful first day in Psychology of Law would alter both of their lives in ways neither one could comprehend for years. Their next interaction improved as Troy recovered from his inept beginning. After several classes, he mustered up the courage to ask her out to lunch. Much to his surprise, she even accepted. Within a few weeks, they ate most of their lunches together, and even occasional dinners. A little over a year later, what started as a casual friendship had developed into much more.

The memories flew through his mind, and a wide grin formed as he thought about how they met. Cate continued to sleep as Troy just stared and dreamed of what was to come as the plane cut through the sky while a rhythmic drone from the engines filled the passenger compartment.

It was a glorious fall day in the nation's capital. The first stop was the Lincoln Memorial so Cate could fulfill her dream. They sat on the steps in utter silence so she could soak in the moment. It didn't disappoint. Troy had been there dozens of times, but never before with the woman he loved.

As expected, they arrived at Georgetown after dark. Troy had a key to the senator's home, and he and Cate made themselves comfortable. The senator was traveling and would not be back until the next day.

The next day they woke up early. The bulk of the day was spent at the National Mall. Cate wanted to see as much as they could, and Troy gladly obliged. Lunch was from a street vendor as they sat on the grass near the reflecting pool. Dinner that evening would be with Preston, and they were told not to spoil their appetites.

After a full day of being tourists, they made their way to the senator's office. Senator Wilcox embraced Troy and Cate warmly, and they received a personal tour of the Capitol. After the tour, Cate changed into an elegant form fitting strapless black dress she had brought for the occasion. Troy wouldn't be the only set of eyes admiring her that night.

The senator took them to an up-and-coming restaurant near Foggy Bottom. The dinner was fabulous, and both Troy and Cate hung on the senator's every word as he regaled them both with countless stories. As was usually the case, many of his stories involved the Cold War. The senator exuded charisma, and Cate could see instantly how he had won each election with ease. He was a remarkable man to listen to for any length of time. After dinner, they all went back to Georgetown for the night.

The next day, Troy and Cate visited Arlington National Cemetery and the Pentagon before their flight to New York City. Preston drove them to the airport, wished them both his best and sent them along their way. He made them both promise to come back and visit him soon, and they both readily agreed.

The flight time to New York was brief.

"I could totally see you in DC," Troy said as he leaned over to Cate. "A nice little townhouse in a place like Alexandria, living the big city life." He elbowed her as he said the last part.

"And what about you?" she asked. "Where would you be?"

Troy smiled and paused. "You know where I'll be..."

"Do I?" Cate asked with a raised eyebrow.

"You had better know," he responded.

She laid her head on his broad shoulder, moved closer, and they continued the rest of the flight to New York in relative silence.

Chapter Twenty-One

New York City

After landing at JFK, Troy and Cate took a cab to Grand Central Terminal, which was only a block from the hotel where his father stayed each time he came to the city for the bureau.

They dropped off their bags at the hotel, and Troy suggested they walk for a little while. Foot traffic was heavy on Park Ave as they weaved their way through a melting pot of humanity. After about five blocks Troy pointed to the right and with a sly grin said, "Let's drop in here, shall we?"

Cate's eyes bulged as she recognized the building from pictures she had seen over the years. "The Waldorf-Astoria! Are you crazy? They won't even let us walk in the door."

"Sure they will," Troy said. "You don't have to be a guest to step inside."

"Is that where you take all the other girls you bring to the big city?"

Troy laughed at that one, "I doubt I could afford a Snickers bar from the gift shop at this place. However, I have wandered through the hotel a few times while in the city."

"Is there anywhere you haven't wandered around?" Cate asked as she jabbed him in the ribs with her elbow.

"More than a few," Troy said with a slight grimace. "My bucket list is quite large and distinguished."

"So you think...I mean say," Cate replied with a wink.

Troy held her hand as they walked through the revolving doors and then walked up the flight of stairs to the lobby. He studied her face as she looked around; she appeared mesmerized. They continued past the bank of elevators and came to the main lobby, where a two-ton bronze clock, which was created for the Chicago World's Fair in 1893, stood. The clock was the centerpiece of the original Waldorf Hotel, where the Empire State Building now stands. After it was moved to the Waldorf-Astoria, the clock became a treasured piece admired by all who visited the hotel. The Westminster chimes rang every 15 minutes, to the amusement and annoyance of hotel patrons.

"This is so cool," Cate whispered into Troy's ear as she brushed her lips against the lower part of his earlobe.

Troy felt a tingle as her skin touched his. "Be cooler if we were staying in the Presidential Suite."

Cate pursed her lips. "As if. And how much would that put you back?"

"If you got to ask…" Troy replied with a coy smile.

As they walked towards the clock and the surrounding nickel-bronze cornices and rockwood stone, someone caught Troy's eye, which caused him to pause mid stride. The man on the other side of the lobby froze as well for a moment as their gaze locked.

Chapter Twenty-Two

New York City

Waldorf Astoria

Muhammad Jarah was not a fan of public places, especially the famous ones. More people meant more eyes, and more eyes meant higher odds someone would take notice of his ethnicity. He felt, probably rightfully so, that because of his Middle East heritage, he stuck out anytime he visited high profile locations. And yet, he was instructed to meet Waleed at the Waldorf Astoria in New York City . He did not like coming into the city under any circumstances because of the throngs of citizens, tourists, and massive skyscrapers. New York and similar megacities always felt borderline claustrophobic.

As he walked into the main lobby of the hotel, Muhammad kept his head down and tried not to make eye contact with anyone. Within a minute of entering through the doors from Park Avenue he saw Kadir, who gestured him towards the elevators, where they would head upstairs to see Waleed.

As he walked in the direction of the bank of elevators, Muhammad looked across the lobby and noticed a young man walking towards the gaudy clock. Their eyes locked for only a second at most, but in that time, Muhammad felt a chill run through his body that he could not readily explain. There was something about the young man that instantly set him on edge, more so than usual. The young man, who looked to be in his early 20's, gave an icy glare towards Muhammad.

Muhammad turned away quickly and followed Kadir to the elevators. When he glanced back before he stepped inside the elevator, the young man had disappeared.

Waleed greeted him warmly as he walked into the suite directly behind Kadir.

"Good to see you," Waleed said as he clasped Muhammad's hands.

Muhammad's face displayed no emotion. "Couldn't you find a more inconspicuous place for your visits?"

"Ha!" Waleed exclaimed in a tone of genuine surprise. "I'm a billionaire Muhammad, where do you expect me to stay in America's greatest city? A Holiday Inn Express or Red Roof Inn?"

Muhammad did not look amused with the humorous banter. "I don't know, Waleed, but this place just does not seem to be the wisest choice. I'm sure it is watched closely, there are probably many spies and people here that take notice of someone of your stature."

"As well they should. And guess what? They would no matter where I stayed!" Waleed extended his pointer finger and moved it back and forth before Muhammad's face like the character Babu Bhatt from the popular television show, Seinfeld. *Tsk, tsk, tsk,* he muttered. "No, I like the Waldorf-Astoria. It suits my needs and taste; it is an appropriate place for a law-abiding citizen such as myself when I'm in the city."

"You could have just come to the safe house you procured for me and my men," Muhammad replied.

"I know you are not a fan of such opulence and wealth, but for me, going to Queens would have drawn far more attention. Please relax. You are here, safe, and we have much to discuss."

For the next ten minutes, Muhammad filled Waleed in on all relevant details. He went into detail about the surveillance that was in place, the family's schedule, and general patterns. He explained that besides the house being wired for video and audio surveillance, which Waleed was already aware of, both family vehicles were being tracked 24/7. Aaron's company vehicle, cell phone and company email were being monitored constantly as well. Waleed let him lay everything out uninterrupted.

After Muhammad finished, Waleed asked many questions. "If and when the need arose, you would have no problem grabbing the wife and two children?"

"None whatsoever," Muhammad replied confidently. "Do you feel that will be necessary?"

"I don't know what will be required, but that's why you are here. In case it needs to be done," Waleed said.

"How can you be so sure that Ryker will even find anything of value within the classified files?"

Waleed arched his eyebrows. "I mentioned to you briefly when we were in London about the vision I had."

Muhammad nodded, but his look conveyed the fact he was skeptical.

"The vision revealed many things to me. I can't tell you when it will happen but Ryker will find an important document. It is something I must get at any cost."

"And I'm trailing him and his family why exactly?" Muhammad asked.

"Because I don't know if he will keep his end of the bargain and willingly give me the information he acquires. That is why you are here. I expect you not to fail me if the need arises."

"And I will not," Muhammad said forcefully.

"That's all I need to hear. If you tell me everything is in place, then I am content. All we must do is keep waiting. Things will fall into place, you will see. Remember, we are told in al-Anfal 8:46 to be patient and persevere, for Allah is with those who patiently persevere."

Muhammad shook his head, "I understand," he replied, "It's a lesson I must remind myself of from time to time as well."

"We all must," Waleed replied.

After a few more minutes of back and forth, the discussion concluded. Kadir escorted Muhammad out of the suite and down to the main lobby. He looked around for several seconds but did not see the young man from earlier who so troubled his countenance. He was relieved in a way, but something deep down told him that their paths would cross again one day. Somehow, he just knew it to be the case.

CHAPTER TWENTY-THREE

NEW YORK CITY

After leaving the Waldorf-Astoria, Troy hailed a cab as he and Cate proceeded to their next destination. It was something Cate talked about endlessly when she discussed New York, and Troy wanted to make sure it was one of the first things they did after getting settled into the city.

Troy was still slightly bothered by the man he had seen in the lobby. The man appeared to be Middle Eastern, and while Troy considered himself in no way to be a bigot, he was on edge regarding people from that region of the world after the events that took place on 9/11. It wasn't what the man looked like that troubled Troy; it was how he looked back. The stare was one of a man without a soul, the man's eyes pierced through Troy to his core. He tried to push it out of his mind and bring himself back into the present with Cate, but he found it slightly difficult. The image of the man was burned into his subconscious, and with his near photographic memory of faces, he knew there it would live.

The cab arrived at Central Park. Troy paid for the cab ride, and he and Cate got out. After a short walk, they ended up at Central Park South between 5th and 6th streets.

Cate's smile grew noticeably large as they approached the line of horse-drawn carriages on both sides of the street.

"You sly devil, you," she said as she looked into Troy's eyes. "You listen after all, huh?"

"I tell you that all the time, Miss Downey, I hang on your every word. It all ends up in here," as he pointed to his head.

"And here I thought all this time guys only thought with other smaller parts," she said with a laugh.

"Ouch!" Troy exclaimed with a broad smile as he made his hands into the shape of a dagger and jabbed it into his chest.

Cate picked out the carriage she wanted, all white, it had an array of colorful flowers painted along the side. After Troy paid, the coachman gave them both a steaming cup of hot chocolate, welcomed them, and said the horse taking them through Central Park was named Rusty.

"This is going to be magical," she said.

"It sure will, just as long as Rusty wasn't fed a can of Beefarino today." Troy said as he gave her a distinct wink.

Cate rolled her eyes. "As long as Kramer is not our carriage driver we should be fine."

It was close to midnight when they made it back to the hotel on Park Avenue near Grand Central Terminal. Troy's dad, Matt was still awake. He had got back to the room earlier, completing his third day on site at Fresh Kills, and was eager to hear about their visit to Washington.

"So, Cate what has been your favorite spot in the city so far?" Matt asked.

Cate scrunched her nose. "Well, in my opinion, Central Park was the most fun."

Troy smacked his head. "Wrong word," he said.

"Which one?" Cate asked with a bewildered look on her face.

"Cate, my dear," Matt said. "Opinions are like buttholes, everyone has them, and they pretty much stink." He laughed as the last few words slipped off his tongue.

"That one," Troy said.

Matt continued to laugh.

Cate shook her head. "Mr. Evans, that's nasty."

"Don't get him started," Troy said. "He's got all kinds of dad euphemisms, and that might be the tamest."

"Lovely," Cate proclaimed as he rolled her eyes.

"Just wait until I get to teach my grandkids all kinds of sayings one day."

Troy looked at Cate, "This is where we both remind him, we will live far, far away."

Matt smiled. "You can never escape me. My Dadisms, they will even live in your head long after I'm gone!"

The three of them had a bunch of friendly back-and-forth and stayed up for the next several hours and talked.

———— ◆○◆ ————

Shortly after two-thirty in the morning, they called it a night, Cate got the queen-sized bed, Matt was adamant of that, and there was no negotiating. Matt and Troy crammed onto the sleeper sofa. Since Matt snored like a locomotive, Troy buried his head in a pillow and finally dozed off after what seemed like an hour.

The next day, Matt was back to work on Staten Island while Troy and Cate played tourists, roaming around NYC. They visited the memorial that had been set up at the World Trade Center site to start their day. As the day progressed, they visited Times Square, Rockefeller Center, and several other famous New York City landmarks. Troy, being a kid at heart, insisted they stop by FAO Schwarz.

Cate loved every moment.

The next day was the end of Matt's first rotation. The three of them would fly home late that night. Troy and Cate stayed busy as they walked across the Brooklyn Bridge and even made the ferry ride out to the Statue of Liberty and Ellis Island. Troy was a huge history buff, and he was grateful to visit some sites he had never visited during past trips to New York.

Late that evening, as their plane went across the flyover states, Cate leaned over to Troy and gently kissed him on the cheek. She thanked him for a wonderful trip and let him know on very clear terms she hoped it would be the first of many to come. Troy smiled, he slowly and affectionately rubbed her face with his muscular hands and told her that had better be the case. Soon they dozed off together, the busy days taking their toll on both.

⸺◆⸺

Matt looked over from his seat across the aisle and just smiled. His mind thought of how darn cute the grandkids would be that Troy and Cate might produce one day.

Chapter Twenty-Four

Drexel

Troy and Cate were at his parents house the next weekend after classes got out Friday. After breakfast, he helped his mom clear the table before going outside where he found Cate on the front lawn stretching. The pink sports bra and skin-tight workout shorts distracted him, and she caught him staring.

"Like what you see?" She asked before running her tongue along the outside of her top lip.

"If you're trying to distract me," he said before a pause. "It's working."

"Good, cause I'll still kick your ass on the obstacle course while you're checking mine out."

Troy laughed out loud. "That's going to be hard to do when I'm 50 feet in front of you and not looking back."

"Cocky, aren't we?" Cate asked.

"Confidence sometimes gets mistaken for cockiness."

"Just remember second place ..." Cate started to say.

"Is the first loser," Troy finished her statement.

Cate was fast that day, but Troy was right. He dug hard and outpaced her every time they went through the gauntlet. Cate let it be known that it pissed her off. She was too damn competitive to be glad when Troy beat her.

Matt joined them on the course later in the afternoon and realized quickly that at just under fifty, his old body was no match for these two just entering their twenties. Matt prided himself on being one of the most physically fit agents his age. Yet, he had to push himself to the near breaking point to keep up with Troy and Cate. As the afternoon wore on, the three of them engaged in some target practice.

Early in his career with the FBI, Matt had signed up for a marksmanship contest that the Bureau held once a year for its agents. He had consistently ranked in the top five percent of shooters who took part. While in his early thirties, he won the whole competition. It filled him with joy when Troy began shooting just as well as he did. Surprisingly, that day came when Troy was sixteen years old. Quite simply, Troy was a natural shot. Matt knew Troy would make an excellent agent. In fact, in his dreams he saw Troy climbing to the very top of the Bureau.

⎯⎯◆⎯⎯

A few hours later, they were all back in the main house. Matt and Amy sat on the front porch chatting. Troy and Cate were in the great room with a college football game on the television.

Troy squeezed her thigh. "Pretty good shooting out there, babe!"

"Thanks," Cate said with a wide grin as she patted his firm hand. "I had an excellent teacher."

"Well, I don't think there is any doubt about that."

"I am referring to your dad, of course, Mr. Cocky," she said as she delivered a playful punch to his muscular shoulder.

"So was I," Troy replied with a laugh. A moment passed, "Seriously, Cate, I'm impressed. Besides my dad, I don't think I know another person who can shoot as well as you."

"Two in the chest, one in the head right," she said.

"Never forget that one...it may save your life one day."

"Or yours," she countered, "Although you know the average FBI agent doesn't draw their gun, let alone fire it over the course of their career, right?"

"True," Troy nodded. "But for those that do, being prepared is what can make all the difference in a life and death situation."

The college football game ended, and Troy started channel surfing, which drove Cate slightly neurotic. After about five minutes, Troy settled on a cable news channel. The segment that played was about the covert special operations war that was taking place across the globe in Afghanistan. They both fell silent as they watched.

After it ended and the talking heads started debating the segment, Troy switched off the television.

"I could so see you doing that," Cate said.

"What being a well-dressed, overpaid, loudmouth on a major television news program? I guess I'm quite dashing if I think about it," Troy said with a wry smile.

"No dumbass, I could see you leading a group of Special Forces soldiers into Afghanistan."

"Me? Really?"

"Definitely. Did you ever consider joining up with the Army and being that kind of guy?"

"No, not really," Troy shook his head. "I mean, Pops served in the Army before his career with the Bureau began and all, but I never gave it serious consideration. For as long as I can remember, I wanted to be like him and be a special agent. No other occupation really interested me."

"No secret desire to run around with a bunch of guys and play cops and robbers in the mountains or desert? Go smoke the bad guys?"

"Nah!"

"And no exotic girlfriends sprinkled throughout the world? Or be like the Navy guys and boast about a chick in every port?" Cate asked in a suddenly sultry voice.

Troy smiled, "I got a super-hot chick right here." He slapped her leg playfully. "And anyway, broads cost lots of money, and I don't think I could afford a harem on a grunt's salary."

Cate just shook her head. There was silence for a few seconds. "I still think you would be one of the best soldiers the US Army had ever produced!"

Troy looked pensive for a moment, "No thanks. I would rather be one hell of an FBI special agent with a smoking hot wife and a few rug rats running around."

"And who you going to find to give you a couple kids exactly?" Cate asked with her eyebrows arched.

Troy winked and made a clicking sound with his tongue and cheek. "Some sleazy broad I know."

"Good luck with that buddy, hope she does your laundry and makes your dinner every night too!" Cate frowned.

"She'll learn."

Cate playfully pushed Troy to the ground as an impromptu wrestling match began. As they squirmed and grabbed at each other, Troy's leg slammed hard into the television entertainment center with a loud thud.

From the front porch, his mom Amy wrapped loudly on the window. "Settle down in there, you two!" She said in a stern yet playful tone.

"You break it, you buy it," Matt added. "And we all know college kids are piss poor."

"And above all, don't forget we're too young to be grandparents." Amy yelled as she nudged Matt.

That comment quieted things down in a hurry.

Chapter Twenty-Five

New York City

November 2001

Matt Evans walked off the plane at the JFK airport in New York and saw he had three new voicemails. He played the first message and smiled. It was an encouraging message from his wife, Amy, who called to tell him she loved him. Amy always knew when he needed a little pick me up.

The next message was brief. It gave an address and basic directions to where he needed to meet for dinner.

The third message proved to be a downer. It was from the Deputy Director of the FBI, who led the day-to-day logistics on Operation Recoup. Because of a scheduling conflict, Matt's team would need to pick up an extra day on their rotation. Matt sighed at the thought of one more day away from home.

While he was glad to do his part and help the Bureau, this project proved difficult. Besides the mental strain, the shifts were long, and one day seemed to blend into another. The five-day rotations were proving to be challenging for all six of the teams involved.

One hour later, Matt found a parking space on the busy residential street and walked up to the front door of the brick row house. After two loud knocks, he heard the dead bolt unlocking, and the door opened to reveal a smiling Sally Ryker, wife of Special Agent Aaron Ryker.

"Mr. Evans, please come in," she said warmly.

Matt returned the warm smile, "Please call me Matt, my father was Mr. Evans, and I feel old enough as it is these days."

"I understand," Sally said. "And I can attest that two little kids will add years to you."

Matt entered the home and a few minutes later was introduced to the Ryker's two young children, Lacy and Alex. During their first shift, Matt and Aaron began discussing their families. Matt had expressed an interest in meeting Aaron's wife and children the next time he was in town. A few days before this trip, Aaron had called and invited him to dinner at his home in Queens.

As Matt walked into the Ryker's home, a cell phone rang across the freeway in the Astoria section of Queens.

"You need to pull up your live feed from Ryker's house," the voice said on the other end of the call.

Muhammad Jarah walked out of the kitchen and to the oak coffee table in the sparse living room where his laptop sat. He flipped it open, logged in, and a minute later watched the secure feed.

"How long has Evans been there?" he asked angrily.

"Less than ten minutes."

"Any idea what he is doing?" Muhammad asked.

"It looks like they are having dinner. The conversation so far has been mainly chit-chat."

"Stay on top of it, I want a full transcript of what they say. We need to know if our operation is blown. So help me, if Ryker tells Evans about our plan, I'll go over and kill his family before his eyes tonight. Betrayal will not be tolerated."

"Of course, I will update you if anything occurs."

The line then clicked off.

Muhammad thought about this newest development. He knew Waleed needed to be informed, so he immediately placed a call to London.

Sally had made a lasagna dinner tastier than what you would find in Little Italy. Matt enjoyed not only the company that evening but a pleasant home-cooked meal to start his long stretch away from his own home. Matt had almost forgotten what a meal was like with young children, it warmed his heart and brought a smile to his face.

After dinner, Matt told Aaron that they would pull a sixth day on this rotation. He could tell from Aaron's reaction that it was not welcome news. Matt was perceptive, and he knew something was troubling Aaron. When he asked him if everything was ok and Aaron responded it was, he did not pry. After talking for a little while longer, they called it a night since they both knew the wake-up call would be early. Matt thanked Sally for a wonderful dinner, shook Aaron's hand and then walked out to his rental car, disappearing down 25th Avenue a few minutes later.

◆

Ten minutes later, Muhammad put down the transcript from the evening and called Waleed.

"It appears to be purely a social visit," Muhammad said.

"Perhaps," Waleed replied. " But it makes me believe that my suspicion may be correct. You and the other men must be vigilant."

"We will be," Muhammad said.

"Anyway, I believe this is the week that the document will be discovered."

Muhammad cleared his throat. "I thought your vision didn't reveal specific details?"

"It didn't. My intuition says it'll be this week. From what I have gathered, more than half of the files have already been recovered. I know the time is running short, it must be soon."

"We will be ready for whatever takes place."

"I know you will not fail me," Waleed said. "Our mission is too valuable, we must have that document, no matter what needs to happen in order to retrieve it."

Chapter Twenty-Six

Fresh Kills

The three men who sat on Aaron Ryker's right examined the newest batch of mostly green and yellow metal boxes, oblivious to the voice he heard inside his head. They could not see the earbud within his right ear canal, yet every time his handler abrasively barked an order, Aaron swore the three men had to hear it as well. The four of them plugged away box by box, file by file. Every now and then, a red box would be placed on the table, and the men would glance at each other as it was inspected.

The voice in Aaron's ear reminded him countless times, "Aaron, we can't see the document, lean down lower so we can get a closer look." The sound of the voice sickened Aaron, and yet he obliged each time.

An American flag pin he wore above the pocket on his dress shirt was a marvel of modern technology. The ornate flag held an extraordinary digital camera that transmitted crystal clear images of everything he saw to Waleed's secure server. It also contained a highly sensitive microphone that could pick up any sound within 30 feet.

Before his first shift on site had begun several weeks ago, he had a final meeting. Besides extremely specific instructions, Waleed provided him some sounds he could make while on site at Fresh Kills. These noises would be a way for Aaron to answer the questions they asked via the earbud without arousing suspicion. When Aaron made the sound "hmmm" that would be answering "yes". If Aaron made a "sighing" sound, that meant "no".

That first day onsite, all his team members commented on the ornate flag pin he wore. Their positive comments only drove the dagger further into his heavy heart. The next day the others, including Matt Evans, had patriotic flag pins as well. *If only they knew*, Aaron thought to himself.

Lexi LeClair, a member of the FBI's counterterrorism division, and the only woman onsite, even wore a flag pin that next day. Lexi acted as a liaison between the multiple groups examining the documents and headquarters. When or if a problem arose and someone needed advice, then "Lexi Lou" as they all affectionately called her, reached out and got clarification from senior leadership in Washington.

Up to that point, Aaron was surprised he had not been asked to remove any of the documents. Each time the voice would harshly say to, "move along."

Matt Evans rolled up his sleeves and worked alongside the others. He was careful in observing his team at work. Matt watched their technique, studied their body language, and listened to what they said. As he surveyed them, patterns emerged for each member.

Of the four men, Special Agent Ken Flemming from the Milwaukee field office proved to be the talker of the group. He talked constantly, and it didn't really seem to matter if anyone listened either, he just liked to talk. Special Agent David Woods of the Richmond office appeared to be the quiet one. He said very little, and when he spoke, it usually ended up being profound. There was no chit-chat with David. Special Agent Marco Santiago from the Orlando office quickly established himself as the loud one. He did not talk excessively, but when he spoke everyone could hear him. Once he got started on sports, especially the Miami Heat, he would give Ken a run for his money.

Then there was Aaron Ryker. Matt considered himself a keen observer, but something about Aaron seemed off. Matt talked with him more than the others, yet still there was something going on that he couldn't pinpoint. Aaron had not given him any specific reason to worry, but Matt did anyway. The glances Aaron gave from time to time revealed a nervousness that the other three men did not outwardly display. Then there were the sounds he made. Aaron constantly made either "hmmm" sound or sighed loudly. No one had mentioned it yet, at least not directly to Matt. However, it seemed to get more prevalent and slightly annoying.

Aaron Ryker had observed the extra attention he received from Matt Evans. A few days prior, he informed Waleed of it during their nightly call. Waleed assured him 'not to worry about Matt Evans and continue as planned.

Part of Aaron wanted to get caught. He was having trouble sleeping. His wife, Sally, noticed. She knew he couldn't talk about his day, so she praised him for his hard work and service to his country. Although he had not taken a single piece of paper out of the site, Aaron already felt like a traitor, and Sally's words only made it worse. His mind constantly raced, trying to figure a way out, but so far, he hadn't come up with any realistic ideas.

As another day came closer to an end, he felt his pulse race. Suddenly Matt was at his side. "You feeling ok Aaron? You look like you're sweating. Everything alright?" Matt asked in a concerned tone.

Aaron did his best to compose himself, "Yes, sorry, Matt, I think lunch did not agree with me. My insides have been turning all day. Felt like I was going to barf earlier."

"If you need to leave early, I understand. We only have an hour left today. I can take your place," Matt replied with sincerity in his voice.

In his right ear, Aaron did not hear the voice of his handler, but instead it was Waleed. "Tell him you'll power through. You are not to leave. Do you understand Aaron?"

"Hmmm," Aaron muttered.

"What's that?" Matt asked with an eyebrow raised, "Didn't catch what you said buddy,"

Beads of sweat now trickled down the back of his neck, "No, I'm good, Matt. I'll be fine. I want to stick it out with the team and finish the shift. I just need a good night's sleep, and I'll be better in the morning."

Matt looked him over. After several long seconds, he said. "Ok, the offer stands though, if you need to bug out, don't hesitate. Understood?"

"Absolutely, and I appreciate the concern," Aaron said.

One hour later, Aaron was being frisked by the security team as he left the building. As was the case every time they passed him through security. Two minutes later he was headed for his car.

Once in his car, he followed the same pattern he had after every other shift ended. He removed the secure phone from under his seat and called Waleed.

"I don't think I can do this anymore," Aaron said as he pulled out of the complex.

"Do what?" Waleed asked.

"Steal documents from the United States Government. I can't sleep anymore, and can't take the praise from my wife, Waleed. I just want out."

"Look, Aaron," There was then a brief pause as Waleed chose his words cautiously. "We have an agreement. You live up to your end and I'll live up to mine."

"And if I can't?" Aaron asked.

"It's been a long day and you're tired," Waleed replied. "I hear it in your voice. Get a good night's sleep. Hug your kids. Kiss your wife and start fresh in the morning. I'm sure when that occurs you will muster the strength to complete the task. One more day and this shift ends. Maybe tomorrow will be the day you find something of interest, and it will all end. Ok?"

Aaron was not convinced, but he did not have the strength to argue anymore. "Ok, Waleed. I understand."

"Good. Tomorrow will be over before you know it."

The call ended. Aaron finished his thirty-minute ride to Queens in silence.

———◆———

Waleed immediately called Muhammad.

"You hear that?" Waleed asked.

"Every word," Muhammad said. "What do you want me to do?"

"Let him sleep."

"That's it?" Muhammad asked.

"Leave the package on the front seat of his car so he sees it first thing in the morning. After he looks at it, have a little chat with him man to man. You know what to say."

A sinister smile formed on Muhammad's face. "Absolutely."

"We're close," Waleed said. "A hunch tells me tomorrow is the day it is found."

"A feeling can be wrong," Muhammad said.

Waleed replied emphatically, "Not this time!"

CHAPTER TWENTY-SEVEN

QUEENS, NY

NOVEMBER 7, 2001

The sun remained shrouded beneath the eastern horizon as the alarm clock next to Aaron's bed chirped. For a few seconds, he continued to stare at the ceiling as he had for the past five hours. He reached over, turned off the alarm and started his normal routine. Sleep eluded him all night, and the knot within his stomach grew harder as the hours dragged on. Forty-five minutes later he sat at the table, his hot breakfast getting colder by the second.

"What's troubling you, honey?" Sally asked tenderly as her hand reached across the table and rested atop his clammy hand.

"Nothing," Aaron said in response. His voice in no way convincing himself or his wife.

"I know you better than that. Is there something you want to talk about?"

"I can't," he replied.

She bit her lip slightly, "Is it this project?"

"Yeah," he said in a tone devoid of emotion.

"You're almost done. This might be the last shift, right?"

"Maybe. At least, I hope it will be."

"Finish strong," she replied. "I believe in you."

Sally left the room, and Aaron pushed his food around the plate, but never really took another bite. Ten minutes later, he walked upstairs where Alex and Lacy lay asleep. He started in Alex's room first and sat by his son's side. After a few minutes of rubbing his head, he gently kissed his son's cheek and slipped quietly out.

Next, he walked across the hall to Lacy's room and just stood in the doorway for several minutes. He watched as her tiny chest slowly rose and fell with each sleeping breath. As he stepped into the room, he gave her a kiss on the cheek then and silently left.

Sally was in their bedroom getting dressed. He said nothing but gave his wife a hug and a kiss before he told her he loved her. As Aaron headed downstairs, he gathered his backpack and credentials and slid his FBI issued Glock 23 .40 caliber pistol into the holster as he made his way out the front door.

It was a cool fall November morning in Queens; he took in a deep drag of the brisk air and walked down the stairs and over to his Ford Crown Vic.

As he unlocked the door, he was startled to see a large manila envelope on the driver's seat. He knew without a doubt no such envelope had been there when he got out of the car the night before. *What the hell is this?* He asked out loud.

Aaron snatched up the packet and stood straight up, looking around to see if anyone was close by. Seeing nobody, he got back into the car, closed the door, and opened the envelope.

Inside he found a large stack of 8x10 pictures. Puzzled, he recognized the first picture was of his wife Sally's car. Aaron quickly flipped to the next picture to see that it was a street level picture of his home. The next few pictures caused his pulse to race as they appeared to be pictures taken from inside his house. Two of the snapshots included bedroom photos that could only have been taken inside Alex and Lacy's rooms.

The pulsating he felt turned into pure rage as he continued through the stack of pictures and now saw one that showed his two children coming out of school together hand-in-hand with smiles on their faces. The next photo showed Sally and the children as they played in a park only a few blocks from the house.

Suddenly he flipped back to the photo of the kids coming out of school. A man was directly behind them in the photo, and that same man was near them as they played together at the park. The next few photos pushed him over the edge as that same man was sitting on his children's bed by himself with a blank glare upon his face. Several more photos showed the man in various rooms of the house. Aaron was livid, and his mind raced a mile a minute.

The person in the pictures was Middle Eastern, and his demeanor sent chills running through Aaron's body. A large bang on the glass window to Aaron's left startled him and brought him back to reality. He looked over quickly to see that very man bent over staring directly into his eyes. Aaron instinctively reached for his sidearm, but the man brandished his own weapon. It was trained right on Aaron's face.

The man calmly said, "Open the window, Aaron, and keep your hands firmly on the wheel where I can see them."

Reluctantly, Aaron obliged as he rolled down the window, "Who the hell are you?" Consumed by anger, he hissed the words, "And what the hell do you want with me and my family?"

The man calmly continued to stare into his eyes and without emotion said. "I'm the Angel of Death, and what I want is your complete and undivided attention."

"Well, you have it," Aaron said. His hands were squarely on the wheel as they now began to involuntarily shake.

"Calm down, Aaron. You have a job to do today."

Realization struck Aaron like a sledgehammer. "Waleed sent you?" he asked with shock in his voice.

"It doesn't matter who sent me, I'm here to make sure you keep your end of the bargain."

"And if I don't?" Aaron replied with a tone of defiance.

The man leaned further in and smiled. A moment passed before he spoke. "If you fail to deliver what is required, then before you can raise a finger to protect them, I will snatch your family away." He was quiet for a minute as he let that line sink in. "And will mail them back to you piece by piece. I'll start with the little girl. Then I'll move on to your wife. Your son will meet the same fate last."

Instinctively, Aaron's hands came off the wheel to grab the monster, but the man reached inside the car and caught both of Aaron's hands with his one free hand. His powerful hand felt like a vice. He put Aaron's hands back on the wheel and squeezed them until they felt like they might be crushed.

"I realize you want to protect your family. I respect that, but we both have a job to do here, Ryker. If you fail in your task, or if you attempt to notify the FBI or anyone else, I will be compelled to do what I've already discussed. Do you understand?"

Aaron was trying to control himself. His head was about to explode, and if he were twenty years older, he would probably be in danger of having a stroke. Mustering all the resolve he could, Aaron grit his teeth and simply responded, "Yes."

"Good," the man replied. "Then we have an understanding. You deliver what is requested, and I won't be forced to kill your family." The man removed his hands and took a step back. "Now, I think you have somewhere to be. Don't be late, Aaron. We wouldn't want Matt Evans to be even more suspicious than he already appears to be.

A white van pulled up beside Aaron's car. The man casually turned away, stepped into the open back door, and the vehicle disappeared down the road a minute later.

Aaron sat stunned in the car. He was lost in his own thoughts for several minutes. As he started the Crown Vic and headed towards Staten Island, a thought crossed his mind. *How the hell am I gonna get myself out of this mess?*

Chapter Twenty-Eight

Fresh Kills

Aaron made his way through security to find Matt Evans waiting for him on the other side of the checkpoint.

"Hey buddy," Matt said in a concerned tone. "You still look like hell. Not feeling any better today?"

Aaron lied, at least somewhat. "Stomach is feeling a little better but spent a lot of quality time on the porcelain pony last night. Didn't sleep nearly enough, and I'll be glad when this shift is over today."

"Sure, you can make it?" Matt asked.

"I'll be ok. We have a job to do," Aaron said. "Whatever doesn't kill you makes you stronger, right?"

Matt smirked. "Yes, the bureau has really beaten that mentality into all of us."

"That they have."

"Well, if anything changes or you feel like you need a break, let me know. I'll cover for you."

Aaron nodded. "Thanks, Matt."

"We're in this together, buddy, and are going to see it thru till the end. Then we can all go back to our regular lives."

Aaron smiled weakly. He had made one stop on the way in. His gas tank light came on, and he stopped at a 7-11 located a few blocks from his house in Queens. The entire drive, he thought of nothing but the pictures in the packet he found on the front seat of the car. He concluded his house must be bugged with cameras, microphones, the works, and figured the car was probably being tracked as well.

Although his BlackBerry was FBI issued, he wondered if Waleed and his men could hack into that as well. Anything seemed possible at that moment. When he stepped inside the 7-11 to pay for his gas with cash, he also made another purchase; it was something he figured maybe needed before this whole sordid event came to some sort of conclusion.

The morning flew by for Aaron. His handler's voice seemed even more abrasive and gruff as the hours slipped away. Very few red core secret files passed before him. Aaron assumed Waleed himself would monitor the feed after what had occurred at his house.

Aaron's contempt and hatred for Waleed had grown with each passing minute.

At lunch, he refused Matt's offer to get some fresh air and go for a walk. Instead, he opted to sit in the car alone and eat. He kept his coat on, which covered the American flag pin he wore, and turned up the talk radio station.

Aaron took those few precious seconds to perform the setup on the item he purchased at the gas station. He prayed he would not need it, but his gut feeling told him he would.

The pace inside changed after lunch. Another dump truck had arrived, but this one carried the mother load. One after another, red-colored metal containers made their way across the sleek stainless-steel table. During prior shifts, they encountered them from time to time but never so many. Tensions in the room were noticeably higher since many of the red boxes appeared to be damaged. The men all exchanged pensive glances as they removed the secrets documents to inspect them.

Matt hovered much closer to the men as the red containers piled up.

There was a sudden change in his handler's voice. More questions were being asked of him, and he was frequently told they needed a better image of the items he inspected. While he examined the fifth red container in a row, a curious thing happened. The handler's voice went silent. At first, Aaron thought maybe the signal was disrupted somehow. He became excited at the prospect.

His excitement was short-lived and morphed into anger as the regular voice he heard was now replaced by another voice. He knew this voice all too well and never wanted to hear it again.

Waleed tried to sound calm and reassuring, but Aaron knew the stakes were raised now that he was under the watchful eye of Waleed himself.

Then it happened. On the thirteenth straight red colored metal container everything changed.

Waleed had been strangely quiet for a while until Aaron picked up the thirteenth container, which appeared to have significant damage. The left side of the three-inch-high container was visibly crushed down several inches. Blackened burn marks were visible on all sides of the thick container. Aaron tried to open the top, but it wouldn't budge.

From the far side of the table, Matt watched him struggle. "You need a hand with that one, Aaron?" he asked.

"Keep him away," Waleed said in an angry tone from deep within his ear.

"No, I got it," Aaron replied as he waved Matt off.

Aaron had to use a pry bar, like he had done with several others, to force the lid open. After several rough tugs, the lid gave way, and he could lift the entire top off the metal container. Glancing inside, he saw that the document it contained was still intact. It appeared to be quite old. It also looked like it suffered some water damage.

Aaron reached up and positioned the bright light that was directly above him to get a better view of the contents. As he peered within, the first thing that caught his eye was the large font at the top of the page read "The Zechariah Option."

Before he could see much of the document, Waleed's voice returned. The normal even tone was replaced with great excitement.

"Lean in closer, Aaron, I need a closer look at this one!" Waleed exclaimed as his voice raised an octave.

Aaron did as instructed and glanced closer at the document. His eyes involuntarily stopped as he saw the word *nuclear* several times. It was a Cold War document from the language in just the first few lines. Before Aaron could read more, Waleed broke his concentration.

"Aaron, this is it. I need this document. We need to go with our primary contingency plan. Do you understand?" Waleed asked.

A few seconds passed, and Aaron had said nothing. His mind raced.

Waleed's voice broke the silence. "Aaron, I don't have to remind you of the visit this morning and what that man can do, right? As far as you know, he could be in your home right now with your family. We've had good dealings in the past, Aaron. I've been generous with my payments to you, and will continue to do so in the future. You will be done after this one document, I promise. Do you understand?"

Aaron replied with gritty teeth to this with the "hmmm" sound.

"You're making a wise choice Aaron, I am sure Sally, Alex and Lacy thank you for your courage and determination. Now, I need you to confirm that we will go with the Alpha plan.

After a tense few seconds, Aaron replied with the "hmmm" sound once more.

Aaron knew the distraction would only be brief, and he would need to hurry. He made sure the lid was completely open and then quieted his mind so he could hear the next words Waleed would say.

"I will count down from five," Waleed said. "When I say *NOW,* it will happen."

Aaron waited a few seconds.

Then the countdown began. "Five, four, three, two, one...*NOW!*"

Suddenly, the lights throughout the whole complex shut off. The entire room was thrown into blackness. Marco, in his loud tone asked, "What gives?"

The emergency lights, which should have immediately illuminated, did not come on. This gave Aaron the time he needed.

Aaron quickly and quietly removed the old brittle document. He made several concise folds and stuffed the document down into his pants, where a hidden inner lining had been sewn. Next, he reached down to his jacket, which hung off the back of his chair, and quickly removed the hidden lining and the document that was contained within. He placed the document in the red container. It all took less than 15 seconds to make the switch. Waleed asked if the document was secure. Aaron responded with his typical "hmmm".

The light blinked on. The four men all looked at each other. Aaron the first to speak. "What the hell was that all about?" he asked.

Waleed told Aaron he did, "A great job," as the lights turned back on.

Matt Evans was at the far end of the table with a perplexed look on his face. After several minutes of discussion, Aaron carried the red container to the far wall and placed it into one of the safes.

Aaron's heart raced at an incredible rate. It felt like it was going to pop out of his chest. He noticed almost immediately that the power outage had caused some additional personnel to arrive in the building. There was a lot of activity in the control room at the far end of the room. The team continued to work, and within a short period, things seemed to settle down, and no more words were spoken at the table about the outage.

Forty-five minutes later, the shift was over. Aaron and the other three men were headed to the security checkpoint. The entire plan would either fall apart or go smooth as butter. Part of Aaron wished he would get caught with the document in his pants. Then he thought of Sally and his children and wondered what would befall them if that occurred. His concern was for nothing since like other shifts, the security check was fairly quick and his normal pat down was even skipped. Aaron walked through the metal detector, and the security guard waved him through and told him to have a pleasant evening.

"Good job, Aaron," Waleed said as Aaron passed outside the security area, "You're almost done."

Aaron was free and clear. Or so he thought as he stepped out the main door and breathed in the cold evening's air. Then suddenly Matt Evans distinct voice beckoned from behind him. Aaron turned to see Matt headed straight for him.

"Hey Aaron, wait up a minute. I need to talk to you."

Aaron's heart pounded against his chest as a lump formed in his throat.

Chapter Twenty-Nine

Fresh Kills

Aaron's nervous grin was hard to disguise as he turned to face Matt, who quickly approached. The guilt he felt began to really take its toll.

"Hey Matt, what's up?" Aaron asked.

"Just need a few moments of your time before you take off," Matt said.

"Of course," Aaron replied.

Matt stood just a few feet away. He was slightly taller, so Aaron had to look up just a little to make eye contact. Matt reached out and grabbed Aaron's left shoulder.

Aaron half expected Matt to say, *What the hell did you take when the lights went off?* But he didn't.

"Look, buddy," Matt cleared his throat. "I know you've had a rough day with this whole stomach issue."

"No worries," Aaron shrugged. "Like I said earlier, I'm feeling better. Things seemed to improve as the day went on."

"Glad to hear it," Matt smiled. "Anyway, I just wanted to let you know how much I appreciate all your efforts."

"All part of the job."

"Yes, I know, but I've been with the Bureau long enough to know often people get placed in stressful situations. Their superiors expect them to perform at the highest of levels, and they never get the recognition they deserve. I know how hard it is to have little ones at home and juggle the special agent role."

Aaron nodded and looked down at his shoes. "My family knows the drill, as I'm sure yours does as well."

"True, but I also remember what assignments were like when I worked my ass off and no one noticed. I vowed never to treat my people that way if I were ever in charge. So, I just want you to know that I really appreciate your efforts. This project has been draining as hell, but I really believe what we are doing has been valuable to the national security of the United States. Since I was informed today at lunch that this will probably be our last shift, I just want to take a moment and say thanks."

Aaron was at a loss. He could feel Matt's sincerity in his praise. The words struck like a dagger. Each kind word made him feel more and more like a coward and a hypocrite. The document stuffed in his pants affirmed the fact that he was a traitor to his country. Only God knew what may occur in the future because of his actions. Yet he didn't know what else to do. His family's life was at stake. Part of him wanted to reach out to Matt and tell him the truth, but his instinct to protect his family prevented him from doing so. Even though he was sure Matt could see right through his smile, he reached out to shake his hand anyway. All he could say was, "Thanks Matt, kind words mean a lot to me, and yours sure struck a chord."

"You'll keep in touch, right?" Matt asked.

"Absolutely," Aaron said. "You'll hear from me real soon."

"If you ever want to come out to Idaho with Sally and the kids, Amy and I would be glad to have you stay with us. The kids would probably love the fresh mountain air, and there are tons of things to do."

Aaron felt another stab in his heart with the simple act of kindness. "Thanks, Matt, I would like to take you up on that offer one day."

With that, the two men turned from each other, and Aaron proceeded to his car. His evening's work was far from over.

Matt had meant every word he just said, but something felt off. He had that same gut feeling several times over the past few days about Aaron. Unable to put his finger on why he felt that way, he headed to his rental car and tried to shake off the feeling he knew deep down must mean something. Unsure what else he could do or so, he had a flight at JFK to catch, so he proceeded to his rental car.

Aaron was not in his car for more than five seconds before the secure cell phone rang. He reached under the seat, retrieved the phone and answered. The call was brief. Waleed wanted to verify that he had made it out successfully with the document. Even though he still wore the flag pin so Waleed should know he made it out safe. Aaron assumed it must be a way for Waleed to play his mind games. Instead of questioning him, Aaron acknowledged he had the document in his possession. Next, Waleed gave him specific instructions on where the drop would take place. After Aaron confirmed he knew exactly where Breezy Point Tip was located as the call ended abruptly.

Aaron considered the drop location and figured he was as good as a dead man. He had been to Breezy Point Tip many times. On warm summer days, his family enjoyed the 200-acre isolated beach that was part of the Gateway National Recreation Area. The tip made up the most southern point of Queens, close to his home. Unfortunately, Aaron also knew it happened to be one of the most barren areas in all of NYC. A perfect place to deal with someone in absolute seclusion, and if necessary to dispose of their body. Aaron knew from numerous investigations as a special agent that the mob in particular loved to take informants out to that very beach to silence them for good.

Before he put the car in gear, Aaron removed the American flag pin and placed it in the center console. Next, he reached into his pants and pulled out the Core Secret document.

As he read through the document, his body filled with dread. Aaron knew now why Waleed wanted it so badly. He wondered why fate would allow him to find it and wondered how Waleed could even have known of its existence. Waleed was a liar, plain and simple since this was no document to give him a leg up in the business world. It would be used to strike at the United States.

As if waking from a stupor, his resolve emerged. He knew at that moment there was no way in hell he could allow Waleed to take possession of this document. The question became what to do with it and how to protect his family.

Just then, he had a thought. A long shot to be sure, but he felt like he had no other choice. For the sake of Sally, Alex, Lacy and even his own life, he had to take the chance.

His car pulled out of the FBI's secure location as the plan came together in his mind.

Several minutes later, he took a right-hand turn onto Arthur Kill Road, only a mile from the freeway. He had no way of knowing if his hastily assembled plan would actually work.

Fate would be the one to decide.

⸺◈⸺

Once Aaron's car was on the main road, Waleed's men started their pursuit. Each evening, two men shadowed Aaron as he traveled home. As was normally the case, they stayed far back so he would not notice the tail. Every day they drove a different vehicle so that Aaron would not pick up on their presence. That night they followed him in a gray Toyota Camry.

The passenger got on his secured radio. "Target is on the move, we are in pursuit."

Muhammad's voice came over the other side of the radio, "If he deviates in any way let me know immediately."

"Understood," the passenger replied.

⸺◈⸺

For the benefit of the microphones he was certain were in his vehicle, Aaron forced out a long and loud fart. "Awe my stomach," he muttered in mock discomfort.

Right before he reached the freeway, he pulled into the gas station on his right. Holding his stomach for the benefit of anyone who watched, he ran into the convenience store with haste.

The car was bugged, but with microphones only.

As Aaron's vehicle pulled over and he rushed out and into the store, the passenger radioed Muhammad. "What do you want me to do? He sounds sick." The man inquired, "Should I follow him inside?"

"No," Muhammad said. "Stay in the vehicle, but watch closely though, something seems wrong about this whole thing. Does he have his phone with him?"

The tracking device within the phone showed it was still in the car, it had not moved after the car stopped and Aaron ran inside. "Negative," the passenger replied, "The phone is still in the car."

"Did he have anything with him when he ran inside?" Muhammad asked.

"No, not that I could tell," the man replied. "His hands appeared empty, although he had his coat on, so I can't be sure what he brought in."

"Yes, the coat must be blocking the camera embedded in the pin. We lost the video image several minutes ago. Just stay on him," Muhammad replied with a hiss. "Make sure he doesn't pull a fast one on us and go out the back."

"Understood," the man on the other end of the line said as he swallowed hard.

Chapter Thirty

Staten Island

Aaron knew he had only minutes before his watchers became suspicious, if he even had that long. He wondered if Waleed would send someone into the gas station after him.

He removed the burner phone he had bought earlier that day and placed a single call. It was a number no special agent ever wanted to call. The person who answered the phone asked for his authentication code.

Aaron gave his code and waited.

"What do you need, Special Agent Ryker?" A woman's voice asked.

"My family is in imminent danger," Aaron replied.

"Location?"

Aaron provided his home address in Queens and added, "I need an Emergency Response Team (ERT) there immediately.

"Understood," the woman said. "And you?"

"I'm not with them. I don't have time to explain, but I need my family secured."

"Can the ERT commander reach you on route at this number?"

"Yes," Aaron said quickly.

The call ended. It lasted less than two minutes. Aaron then typed a simple yet direct email on his bureau issued Blackberry. He hoped the recipient would forgive him for what he had almost done. Events were now set in motion that could not be undone. Aaron knew between the phone call and email, his fate was sealed.

Four minutes after walking into the convenience store, Aaron walked out and got into his vehicle.

"Target has emerged and is on the move again," the man shadowing him said.

"And?" Muhammad Jarah asked.

"It looks like he is clutching a half-drunk bottle Pepto Bismol in his right hand."

"Nothing else?"

"No."

"Stay on him," Muhammad said. "I have a suspicion he is not going to Breezy Point. If he deviates from his course, call me. I am preparing an alternative plan if the need arises."

Muhammad sensed something wasn't right. He called his team surveilling the Ryker home several blocks from where he currently was parked. The team reported nothing suspicious as the family had been home for several hours and no one had come or gone.

He followed his instincts, started the car, and proceeded across the Queensboro Bridge heading towards Manhattan. As he crossed the East River, he headed south on the FDR Drive. His next call to the team at Breezy Point Tip. He instructed them that if Ryker failed to show, he may need them to move quickly.

Fifteen minutes later, Aaron crossed the Hudson River on the Verrazano-Narrows Bridge. As soon as he failed to turn onto the Shore Parkway and instead continued to Interstate 278 towards the Brooklyn Bridge, the gig would be up, and Waleed would know where he was headed. He would have to drive like a bat out of hell if they tried to overtake him.

The entire drive from Fresh Kills, Aaron had been reaching around the dashboard and seats trying to locate the microphone, which he knew surely must be in the car. It took a while and was difficult as he drove, but finally he found it. With one quick motion he dislodged the half-dollar sized bug and rolled down his window. The bug and the American flag lapel pin were tossed out of the window in one swift motion.

Suddenly, the burner phone rang. "Yes," he said as he answered nervously.

"Special Agent Ryker, this is Mitch Farnam with the ERT. Sir, we are almost at your home in Queens."

"Protect my family, Mitch." He said as tears formed in his eyes.

"We will, sir, do you require protection as well?"

"Probably, I'm on my way to the Manhattan field office. A document in my possession is wanted badly by some undesirable men."

"Who?"

"Very dangerous men who are determined to do great harm to our nation."

"I can send a team to you, Aaron. Just pull over and give me your location."

"No. I can't stop the vehicle. I need to keep moving. These men are following me. Have a team near the Federal Plaza office, hopefully I won't need them."

"Hold on," Mitch replied, "We are at your house."

Aaron heard the sound of screeching tires and heavy footfalls before the line went quiet. For the next ninety seconds he heard nothing. Just the throbbing of his heart as his pulse raced. It was the longest minute and a half of his life.

Mitch's voice returned, and he sounded slightly out of breath. "Aaron, we have your family. They're safe and all accounted for. We are going to proceed to a secure location until the situation is resolved."

"Thank you," Aaron said as a wave of adrenaline pulsated through his body. "Tell my wife and children I love them and will see them as soon as I can."

"Will do, Aaron," Mitch said. "And you be safe."

Aaron disconnected the call and wondered if he would ever see his family again. He knew with virtual certainty he would be branded a traitor for his actions up to that point. Aaron shuddered at the thought of how things would shake out, but for now pushed those thoughts aside and considered his next goal. Making it safely over the Brooklyn Bridge.

Muhammad's cell phone rang twice just a few minutes apart. The first call informed him they had lost audio from Ryker's car and that the vehicle did not pull onto Shore Parkway as expected. Immediately Muhammad knew Ryker must be headed to Manhattan, and that meant only one thing: 26 Federal Plaza. Muhammad knew he would have less than fifteen minutes to acquire Ryker before the entire mission was lost, an unacceptable outcome.

The second call came from his team in Queens, just down the block from the Ryker's house. His man explained how three black Suburban's pulled up and a large tactical force descended on the home. The family was now untouchable.

Muhammad slammed his hand on the steering wheel as he proceeded down the FDR Drive. *Ryker must have made a call when he stopped at the convenience store. We just got played.*

Chapter Thirty-One

Manhattan

Aaron checked his rearview mirror and tried to locate the tail he knew must be there. As his eyes darted between the road in front of him and the rear mirror, he saw it, the same gray Camry had been several cars back as he left Staten Island.

He pulled onto the Brooklyn Bridge and knew he had less than eight minutes until he arrived at his destination.

As he crossed and then exited the bridge, he took a right onto St James. After he made a left-hand turn on Worth Street, he would only be a few blocks from 26 Federal Plaza. His hands visibly shook as he held a death grip on the steering wheel.

The passenger in the gray Camry confirmed to Muhammad their location, about 50 feet behind Ryker.

"Get closer to him, and let him know you're there," Muhammad said in a forceful tone. "I need him to gain speed quickly. I am in position and ready."

The Camry sped up and closed in, turning the fifty feet into less than five within a matter of seconds.

Ryker watched the rearview mirror. *Damn! Here they come*, he muttered out loud. Instinctively, he dropped the pedal to the floor and did his best to evade the approaching Camry.

As his speed increased, Aaron saw a problem up ahead. A large garbage truck blocked his lane about a thousand feet further down St James. Fortunately, there was no oncoming traffic at this time of night. Aaron figured he would jump over to the oncoming lane at the very last moment and swerve around the parked truck.

His eyes darted between the approaching garbage truck and the Camry on his tail. His speed remained constant, and the Camry was now almost close enough to touch his back bumper.

The Camry suddenly dropped back.

What the hell? Aaron thought.

Suddenly, a white van appeared in the oncoming lane next to him and matched his speed. Aaron tried to do two things. First, he pulled hard to the left and made contact the van to muscle his way over. Second, he slammed hard on the brakes.

Neither worked, and with tremendous force his car smashed into the back of the garbage truck. Aaron's car crumpled like an aluminum can, and it all went black.

⸻◆⸻

The sound of the horn blaring brought Aaron back to reality. He could not feel much of anything except the warm blood that oozed from his nose into his open mouth. Every fiber of his body ached as pain shot out from every limb.

His head was pressed against the steering wheel, and he couldn't move. All Aaron could do was look out the driver's window. In horror, he watched as the man who caused this hellish existence calmly climbed out of the white van and walked towards him.

The man held a large caliber handgun in his right hand as he approached the side of the car with a grin on his face as he spoke.

"Agent Ryker, you survived. I'm quite shocked," Muhammad said. "You are quite a clever man after all. Very smart to have your family taken into protective custody. One way or another, I will see that they join you in the afterlife before long."

Aaron's eyes narrowed as rage grew from within. But he couldn't do anything about it.

"Oh, and I'll take that document now," Muhammad said.

Aaron tried to protest, but blood filled his mouth, and he couldn't utter a word.

Muhammad raised his gun and fired two quick shots into Aaron Ryker's skull, splattering his brain all over the roof and passenger seat.

As Muhammad reached into the vehicle past the lifeless body, he found what he was looking for within seconds. He glanced at the document to make sure it was what he needed and turned around without a second look back. He climbed into the white van and sped up rapidly.

Muhammad failed to notice the ATM machine directly across the street from the accident scene.

As the van sped away, he made a single call. "I have the document, and Ryker is dead."

"Very good," Waleed said, "I want it delivered personally to me. You know where I am."

"Understood," Muhammad replied, "I'm on my way now."

CHAPTER THIRTY-TWO

JFK Airport

Matt Evans cleared security at JFK, a place where he had been spending far too much time lately, and sat at the departure gate ready to board the flight home. He sat back in the uncomfortable airport chair and closed his eyes as he waited for the plane to board.

His cell phone vibrated, and as he glanced down, he noticed it was a New York area code. "Matt Evans," he said in a tired voice.

"Matt, it's Chuck Parsons."

"Chuck, hey buddy. How is my favorite super special agent in charge of the big city field office?" Matt remarked with a hint of friendly sarcasm.

Chuck and Matt had known each other for a long time, and Chuck always busted Matt's balls since he was in charge of the prestigious NYC FBI field office while Matt headed the tiny Boise office.

"Where are you?" Chuck asked in a very serious tone.

"JFK, just about to board my flight back home. Why?"

"There's been an incident. I hate to do this to you, but I really need you to get some transportation and make your way to lower Manhattan ASAP," Chuck said.

"Why? What happened?" Matt could not hide the concern in his tone.

Chuck cleared his throat and paused before he replied. "It's Aaron Ryker. I hate to tell you this, but he's dead. We just found him in lower Manhattan about ten minutes ago."

"What the hell? I was just with him an hour ago. What happened? Was it a car accident?"

"Yes, he was involved in a car crash, but it was no accident, and that's not what killed him," Chuck replied somberly.

"Then what did?"

"Two bullets to the head," Chuck said.

"Jesus," Matt answered, "I'm on my way."

Chapter Thirty-Three

Manhattan

Waleed sat in the plush leather chair in his Waldorf suite and read the Zechariah Option document slowly, studying each word carefully. The bottom right corner was missing and had minor water damage. Some words were hard to make out, but not impossible to read. At last, he read the last words, put his head back, looked up towards the ceiling, and smiled.

"What does it say?" Kadir sat on the edge of his seat only a few feet away.

"It says enough for us to start our quest since Allah has found favor with us, gentlemen." Waleed exchanged glances with Kadir and Muhammad, who both sat across from him. "The document is vague as to the location of the device, but there are clues sprinkled throughout the text. I have several cryptanalysts I will bring in to examine it and provide me a more detailed assessment."

"It really states the United States hid a nuclear weapon during the peak of the Cold War?" Kadir asked.

"Yes, that is precisely what it says," Waleed stared at Kadir and then back at the damaged document.

"And what do you intend to do with this nuclear device when you find it?" Muhammad asked.

Waleed smiled. "I plan to destroy the United States with it." He said the words coolly, without a hint of doubt or concern.

"One device cannot destroy the entire nation," Muhammad stated matter of fact.

"You're right," Waleed said as he tapped his temple with his index finger. "The nuclear explosion itself cannot reap such destruction. However, using the weapon in the way I intend will most certainly bring an end to the United States as we know it, Muhammad."

"Your target is not Washington or New York?" Muhammad leaned forward in his chair.

"No," Waleed shook his head. "Destroying a single city is a fruitless endeavor. I intend to destroy the great Satan from sea to shining sea."

Muhammad rubbed his chin. "How?"

"All in good time. I will reveal all when the time is right," Waleed replied with a sly grin.

Chapter Thirty-Four

New York City

Matt knew none of the details as he walked out of the airport terminal, but his first call was to Amy. After he explained what he knew, Matt assured her he would come home as soon as possible. He hailed a cab and half an hour later stood inside the yellow taped off crime scene.

Chuck Parsons met him and took him over to the grisly scene.

Aaron's car remained partially under the dump truck. His lifeless body still slumped against the steering wheel. With his face mainly intact, the back of his head was almost completely blown off by the force of the two hollow point rounds fired from point-blank range.

Matt looked at him for a few moments and then looked away. As he surveyed the street, he noticed the bank ATM directly across from the crumpled car and accurately figured the camera would prove invaluable.

"Get the images from that ATM camera," Matt said as he pointed across the street.

"Already on it," Chuck said before he led Matt over to his bureau issued car.

The two men leaned against the hood of the vehicle.

"We know you were the last person seen with him. Matt. Any help you can provide would be great. Did he say anything suspicious or act differently today?"

Matt told Chuck a synopsis of the past few weeks.

"Besides not feeling well today, he said nothing to make you suspicious?" Chuck asked.

"No, nothing comes to mind. He made some weird noises when we were working at the facility, but at the time I figured maybe it was nerves or even allergies." Matt said.

"Well, whatever might have been going on, this was an execution style hit," Chuck said.

"It sure looks that way. I suspected something was going on, but he indicated nothing specific when I asked him questions. In fact, he seemed to deflect anytime I pressed him. Aaron was a standup guy as far as I could tell."

"One of our best special agents."

"Did he have any cases he was working on that had mob ties or any organized crime cases?" Matt asked.

"Not sure at the moment. We'll be going over his case log with a fine-tooth comb in the coming days, though. All I know right now is that shortly after leaving the Fresh Kills facility tonight, he made a call to our FBI Emergency Response Team. He gave his info for authentication and then said his wife and two young children were in imminent danger. He requested a tactical team be deployed immediately to ensure their safety."

"And?" Matt asked.

"The team arrived within fifteen minutes of his call to secure his family. They were successful in doing so. Right before you arrived, I talked with one of the tactical team members. He spoke with Aaron after they removed his family."

"What did Aaron say?" Matt asked.

"Aaron said he had a document in his possession that some very dangerous men wanted and felt his family was in imminent danger. He told the agent he would bring the document to the field office in Manhattan and asked to have a team on standby in case they were needed."

"That's what he said precisely? That he had a document?" Matt asked.

"Yes. The tactical team member is giving a full written statement right now."

Matt zoned out and then realized something he should have pieced together much quicker.

"Hey Matt! What is it? What are you thinking?" Chuck inquired as he snapped his fingers several times and pulled Matt back into reality.

Matt shook his head slightly, "Sorry Chuck. I just realized something, I need to get back to Fresh Kills and review some security tapes from today."

"Why?"

"There was a power outage earlier at the facility."

"I heard. What does that have to do with this?"

"Not sure, just a hunch."

Chuck nodded his head, "Your hunches usually scare me. Let me know what you find out, ok?"

"Will do," Matt said. "By the way I took a cab here, do you have a vehicle I can use for a little while so I can drive to Staten Island?"

"Of course," Chuck said as he summoned one of his agents and instructed the man to provide Matt a car.

Ten minutes later, Matt drove across the Brooklyn Bridge on his way to Fresh Kills for the second time that day.

Chapter Thirty-Five

Fresh Kills

Matt poured another cup of coffee as he reviewed the surveillance footage until his eyes wanted to fall out of their sockets. He told the technician who helped him sort through the footage to focus on the container Aaron worked on when the power went out. The contents of that Core Secret box concerned Matt tremendously.

Since the files processed that day had already been flown back to FBI headquarters, Matt waited for the call from D.C. telling him what they discovered inside the box Aaron examined during the power outage. In the meantime, he continued to review the surveillance tapes frame by frame.

When he arrived several hours earlier, he told Earl, one of the technicians, what happened. Together, they scrutinized the security tapes and looked for anything suspicious. Matt told Earl to start the playback immediately before the power outage. Nothing appeared out of the ordinary. The system even recorded when the time the power was out. Matt asked how that was possible.

Earl explained that the cameras were on a dedicated power source. Even though the room was pitch dark, the cameras kept filming.

Several hours into their analysis, they seemed to have hit a brick wall. Matt instructed Earl to start at the beginning of the day. Although it was a long and meticulous process, Matt was sure something would turn up. After two hours, they still found nothing.

"Say, Earl," Matt said as a thought occurred to him. "What was the total time the power was out?"

Earl looked at the footage and the timestamps, "One minute and thirteen seconds," he replied, "Why?"

"Anyone figure out why the emergency backup lights did not illuminate?" Matt asked.

"Nope," Earl replied, "They are still digging into that snafu."

"Hmm... And what about the cameras? They need light to record an image, right?"

"Of course, the cameras only recorded darkness during the time the power went out.

"And there were no thermal lenses or anything like that installed?"

Earl grinned and slapped his leg hard. "Jeez Matt! It never even crossed my mind! Yes, we have Flir thermal imaging lenses on select cameras, but not all of them."

"Can you see where they're mounted and what they recorded during the outage?"

"Sure can," Earl said as his fingers moved at a high rate of speed over the keyboard and his mouse. After a few minutes, he grunted. "Not finding what I'm looking for. Let me grab one of the other techs who knows that stuff better. Give us fifteen minutes, ok?"

"I'm not going anywhere," Matt said as he sipped at his now lukewarm coffee.

Twenty minutes later, Matt, Earl and one of the other technicians, Tate, were huddled around the bank of monitors.

Tate pointed to the center monitor, "Ok this one here is the best angle we have. Check this out. The camera is on the wall, slightly off center behind Aaron, who is on the far left of the images. It allows us a clear view of everyone for the entire time of the power outage."

The footage began, and Matt was immediately surprised at the clarity of the images that had been captured. This was not a fuzzy figure shaded in orange and red. Instead, the men looked almost whitish and ghostly, and their movements were easy to make out.

The first thing Matt noticed was that the men barely moved once the power went out. That is except Aaron. Even when the room went black, Aaron continued crouching down over the metal box before him. In fact, his movements appeared to increase. Since the image was from the back, they couldn't make out what he was doing. After a few moments, Aaron stood fully up, turned slightly and moved his hands downward.

Matt shook his head in frustration.

Aaron then turned fully around toward the chair behind him and reached for something. After a few seconds of hand movements, he appeared to cradle something in his hand. He then turned back away from the camera and leaned over the metal box once more. Finally, he stood up and remained still until the lights came back on.

He knew how long the power would be out, Matt said half to himself, half out loud.

As the thermal image gave way to the normal images, Earl heard what Matt said under his breath. "I think you're right. And unless my eyes deceived me, I think we just witnessed Special Agent Aaron Ryker remove a document from the box, place it on his person and then replace it with something from his jacket."

"That is exactly what we saw," Matt said as he nodded slowly.

"But what did he take?" Earl asked.

Matt shook his head, in both disbelief and frustration. "I don't know, but whatever it was I feel pretty damn sure he paid for it with his life tonight."

⸻◆⸻

Over the next hour, they pieced together all the camera angles right before the lights went out.

"Can you get me a glimpse of what was in that container he had?" Matt asked.

"We can try, but I can't make any promises," Earl said as he stroked his chin. "When we set up the cameras before the project started, headquarters made it clear that none of box contents should be recorded. We were pretty careful about those angles we used. No cameras were mounted in a way that would clearly record the documents on the tables."

"Well, shit," Matt said, unable to hide his exhaustion or frustration. It showed in his words and tone. "There goes that idea."

"Not so fast," Earl replied with a smile. "These cameras are the best money can buy. Even though there was no camera directly overhead, we may have caught something from an angle. It may take some time, but I can pull the various camera angels and see what we got."

"Sounds like a start," Matt patted Earl's upper arm.

"If we have any image of the document though, it will probably require some enhancement to actually make anything out."

"You're saying it may be a while?"

"Exactly."

"Work your magic," Matt said. "We need to know what document he stole."

"You might as well grab a hotel room and get some shuteye."

"Think I will since I'm beat." Matt thanked Earl for all his efforts, stood up, and walked towards the security checkpoint.

A few minutes later, Matt Evans was outside in the cold early morning air. Just then, his cell phone rang.

The call was brief. The agent on the other end was from FBI Headquarters in D.C.. He confirmed Matt's suspicions that the Core Secret box Aaron had been examining when the power went out held a fake document.

Matt hated to admit it, but they now had concrete proof that Aaron Ryker had been a traitor. His heart sank at the news since he knew something was off about Aaron, but he would never have suspected him of treason.

An hour later, Matt had trouble falling asleep. He opened his laptop and checked his email. The email from Aaron Ryker spiked his pulse. The timestamp showed it was sent at 8:16 PM EST. As Matt read the brief email, he became more distressed and immediately forwarded the email to Chuck. He knew they would discuss it in the morning.

Chapter Thirty-Six

Drexel

As he stretched out his arm, Matt's hand slid against the smooth skin of his wife, Amy. She held his muscular hand and placed it on her stomach. It was Saturday morning, and Matt arrived home around 1:00 am from another trip to Washington. After whispering a few words in her ear and giving her earlobe a slight bite before they tenderly kissed.

After leaving the Fresh Kills facility the morning after Aaron's murder, Matt went directly to his regular hotel in Manhattan and crashed for eight hours. The sound of his cell phone ringing woke him up. It was the director himself. He wanted Matt in D.C. immediately. The Director explained that a Gulfstream V idled in Teterboro, New Jersey, and Matt was not sure if he should feel honored or scared since the Bureau had never sent a private jet for him before.

The next two days proved intense as Matt met with a myriad of agents and faced repeated questions about his team. At that point, no one knew what Aaron Ryker had stolen, but they knew it was a Core Secret file. Based on the ATM footage retrieved at the crash scene, it appeared the man who took Aaron's life removed something from the vehicle. The logical assumption believed it to be whatever document he took from the secret facility.

Following his time in D.C. Matt flew back to New York to aid in the investigation. On the second day in the city, Matt was called into Chuck's expansive office on the 42nd floor.

"What's up, Chuck?" Matt asked with a wide smile as he walked into the office where Chuck sat stoically. Matt's humor might be slightly immature at times, and he told those who rolled their eyes at him that his sense of humor kept him young.

Chuck looked up from the file he examined, "Never tire of that line, do you, Evans?"

"Nope," Matt said, "You called?"

"Yes." Chuck stood and handed a file to Matt. "Ever seen this guy before?"

Matt stared at the photo. "No, the face does not look familiar. Should it?"

"This is the man who put two bullets in Ryker's head."

"This is the image we captured from the ATM?"

"Yes, it is. Our technicians had to do a lot of cleanup on the images since ATM cameras are good close up, but utter shit further away."

"Do we have a name?" Matt asked as he raised an eyebrow.

"Does the name Muhammad Jarah ring any bells?"

Matt thought for a minute before it came to him. He slapped the side of his leg. "Hell, yes! That's the guy the Bureau wanted for the 1994 incident in Philly right? He's on our most wanted list."

"Excellent memory. The techie guys say the probability rate is 96 percent, which is good enough in my book."

"Any leads on where he is?"

"No, we've pulled in everyone we can and have been scouring every image recorded in New York since then. So far, no luck. If he's still here, we will find him."

"Any idea yet what Aaron stole?"

"No updates on that. As soon as I learn something, I'll fill you in ASAP. The director is all over my ass. Ryker was my man after all, and I'm taking a lot of heat since he apparently went turncoat on us. I recommended his placement on the team."

Matt frowned. "It's not your fault, and you know it."

"You and I both know it's always our ass on the line when one of our guys screws the pooch. Shit doesn't flow uphill."

"You're not wrong."

"I hear DC wants you back tomorrow," Chuck said.

"Yes, Thursday and Friday, then I finally get to go back home. I'm ready to see Amy and Troy. The last seven days have been hell."

"Keep that chin up, sissy. You'll be breathing that dreadful fresh mountain air again before you know it."

"You need to visit my little po'dunk office in Boise. The clean air may do your old lungs some good," Matt said.

"Nah, the grime, grease and filth of the city has preserved my body for this long. No need to screw it up at this stage in life."

That both laughed.

⸺◆⸺

As noon rolled around, Matt and Amy finally made their way out of the bedroom. After a nice long shower together, they dressed and headed to the kitchen to make lunch. Thirty minutes later, at the very smell of food, Troy and Cate pulled in the driveway for their typical weekend at home.

The four of them talked at length over lunch. Matt told them all as much as he could about his time in New York and Washington. Troy peppered him with questions, some Matt could answer, others he could not. Amy and Cate just listened.

⸺◆⸺

Matt's first day back in the office after several weeks proved frantic. Everyone wanted to know what occurred. He told them what he could, which was not enough. By midafternoon, things had returned to normal. Matt sat at his desk reviewing a case file as his office phone rang. He answered and had a brief discussion with the familiar voice on the other end of the line. About halfway through the conversation the man became quiet.

"What is it?" Matt asked.

"Look, what I'm about to tell you...I didn't tell you. You got that, Matt?"

"Sure, Earl. I hear you loud and clear. My ears are open, but my lips are sealed."

"It took a while, but we finally found a camera angle that caught an image from the top portion of the document. The initial screenshot was terrible. I had to run the image through a lot of special programs to clarify it. In the end, I could only make out the top three words at the center of the document."

"Well? What did Aaron Ryker take that ultimately cost him his life?"

Earl paused for a moment, not to add any drama, but he was genuinely concerned about telling Matt what he knew. After a few seconds, he continued and said only three words.

Matt considered the words for a moment before he asked, "What the hell is The Zechariah Option?"

"That's just it," Earl said in response, "Nobody knows. And I mean nobody. No one I've spoken to has a clue. Anyway, once we got the name, it didn't take long before people way above our pay grade swooped in. They took everything, man! And I do mean everything! Every computer, every hard drive, every piece of equipment we used over the last two weeks."

"They took them back to the Hoover Building?"

"No, they destroyed them. Every piece, they burned them up like some Old Testament sacrifice in the parking lot. Swept up the debris and left with it. We were told in no uncertain terms that we saw nothing."

"And what did you do?" Matt asked in an incredulous tone.

"I shut my mouth, that's what I did. I like my job, Matt, and I ain't about to lose it, especially over some biblically named document."

"Yet you called me..."

"Figured you at least ought to know, Matt, it was your man that stole the document then took two bullets for it. Just be careful, and you didn't hear it from me."

"Scout's honor," Matt said. "I'll take The Zechariah Option to the grave."

Chapter Thirty-Seven

London

December 2001

Waleed read the document hundreds of times after Muhammad brought him the worn parchment of The Zechariah Option. The more he read, the more he believed not only was the story true, but that he and his men would find the missing device lost to time.

As soon as Ryker had been dealt with, Waleed headed home to London. Two cryptanalysts awaited his arrival, and for the first couple days, he left the men alone so they could work. A shrewd businessman by trade, Waleed knew that when you paid the best people to do a job, you gave them the latitude to do the work.

After three days, they provided Waleed with some valuable details. The weapon was most certainly hidden around the year 1963. With a large-scale public works project used as a cover to hide the weapon deep underground. The document indicated they hid the device behind a large vault door. The cryptanalysts were also certain that the construction of a new dam served as the public works project used as a cover. Although The Zechariah Option document did not provide a specific location, it indicated the western part of the United States was the ultimate resting place of the device. The text provided multiple references to water, mountains and even a lake. Besides a few vague references to the terrain, one specific line of text stated, "*To find the passageway which leads to the vault one must pass before the Hand of God.*"

A web search of that phrase *Hand of God* contained many possibilities.

An extremely secretive plan, the document indicated only seven men knew of The Zechariah Option project. That number included two senators, who came up with the original idea. However, their identities proved to be a mystery since the two signature lines in the bottom right corner of the document were part of the missing piece. Only the beginning of the two lines that started with the words "United States Senator ..." remained.

Once Waleed felt certain the two cryptanalysts scrutinized the document and extracted all the information, he gave each man a large duffel bag filled with cash. He left the men in his personal study and walked down the two flights of stairs to his wine cellar. When Waleed returned, he opened a bottle of 1963 Taylor Fladgate Vintage Port from Portugal. They looked surprised as he opened the nearly 40 years old bottle. After he poured each man a glass, he sat back and watched with amusement as they enjoyed a parting drink. A short time later he said his goodbyes and the two men climbed into the back of his limousine for the drive to Heathrow International Airport.

Within 10 minutes of leaving South Carriage Dr. the two men were fast asleep. The tasteless sedative that lined the wine glass worked quickly. The limousine did not go to Heathrow as expected but went directly to a heavily industrialized area in east London. Three men awaited the car's arrival and unloaded the sedated men onto a large plastic tarp in the center of the vast warehouse. Without hesitation, the man on the left removed a .40 caliber pistol with a threaded silencer and placed two shots in the center of each man's forehead. The plastic tarp was rolled up, and the two bodies were loaded into the back of a black van. From London, the drive south to Brighton took just under two hours. Darkness engulfed the shore. It was a moonless night. The van was met at the dock by several men, who quickly unloaded the tarp containing the two bodies. After loading the corpses onto the boat, heavy weights were chained to them. The fishing vessel traveled about five miles out to sea, where the bodies were dumped. The two cryptanalysts would spend eternity at the bottom of the English Channel.

Waleed wasn't one to leave witnesses alive, no matter how helpful they may have been. The two duffel bags of cash were opened and dispersed to the men who buried the bodies at sea.

The next week, Waleed formatted his plan and sent two teams of trusted men to the western part of the United States. These men were instructed to scout out some dams that might be probable locations for the hidden vault. Of course, the men were only provided limited information, and nobody knew the content of this mysterious vault they were required to locate.

Waleed waited each day for calls to come in from the two teams. Each day, the teams told him the same thing. Nothing of substance was discovered at any of the dams over the two-week period.

The Big Bend Dam in South Dakota, completed during July of 1963, initially proved to be a likely location. However, when the team arrived to reconnaissance the dam, they knew immediately the topography didn't match the description on the document. Next came the Glen Canyon Dam in northern Arizona, followed by the Yellowtail Dam in south central Montana. However, upon intense inspection, none of them featured the geographic descriptions in the document.

With roughly 75,000 dams in the United States, the list of sites to visit appeared overwhelming. The document specifically stated it was a concrete structure, which narrowed the list. After visiting many of the larger dams, the two teams looked at smaller dams. Several weeks into the search, they still did not find the correct site.

Waleed became frustrated, and the sense of exasperation boiled over one night at 9:30 PM on a Monday. With Waleed reading in his study, a gentle knock at the door drew his ire. "Enter," Waleed said in a voice that did not mask his displeasure.

"I'm sorry to disturb you, but the teams had no luck today." Kadir could see the sneer on his boss's face as he moved closer.

Waleed shook his head. "This is unacceptable. Allah has found favor with us, but we are squandering the opportunity he provided us with. The team needs to do better, and we need to narrow the search."

"Any specific ideas?" Kadir asked. "The teams are working hard, but nothing matches the descriptions provided in the document."

Waleed rubbed his chin vigorously as his mind raced. Suddenly, a thought occurred to him. "Yes, I have just realized something."

"What's that?" Kadir asked as he rocked back and forth on the heels of his expensive Italian shoes.

"Something we should have focused on before now. The bottom right portion of the document that is missing."

"The names of the two senators who you believe authorized this project?"

"Yes, precisely."

"What about them?"

"If we could identify those two individuals, it may give us answers where they hid the weapon."

"There are 100 possible senators who could have signed that document in 1963, and many are probably already dead," Kadir stated. "How do you suggest we go about tracking them down?"

"I need you in Washington. I think it will be necessary for you to travel to the National Archives."

"And what am I looking for exactly?"

"I'm not sure," Waleed said. "But I know the Archives has a section called the Center for Legislative Archives. Its role is to preserve and make available for research the historical records of both the House and Senate. My thought is to go there and pore over as much information as you can. Start with the years 1962 and 1963. Look for any mention of the word Zechariah. Take special care in looking over anything that deals with nuclear weapons. You will find many such items, I'm sure. In fact, keep a keen eye out for the Senate Armed Services Committee transcripts. I would not be the least bit surprised to find that our two senators were both a part of that committee during the early 1960's."

Kadir smiled, "That is a very astute observation, Waleed. I would not have thought of looking in that direction. How long should I plan on being there, and what type of access do I need to enter the Archives?"

"You'll need to stay until we uncover some clues. The Center for Legislative Archives is open to attorney's, historians, and scholars. We can create a cover story for you and give you an appropriate ID and background to make you blend in."

Kadir bowed slightly and walked backwards away from Waleed. "As you wish. I'll do my best."

"You have never let me down before, and I don't expect you will start now." Waleed stood and patted Kadir on the shoulder. "Go with Allah's blessings. And may you find favor in his eyes."

Chapter Thirty-Eight

Georgetown

Senator Preston Wilcox struggled to fall asleep even after the two glasses of scotch before he laid down. After what seemed like several hours of restlessness, his exhausted body finally overrode his active mind, and he drifted off to a tumultuous slumber.

Less than an hour later, the nightmare began.

He found himself walking through the woods at his ranch in Drexel, something he did daily during the month of August when Congress took a recess and he flew home.

The sun peered through the gaps in the forest canopy and warmed his face. As he walked up a large incline, he could see a clearing before him. When he reached the open space, he did something he had not done in many years, and laid down in the tall grass. Preston basked in the summer sunlight and felt like a young child once more.

A metallic sound startled him as he lay on the grass. The sound didn't come from the tree line, but from the valley below. He slowly rose from the alluring grass and made his way to the edge of the clearing, where the ground dropped dramatically. This spot afforded him a clear view of the valley. As he glanced down, he saw Lake Drexel, and to the east, the concrete dam, which had been built as a cover for The Zechariah Option.

Then the noise came again, louder this time. The ringing sound perturbed him greatly. He looked around, and after a few moments saw movement out of the corner of his eye just past the dam on the far hillside. His heart sank as his eyes watched three men emerge from one of the long ago sealed off mine shafts.

Preston recognized the spot instantly and yelled, "No, not that one. Anyone but that one," but no words came from his mouth. Yet somehow, even though he made no sound, the three men heard him. They looked in his direction. One of them made eye contact with him, smiled and mouthed the words, *Thank you, senator.* Those three words caused shivers to run down his spine. He knew at that moment that the clanging sound he had heard was the sound of the vault door being opened somehow. But how could they have known where to look? And who were they?

He took a step forward but forgot he was at the edge of the steep cliff. Losing his balance, he startled to tumble. Preston found himself in freefall only a few feet away from striking the rocks below when he awoke with a shudder.

—◆—

Sweat flowed as Preston emerged from his nightmare. He had not fallen, and he was not in Idaho. As far as he knew, the hidden nuclear weapon remained buried in its underground vault. As he sat up, and after several minutes paced around the room. Without a doubt, he knew he was the only living soul left who had been part of the project, and according to Dick all documents about the project had been destroyed.

Yet, a nagging concern welled up from deep within. He learned the hard way Dick could not be trusted. If only he had known that back in 1962 before the two of them had come up with the plan.

Even after almost 40 years, it still sickened Preston to know what Dick did to those five men under the guise of giving hope to the nation if the unthinkable happened and the United States and the Soviet Union engaged in an all-out nuclear war.

Chapter Thirty-Nine

September 1963

The darkness within the old mineshaft proved difficult to fathom. A few times when they descended, the lights flickered and even went out for a minute. During those moments of pitch black, Preston could put his hand in front of his face and not see it. It reminded him of the time he and his wife, Sarah, had visited Maui. They, like most tourists, took the scenic road to Hana. The beautiful 64-mile winding roadway led them to black sand beaches and several waterfalls along the roadside. At lunch, they stopped at a lava tube and paid for a personal tour. The man who took them deep underground wanted them to experience what pitch dark really meant. Deep into the lava tube, Preston, Sarah and the guide turned off their flashlights.

Preston had that feeling once more while in the old mineshaft, and he didn't enjoy it anymore than the similar experience in Maui. He and Dick watched as the workers maneuvered the five-hundred-pound nuclear weapon into the concrete vault. Dick pulled the heavy steel door shut with a loud *thud* sound that reverberated throughout the narrow tunnel. With the lock mechanism fully engaged, the two senators and five men they entrusted with The Zachariah Option project proceeded out of the mine shaft together. Dick instructed the men to go straight to Preston's house while he and Preston stayed behind.

As instructed, the five men got in the car and left. A few minutes later, four men arrived in a pickup truck. One of them was Jack Harding. Senator Griffith handed over a black briefcase. Jack opened it and smiled as he viewed the contents.

Preston looked towards the tunnel entrance. "Seal it up, Jack. No one ever goes in that shaft again. Understood?"

Jack nodded, and then patted the briefcase, "We can take care of that, senator. I seem to recall shaft 134 here has some sort of methane gas leak and needs to be sealed up." He winked slightly and then turned to the three men he brought. "You heard em' boys, 134 here is dangerous. Seal her up and double-time it. Dinner is on me if you bust your ass."

The men looked at each other, grinned and got to work. In less than an hour, shaft 134 looked like many other abandoned mine shafts across the hillside. By then, darkness settled over Drexel.

Soon the two senators were on their way through the valley towards Preston's house that overlooked Lake Drexel. A mile before they arrived at his house, flashing blue lights and several stopped cars blocked the roadway. Preston pulled his truck off the side of the road and preceded on foot to the emergency vehicles.

The accident scene appeared horrific. The black two door Buick Riviera lay crushed between a logging truck and a massive white pine tree. As they walked up to the scene, Preston and Dick knew the occupants of the Riviera were all dead. No one could have survived that wreck. They also knew who was in the car since it had just left the gold mine an hour before.

Preston stood on the side of the road in shock. He went straight up to the sheriff currently taking statements from several eyewitnesses to the gruesome scene.

The sheriff nodded his cap as he saw Preston approach. "Senator Wilcox," he said in a somber tone as he shook Preston's hand.

"Phil," Preston replied

"Pretty grisly scene," Phil pointed back behind where he stood. "Is everything ok? You look as white as a ghost, senator."

Preston swallowed hard. His words came out slow. "I...I knew those men, there...um...were five victims, right?"

"Yes sir," the sheriff replied. "I don't believe they were from around here, though."

"They weren't," Preston said. "They were guests of mine. Federal government employees in town for just a few days. What happened?"

"Still piecing all the details together, but it appears the logging truck either lost control or its brakes went out. Plowed right through the intersection and slammed into the Riviera. That big old white pine tree stopped them all. Appears the five men in the Buick died immediately."

"What did the truck driver say?" Preston asked.

"Nothing," the sheriff said. "He died as well. The impact of the crash sent him right through the windshield. Snapped his neck like a twig. Dead men don't tell us squat, senator."

"Ain't that the truth," Dick said with raised eyebrows as he stood behind Preston.

The two senators stayed for half an hour before they got back into Preston's vehicle and proceeded home. The rest of the drive was in utter silence. Two days later, the men headed back to Washington. Preston still very much upset about the death of the five men while Dick seemed detached from the whole incident.

• ❖ •

Several weeks later, Dick visited for dinner. Sarah remained at Drexel for an extended stay home. The conversation started light and focused on mainly politics. However, something nagged at Preston, and he wanted to bring it up several times over the past few weeks. Because of his close friendship with Dick, he remained quiet. That night he didn't feel like holding it in any longer, so he summoned the courage to ask a tough question of his friend.

"Dick, you didn't seem upset about the accident in Drexel. Why is that?"

Senator Griffith smirked slightly but did not reply immediately. Instead of answering the question, he responded with one of his own. "You do you realize we completed our objective, right Preston? We set out to do a great thing for our nation. We hid a weapon that those damn Ruskies can never find. God help us, but if nuclear war befalls us, America will still have a weapon at its disposal."

Preston felt uneasy by the way Dick replied. "And you and I are the only ones that know about it now, right?"

"Correct," Dick said smugly. "The incident in Drexel certainly shrunk the circle of who knew about The Zachariah Option project."

"You mean accident. The accident in Drexel, not incident," Preston replied.

Shaking his head back-and-forth Dick replied, "No, I meant incident. It was part of my plan to ensure that only the two of us knew about the mine shaft and what it contains."

Preston looked back in anger, "Are you admitting it was not an accident, and you had those five men killed?"

"I mean, technically speaking, it was six. Don't forget about the driver of the logging truck. All their deaths were necessary. Might I remind you, loose lips sink ships, Preston. Don't be naïve. There were five people too many that knew what we did out there."

"But those men were innocent. They didn't deserve to die."

"They served the greater good of our United States," Dick said without a hint of remorse. "I made arrangements, and their families will be well compensated."

"I never took you for a killer," Preston said through gritted teeth.

Dick's eyes narrowed, "And I didn't take you to be such a pussy. People die, plain and simple. If that weapon is ever needed one day, it will be because a nuclear holocaust has occurred. And you bet your ass a hell of a lot of people will be dead if that happens."

"I can't let your actions stand," Preston shook his head, "Hiding the weapon for the greater good is one thing, but murdering innocent people to cover it up is unacceptable."

An uncomfortable silence filled the room as the men just glared at each other.

"I'm sorry, but I cannot allow this," Preston stood suddenly.

"What are you going to do?" Dick asked as he stood and inconspicuously picked something up from the place setting. Then he added, "Do you plan to turn me in?"

"If I must, then yes."

"It looks like I left one too many witnesses," Dick yelled as he lunged across the dining room table with the concealed steak knife in his right hand. He aimed for the heart. Dick may have been old, but his motion was faster than most men his age.

The sudden movement surprised Preston, who turned to his right just in time for the knife to miss his chest by an inch. The blade cut the sleeve of his dress shirt but did not pierce his flesh. With his left arm he swung down and slammed Dick's body hard into the solid oak table. Dick still had forward momentum. The movement caused him to slide off the end of the table. His arms were away from his body and unable to break his fall. As his head crashed into the solid wood floor, a distinct cracking sound reverberated around the dining room. Preston took a step forward where the body came to rest face up after rolling over after he hit the ground.

Dick glared toward the ceiling, his lifeless eyes stared past Preston. The whole thing happened so quickly, Preston didn't know what to do. After several anxious minutes, he sat down and thought. A plan took shape.

About two hours later, Preston sat in the passenger seat of Dick's car. Dick's lifeless body in the driver's seat. Preston propped up the corpse as best he could. He put several beer bottles in the car, even poured one out on the floorboard for good measure, sure to spill some on Dick's clothing as well. The car was running but in park; it idled on top of a moderate incline. At the bottom of the hill, the intersection was "T" shaped. A large stone façade apartment building lay at the bottom of the hill.

Preston said no last words. He got out of the passenger seat; made sure he wiped off any prints he may have left and walked around the car to the driver's side. Reaching in through the open window, and using his gloved right hand, he took the car out of park and placed it into drive. The car slowly proceeded down the hill but gained speed as gravity took over. It passed through the intersection and struck the stone building with a decent amount of force. The sound of the crash decidedly louder than Preston expected. It would certainly draw people out of their homes rapidly.

Preston watched the events occur, turned and then walked back to his home.

◆◆◇◆◆

Thirty-eight years passed, and Preston recalled all the events as if they happened mere minutes before. His mind left that distant scene and thought more about the nightmare that had awoken him. There was something he had to do, it should have been done a long time ago. Someone besides himself needed to know about what occurred so many years ago. They needed to know about the hidden weapon. He could not take the secret to his grave. Preston knew there was only one person he could trust with such vitally important information.

Within forty-five minutes, he completed the letter and map. Preston re-read it two more times than placed it in an envelope. After writing the name on the outside of the large manila envelope, he placed it inside the safe in his office with his other last will and testament documents.

Chapter Forty

Washington D.C.

Matt Evans found himself back in D.C. the week before Christmas, not exactly his idea of celebrating the holidays. Fortunately, he had a Park City ski trip with Amy, Troy and Cate the day after Christmas to look forward to. Matt planned for it to be an enjoyable break from the nonstop workload over the past three months.

Pat O'Shea called Matt on Wednesday. Since he was in town, Pat asked if they could have dinner. Matt agreed, and they decided on a time and place.

As Pat walked into the new restaurant on H Street NW, only six blocks from the White House, he saw Matt at the bar nursing a Guinness.

Matt saw Pat arrive, grabbed his drink, and walked over to his friend. After they shook hands and said hello the maitre'd showed them to their table.

"You are ok with sushi, right?" Matt asked as they took their seats.

"Of course," Pat said. "After all, I'm Irish. We eat anything put in front of us as long as we aren't buying."

Matt let out a laugh at his friend's humor. "Ah, and here I thought you Irish lads did was drink till you passed out or pissed yourselves."

Pat smiled. "We've been known to do that too when we aren't devising our plan of world domination."

They ordered dinner, and the two men caught up on how things were going. They had not seen each other since early October and had only spoken a few times on the phone. The events after 9/11 had kept Pat traveling much more than he liked. He had only been home a few days every other week since the terrorist incident occurred.

"What's new at the NNSA?" Matt asked.

Pat shook his head and sighed, "Part of me wants to shoot the next dock worker that reports an unusually high Geiger count. We're being run ragged with high readings workers are reporting."

"Nothing dangerous has been found?"

"No," Pat said. "I shouldn't complain. These guys are just doing their job, but it's hard with limited resources to run down every concern that gets lobbed our way. Feels like we are just chasing our tails."

"How about that cargo ship in New Orleans you told me about, the one that departed Yemen? Anything ever come from that investigation?"

"No, the trail went cold."

Before long, the discussion turned to the events that had taken place on Staten Island and Manhattan.

"Whatever happened to the murder investigation involving Agent Ryker? Any progress? Muhammad Jarah, right? We even got a BOLO for him at the NNSA."

"Yes, that's him. There's nothing to report. The intelligence agencies claim he slipped out of the country on November 8th. Interpol said they have credible intelligence he was seen in Algeria during late November. The president authorized a strike on a training camp where they believed Jarah to be holed up in outside of Ksabi. The Delta guys went in for him. They killed several guys, captured some, but they didn't find him. Unfortunately, he's out in the wind."

Pat nodded slightly, "Any truth to the rumors that Ryker took something out of that secret FBI facility, and that's why he was killed?"

Matt looked genuinely surprised at what Pat asked, especially since it was completely accurate. "Where did you hear that?"

"The feds all talk, Matt. I'm sure you can't say anything, but that's the word on the street. Nobody knows what he took or what really happened at Fresh Kills, but there sure as hell are a bunch of rumors floating around," Pat said as he took a long swig of beer the waitress brought a few minutes before.

Matt frowned slightly, and replied, "Can't confirm anything you just said, Pat. I can tell you Ryker is dead and Muhammad is the person we believe is responsible for his death. But as for what we were doing in Fresh Kills, sorry, my lips are sealed."

"I understand. That's why I like you, Matt. The government needs more men like you. Maybe you should run for office one day."

"Hell no!" Matt exclaimed a little too loud for the size of the room. "We already have one adopted politician in our family, good ole' Preston. We sure don't need an Evans to run for office."

"Troy might get that chance one day. You said he is gonna follow in your footsteps. Maybe he'll be the director one day. Or maybe he'll work for the president."

With that comment, a big smile formed on Matt's face, "You never know, Pat. The only thing that scares me is how passionate he can be. He never forgets a face and can hold a grudge. I keep telling him he will have to control his temper. When he works for the Bureau one day, he'll come across his share of dumbasses and will have to resist the urge to put them in their place. Especially the bureaucrats. Troy won't enjoy working with them if he climbs the ranks one day."

"NNSA isn't any different, I deal with that kind of shit all the time."

Matt shifted the conversation, "When will you be heading out west with the family?"

"Middle of March," Pat said. "The kids have never been past Tennessee so we thought we would take them for a western adventure on their winter break."

"Any chance you'll be near Boise? Amy and I would love to have you all stay with us for a few nights."

"Thanks for the offer, Matt, and yes, I think we may swing by Boise. I'll run it by the misses when I get home tomorrow."

"Good deal," Matt said. "Just give me a little heads up and we'll have some fun planned for the kids. I'd love for you to meet Troy as well."

"I would be honored to meet all the Evans crew."

—◆—

The cold breeze greeted Matt as he left the sushi restaurant. After a quick call to Amy, he rang someone else. "Hey old man, you still up?" he said as the phone connected on the second ring.

"Of course," a distinguished voice responded.

"Mind if I stop by for a nightcap?" Matt asked.

"There is a twenty-five-year-old bottle of Macallan sitting here on my desk waiting to be opened. Come on over. You still remember where I live, right?"

Matt laughed, "Yes, Preston, I believe I have been to Georgetown a few times over the years."

"Then get your ass over here, I ain't getting any younger after all."

"On my way, senator."

Chapter Forty-One

Washington, D.C.

January 2002

Waleed had very few genuine friends, men he could entrust with secrets or share his innermost thoughts. Instead, he hired people at least as smart, if not smarter than himself. However, he certainly did not hire those people because he liked them or wanted to be friends with them. No, they were employed because they served a purpose, and in many cases brought an exceptional skill set. Some could perform certain tasks with extreme efficiency. While others did things he demanded, since those tasks were well below his means and status. Waleed saw most people he encountered as pawns, and he would move them around the chessboard of life in both offensive or defensive moves. They certainly were all expendable. With no exceptions.

Unfortunately, Kadir Bashara was no different in Waleed's eyes. Sure, Waleed would openly profess they were longtime friends, but deep down Kadir was in his life because he served a specific purpose and performed certain tasks with precision. No more, no less. It wasn't personal, just business.

Kadir had many amazing gifts. One of those included the fact that he had a photographic memory, and rarely, if ever, forgot a single detail. If he read something years before he could not only tell you what he read, but what page, paragraph and line number.

Because of this unique gift he possessed, Waleed dispatched Kadir to the National Archives. Waleed needed someone who could assimilate as much information as possible in order to discover which two United States Senators crafted The Zechariah Option.

Kadir might be a pawn, but he was a trusted pawn that had never let Waleed down.

———◆———

Every day for almost a month, Kadir left his plush hotel, the historic Hay-Adams on Sixteenth and H streets, walking the 1.1 miles to the National Archives building at 700 Pennsylvania Avenue. As he passed the Treasury Building, he would look to his right and just get a glimpse of the White House. He held contempt for the man who sat in the Oval Office. Kadir longed for the day when the United States would be brought to its knees. If his efforts in the National Archives could aid in that, then his time in D.C. would be well spent.

Kadir's cover was quite clever. He had fake credentials, created by one of the best illicit firms in London, which listed his name as Samuel Cohen, an assistant professor at Oxford University. The cover story explained Samuel was part of the Rothermere American Institute, a new institute at Oxford dedicated to the interdisciplinary and comparative study of the United States of America. When asked about the purpose of being in Washington, he explained that his National Archives research each day was to write an in-depth article on the United States Senate and the Cold War with the Soviet Union.

For over a month, Kadir entered the Center for Legislative Archives and requested volumes of reports, including transcripts from senate hearings and committee meetings. The staff appeared exited to hear about his writing project on the Cold War and were very helpful in retrieving whatever documents he requested each day. Within a week he memorized the coffee habits of all the ladies on staff, sure to bring in their favorite, grossly overpriced drink. Kadir knew how to win over and impress people, especially the attractive ones.

During the day, Kadir worked tirelessly at the Center, while at night he compiled his findings and tried to find the clues that would unravel the mystery. The tedious task proved arduous, but one he was well suited to accomplish.

Kadir labored daily in the research room and read page after page from the senate documents, which had been meticulously preserved from 1962 to 1963. Senate bills, transcripts of speeches, and various committee meeting minutes flew past his eyes at an incredible rate of speed.

After a few weeks, the days bled together. Before he knew it, he had already been in D.C. for three weeks. Christmas slipped by, and New Year's Day arrived. The Archives remained closed for the holidays, but the assistants gave Kadir a stack of photocopies to review.

Kadir sat upright in his hotel bed. One of the assistants, Tracey, a petite blond with legs that stretched on for miles, had put a red check mark on the transcript for the Senate Committee on Armed Services. The check mark indicated that something in the transcript might be beneficial to his research project. He had given the assistants a comprehensive list of items to notate. He paid special attention to this document. Like many of the pages that he had been reading for the past month, there were lines that were redacted because of their classified nature.

Kadir read through the document, as he had countless others over the past month. Initially, nothing seemed remarkable. Then suddenly, some dialogue caught his eye on the ninth page of testimony. A debate between a handful of senators raged on. They appeared to be discussing the risk of a nuclear holocaust.

With each line he read, Kadir's pulse quickened. As more of the discussion unfolded, two senators statements stood out from the others. Kadir picked up on something that countless historians and research analysts simply glossed over during the past 39 years. The conversations played out like distant ghosts from the past. It gave Kadir chills as he read the transcript from March 25, 1963.

Come now, Senator Griffith, do you really believe the Soviets will launch their missiles? Let's be serious here, we're on the record after all. The Soviets are not fools. They know if they launch; we launch. I feel quite certain mutually assured destruction will dissuade them from choosing that course. The distinguished senator from New York said.

I don't know what the Ruskies will do, sir, Senator Griffith replied. *But I know we need to be prepared for all scenarios that may occur. And that of course involves all-out war with the Soviets, and a possible nuclear winter if they launch.*

May God have mercy on our souls if that occurs, Senator Preston Wilcox of Idaho said.

Amen, Senator Griffith added.

The senator from New York replied, *I doubt God will have anything to do with things if nuclear war befalls us, gentlemen. It's not like the good book discusses nuclear warfare.*

Maybe you should read your Bible closer, senator, Senator Griffith said.

Take a look at Zechariah, Senator Wilcox stated.

Chapter 14 verse 12, Senator Griffith added.

━━━◆━━━

The debate continued for several more lines, but Kadir didn't really pay any attention after the last comments from Senator's Wilcox and Griffith. The exchange was just what he was looking for. He re-read it several more times. Once he was sure, he picked up the phone. Waleed answered, and Kadir read the transcript to him.

"I believe you may have found our two senators," Waleed stated in an enthusiastic tone.

"Yes, I think so," Kadir replied.

"Tell me about the two of them?" Waleed asked. The curiosity apparent in his tone.

Kadir studied all the senators from 1962 to 1963. He picked up the hand-written notes he had on each one. "Senator Griffith died in 1963. He apparently had too much to drink one night and crashed his car into a building in Washington. Snapped his neck like a twig."

"And Wilcox?" Waleed asked.

"Still alive. In fact, he's still in the United States Senate. Wife died several years ago, he lives alone in Georgetown."

"You feel confident they are the two senators responsible?"

"It's very likely based on what I read, but I'll keep digging to see if I can uncover any more evidence," Kadir said.

"Based on what you find, we may need to pay the senator a visit," Waleed said in a firm tone.

"When?" Kadir asked.

"January third," Waleed said.

"Then it sounds like I have a lot of work to do in the next 36 hours."

"We both do," Waleed replied before he quickly added, "And Kadir..."

"Yes?"

"Good job, I knew I could count on you!"

The line disconnected

Kadir sat back and cracked a smile, it was one of the few smiles he had displayed in the last month. Of course, that did not include the days Tracey wore her tight red skirt at the archives. Those days he cracked more than a smile as she passed him each time. On those days, Kadir made it a point to request as many documents as Tracey would retrieve. He did not see a ring on her finger, and a few times even thought about asking her out for dinner. His judgment held him back, and instead he took a mental snapshot of how she looked in that skirt. His photographic memory etched each curve of her figure into his memory bank.

Chapter Forty-Two

Georgetown

Preston stayed up late, a habit he picked up as a young man and never shook as he got older. After finishing some last-minute changes to the senate bill he sponsored, Preston poured himself a nightcap. Now in the downstairs study, he sank into his leather recliner and took a slow sip. The liquid burned his throat and made him feel not so old for a few minutes. After a second drink, he took his normal spot on the old worn sofa across from the recliner in the study and lay down.

Within a few minutes, Preston drifted off to sleep. Not long into his restless sleep cycle, a sound startled him.

Preston awoke and sat upright as quick as his aged body would allow. The room was pitch dark, and he couldn't see anything even with his eyes open.

Is my mind playing tricks on me, he thought, *Or did I hear a thud?*

As he swung his legs down to the ground, he sensed a presence. The lights in the study came on suddenly as he involuntarily jerked backwards. The bright light temporarily blinded him as he raised his hands to cover his eyes from the sudden burst of light.

A calm voice spoke, "Please, Senator Wilcox, don't be startled. We mean you no harm."

The man seemed to have a slight British accent thought Preston. "Who the hell are you? And what are you doing in my home? I'm a United States Senator, for God's sake!"

"I know that, Preston. In fact, that's why I'm here," the voice replied.

Preston's eyes had finally adjusted to the light, and he could now make out the image of four men in his study. Two of the men were quite burly. They were most certainly a security detail of some sort, Preston assumed. The men were close to him, one on each side of the sofa. A third man stood in the background. He appeared to be looking around the study, his back turned slightly away from the rest of them.

The man doing the talking stood directly before Preston. He was close enough to touch. The man was very well dressed and clearly had money. The man looked to be Arab, yet his clothes were European with professionally styled jet-black hair, and a well-manicured goatee.

"I have a security system," Preston said in a concerned tone, his octave raised a few notes higher than normal. "The authorities are most likely already on their way. If you leave now, you may have time to escape before they arrive."

"No, you had a security system," the well-dressed man said in a firm tone. "My associates disabled the system. Sorry, senator, it was in all of our best interests. No one will come tonight."

"What do you want?" Preston asked. With anger clearly displayed in his facial contortions, and also in his voice inflection.

"I need to ask you a few questions."

"Regarding what?"

"Silly me, I forgot to introduce myself." The mysterious man extended his hand. "I am Waleed bin Abdulah. We have not had the pleasure of meeting before now, senator."

Preston did not extend his hand to meet Waleed's. He glared at the man before him and recognized the name immediately.

After a few seconds, Waleed withdrew his hand.

"I must be a special person to have the House of Saud here in Georgetown tonight, but I don't believe in being cordial when someone breaks into my house in the middle of the night. Nor do I care for threats, or whatever you are here for, Prince Waleed," Preston said harshly.

"Threats? I have not threatened you, Senator Wilcox. I merely want to talk. And please no need for the formality, I am merely Waleed. I dropped the prince title years ago."

"I have an office and visiting hours at the Russell Senate Building if you need to talk," Preston said.

"That's just it senator, the matter we need to discuss is slightly sensitive. It's not something I could make an appointment to go over. I would not want to discuss something like this in your stuffy office space on Capitol Hill. No, your study here in Georgetown is quaint. It has a very homey feel, which is why it's the perfect place to discuss our matter."

"And what would that be?" .

A wry smile formed at the corner of Waleed's lips as he replied, "Why, The Zechariah Option of course, my dear Senator."

Preston's eyes gave no hint of acknowledgement. His years in the United States Senate had taught him to present a killer poker face when needed. "I don't know what in the hell you're talking about, Waleed." Inside his stomach twisted and turned. His worst nightmare was coming true.

"Ha," Waleed replied with an audible laugh, "You know exactly what I am talking about, Senator Wilcox. Besides, don't try to bullshit a bullshitter."

"I'm not in the habit of lying, sir," Preston replied.

"That's rich coming from a United States Senator." Waleed handed Preston the transcript that Kadir discovered. "Maybe this will jog your memory? If not, I can fill in a few blanks for you."

Preston read the old transcript. When he finished, he stated, "I don't have the foggiest idea what you or this transcript is referencing."

"Let me tell you what I know," Waleed said.

Over the next five minutes, Waleed discussed the Zechariah Option. In fact, he pulled out a photocopied version of the official document and read it word for word. As he did, he could see out of the corner of his eye telltale signs that Senator Wilcox knew what he was talking about. Preston's eyes betrayed him; they were a portal to his soul. Waleed briefly mentioned how they had come into possession of the document and how Kadir had tracked down the two senators.

Still, even after everything Waleed explained, Preston remained stoic. "I don't know what this Zechariah Option was or is, but I can tell you, Waleed, if I knew anything about it, I would take that secret to my grave. I'm an old man. My wife died some time back, and I have no reason to continue living. You might as well have your roughnecks over there start beating me to a pulp. In the end, it won't matter. I know nothing and I'm ready to meet my maker tonight."

Waleed shook his head, "I think you are lying, Senator Wilcox. Of course, you are a United States Senator, so let's be honest with each other, you lie for a living, don't you? But no, I would not lay a hand on you. I respect my elders. These two men here could snap your neck like a twig. Just like what happened to Senator Griffith's neck. You're right, you probably would take the secret to your grave. Beating you won't work, and I have nothing to hold over your head."

"Sounds like you have few options," Preston said.

"Ahh," Waleed replied, "But, I have other ways to make you talk."

⚬

Two men with thick necks and bulging muscles plunked down on either side of Preston and pushed him to the center of the elongated sofa. Both oversized men reached out and held his arms down at his sides with ease.

Preston didn't resist since he knew it was futile.

Waleed kneeled before the senator as Kadir walked up behind him and handed him a syringe filled with clear liquid.

"Sodium pentothal?" Preston asked as his eyes grew wide.

"No," Waleed shook his head. "This is not some Cold War spy novel, senator. Sodium pentothal is quite an unreliable way to gain necessary intel. You would go on blabbering incoherently all night and never give me anything but useless dribble." Waleed held up the syringe and smiled as his finger flicked the needle. "No, what I have here is much better than that old school truth serum. I prefer to call it liquid honesty. The chemists at the Central Intelligence Agency concocted it a few years back. It has been highly effective in test subjects so far. We will see how it works tonight."

"Go to hell," Preston said as he winced while Waleed pressed the cold steel needle into his vein.

"You first, senator," Waleed replied. He repeated the phrase, "You first!" while he pushed the stopper.

Almost immediately, Preston relaxed. In fact, his body went limp within seconds. The two large men on either side of him had to physically hold him up. Waleed checked the older man's pulse to see if he was still breathing.

"Is he dead?" Kadir asked with a hint of concern in his voice.

"No, it will pass," Waleed stated in an icy tone. "The cocktail of chemicals needs to do its job. Just give him a few minutes, and he'll sing like a canary."

Like clockwork, two minutes later, Preston's head slowly rose from where it rested on his sternum. A wide grin replaced the stern, angry look on his face before he passed out.

"Feeling ok, senator?" Waleed asked.

"I'm quite well, my good man," Preston in a tone that could best be described as bubbly. "I sure like whatever it is you gave me."

"Of course you do," Waleed said. "What's that you American's like to say? Oh yes, that's right. I bet you feel like the prom king in the back of mom and dad's station wagon with his date after the big dance. Don't you, old boy?"

Preston slowly smiled, "You sure as hell ain't the prom queen."

"You remember who I am?"

"A pompous asshole, who should go back to Saudi Arabia and take the rest of the ragheads with him."

"Ha," Waleed responded with a boisterous laugh as he turned to Kadir, "I believe the liquid truth is working just fine." He then looked back to Preston, "You're a funny old coot, senator. You may grow on me before long."

Waleed started a few questions just to get a baseline confirming the senator was giving him truthful answers. He started with questions like Preston's age, hometown, date he got marriage, and bills he had sponsored. The senator answered each question honestly.

After several minutes, Preston interrupted, "Say, Waleed, can we continue these questions from my office chair. It sure is uncomfortable sitting here on the sofa between these two large oaf's you brought to restrict my movements. I'm an old man after all."

Waleed considered the request. "Sure, Preston," he replied and gestured to the leather chair behind the desk, "My associates, or oaf's as you like to call them, will guide you over to your seat. Get comfortable. We have a lot to discuss, and it may take a while."

⚬

Waleed's first question was blunt. "How did you get the nuclear weapon out of the arsenal with no one missing it?"

"Ahh, right to the 64,000-dollar question, huh? You'll like this story, Waleed." For the next five minutes he explained in explicit detail the way he, Senator Griffith, and the five other men did the impossible.

Waleed was on the edge of his seat as he sat across from Senator Wilcox. It was a fascinating story, but about to be interrupted.

One of the bodyguards received a call. The concern on his face evident. "Dammit!" The man cursed as he crossed the room and frantically examined the underpart of the desk.

"What is it?" Waleed asked.

"Silent alarm. Must be an independent, cellular only signal. He must have triggered it somehow," The bodyguard searched under the desk, and found the silver button.

Preston raised his arms like he was giving up to robbers, "Oops! Guilty as charged!" he exclaimed with that goofy smile on his face. "HELP, I've fallen and I can't get up! It's like that old Lifecall commercial from back in the late eighties."

"How long do we have before the authorities arrive?" Waleed asked in a frantic tone.

"Three to four minutes."

As Kadir handed Waleed another syringe they both knew he only had time for one or two more questions.

"Where the hell did you hide the nuclear weapon?"

"Pffttt ... why Drexel, of course! Where else would it be? I couldn't stick it up my ass now, could I? It had to be somewhere close to home, yet somewhere that would not be targeted if the Soviets nuked the United States. Drexel was not on their radar. I needed to monitor it, keep it from men like you," Preston spoke the words casually, in a matter-of-fact manner. "We had the dam and Lake Drexel built as a cover, and it worked flawlessly."

"Where exactly in Drexel is the bomb?" Waleed asked as he knew his time was up and he pressed the needle into Preston's flesh.

"An old, abandoned gold mine shaft owned by Jack Harding next to the dam. There are hundreds of those shafts. We had the dam builders construct a vault at the end of one of the mine shafts deep within the mountain," Preston said with a wide grin.

"Which one?"

"The one boarded up of course."

"Aren't they all sealed?"

"Yup."

"But which one?" he asked while pressing the syringe further into his arm.

"No clue," Preston answered. "That was a long, long time ago, and the shafts don't exactly have house numbers mounted to the outside of them."

Kadir interrupted, "We are out of time. I hear sirens in the distance."

Waleed was pissed. To have come so close and be outsmarted by an older man. The information provided would just have to be enough.

Waleed depressed the stopper, and the amber colored liquid entered Preston's vein.

It was a warm sensation, quite a different feeling from what he had been admin-istered before.

"Tell Sarah I said hello," Waleed spoke the words in a sarcastic tone.

Preston smiled as the tingled pulsated through his veins. "Ah, I can't wait to embrace the love of my life once again."

As Preston finished those words, his head slumped down towards his chest.

Waleed checked his pulse. He was gone.

Two minutes later, Waleed, Kadir and the bodyguards exited through the back door. Not before they enabled the alarm system once more. Sixty seconds later, the authorities burst through the front door and proceeded into the house. They found the senator dead in his leather office chair. The EMS on site concluded he died of an apparent heart attack and must have triggered the silent alarm while he sat in his chair.

Chapter Forty-Three

Drexel

A little after 2 AM, Matt and Amy finally climbed into their bed. They had arrived home from Park City, Utah, late in the evening. The conclusion of one of the most enjoyable weeks the family had ever spent together. Part of what made it a great week was that Cate's family had vacationed with the Evans family. The first vacation the two families had all taken together could not have gone any better.

Matt had only been asleep for about an hour when his cell phone rang. At first, he hardly stirred, but by the fourth ring, Amy gave him a not-too-subtle nudge. He rolled over to the nightstand and picked up the phone. "What?" he answered, still mostly asleep.

"Matt, I'm sorry to have to call at this time of night," a female voice said.

Immediately Matt awoke as he recognized the voice and looked at the clock on the nightstand. The time read 3:30 AM, and he knew in an instant there would only be one reason why Senator Wilcox's personal secretary would call him at that hour.

"What happened to him, Loretta?" Instead of a response, he heard the sobbing sound on the other end of the line.

Matt knew his dear friend was gone.

Loretta composed herself and told him everything that happened.

After Matt hung up, Amy embraced him. He got up and made himself a cup of coffee and waited until dawn to tell Troy, knowing his son would be devastated at the news of Preston's passing.

Hours later, once Troy awoke, Matt told him the news. Troy wept, as did Matt.

Troy called Cate soon after his father told him, and she said would leave after lunch and drive from Coeur d'Alene. He tried to talk her out of it, but she knew he needed her now.

Later that day, Matt made a few calls to Washington. His first call was to the Capitol Police. Matt knew the chief of police personally, so he called him directly. The Chief explained that the silent alarm had been triggered, and the D.C. Metro police force arrived on site in less than 10 minutes. Since the emergency call came from a United States Senator, the Capitol Police came five minutes later. The Chief assured Matt that he made it to the house within the hour of the senator passing and had gone through the scene himself. Nothing appeared out of place, and all law enforcement onsite agreed it was a clear-cut case where old age had finally caught up to the senator. The cause of death would show on the death certificate as a heart attack.

Four days later, Preston's family and friends gathered for the funeral at Grace Community Church in Drexel, Idaho. Preston had touched many people's lives, and several thousand people attended the wake, while the funeral included only close family and friends. Preston wrote out specific instructions for his arrangements and explicitly stated he did not want any over the top remembrance. The senate leadership pushed for his body lie in the Capitol rotunda, but Matt Evans, the executor of Preston's will, politely refused the honor. As executor, Matt had the ultimate responsibility for the funeral plans. Preston had been clear years before when he told Matt how he wanted his funeral. Besides a simple funeral, Preston made it clear he wanted to be laid to rest in his family plot near his dear wife Sarah.

All senior leadership in the House and Senate showed up at Drexel to pay their last respects. There were a few heads of state who made the long trip. Preston impressed many people over the years and had many admirers. Even the President of the United States traveled to Drexel, although his appearance at the wake proved to be brief. He knew the senator well and had great respect for the man, who had served the people of the great state of Idaho for 39 years. Since Preston had few living relatives, the president stopped at the pew where the Evans family sat to offer his condolences.

After the simple, yet upbeat service concluded, the Evans family and select others had a gravesite service at the Wilcox family plot.

An hour later, everyone else left the gravesite, and only Matt and Troy remained. Troy had his arm around his father's shoulders, and they just stood there and watched as the workers completed their task of interning Preston's remains into the ground.

For a while, neither one said anything.

Troy broke the silence. "He was one of the good ones, Pops. I know he lived a full life, but I'm torn up that he left us. Sure wish I had a chance to say goodbye."

Matt smiled slightly, "He loved you like a grandson, Troy and had told me many times over the years that he and Sarah were better people for having us in their lives. We were blessed to share this life with both of them."

"We lose the ones we love," Troy said somberly.

"Yes, yes we do," Matt said as he embraced his son. "We sure do."

CHAPTER FORTY-FOUR

LONDON

Within an hour of leaving Senator Wilcox's home in Georgetown, Waleed, Kadir and the two bodyguards were headed east on Waleed's private jet. Six hours and forty-two minutes later, they landed outside of London at a private airfield, where most of the elite in London house their jets. He was whisked back to Knightsbridge in his silver Maybach 57.

After a week back home, Waleed rarely left his study on the second floor. He ventured out for dinner only once to his favorite ultra-trendy west London restaurant, but otherwise remained behind closed doors, informing Kadir he needed solitude to plan his next move carefully.

Periodically, Waleed emerged to give Kadir a few tasks to complete. Few people in the household saw him that week. He sent his four wives to Paris for ten days. They were given his black Amex card and were ecstatic about leaving London with the freedom to shop nonstop in the City of Light.

On the seventh day, Waleed emerged from his study and made his way down to the main floor. Kadir sat in the front parlor conducting internet research as Waleed had requested. When he saw Waleed come down the stairs dressed in a blue shirt with white pants, Kadir stood up and smiled. "Glad to see you have emerged from your study. Has your time been enlightening?"

"Very much," Waleed said in a confident tone. "I feel renewed and believe my plan is the correct path to take. There are still some logistics to compete, but you'll help fill in any gaps. What progress have you made with the latest item I asked you to research?"

"I'm almost finished," Kadir pointed to his computer. "As expected, there are many platforms available; thousands, actually. Leasing one will not be difficult. How do you want me to proceed?"

"We can't use any of my legitimate businesses or any entity that can be tracked back to me. I'll need you to fly down to the Bahamas, Nassau, and open several LLC's on Monday morning. It must be untraceable, so you'll need to take a commercial airliner. Stay at the Atlantis resort, many businesspeople stay there." He reached into his pocket, produced a large stack of currency that he had retrieved from the safe in his private study and handed it to Kadir. "Get there early Sunday and do your best to fit in. Enjoy the water park on site, gamble, and have a nice dinner. Maybe even enjoy the company of an attractive woman if the opportunity presents itself."

Kadir smiled, "I believe I can do that."

"Good. Then on Monday morning you will go into the First Caribbean International Bank on Shirley Street and ask for this man." Waleed handed Kadir a business card. "Then give him this envelope, it contains $50,000 USD. Tell him you need three LLC's opened, and the normal process needs to be expedited. The money will ensure that will take place." Next, Waleed produced a sheet of paper that contained the four names of the legal entities that needed to be created. All relevant information was included on the paper."

Kadir looked over the names and smirked.

Waleed continued, "If the Americans ever start digging into anything, I want them chasing their tails as much as possible. The Bahamas are a haven for all sorts of transactions. The Americans have no jurisdiction there, but that doesn't mean that they don't stick their noses where they don't belong from time to time. After the process of creating the LLC's has begun, you will return to London."

"None of these names can point back to you?"

"No. My contact at the bank will set them up, and no questions will be asked. Your fake credentials will be delivered tonight." He then gave Kadir a last piece of paper. "Here is the name that will be on your passport."

Kadir's eyes grew wide as he read the name. "Is that wise?"

"It is."

"What if he finds out?"

"He won't. We may need a fall guy if anything goes wrong. The American's would have no trouble believing he was responsible for what will take place."

"I agree, but they will know he had someone fund him. He doesn't have the money to sustain any operation of this scale."

"Leave that to me. We will cover our tracks. Plus, I can make it seem like someone else is funding the operation."

"As you say."

Waleed continued discussing the plan, "It will take about 15 days before the LLC can make any purchases, but by that point we will have returned from our scouting trip."

"Are we headed to Drexel?"

"Yes. I needed to let everything settle down before we ventured out there. My contact in the West Wing informed me that the president would show up for the senator's wake before it was public knowledge. That little town had countless federal agents, various dignitaries, and elected officials, so we needed to keep our distance. Besides, the bomb's not going anywhere. Now that the only living soul who knew about it dead, we have whatever time we need."

"What happens after the scouting trip?"

Waleed rubbed his chin as his mind went in several directions. "Then we see where things stand. You may not return from Drexel."

"What do you mean?" Kadir asked with a perplexed expression.

"I have made some inquiries about the town. The largest employer is a company named Siberdrive. It's quite fascinating. Siberdrive is a technology company that has several government contracts. The company creates system components for Unmanned Ariel Vehicles, or drones as they are calling them now. The company was started in the 1970's and almost immediately received government contracts. I suspect that Senator Wilcox handled that. Drexel is in the middle of nowhere. When you have a respected United States senator from your town and the largest employer in town is reliant on federal funds, some back scratching must be going on somehow. And guess who owns it?"

"Not a clue," Kadir said.

"Jack Harding."

"The man that Senator Wilcox mentioned?"

"Precisely."

"Fascinating."

"My initial thought is to get you and another one of my people on staff at Siberdrive. It would be a perfect opportunity to get familiar with the town and start looking for the weapon at the same time. We still have lots of details to work out, but it's a start."

Kadir nodded in agreement. "How do you propose getting us hired?"

Waleed smiled, "I have numerous contacts in the government. I can pull some strings for some bright British citizens who are looking for opportunities in the United States. I looked at their job postings, and I saw several positions that should work. Drexel is an hour north of Boise, basically, it is in the middle of nowhere. I don't think they have top talent vying for jobs around there. If a recommendation is provided, I believe it will be quite easy to get you hired.

"Besides the oil platform in the gulf, how are we going to utilize the remaining three LLC's?" Kadir asked.

"We need to make three additional purchases."

"Buying what?"

"Property," Waleed said.

"For what exactly?"

The grin on Waleed's face grew larger before he answered, "Why judgment day of course!"

Chapter Forty-Five

Drexel

February 2002

For over three weeks, Kadir settled into Drexel. He easily secured employment at Siberdrive under the name Thomas Smith, from London, England. His documentation looked impeccable, and he passed his background check with no issues.

His introduction to life in Drexel had been some of the coldest temperatures the town had experienced in over one hundred years. Kadir was used to some cold weather in London, but those initial days in Drexel never got higher than 30 degrees, and it snowed just about every day. The extreme weather proved to be an unfamiliar experience for Kadir, and not a pleasant one.

When not working, Kadir stayed at the house he shared with Zayan Faraj. Zayan being the other man Waleed handpicked to join Kadir in Drexel. Zayan was a very bright computer programmer, and intimately familiar with the software used by Siberdrive.

When they were not at work, the two men discretely began their search for the nuclear weapon.

Drexel had a tiny public library located right on Main Street in downtown. Kadir made it a point to visit there as often as possible. Proud of its gold mining heritage, the town kept detailed records about the mining operations at the library. Kadir did not want to raise suspicions, so during his first outing to the library he befriended the library's Director Frank Henson. Come to find out Frank's family had emigrated from England when he was a child. Once Kadir told Frank about his British origins, the two men formed an instant connection.

Frank considered himself the resident expert on the gold mining operations in Drexel and much of Idaho. When Kadir professed passionately his love of the gold rush era, the two men had yet another thing in common.

Over drinks one night at Hannah Flanagan's, an Irish pub in downtown, Frank told Kadir much about the Harding family and their ties not only to Siberdrive but also to the gold mining history in Drexel.

On Kadir's third Saturday in Drexel, he and Frank were in a conference room at the library looking over old schematics and mine shaft diagrams. They were deep in a discussion when Kadir asked, "Do you think there is still gold in those old mines, Frank?"

Frank let out a potbellied laugh, "Well, if you were to hear Jack Harding say it, absolutely not! But I don't believe old Jack. Even though the mine operations were shut down several years' back, I think there sure as hell is gold left in those mountains."

"So why doesn't he continue the gold mining operations?"

"Hard to say. Jack says it's all gone, but others believe the cost became too great for the Harding's and they closed up shop."

"And what do you believe," Kadir asked.

Frank looked around before he spoke and lowered his voice slightly. "I think old Jack makes a lot more money off that Siberdrive business. And don't take offense, but it's easy money. At least for Jack. The government contracts have been steady for a long time, and they've been very lucrative for the Harding family. Mining gold is hard work, and if you don't produce enough to cover your costs, you can lose your shirt quickly. In fact, Jack had a hard time turning a profit for a while. That all changed in the early 60's."

"What happened that turned things around?"

"Well, for one thing, the Army Corp of Engineers came in and work began on Lake Drexel and the dam. Jack had to switch around his mining operations and dig in some different places. After he started digging in other spots, the gold revenue skyrocketed. I guess you could say the whole dam project, pun intended..." A wide smile formed on Frank's face before he continued, "Really helped Jack out in more ways than one."

"Interesting," Kadir said in a soft tone as he pursed his lips.

"There are even a few rumors that started soon after the dam was completed."

"Which ones?"

"One worker on the dam project was the father of one of my buddies growing up. His dad swore they even poured some concrete and lined an old mine shaft. Even built some enormous vault at the end of the tunnel."

"What for?" Kadir asked. "That sounds odd."

"I agree, and I believe it was true. I think Jack wanted somewhere safe to store his gold."

"Has anyone ever seen that tunnel?"

"Nope, as kids we broke into a bunch of them to look for it. But we found nothing besides old mining gear, and lots of dust."

"I would love to see the tunnels for myself," Kadir said. "I've always been fascinated by the old mining stories I've read about since I was a little boy."

"Be glad to show you inside a few one night," Frank said with a warm smile. "Course it would be just between us. Old man Harding would have a fit if he knew anyone was roaming through the old tunnels. Acts like he has the Ark of the Covenant buried in there."

"Do you mind if a friend of mine tags along, a fellow Britain who works with me at Siberdrive. We share an apartment to save money. He likes a good adventure, but gets a little scared and may mess his breeches if it's too creepy."

"Breeches!" Frank exclaimed with a chuckle, "You Brits talk funny. But if you want to give him a good fright, I'll take you guys to some of the darkest and longest tunnels in Drexel."

"Thank you."

Frank took Kadir and Zayan to the mine several times. The first time they visited the old mining area, Frank referred to a strange rock formation at the base of the mountain. "They call it the *Hand of God*," he stated.

Kadir smiled as he knew without a doubt they had found the right place. The bomb must be somewhere close. He called Waleed later that day to tell him about the *Hand of God* reference.

Waleed sounded thrilled about the progress Kadir had made.

Those initial explorations with Frank proved to be invaluable as Kadir learned things that no book or research could have taught him. It also confirmed a sneaking suspicion he had that not all the tunnels were mapped. Even though he had a full blueprint of the mines, the list was incomplete. Kadir realized it might take longer than he originally thought to locate the correct tunnel.

The days at Siberdrive passed quickly. The department Kadir worked in was on the third floor of a four-story building, the largest structure in Drexel. There were twelve people who worked in the research and design division (R&D) where Kadir and Zayan were assigned. They worked in cubicles next to each other. To the right of Kadir sat Paul Brighton, who knew Kadir and Zayan only by their aliases, Thomas and Christopher.

⊲◉⊳

Paul kept to himself mostly, a trait not uncommon in the world of information technology. He said very little to the two new men who worked at the company. Besides the fact that they had both moved recently from England, Paul knew relatively little about them, but he could look at them and know their ancestors were not native to England.

The unmanned aerial vehicle technology constantly evolved, which meant the bright minds in the R&D department at Siberdrive were at the forefront of the technology.

Paul found one thing very curious about the two new workers. A few times during the day, conversations would occur between the two new men. Most of the time it appeared to be benign work talk, but sometimes the talk centered on after work activities. The conversation sounded cryptic. What Paul found most curious was that their discussions were not always in English. Most people would not recognize the language they spoke, but Paul recognized it immediately.

Paul's older brother had been in the Army for over six years. When the Army tested him, he scored high on the language aptitude test. The Army asked if he would be interested in being an interpreter. His brother agreed and for the next two years took on an intense language school. After he finished the program, the Army assigned him to a division based in the Middle East.

Paul's brother spent some of his time on leave teaching the new language he learned to him. Paul was good with languages and picked them up quickly. He had mastered not only Spanish but also French while in high school. When his brother challenged him to learn the language the military was teaching him, Paul bought computer software to aid in his learning and within a year spoke it fluently.

The first time he heard Thomas and Christopher utter words in Farsi, his ears perked up. He had heard no one in Idaho besides his brother speak those words. This made the men stand out in his mind. From overhearing the conversations these men had said in Farsi, Paul learned the two men spent their evenings exploring the old, abandoned gold mines that surrounded Lake Drexel and the dam. Paul found that to be odd.

Odd indeed.

Chapter Forty-Six

Drexel

March 2002

Fresh snow blanketed Drexel from the previous night's storm, making the roads slippery and driving conditions less than optimal. The Evans family farm looked like a picturesque postcard with towering snowcapped mountains in the backdrop. A steady stream of smoke emerged from the fireplace and made its way steadily upward.

Matt greeted his friend Pat O'Shea with a hug as he got out of the car.

"Thought the snowy roads might scare you away," Matt said as the two friends embraced.

"Nonsense," Pat replied. "You realize it does snow in Tennessee, where we live, right?"

Matt shrugged. "East Coast snow doesn't hit as hard as snow around here."

Both men laughed.

Pat's wife Eva and their three adorable children got out of the car, approaching the porch where Amy, Troy, and Cate waited. After the introductions took place, Amy ushered them all inside, where a nice roaring fire greeted them, as did tasty treats and hot chocolate. The O'Shea family felt at home immediately.

The two families spent a while talking in the living room while the children played. When the kids got restless, Matt showed them downstairs to the basement, which had been converted to a game room for Troy and his friends when he was younger. It held a pool table, several arcade games, a large TV, and gaming consoles.

Upstairs, it was getting close to dinnertime. Amy, Eva and Cate ventured into the kitchen to work on dinner. Matt and Pat talked shop while Troy listened in.

"The Bureau is hearing a lot of chatter about various nuclear threats. Any truth to any of it?" Matt asked.

Pat sighed slightly, "Hard to say buddy, the threats and intent are surely there, but whether the bad guys can get their hands on nuclear material is the unknown variable. I've hardly slept in my bed for the last six months due to all the threats that have been investigated. None of those concerns have been realized, but some say it's just a matter of time."

"Matter of time before something nuclear is used?" Matt asked.

"Yes," Pat said as he let out a deep sigh. "The popular consensus is that a dirty bomb will be the most likely way they will attack us. Getting their hands on an actual nuke is extremely difficult. However, acquiring radioactive material is not tough, and all they need to do is mix that material in with a conventional bomb and BOOM!" Pat slapped his hands together, the sound reverberated off the walls.

Matt shook his head slightly, "But from what I heard, a dirty bomb wouldn't have much radioactive fallout. The radiation exposure would probably be minimal."

"That's true," Pat nodded. "A dirty bomb attack probably wouldn't result in mass casualties, but psychologically it would achieve the desired results. It would cause a countrywide panic and spread terror. That can be just as effective as killing a lot of people or destroying physical property."

"I guess that makes sense," Matt said.

"Look at the Cold War," Pat continued. "The mere threat of nuclear war with the Soviets was enough to change the way our culture handled things. I mean from the 1950's until the 1970's our county had air raid drills at public schools. Like getting under a desk would really have saved any lives if the nuclear holocaust took place. Just the threat is sometimes all you need. Fear is a great tool, and terrorists know it. They're actively trying to obtain nuclear weapons and are more than happy to express that threat verbally to scare ordinary people. The question is what do we do about it?"

"We get them before they get us," Troy jumped into the conversation.

"Uh oh, here comes my cowboy," Matt said with eyebrows raised.

"So, are you gonna join the military and be one of these special forces guys going after Osama?" Pat asked.

"Me?" Troy replied with a raised eyebrow. "Nah, nothing like that. I'm gonna join the Bureau like pops here. Be part of the new counterterrorism division, it's only been around a few years, but that might be a good way for me to serve my country."

"They would be honored to have you, son," Matt said as he leaned over and struck Troy's shoulder. "Of course, they might court Cate before they come after you," he said with a smile

"Yeah, I hear your girlfriend wants to be an agent as well. Your dad says she shoots better than you," Pat ribbed Troy in a good-natured way.

Troy shook his head and smiled, "What can I say? I'm not only an expert shot but an outstanding teacher. Taught her everything I know. She doesn't have my moves on the dance floor though," Troy said as he elicited a laugh at the end of the statement.

"I heard that," Cate said from the other room.

"Ouch," Matt. "Sounds like Mr. Smooth Operator here just got busted by the real boss."

"Why don't you dance that cute butt of yours into the kitchen and help the women cook," Cate stated. "We already know your mouth can talk, let's see if your hands can work as fast as your lips move."

Troy shook his head, "Coming, dear," he mocked in a high-pitched voice.

"It only gets worse when you marry them, son," Matt said with a laugh.

"Matthew Evans, I heard that trash," Amy hollered from the kitchen.

The two Evans boys looked toward Pat, who did not utter a word. "I might be Irish, but I'm no idiot. I know when to shut my mouth," he added.

"Well, that's a first!" Eva exclaimed from the other room.

They all laughed.

———◦———

After dinner, Troy and Cate left. There was a small coffee shop located in downtown Drexel that stayed open late on Saturday nights.

Matt and Pat headed out to the back screened-in porch. Matt had a small fireplace in the corner, and even though it was bitter cold outside, the fireplace gave off enough heat to make the area comfortable. They lit up cigars and talked for a while.

At first, they talked about the loss of Preston.

"Sorry to hear about his passing," Pat said. "If I were not overseas when it occurred, I would have come to the funeral. It was nice to hear that even the president paid his respects. The rumor mill said he left a lot to charity, that was decent of him."

"Yes," Matt said. "I was the executor of his will. He really had no living family to speak of since Sarah passed away. Sadly, they never had children, His estate is still working its way through probate. The lawyer called me last week to say he had the contents of Preston's personal safe, which is being shipped to me. He left his house in Georgetown to Troy actually, which was a pleasant surprise. It was a house Troy spent time in as a teenager, he stayed with them one full summer, and it meant a lot to him. Not sure what he will do with it, but if he gets a job in D.C. at the Bureau, it would be a nice place to live. Much nicer than most federal agent's homes in the beltway."

Pat nodded. "That was awfully kind of Preston."

"The ranch here in Drexel will be sold at some point, the proceeds will be given to several children's charities," Matt continued. "Amy and I were left a small cabin on a ski resort in Utah, and Preston left his lifelong secretary in Washington enough money that she can easily retire. He was very generous to those he cared for. His loss was profound for all of us."

After a little while, the conversation turned back to the events from the previous fall. "Still no updates on the Ryker case?" Pat asked.

Matt did not respond and instead asked for Pat's cell phone. Pat handed it over without question, and Matt turned the phone off and removed the battery and SIM card. He then placed the phone on the table before Pat.

"What was that for?" Pat asked with a curious expression.

Matt shook his head, "Just some rumors I am hearing about the boys over at the NSA. Better safe than sorry."

"I get it," Pat said.

"Regarding Ryker, it seems like the more questions I ask, the more I get stonewalled. It's almost like the powers that be want to ignore what occurred."

"Is someone hiding something?"

Matt pondered the question for a moment, "There are some suspicious things that took place, that's for sure. Someone wanted to sweep it under the rug." Matt looked directly at Pat as he uttered the last few words.

Pat returned the stare, "I know he took a document."

Matt was quiet for a moment.

"Aren't you gonna ask how I know?" Pat asked.

Matt didn't bite. It was turning into a one-way conversation.

"The NNSA was read into the events of Fresh Kills, Matt. I know more than you think."

Finally, Matt broke his silence, "Ok then tell me what the document was titled?" Matt trusted Pat, but he was unsure how much he should tell him.

"I don't know that, no one knows, I just know the document was a Core secret. Some people very high up the food chain would stop at nothing to pretend the document doesn't exist."

"Maybe it doesn't," Matt said. "Or maybe the document was worthless, just an old forgotten piece of paper from years past."

"I doubt that since too many panties in a wad about it, and why Muhammad Jarah killed Aaron for it."

"Good point. I'm convinced he was just an enforcer, a glorified, and brutal delivery person, but we haven't been able to figure out who employed him. I asked a lot of high-ranking officials, and from what I could tell, no one knows what the document referenced."

"Did you see it?" Pat asked.

"Just the title," Matt responded honestly.

"And?"

Matt put his head in his hands as he spoke. He wondered if he was about to make the biggest mistake of his life. "No one knows what the hell The Zechariah Option is. Like I said, it may just be a worthless piece of paper."

⸺◆⸺

It was quiet. Pat didn't reply.

As Matt lifted his head from his hands, he looked over to his friend. Pat looked back, with eyes as wide as saucers.

"What?" Matt asked.

"Damn!" Pat exclaimed.

"Damn what?"

"Damn, the rumors are true.""What rumors?" Matt moved closer to the edge of his seat.

"About a hidden nuke."

"A what?"

"It's like the story of the boogeyman," Pat said as he shook his head quickly. "Nobody thinks it's real, but it still scares the shit out of you when you hear it."

"Tell me everything you know," Matt said.

For the next fifteen minutes, Pat told him everything he had ever heard about the hidden nuclear weapon. Granted, it wasn't much more of an old wives' tale as far as he knew. However, the stories were passed down through many within the NNSA, and they all had one common denominator. They all called the highly secretive project that no one would ever admit to The Zechariah Option. By the end of the conversation, neither man knew what to believe. And neither one knew if what was taken by Muhammad Jarah back in November should cause the United States and its protectors grave concern.

CHAPTER FORTY-SEVEN

DREXEL

Troy and Cate settled into their normal corner table at the coffee shop when a familiar face walked inside the place.

Paul smiled broadly and walked right over to the beaming couple.

Troy pushed a chair out with his foot, and his friend sat down. They had not seen each other since before the holidays. At first, the discussion focused on the ski trip to Utah and then how Paul spent his holiday.

Later, the subject of work came up, and Paul told them how busy things had been at Siberdrive. He explained how they staffed up over the past few months and his department had hired two new guys.

"They good guys?" Troy asked.

"I guess," Paul said in a tone not entirely convincing. "I mean, they are ok. They mainly keep to themselves. Apparently, they're both British nationals, but I think they were born in the Middle East."

There weren't many folks from that region of the world in the Boise area. As Paul talked about the two men in greater detail, Troy could sense that something about them was off in Paul's opinion.

Troy asked, "So what bothers you about them? I'm sure it's not the shade of their skin color since you know all about that."

"No, it's certainly not that, but they talk sometimes in hushed tones."

"And?" Troy asked. "That's not super weird."

"And they speak in Farsi," Paul said.

"That's strange," Troy said. "Especially since few folks around here speak Farsi. But you suspect they are from the Middle East, so that wouldn't be super unusual."

"Do they speak Farsi in front of everyone?" Cate asked.

"No," Paul said as he shook his head. "That's what bothers me the most, they only speak it when they believe no one is listening."

"You understand Farsi," Troy said. "So, what are they saying to each other?"

"They talk about the old abandoned gold mines. Exploring them or something."

"Maybe they're just private. Don't want people to know much about what they do in their downtime," Cate said.

"Maybe," Paul shrugged. "Like I said, they keep to themselves, but something feels weird about them."

"Sounds a little suspicious if you ask me," Troy said. "You want me to have my dad do some digging for us?"

"No, nothing like that. It's just a vibe I get. I may follow them one night and see if they really explore the old mines."

"We had our fair share of doing that over the years. If you want, I'll come with you."

"That might be a good idea," Paul replied.

"Hey! What am I, chopped liver?" Cate crossed her arms over her chest. "Don't I get to come on this boy's adventure?"

"Of course, babe," Troy said sweetly as he reached over and patted her leg. "Stakeouts are pretty boring though."

"Oh, I'm sure you two charmers can entertain me. Tell me about all your high school conquests. I'm sure the star quarterback and his number one receiver have all sorts of cheerleader stories to share."

"That will be a brief conversation," Paul said.

"Yeah, as in nonexistent," Troy added. "We went to Drexel High, this isn't Beverly Hills, 90210."

The three of them chatted for another thirty minutes until the coffee shop closed for the night. Paul said goodbye, climbed into his car parked right outside the coffee shop, and headed home.

Troy and Cate held hands and took a walk. A few minutes later they crossed Valentine Street, and she gave his arm a tug to the left.

"What do you want?" Troy asked in a playful tone.

Cate tilted her head toward the store across the street. "A Blockbuster movie sounds like a fun way to end our night."

Troy sighed. "I probably owe them a fee for the last movie you brought back late."

She feigned surprise, "Who, me?"

"Yes, you, the queen of keeping movies past their return date."

Cate pouted. "If you get me a movie, I'll cuddle with you."

"And?"

"Maybe I'll make you some chocolate chip cookies," Cate said as she gave him an elongated wink.

"That's it?" Troy asked.

"Well, if you're really good, I'll let you rub my feet."

As they walked into the video store, Troy opened his mouth to respond.

Cate gestured to the two little kids by the front door. "Little ears, Mr. Evans, watch what your words."

Troy smiled. "It's almost like you knew what I would say in response."

"I know how your brain works, like the back of my hand, babe."

With a wide grin, Troy gentled patted her backside as they turned down one of the video aisles and were away from the gaze of the two kids. He let his hand linger long enough that she swatted it away after several seconds.

Chapter Forty-Eight

Boise

April 2002

Waleed's private jet had landed earlier than expected, and fifteen minutes after he walked off the plane, he climbed into the black Lincoln Towncar in front of the Grove Hotel in downtown Boise. As usual, he had his two bodyguards with him. Waleed told them to keep their distance. Boise, after all, was not a dangerous place.

After he checked into the hotel, he went outside and took a walk. Kadir would not arrive for at least forty-five minutes, which gave him a few moments to himself. As he walked down South Capitol Boulevard, the two bodyguards followed well behind.

It took less than seven minutes to walk the four-tenths of a mile to the Boise State Capitol. Waleed thumbed through the visitor's guide he picked up near the entrance to the property. The building had been completed in 1912 at a cost of just over two million dollars. Waleed smirked when he read the amount since he had numerous Italian sports cars worth more than that. The pamphlet stated the architects drew their inspiration from Saint Peter's Basilica in Rome, Saint Paul's Cathedral in London, and the U.S. Capitol in Washington. Waleed had been to each place and could recognize the similarities easily. The prominent dome cut into the clean air and stood out amongst the skyline. Atop it stood a bronze eagle measuring five feet seven inches tall, which he thought ironic since he was the same height. Waleed walked around the impressive building and then ventured inside for a few minutes. Fascinated by architecture, Waleed felt that many of the U.S. State Capitols were exquisitely designed. The Capitol in Sacramento proved to be one of his favorites, and it didn't hurt that one of his favorite steakhouses, a block from the Capitol, served crème brûlée to die for. His mouth suddenly watered.

After spending some time in and around the Capitol, he headed back to the Grove Hotel and walked through the lobby doors just as Kadir arrived. Even though they spoke daily by phone, they had not seen each other in six weeks.

After pleasantries took place Waleed pointed to the door. "Let's take a walk. The Boise Zoo is only ten minutes away, and it would be advantageous to stretch our legs."

As they started down West Front Street, Kadir asked, "Is it wise for us to be seen together in public?"

Waleed smiled warmly, "I doubt think anyone will recognize me at the zoo in downtown Boise."

They were standing on the corner of West Front Street and 6th Street waiting for the crosswalk to change colors.

Waleed had hardly uttered the words when he put his arm out to stop Kadir from crossing the street as the crosswalk indicated they could safely walk. "Wait," he said.

"What is it?" Kadir asked.

"Irony," Waleed replied.

"Excuse me?"

Waleed pointed to his left across the street with his eyes. "See that man and his two associates over there walking into the restaurant."

"The one in the blue shirt?"

"Yes," Waleed said.

He squinted for a moment, "Is that who I think it is?" Kadir asked as a shocked expression spread over his face.

"The one and only. His office is on the same block as the hotel."

"Matt Evans, the Special Agent in Charge of the Boise office..." Kadir said as his voice trailed off.

"It's a small word, but it's no problem. After all, Agent Evans has no clue who we are, even if we know much about him. I find it ironic that our paths came that close to crossing."

"Is it safe to talk? Should we be concerned he's here?"

"No, we are fine," Waleed said as he waved his hand in the air. "Let's continue our walk. I have much to tell you as we tour the zoo."

⚬

Waleed purchased tickets and slowly moved from exhibit to exhibit. He told Kadir about the purchases that had been finalized over the past few weeks.

"You have been busy," Kadir said.

"We both have been. I think everything is in place."

"I understand why you leased the oil platform but tell me about the plan for the other two properties."

"I have not decided on the location to start the attack. Part of that will be determined by the size of the weapon once it's located. I'm preparing for numerous contingencies. While the platform is my primary location, it may be difficult to acquire what I need to utilize that site. Second, even though we have attracted no attention so far, that could change at any minute. The other locations may be needed."

"As a diversion? Or backup?"

"Yes, that is a very astute observation. Better to have several options on the table instead of being pigeonholed into just one."

"The three locations are certainly spread out throughout the United States," Kadir said.

"The workers are already on site at the oil rig, it will take a month or two to construct what I requested."

"Understood."

Waleed rubbed the side of his face. "Still nothing new to report from the search of the tunnels?"

Kadir sighed. "The process is tedious, and the diagrams I have are incomplete. There are certainly mine shafts I still don't know about. Finding them all may be problematic."

"What other resources do you need? More men?" Waleed asked.

"No. More men may draw attention. Drexel is a small town. Zyan and I already stick out. Plus, I'm sensing some extra attention from one man we work with. I feel he doesn't trust us. A few times I believe he has overheard Zayan and I speaking in Farsi."

"Did he understand what you said?"

"I don't see how he could. Farsi is not a common language around here. Even if he did, we spoke in code. There would be nothing we said that could give away our true intentions."

"Still," Waleed said with a stern look on his face. "You need to be more careful. Remember, after the events of 9/11, Americans suspect foreigners, especially those who appear to be of Arab descent. Can you befriend this man? Maybe set his mind at ease?"

Kadir pondered the question for a moment before he shook his head. "No, not this one. I don't think he is to be trusted."

"Then be careful around him, and if he becomes suspicious, eliminate him."

"Waleed, this is a small town. If people turn up dead or missing, I'm sure the people from out of town will be the first to be suspected."

"Valid point," Waleed said. "Anyway, as you get closer to completing our mission, I think it might be necessary to send for an acquaintance of ours."

"Who?"

"You know who," Waleed said.

"I thought after New York he was done. His slate was clean, and he no longer owed you."

"That is correct, but I believe I have a way to pull him back in for one more job."

"Whatever you think is best."

"Is there any technology that can get you that may aid in the search?"

"I don't think so," Kadir said as he considered the question. 'Although, come to think of it, there may be something, or someone that may know where to look."

"What or who might that be?" Waleed asked.

"Jack Harding."

Waleed gave an inquisitive shrug.

Kadir continued, "I befriended a man named Frank Henson, who works at the library. He has lived in Drexel his whole life, and his father even worked on the dam construction back in 1963. He told me just last night over coffee that he feels certain Jack keeps his own complete set of diagrams in his personal safe at home. Like I told you before on the phone, Frank claims Jack had a secret concrete compartment built during the time the dam was constructed. According to Frank, his dad spoke of it once in hushed tones, and said he helped pour the concrete. Supposedly, Jack stores a large amount of gold in the vault. I wonder if the vault in question really holds the weapon."

"Is Frank's father still alive? Maybe he can show you the location of the tunnel?"

"I asked. His father died in the early 1990's, and Frank does not know which tunnel holds Jack's mysterious vault."

"Well, I can't imagine the senators would have brought Jack into their plan," Waleed said.

"No, you are probably right, but what if they utilized Jack's knowledge of the mine and never told him what they were hiding? Think about it. Maybe they told him it was some government secret. After all, Jack was friends with Senator Wilcox for many years, and Jack's company got some extremely lucrative government contracts soon after he started a technology company. I might be jumping to conclusions here, but I find it no stretch to imagine those government contracts were payback for him turning a blind eye to what they did all those years back."

Waleed nodded, "Your hypothesis has merit. We should pursue it. How do you want to deal with Harding? I doubt he will voluntarily divulge any information."

"There's always liquid honesty," Kadir said.

"But remember, you told me it's a small town. A murder or missing person would cause suspicion."

Kadir smiled widely from ear to ear. "Jack is an old man, I feel certain he can meet a timely and expected end based on his age. After all, Senator Wilcox met a similar fate, and no one was the wiser."

"Kadir, I like the way your mind works," Waleed responded with a devious smile.

"I had the best teacher."

The two men now stood before the lion exhibit.

Waleed leaned against the bar and glanced down toward the mighty beasts. "The lions are my favorite of all Allah's creatures, Kadir. Do you know why?"

"Of course," Kadir immediately responded. "He is the king of the beasts. You are a prince. You respect his regal authority."

"Hardly," Waleed said with an audible laugh. "No, I respect the versatility of lions. Sometimes they are in charge of a pride, while other times they are nomads. During periods of life, they are aggressive hunters, while in other instances they let the females do all the hunting. They can be predators or merely lounge around for 20 hours a day and do nothing. However, ultimately a lion is a survivor, he does what he needs to survive. No more, no less. I respect that."

Chapter Forty-Nine

Drexel

Paul slouched in the front seat of his 1998 forest green Nissan Altima. Next to him in the passenger seat was Troy. Cate sat in the backseat.

"Why are we going to all this effort, again?" Cate asked as she looked back and forth between Troy and Paul.

"Because it's the right thing to do," Troy replied from the front seat.

"It just feels like we need to see what they are up to," Paul said.

"Not having fun yet, babe?" Troy asked.

"Uhh...No! Stakeouts are boring," Cate replied.

"Better get used to them. We may do a lot of them when we work for the Bureau."

"I guess," Cate replied.

"Sorry, I don't have any donuts. You cops eat those on stakeouts, right?" Paul asked in a sarcastic tone.

"Funny one, Paul," Cate said. "Feds don't eat donuts."

"That's right, I forgot. The Bureau has the highest standards," Paul said. "Chocolate filled croissants, right?"

"Watch it, nerd," Troy said.

"You bring the gear, Mr. FBI?" Paul asked.

"Of course. Pops is out of the country for a few weeks, so I borrowed a few toys."

"Where is dad this time?"

"Jordan. He's over there with a large contingency from various agencies. Apparently, there was an attack at some safe house used by the spooks. The Bureau had staff there when the shooting started. Several men died, so all the agencies are over there investigating what happened. The terrorists used some sort of radioactive laced bomb in the attack. Has everyone freaked out. Even Pops friend from the NNSA, Pat O'Shea went."

"I like Pat. He's a cool guy," Cate said.

"What the heck is the NNSA?" Paul asked with a puzzled look on his face.

Troy smiled as he turned around and looked at Cate. "Told you, babe, nobody knows who they are. Here we have an organization that safeguards our entire nuclear weapon stockpile, and even smart dudes like Paul here have no clue."

Paul frowned. "Hey man, you ever watched the Tonight Show with Leno?"

"No, not much of a late-night TV kind of guy," Troy said. "Why?"

"Well, if you get a chance, check out his Jaywalking skit. Half the people in this country don't even know who the vice president is. Compared to most Americans, I'm like Einstein."

Cate was the first one to notice the movement, "Ok Mr. Einstein, while you're blabbering, the suspicious guys just walked out of their rental house." She pointed to the house down the road.

Kadir and Zayan, or as Paul knew them, Thomas and Christopher, walked out of the house and got in the charcoal gray pickup truck. They held duffel bags in each hand and placed them in the truck's bed before they climbed in.

"Looks like they are heading out for more than just an evening drive," Troy said.

"This is the third time I've parked out here and watched them. They carry the same bags every time."

"Have you followed them after they leave?" Cate asked.

"Only once," Paul said. "I drove all the way to Lake Drexel. I stayed on the main road and kept going when they pulled off onto the old access road that leads to the mines."

"The one off of Lincoln Boulevard?" Troy asked.

"Yes, that's the one. So, what do you want to do? If we follow them on that access road, it will be a dead giveaway we're tailing them."

"You're right," Troy said. "Keep following them at a safe distance until they turn off. Then keep driving another quarter mile or so. The next right will be the entrance to Burton State Park. Take that turn and then follow the road until it dead ends. From there, it's only a short walk to the mine."

"But it's pitch dark," Cate said. "How are we going to make our way through the woods?"

Troy reached into the bag and pulled out three sets of night vision goggles, "We can easily make our way through the woods with these bad boys on."

"Well, don't you just think of everything, Cate said as she rolled her eyes.

—◆—

Kadir and Zayan had spent the better part of the past six weeks methodically exploring the tunnels each night. The entrances to the tunnels were all boarded up, but Kadir learned from his adventure with Frank that a simple pry bar was all that was needed to remove several boards and climb into the dark tunnels. He also learned that many of the tunnels connected. The deep, dark subterranean passages were mazelike.

According to Kadir's notes, they had already explored 29 tunnels. They had found some obsolete mining gear, but no sign of any concrete vault.

Kadir knew it had to be somewhere in the mountain, but so far, the vault eluded them. He believed the tunnel they needed was not on any map. As each night blended with the last, he felt their best option would be to pay a visit to Jack Harding.

—◆—

After they arrived at the end of the park road, Troy, Cate, and Paul used the goggles and quickly made their way through the thick grove of trees. Within ten minutes they emerged from the woods of Burton State Park and could see the mountain and many of the entrances to the old, abandoned tunnels.

Troy picked up on movement about a third of the way up the side of the mountain. "There they are," Troy whispered as he nudged both Cate and Paul.

"Yes, I see them," Cate said.

"Me too," Paul added.

"Let's watch and see what they do," Troy suggested.

The two men approach one of the entrances. Heavy wooden timbers were on either side and above each shaft. Thick boards had been nailed to the front of the beams, closing off the entrance.

With ease, the two men removed pry bars from the long duffel bags they carried and within five minutes enough boards had been removed to allow them to squeeze through the opening. It appeared both men wore helmets to light the passages.

Troy watched the two men climb through the opening and disappear. A few minutes later, the dim light that showed through the opening vanished as the men made their way further underground.

"What now?" Paul asked.

Troy pondered the question for a moment, "You and Cate sit tight. Monitor the shaft they just entered. If they come out, call me on the two-way radios we brought." Troy verified they were both turned on and set to the right channel.

"Where are you going?" Cate asked with a hint of concern in her voice. "You're not going to try to get closer, are you?"

"No," Troy said. "I want to hike down and look at their pickup truck. Maybe they left something in there that might give us a hint what they are doing."

"Be careful," Cate reached out and touched his arm.

"I will," Troy said as he kissed her cheek. A second later he turned to walk away, but looked back over his shoulder, "Keep her safe."

Before Paul could reply, Cate spoke, "Troy Matthew Evans, you know damn well I can take care of myself."

Troy smiled as Paul looked at his friend with a slightly troubled expression,

"I like to piss her off sometimes," Troy said. "She's hot when she's pissed."

"You can be a dick sometimes," Cate stated. "You know that?"

Troy had a big smile on his face, "Love you too babe, I'll be back in a few."

A few minutes turned into forty minutes. Cate and Paul appeared anxious until finally Troy returned. The look on his face made it clear he found something.

"You were gone way too long. What did you find?" Cate asked.

"Sorry," Troy pulled out his digital camera and showed the pictures he took. "I poked around the truck for a while. Anyway, they have a schematic of the whole gold mining operation. My guess is they are searching one shaft at a time and crossing out which ones they have explored so far."

"What are they looking for? Gold?" Paul asked.

"That's what it seems like," Cate said.

Troy was quiet. His eyes revealed that his brain was hard at work.

"What is it?" Cate asked.

Troy rubbed his chin, "Maybe they are after something else?"

"Like what?" Paul asked.

"Not sure. But whatever it is, they apparently haven't found it yet."

"Maybe they are just spelunkers," Cate said.

"No way, they would look for caves, not mine shafts," Troy said. "They are after something. I just know it."

Just then, a faint light emanated from the tunnel again. The two men emerged a few minutes later. They still held the bags in their hands as they crawled out of the tunnel. They nailed the boards back onto the solid timbers, closing the tunnel once more. A few minutes later, they put their helmets back in the duffel bags and proceeded back down the mountain and towards their pickup truck.

Troy, Cate, and Paul watched silently from about three hundred yards away and waited until the truck started up and drove away. After a few more minutes passed, the three of them hiked over to the tunnel the men had emerged from. Using some equipment Troy had packed, they removed the worn boards easily and made their way into the tunnel.

Two hours later, they emerged. They had followed the footprints the men had made and explored the tunnel. They found nothing.

Cate was the first to speak as they made their way back into the chilly night air. It was now close to 3 A.M.. "Well, that was a bust."

"We need to keep a closer eye on those two, Paul," Troy said.

"What do we do next? Paul asked.

"We need to come up with a game plan," Troy said. "Can the three of us meet this weekend?"

"Sure," Paul said. "And in the meantime, I'll keep my ears open tomorrow at work. Maybe they'll slip and speak Farsi again."

"You're gonna be a tired hombre tomorrow at work, Paul," Cate said.

"Hey, I'm still young," Paul replied. "And anyway, that's why they make Mountain Dew!"

"Ahh, the nectar of the god's," Troy said with a chuckle.

Chapter Fifty

Drexel

Kadir focused on the house for over a minute before he put his binoculars down and looked at the man who sat to his right. "You'll have to deal with the dog quickly."

"No problem," Zayan said in a confident tone as he gently tapped the rifle slung over his shoulder. "Just one, right?"

"Yes, just one," Kadir said.

Dusk arrived, and Kadir used his binoculars to watch the man move within the house two-hundred yards away. As the man moved away from the kitchen and headed for the back of the house, Kadir saw the light turn on in the study.

The time had finally arrived.

As the two men approached the old stone house on the top of the hill, the 11-year-old Bluetick Coonhound stood up from his bed on the front porch. The 75-pound dog descended the three stone stairs to the front lawn as the two strangers approached. His head raised upward to let out a howl.

Zayan saw the dog stir and watched as it came down the steps towards the front lawn. He knew the animal would follow its instinct and let out an ominous bark. Zayan took a knee and raised the rifle. He zeroed in on the dog, exhaled, and gently depressed the trigger.

A muffled *pop* sound occurred as the rifle recoiled, followed by the animal crumpling to the ground.

"Nice shot," Kadir said.

Zayan did not respond. The men quickened their pace, stepped over the dog, and a few seconds later they were at the side of the house. They made their way to a side door close to the study. The old farmhouse had creaky floors, so coming in the front door would betray their presence, and the old man might have time to react.

Kadir turned the handle, but the side door appeared to be locked.

Zayan removed the lock pick tool from his back pocket and disabled the lock quickly. He quietly turned the knob and opened the old hickory door. It was only fifteen feet from the entryway to the doorway leading into the study.

As the two men crept down the hall, one board slightly creaked under the weight of the footstep.

———◆———

Jack Harding sat at the same desk he had for over fifty years. His seventy-eight-year-old body was just about worn out. His muscles ached constantly, and sleep no longer came easily. Jack stayed active because of his work ethic, partially to pass the time, but mainly he knew no other way to live. His life had been centered on hard work, and old age could not stop his insatiable drive. A stack of papers lay before him. The desk built by his father from marble quarried nearby was a gift when Jack started in the family business. The desk faced the window on the far side of the wall, which looked out over Boise National Forest. Jack loved the majestic view.

As he looked over the report before him, a sound broke the silence. At first, he thought it was Scout, but he knew the trusted animal was on the front porch and the sound came from behind him in the hallway.

Jack turned around in his chair to look toward the doorway. Two men stood in the threshold. They both looked familiar. He recognized them as relatively new employees at Siberdrive. Their presence startled him. "What the hell are you doing in here?" Jack asked in a gruff voice. "I sure didn't hear you knock."

"No, Mr. Harding, we didn't knock." Kadir replied as the two quickly approached the desk.

"You should have," Jack said as he reached for a secret compartment under the marble top of his desk.

Zayan lunged at him and had his arm in a vice-like grip before he could retrieve the hidden .357 Magnum.

Jack prided himself on being physically fit in his younger years, and even into his 60's. However, the last decade had caught up to him hard, and he couldn't overpower the younger, stronger man's grip.

Zayan held Jack's arms at his side. Kadir approached and secured his arms to either side of the chair with black zip ties.

"What do you want?" Jack demanded.

"We just need to ask you a few questions," Kadir said.

"About what?"

"The gold mine."

"The mine is shut down. What could you possibly want with the mine? It's empty. The gold is long gone."

"I'm not interested in gold, Jack," Kadir replied with a smirk.

⁕

Instantly, Jack knew what this was about. He had always wondered if someone would come looking for that tunnel. Since Senator Wilcox had died, he figured incorrectly that the secret of the mine would die as well.

"You better plan to kill me, cause I sure as hell ain't gonna tell you bastards anything." Jack spoke in an angry tone as his blood pressure rose by the second.

⁕

Kadir smiled as he flicked the syringe with his middle finger, "You're wrong, Jack. You'll tell me exactly what I want to know."

Jack protested as Zayan held him firm and Kadir shoved the needle into his arm. The clear liquid entered his body. Within seconds, Jack's body relaxed, and he went limp.

A few minutes later, the questions began.

Two hours later, Kadir had everything he needed. He gave Jack a sedative, and he now slept soundly in his chair.

The schematics he had removed from Jack's personal safe were carefully locked up again. A digital copy now in their possession. Zayan expertly wiped down the room, which left only one thing to do.

Zayan entered the kitchen, which had recently been remodeled. It took him only a few minutes to loosen the fitting on the back of the Viking gas range.

Within moments, the smell of the mercaptan was noticeable. The odor could best be described as rotten eggs. Zayan returned to the study, where Kadir waited.

"Ready?" Kadir asked.

"Yes," Zayan said.

Kadir stood over Jack. As he pressed a new needle into Jack's flesh and depressed the stopper. The clear liquid entered Jack's body as Kadir muttered, "Goodnight, Mr. Harding, I thank you for the help. You saved my colleague and me many more miserable nights trudging through those worthless tunnels of yours."

With the deed done, he removed the needle and cut Jack's hands free. He and Zayan left through the same door they entered.

As they made their way out the front of the house, Zayan stopped at the dog's body and bent down. He removed the tranquilizer dart from the animal and checked its breathing.

"He'll wake up in a few hours," Zayan said.

As they made their way down the driveway, Kadir placed a call. "It's done. I have the location of the tunnel."

"And Harding?" Waleed asked.

"He will sleep and never wake."

"Good," Waleed said. "And the evidence?"

"It will look like the old man died from carbon monoxide poisoning, just as we planned."

"Perfect."

"Zayan and I will locate the tunnel as soon as possible," Kadir said.

"I'll finalize the plans to bring Muhammad and his men over."

"He agreed to come?"

"It took a lot of persuasion, but I convinced him."

CHAPTER FIFTY-ONE

AMMAN, KINGDOM OF JORDAN

Matt disliked visiting the Middle East ever since the FBI started sending him there early in his career as a liaison between the Bureau and the local governments. The trips were rarely pleasant and often they only sent Matt and other senior special agents when either someone died or an ominous threat needed to be resolved.

An exception occurred fifteen years ago when Matt took part in an official trip to Syria and flew Amy over after the FBI business concluded. They toured the Holy Land together, and the trip was amazing. It renewed not only their faith but imparted to them hope for the future as well.

This investigation in Jordon proved to be far from amazing. Four CIA agents, three members of the State Department, and two FBI agents were dead in an attack using a radioactive bomb.

Since the attackers used a dirty bomb, Pat O'Shea assisted in the investigation, allowing the two men to work closely together. Matt had not made a new friend in a while, and he welcomed his newfound friendship with Pat for the past eight months.

A cool evening breeze swept across Matt's face as he exited the hotel. Pat and three others from the investigative team were having dinner with him. Jordan was one of the best places to eat in the Middle East, at least according to Matt. Amman contained a bounty of exceptional restaurants. Since most of the agents traveling with Matt had never been to Jordon, he drove them to a great place on Asaad Khaleel Hamdoukh, which served a Jordanian specialty called mansaf.

As the five men sat down to dinner with Matt at the head of the table, Pat sat to his right.

"You sure know where to go for great food, whether it be Amman or Washington," Pat said.

"A man's gotta eat," Matt said as he slapped his stomach. "And I'm clearly not starving."

"So, what is mansaf anyway?" Trent, who was one of the men on the team who had never visited the Middle East with the Bureau previously, asked.

Matt smiled, "It's a mélange of rice, lamb and rehydrated yogurt cooked in a blend of baharat spices and garnished with pine nuts and parsley."

"We got Chef Boyardee here," Pat teased as he nudged Matt.

Matt raised his eyebrows. "Momma taught me years ago not to expect a woman to cook for me. She said, *if a man want's to eat like a king, he better know how to cook like a top-notch chef.* Truer words have no other woman spoke."

Pat raised his Guinness. "This Irish lad can drink to that."

The conversation over dinner jumped all over the place. The investigation was a major topic, but they also discussed Jordanian politics, the Middle East, and even sports as the numerous courses of food were served. They sat in a private room near the rear of the restaurant, which afforded them more privacy to speak openly without fear of prying ears.

Jordon, like almost all spots in the Middle East, was known for having lots of figurative and literal flies on the walls that may overhear any and all conversations and report them back to the powers that be.

Before they poured the last drink, Pat steered the conversation to a serious matter as he shared some recent news. "According to the intel provided to us by folks at the NSA, we may have an additional threat to add to our list on the home front."

"And that would be?" Matt asked.

"An EMP attack."

"I didn't think that was anything new?"

"Well, it's not, of course," Pat said as he took another sip of beer. "The NNSA has been warning about an EMP attack for years. Apparently, the chatter that the NSA has picked up recently mentions it heavily."

"Not to be the ignorant one here," Trent said as he tapped his utensil on the thick table, "But can one of you give me more specifics on what an EMP attack would be? I work for the FBI, but I'm a forensic crime scene analyst. Weapons and explosions aren't my thing."

"Really?" Matt asked. "You don't know what an EMP is?"

"Umm, no," Trent replied. "I've heard the term before, but normally just shook my head. Never really asked any questions."

"You know what happens when a nuclear weapon goes off?" Pat asked in a serious tone.

"Ya, a big mushroom shaped cloud fills the sky, all hell breaks loose, and everything gets destroyed," Trent said.

"Correct," Pat said. "But in that millisecond before the destruction occurs, an electromagnetic pulse is sent out in every direction. That pulse essentially fries or damages all electric equipment, rendering it useless."

"Before the nuclear blast vaporizes everything?" Trent asked.

"Yes."

"And this matters why?" Trent asked. "Everything is blown to shit anyway, so who cares about the pulse."

Pat frowned. "It matters because terrorists are actively trying to acquire nuclear weapons specifically to use these weapons not just to destroy a U.S. city, but our electrical grid."

"How?" Trent asked as he leaned closer to the table. "I thought a nuke would only affect a specific area. Wouldn't they need more than one device to really affect much of our power grid?"

Pat shook his head. "Good question, and to be completely honest, no. They only need one nuke to wreak havoc on our entire nation. They would need a High-Altitude Electromagnetic Pulse or HEMP, in order to fry our entire power grid. Essentially, this requires a delivery system that can launch a weapon very high into the sky before the detonation occurs."

"How high?" asked Trent.

"Probably about twenty-five miles, or over sixty-thousand feet up. That would be enough to destroy the entire United States power grid if it struck near the center of the nation."

"But twenty-five miles is way up there, how could it be launched that high?"

"They would likely need a missile."

Trent's face contorted from a look of intrigue to more of concern. "Can a terrorist group or rogue nation get their hands on that?"

"It's not likely," Pat said. "But not impossible."

"Then the threat is not that dire?"

"Well," Pat replied. "They could settle for destroying only a portion of the grid with a weapon detonated at a lower altitude. No missile needed for that."

"And don't forget," Matt jumped into the conversation. "There are also nations out there that are actively trying to make an EMP type weapon to be used offensively, no nuclear material is needed for those."

"Good point," Pat replied.

"So, we're screwed either way?" Trent asked.

"Nah," Matt said as he slapped Pat hard on the shoulders. "We got a talented group of guys here at the NNSA that are going to stop any such attack."

Pat smiled and shook his head, "Wish I shared your faith, Matt."

"All you need is faith as small as a mustard seed. It says so in the good book, Pat."

"You turning into an evangelist now, Pastor Evans?" Pat asked in a joking tone.

"Only if I beg for money," Matt said as he let out a chuckle.

"In one of his songs, Bono says something about the God he believes in isn't really short on cash."

Matt's eyes opened wide. "I mean, if Bono says it…"

Chapter Fifty-Two

Drexel

After the morning church service ended, Troy and Cate headed to the coffee shop. They sat down in the comfortable leather chairs after placing orders for cappuccinos. A few minutes later, Paul entered.

Troy picked a chair towards the rear of the room that faced the front so he could see anyone entering and or leaving. His dad had taught him an immense amount over the years, and one critical lesson entailed never having his back to a door. He learned sight lines before he could drive and always knew how to get out of a room if something terrible occurred.

Paul told them what he had witnessed at work over the past week. As he spoke, one the local deputies walked in. The officer walked over to the shop owner and spoke for a few minutes in hushed tones. The two men shared solemn expressions, and after a few minutes the deputy left.

Troy listened to every word his friend said, but Cate noticed the change in Troy's body language.

When Paul finished, Troy excused himself for a moment. He knew the coffee shop owner and walked over to the counter to speak with him. A few minutes later, he walked back to where he had sat.

"Well," Cate asked. "What is it?"

Troy shook his head slightly, the look of surprise evident on his face. "Jack Harding is dead."

"Wait, what?" Paul asked.

Troy sat back down. "He missed his Sunday morning visit to Hilda's House of Pancakes. He's been going there for over 30 years. One of his church buddies went to his place. Jack's truck was in the driveway, but he didn't answer the door. The guy called the sheriff, who drove over to do a wellness check. Before they even had the front door half open, the stench of gas flowed out. They got the gas turned off, and a special team came in from Boise to clear the house. They found Jack dead in his study. It seems clear he died of carbon monoxide poisoning."

"Wow," Paul said in a hushed tone. "Jack and his family pretty much built most this town."

"What will this mean for you, Paul, I mean with Siberdrive and all?" Cate asked.

Paul shrugged. "It's kinda hard to say, I guess. I don't think it should affect the company much though. Jack stepped away from the day-to-day operations a while back. He hired Chris Buckets as the CEO about five years ago, and he runs the business. Chris is a visionary, he really believes he can make the company a major defense department innovator, not just a follower. Jack still stopped by each day and had an office as Chairman of the Board but otherwise was rarely involved."

As Paul continued to talk, Troy's eyes narrowed. He looked past Paul. Outside, he saw a man climb out of a blue Ford F150 and walk into the hardware store across the street. Immediately Troy knew he recognized the man's face from somewhere, but he couldn't place where.

Troy had an excellent memory for faces, especially if they stood out. He racked his brain trying to remember where he had seen that man before.

Cate excused herself to the restroom, while Paul went up to order another coffee. Troy meandered toward the large plate-glass window at the front of the coffee shop and stared out the window toward the hardware store.

Several minutes later, the man emerged from the store and headed towards the truck. As the man's head turned toward the coffee shop, Troy eased behind the large drapery that bordered the window.

Muhammad Jarah hated being out in public. Plus, in such a small town he felt like he had a bullseye painted on his back, but he had no choice. Several pieces of excavating equipment were needed to dig that night, and the only hardware store in town was on Main Street. He intended to grab what he needed and get out as quickly as possible.

As he neared the truck, he got the feeling someone was watching him. He paused, turned slightly around to look before pulling his baseball cap low. Seeing no one, he continued to the truck, climbed in and drove away. The feeling of being watched continued to bother him.

———◆◇◆———

Troy peeked from behind the curtain and had his camera phone out. He snapped the man's picture. As the man looked around and before he pulled his baseball cap down, Troy zoomed in and got a somewhat grainy picture of the man.

The man climbed into his truck and pulled away. Troy memorized the license plate number as the truck left. Lost in his thoughts, he returned to his seat. A few moments later, Cate and Paul returned.

His mind raced as images flipped through his brain like a high-speed rolodex. Then, like a quick jab to the stomach, the events back in NYC at the Waldorf came back to him. Even though over six months passed, Troy suddenly recalled the chance meeting like it just occurred.

"What the hell is that man doing in Drexel?" Troy questioned out loud as his brain tried to figure things out. He didn't believe in coincidences.

"What's that, babe?" Cate asked, not sure what Troy had just said.

Troy was brought back to the present just then, "Just something on my mind..." The words came out in a slow, measured tone.

Cate perked up. "Want to share?"

"Maybe later," he replied with a smile.

Chapter Fifty-Three

London

May 2002

Waleed awoke slightly startled after experiencing a disturbing dream. He rarely recalled dreams, and when he did, they almost always gave him a feeling of peace and tranquility. This one had the opposite effect. In the dream, a young man with thick hair and a piercing gaze appeared out of nowhere in the middle of a field with a rifle slung over his shoulder. Waleed did not know the identity of this person, but whoever it was raised the rifle, pointed it at him, and pulled the trigger. The flash of brilliant light and the sound of the bullet exploding from the end of the barrel caused Waleed to shudder as he suddenly found himself in his own bed.

He rolled onto his side and grabbed the alarm clock on the nightstand with his right hand, while his left arm wiped beads of perspiration off his brow. The time displayed as 5 AM local time, still dark in London. Waleed knew he could not fall back to sleep after the jarring moment.

Waleed walked over to the ornate chair near the stone fireplace on the wall opposite his bed and put on the crimson-colored robe draped over the chair. Once he got to the kitchen on the first floor, he brewed a pot of coffee. Everyone else in the house, including his wait staff, was still asleep.

For over a week, he received daily updates from Kadir on their progress. It took two nights after the interrogation of Jack Harding to find the opening of the shaft. Unfortunately, less than 50 feet inside, they encountered their first problem. A cave-in occurred in the past, and they had no choice but to dig around the rubble. The rocks that blocked the tunnel were too big to move with the equipment they could get down the mine shaft.

About 30 minutes later, after he sipped on his third cup of coffee, his cell phone rang. He saw it was Kadir and answered immediately. "Yes. What is it?"

"We made it around the debris," Kadir's clearly out of breath voice said from 4,834 miles away. "We dug until we connected to a parallel tunnel and then cut back to the shaft that Harding said contained the vault.

"And?" Waleed asked as he put the coffee cup down. Hiis body tensed as he awaited the reply.

"And 200 feet further into the tunnel we found the vault door."

"Is it large?"

"Huge!"

Waleed felt a pulsation surge through his body as adrenaline rushed to his extremities. "What do you need to open it?"

"Time," Kadir said in a measured tone. "Muhammad is here, and he has a few ideas. We're trying to figure out how to open it without making a lot of noise."

"That's smart, and anyway explosives could cause another cave in," Waleed said.

"Yes, we considered that. Plus, any noise that large would likely alert someone to our presence."

"Do you have the equipment we discussed so you can see inside the vault?"

"Yes, we will bore a hole through the door and then snake the fiber optic camera inside to look at the contents of the room."

"We need to know how many kilotons it is," Waleed said firmly.

"I know, and we will find that out."

"Good job," Waleed said as he felt joy with the vault finally being located. "Our quest is almost done."

"Allah's vision is close at hand. Just as you said it would."

"The prophet looks down on you with pride, Kadir. Do you need anything else?"

Kadir sounded exhausted, and his reply was direct. "Rest," he replied.

"Soon you shall have just that," Waleed said before the line disconnected.

Chapter Fifty-Four

London

The work on the oil rig was completed ahead of schedule, and the pictures Waleed received looked impressive. He decided that when he arrived in the United States in two days' time, he may have the pilot conduct a flyby to see the structure for himself.

The location on the east coast neared completion as the material needed arrived in New Jersey via a storage container. Next, workers loaded everything onto a semi for delivery to the rural farm he purchased via the LLC's that Kadir set up.

Finally, the team constructing the structure on the west coast land finished two days early. Although that site was chosen purely as a diversion, Waleed had no intention of launching the attack from the west coast.

Through obscure means, Waleed rented a home high in the mountains overlooking the mine in Drexel. He planned to be there within the next few days to observe the progress with his own eyes and be there when the team removed the hidden nuke.

Waleed took another sip of hot coffee as his mind wandered, and he considered all the moving parts his plan put in motion.

Muhammad had arrived in Drexel the week before with three of his most trusted men. Including Kadir and Zayan, there were now six men available. Waleed felt a sudden concern, something he could not readily explain. An idea came to him a few minutes later.

He called into the other room for his bodyguard, Usaim. One reason Waleed brought him onto his security detail was that Usaim's name meant guardian.

Names meant much to Waleed, and he believed the prophet himself spoke through a man's name.

"You called Waleed?" Usaim said as he rushed into the room with his hand inside his dark gray sports coat.

"Yes, I need something."

"Anything."

"As you know, we are headed to the United States for an unknown amount of time," Waleed said. "I believe we need more men."

"Moein and I can keep you safe, sir."

"Of that I have no doubt," Waleed replied as he nodded. "We need to bring more men though to safeguard the weapon. How many trustworthy men who are able to handle themselves can you arrange with short notice ?"

"How much time are we talking about?"

Waleed looked down at his Patek Philippe watch. "Less than two hours."

Usaim remained quiet for several seconds as his glance shifted downward. "I will go to the mosque now, I'm certain I can return with three or four men."

Waleed nodded as he rubbed the side of his face. "Make sure they are unattached; I don't need wives or girlfriends looking for them if we are gone for a while."

"I understand," Usaim said as he turned and walked towards the door. Waleed's voice caused him to turn back.

"Also, take the men and stop at Soho before you make your way to the airport. I'll meet you there later. I have made the arrangements already, and my man at Soho is expecting you. Each member of the team will need new identities, including passports and licenses." Waleed looked at the door. "That will be all."

"Understood," Usaim said as he left the room and hurried outside into the cool London morning.

Waleed drank a few more sips of coffee and thought some more. Pleased by his decisions, he placed a call. "The plane should be fueled and ready," he said to the person on the other end. "File a flight plan for the United States, we are headed for Pennsylvania first. I want wheels up in less than four hours."

Six hours later, Waleed sat in the private study on his 757. The jet flew high above the Atlantic Ocean at 37,000 feet. He and another man were in deep conversation for over an hour.

The man who sat opposite him appeared to ponder Waleed's latest question.

Finally, the man replied. "As long as all the parts I need are onsite and no significant complications occur, I would say thirty-six hours should be enough time to make the modifications."

Waleed smiled broadly. "How is your family enjoying London? It's better than Islamabad, right?"

"Yes, we enjoy London very much," the man said as he bowed in his seat ever so slightly. "My family and I are grateful to you for our new life in the United Kingdom."

"My pleasure," Waleed waved his hand and replied warmly. "I am happy to do so in exchange for your work and absolute discretion."

"I will complete the task as requested," the man said confidently. "No one will ever know what I did for you."

Waleed shook his head, "I know you will do both things, doctor. Once we land in the United States, two of my associates will bring you to the farm I told you about. There you can make the preparations."

"What about the weapon?"

"I'm going to retrieve it personally," Waleed said as he placed his hand on the Koran, which sat on his desktop.

Chapter Fifty-Five

Drexel

The end-of-year exams proved to be harder than normal for Troy. Testing always came naturally to him over the years, but his mind felt cluttered as he prepared for his finals. What Paul told him earlier in the week rubbed him all wrong and made studying difficult.

On the phone call, Paul explained to Troy how he continued to keep tabs on the men as they explored the abandoned mine each night, but something changed when they brought additional equipment. The two men started digging in an area that contained no visible tunnel entrances. Stranger still, soon they were joined by several new men.

Troy had asked if Paul could get a picture of the new men. Paul had told him not from his vantage point.

Paul agreed to meet at Troy's house Friday night after exams wrapped up.

Both Troy and Cate lined up internships over the summer.

Cate flew home to Coeur d'Alene to spend a few days with her parents before her summer internship with the state police investigative division in Boise began.

Troy's internship kept him closer to home. The local sheriff in Drexel practically begged Troy to work with them over the years. He knew it made sense to learn how local law enforcement functioned firsthand, especially after all his father's training since he was a kid. Troy felt the experience with the local police would provide him with a good handle on what things would be like when he joined the FBI after college.

Troy's mom wasn't home the night Paul came over. The two friends sat in his father's study as they both enjoyed ice-cold glass bottles of Coca-Cola.

Matt returned home from Jordan earlier in the week, but his stay proved to be short-lived as headquarters beckoned him back east once more.

Troy had not seen his dad for close to three weeks. Besides being his *Pops*, Matt really was Troy's best friend, and he missed their conversations.

Paul started at the beginning and told Troy everything he had seen since they last spoke.

After a few minutes, Troy interrupted him. "Have you been waiting outside their place every night to follow them to the mine?"

Paul smirked as he shook his head, "No, technology is changing so fast that there really is no need to do stakeouts if you're tech savvy."

"Enlighten me," Troy said as he raised one eyebrow.

"I installed a Wi-Fi based, motion activated camera on the light pole across from their place," Paul said. "Installed it one night after they left for the mine. It piggybacks off an open Wi-Fi signal at the neighbor's house and sends the images directly to my laptop,"

"Pretty ingenious," Troy said. "How did you hack into the neighbor's Wi-Fi?"

"Most people are lazy, they leave the password as *Admin*, the same way it comes from the manufacturer."

"Remind me to update my passwords after we get done talking tonight."

Paul smiled. "I also set up a few cameras at the mine, but those don't have Wi-Fi. No cell signals out there. Those cameras record the images, but I must go there to download them. I go a few times a week."

"Brilliant," Troy said. He asked more questions about the other guys who had arrived. Paul had little to tell him about the four new guys except that they all appeared to be Middle Eastern.

As Paul described the men, Troy took out his cell phone and pulled up the somewhat blurry picture he had captured of the man in the ball cap. "Is this one of the guys?" He asked.

Paul squinted at the grainy photo and then acknowledged, "Yes."

Troy then relayed the encounter they had with the man at the Waldorf in NYC during the fall.

"And you have no clue who this dude is?" Paul asked.

"I don't..." Troy replied as his voice trailed off. A few seconds later he added, "But now that I think about it, I may have a way to find out right here and now."

"How?"

Troy patted the computer that sat on his father's desk. "Right here."

"But isn't it password protected and encrypted by the FBI?"

"It is," Troy said with a wide grin.

"You know his login and password?"

"Well, he doesn't know that I do, but yes. Pops won't admit it, but he has a sweet tooth from time to time. He likes to use the word Bosco a little too often for passwords."

"George Costanza would be proud," Paul said as he rolled his eyes. "You've logged onto his FBI account this before?"

"Are you asking if I have ever committed a felony?" Troy asked with a sheepish smile. "Actually, no, but you have to pop the cherry one day, right?"

"And what are you looking for exactly?"

"The Bureau has a secret database, which is a joint conglomeration with the NSA. Very few people know about it."

"And what does it do?"

"It's essentially a facial recognition database, but it's not fully operational yet. In fact, it has a long way to go before they achieve their goal of archiving an extensive image database. But for now, it's chock full of images and data on any person who has a record or is wanted by various national agencies."

"And you think this guy may be in there?"

"My gut says without a doubt."

"And that gut of yours is never wrong," Paul said as he rolled his eyes.

"Rarely, but there's only one way to find out," Troy gently patted the laptop.

For the next ten minutes, Troy worked in virtual silence as Paul watched him log into the FBI's secure servers using his dad's credentials. Troy was all in now.

As he made his way into the image database, he uploaded the image he had taken of the man.

The bottom right-hand corner of the program displayed a percentage indicator that told the user how far the search had processed, and it crawled at a snail's pace. They grabbed some food from the kitchen while they waited for the results.

Thirty minutes and two sandwiches later, Troy stared at the results, "Damn!" He exclaimed in utter shock.

Paul shook his head, unable to believe what the screen showed.

They both said it must be a mistake.

Finally, after a long silence, he asked Troy, "What the hell are we gonna do now?"

Troy slowly lost the shocked expression and looked his friend in the eye. "I have no idea."

Chapter Fifty-Six

Washington D.C.

Matt returned to his hotel. It had been another long day at the Hoover Building. He did not know when he would return home to Drexel, and senior leadership even mentioned another trip to Jordan might be necessary. The thought of returning there really pissed him off.

That evening, after his last meeting had ended, he met Pat, and they had dinner at the Capital Grille. It brought back lots of memories of Preston as Matt walked into the familiar spot.

As his mind thought about his dear friend, he beamed. At dinner that night, he regaled Pat with story after story about the senator. Some were stories from times they had spent together; others were recounts of events Preston had shared over the years. Lots of laughs were shared, Preston would have enjoyed the conversation immensely.

It was close to 11 PM when he removed his shoes and pants and sat down in his boxers and t-shirt on the sofa. He called Amy, and after they talked for a while, he asked for his son to jump on the call.

"Pops! How are you, old man?" Troy asked.

"Tired son."

"I bet. The Bureau really is sticking it to you on this Jordanian investigation, huh?"

"Been brutal."

"You coming home soon? Mom misses you terribly, she has already called me a pain in the ass, and I've been home for less than three days."

"Sounds like you're filling my role nicely," Matt replied with a laugh.

"Apple doesn't fall far from the tree," Troy said.

"Your internship starts soon, right?"

"Yes, sir," said Troy. "Bright and early Monday morning. I envision it will be a dull summer, though."

"Well," Matt said, "Drexel is a small town and not much happens, but working with local law enforcement will be good for you, son."

"Yes sir. I just can't bear the thought of Cate having all the action this summer while I patrol Camp Drexel issuing parking citations."

"Well, at least you'll be much quicker eating a jelly donut by the end of the summer than Cate."

"Not funny," Troy said as he let out a low chuckle.

"The sheriff is a good man and very excited to have you working with his team this summer. Treat him right."

"Yes, sir, I will."

"I think deep down the sheriff feels with you on the force something exciting may happen. Maybe some action will come your way after all."

"One can only hope."

"What are you up to the rest of the night? I can't imagine you know what to do with yourself without Cate around."

Troy became quiet at the question. It took him a moment to respond. "Heading out with Paul tonight."

"Out with Paul? Drexel closes way too early to have any place to go out to on a weeknight. Plus, doesn't Paul have to work in the morning?"

"Yes, we're just going out for a drive. Shoot the breeze, catch up a little. Maybe throw back a cold one."

"Well, don't keep him out too late," Matt said in a fatherly tone.

"I won't."

"Goodnight, son, I love you."

"Love you too, Pops. Come home soon."

———◆———

Matt picked through his suitcase to find a clean outfit for the next day. As he moved a shirt, he saw the large manila envelope he had packed. The envelope was left over from the Wilcox estate and had been addressed to him. The need to climb into bed overtook any desire to open the envelope at the moment, and Matt decided he would open the envelope on the flight home. Whenever that would be.

Chapter Fifty-Seven

Drexel

The night temperatures dipped down to the low forties, and the moon shone bright as Troy and Paul crouched low to the ground. They parked at Burton State Park and made their way through the woods to a spot that allowed them an unobstructed view of the mine.

Troy peered through his binoculars. The moonlight was bright enough that he didn't need the night vision googles.

"You tell Cate what we found the other night?" Paul asked in a hushed tone.

Troy shook his head, "I love the girl, Paul, really I do, but if I told Miss Goodie Two Shoes that a man on the FBI's ten most wanted list was roaming around the mines, she would call the authorities immediately."

"Maybe you should. This is a big deal, Troy. It maybe more than even you can handle."

Troy rolled his eyes, "We've been over this. I just want to figure out what these guys are doing before we call in the cavalry. When that time arrives, I'll be the first one to say I need help."

"You're not trying to be the hero and single-handedly snag a most wanted fugitive."

Holding his thumb and pointer finger a half inch apart, Troy said, "Well, maybe just a little."

"Cate is gonna be pissed that you left her out of this."

"You're definitely right. She would be livid if she knew I even logged into Pops laptop. But she'll just have to get over it. What's done is done."

Just then, another vehicle pulled up at the base of the mine. Four men emerged from the Ford F250. Troy and Paul raised their binoculars and focused on the men who arrived.

Troy only noticed one of them. "Bingo," he said.

"It's him?" Paul said.

"You bet. Mr. Muhammad Jarah himself."

Troy and Paul watched as the four men climbed up what was now a well-worn path about two hundred feet up the mountain to the tunnel entrance

"You think Thomas and Christopher really are who they claim to be?" Paul asked.

"Not a chance," Troy said. "In fact, once we get back, I'm gonna log back into the FBI database and run a background check on both of them. Did you get the info I requested?"

Paul smiled, "One of the girls in the HR department has a slight crush on me. I sweet-talked her the other day and took her to lunch."

"You sly dog. And?"

"While she went to the restroom, I swiped her badge and made a copy using a key card clone device."

"Where in the world did you get that?" Troy asked in a surprised tone.

"The internet, some Chinese company for only $39.99."

"Did it work?"

Paul reached back to the backpack he wore and removed the documents he had copied from the personnel files. "Perfectly," he replied. "I waited for everyone to go home that night, and I used her cloned card to access the personnel files in HR."

Troy looked at the employment applications with a dull light he pulled from his pocket. "They look legit. Passports are clearly British. I don't see anything suspicious in the info they provided."

"You know what a genuine passport looks like versus a fake one?"

"Of course, Pops taught me."

"Next step?"

"I'll take this copy of the passport and run it through the software the FBI keeps, it should provide us a better background check than Siberdrive uses."

"Pretty cool. Those felonies are adding up."

Troy flipped Paul the bird.

As Troy and Paul looked back towards the mountain, the two men they knew as Thomas and Christopher emerged from the tunnel and were met by the four men who had arrived. After exchanging pleasantries, the six men stood there for several minutes. Then, one of them pointed back to the vehicles.

A third vehicle climbed the old mine road and approached the other vehicles. Troy and Paul turned their attention to the new vehicle. A black Range Rover with heavily tinted windows parked next to the two pickup trucks.

Five men emerged from the Range Rover. Troy zoomed in as close as he could and looked at each man that now stood around the vehicle. The person who emerged from the front passenger seat could not be seen. He wore a head covering that partially obscured his face.

"What the hell is that seventh guy wearing?" Paul asked. "What do they call those things called? Turbans?"

Troy laughed, "No, that's what a Sikh or Hindus would wear. That man has on a keffiyeh."

"Keffiyeh? You take some sort of Middle Eastern or Islamic culture class at Boise State?"

"Nothing like that, but Pops has traveled over there extensively, and he taught me a lot about their culture. I went one time as well when I was younger."

"To the Middle East? I don't remember that, but as many trips as you have been on, I'm not sure even you could keep them all straight."

"True, but I'm sure I told you about the trip. Anyway, Dad took me on a trip to Lebanon. Freaked my mom out that he dragged me along. It was an interesting trip, and I saw a lot of culture, but it was way too hot for my liking."

"Would you ever go back?" Paul asked.

"Hell no!" You won't see me willingly set foot in the Middle East ever again. Once was enough in the sandbox."

"Who do you think these new guys are?"

"Trouble," Troy said. "That's over a dozen guys up here, and they all look to be to be from the Middle East. This is not good."

"You still think there is gold in that vault?" Paul asked.

With a concerned look on his face, Troy replied, "No, no, I don't."

Troy and Paul watched as the group of men headed into the tunnel.

⋅⋅⋅◈⋅⋅⋅

An hour later, the men came back out. Troy could still not see the face of the man who wore the keffiyeh, but the other men all appeared to smile. Several hugs occurred, and the men patted each other on the backs and shoulders many times. After a few minutes and several long handshakes, the group proceeded down the mountain to the three vehicles at the bottom. Five minutes later, they left.

"What do we do now?" Paul asked.

"We go in that damn tunnel and see what made them so touchy feely," Troy said.

CHAPTER FIFTY-EIGHT

DREXEL

The next three days straight, the rain came down without abating. Instead of a dusty footpath, the trail leading up the mountainside to the abandoned mine turned into thick mud. Conditions on the mountain made it impossible to bring any equipment until the ground dried.

Waleed spoke with Doctor Yasir Ghazini back in Pennsylvania by phone after he left the mine shaft, and he even sent images of the device. The doctor confirmed that he could make the modifications to the device. The confirmation pleased Waleed since everything appeared to be going as planned.

Later, he shared with Kadir the entire conversation with Doctor Yasir. Zayan also was in the room when the discussion took place. He had earned Kadir's implicit trust, which meant he had Waleed's as well. In the past, Waleed would have been hesitant to reveal the full plot to anyone but Kadir. But they had come so far and were so close to the end that he spoke freely in front of Zayan. He had, after all, played a critical role in not only the acquisition of the weapon, but he would also play an important role in its detonation.

As Waleed relayed the conversation, Kadir stopped him at one point.

"But isn't that kiloton yield on the small side? Will it be enough?" Kadir asked.

"The good doctor assured me it would be plenty. I trust his judgement. Anyway, the bomb may be smaller than we expected, but it will also be easier to transport."

Kadir stroked his chin slowly, "Yes, that is true. Getting that bomb through the mine shaft is already problematic. If it were larger, that would only exacerbate the problem. Could you imagine if they had hidden a bomb that was closer to 20,000 pounds?"

"Fortunately, the senators were smart enough to realize transporting a weapon that large would be quite difficult. It would have made others aware of their plan. The fact that the weapon is less than five hundred pounds is perfect. Regarding our plan, I believe the vehicles we intend to use to transport the device will work fine, don't you agree?"

"Yes, once the ground dries, we should be fine," Kadir nodded.

Just then, there was a knock on the library door where the three men sat. "Enter," responded Waleed in an authoritative voice.

Muhammad Jarah walked into the room. He wore his typical blank expression. Kadir stared at the man, never knowing how to read him, or if there was even anything to read. His eyes revealed little. They appeared to be a gateway to a very dark soul, one that lived without conscience or remorse.

"Everything is in place, just as you requested," Muhammad said.

"How long will it take you to get there?" Waleed asked.

"The house is about 30 minutes south of Drexel, not too far off Highway 55."

"You have everything you need?"

"Yes. We will enter the house at 5 AM. It will not take long to do what is needed."

"Make sure the scene is bloody," Waleed said in a bitter tone.

Muhammad's expressionless face contorted to one best described as gleeful. "I'll make sure it flows."

"That will be all for tonight. Kadir and I still have much to discuss."

Muhammad nodded his head, "As you wish," he said as he turned and walked out the door.

Kadir shuddered involuntarily. Just being in the man's presence gave him the chills.

"You're sure what Muhammad is going to do is necessary?" Kadir asked after Muhammad had left.

"Vitally," Waleed said. "It is essential that local law enforcement and state agencies have their hands full. I don't want them anywhere near the mine when we remove the weapon. It's unfortunate, but trust me, it is essential. The infidel's losses will only glorify Allah."

Chapter Fifty-Nine

Drexel

Troy and Cate curled up on the couch before a small fire in his parents' living room.

"How have the first few days been with the state police?" Troy asked. "But before you answer that, it was a pleasant surprise for you to drive up for dinner." As he said the words he kissed her cheek affectionately.

"Well I'm just that kind of gal," Cate replied as she turned towards his lips and pressed hers into his.

The kiss lingered just long enough but didn't turn into anything more.

"Jeez, the days we don't share a kiss can be rough."

"Same here," Cate replied with a wide smile. "The job has been fine, but I've definitively missed you. What have you been up to during your week off? Ready to serve with Drexel's finest?" Her questioning tone slightly sarcastic.

"Humph," Troy replied with a grunt. "Sheriff Barnett has called me every day this week. He apparently has a growing list of duties for me."

"I think Roy has been waiting a long, long time for you to put on the brown and gold uniform," Cate said as she gave him a playful jab with her elbow.

"You bet he has, I think in some twisted way he thinks I'll spend the summer interning with him and then give up my dream of joining the FBI and stick around here to work for him. As if..."

"You'd make a sexy Barney Fife," Cate said with a wink as she slowly ran her tongue along her upper lip. "Just think of how many illegal mule deer crossings you could prevent in your career."

"Shoot me now," Troy replied as he rolled his eyes. "If I'm still in this town after graduation, I've made some pretty piss poor choices."

"Aww, come on. You love Drexel. After all, it's your home."

"Sure is, but that doesn't mean I want to spend my life here and grow old within this valley. It's a big world, and I plan to explore a hell of a lot of it."

"Trust me, I get wanting to spread your wings and get out from where you've grown up." Cate then went into details about her first several intern days in Boise. She explained that the work was fairly interesting, and she planned to learn a lot about the investigative process.

⟢✦⟣

"Heard from your dad this week?" Cate asked.

"Yes," Troy said. "Talked with him last night. Sounds like he is booked on the last flight out of Dulles tomorrow, so he should be home late."

"This Jordanian investigation has been all-encompassing. How exactly does a Special Agent in Charge get stuck on lots of high-profile cases?"

"He's the man, no other word to describe him. The FBI knows Pops is the best of the best, if they want to get to the bottom of something, they go to him."

"Does the apple fall far from the tree?" Cate asked.

"You tell me."

Cate laughed, "The last thing you need, Mr. Evans, is a bigger ego. You already know you're the man. More importantly, you know you're my man." She said as she drew him in closer for a mini make-out session.

After a few minutes, she pulled away slightly. "Well, Mr. Hot and Heavy, we are officially seniors now."

"That's right, Ms. Downey," Troy said. "Only one more year left."

"Till..."

Troy cut her off, "We're done with school and headed to Washington."

"And..." Cate looked down at the ring finger on her left hand.

"You missing something on that hand?" Troy asked in a coy tone.

"Yes, I am in fact," Cate replied with pursed lips.

"All in good time, my love."

"When will that be exactly?"

Troy smiled, "When you least expect it."

"Uh, that would be right now," she said.

"Ok, when you least expect it, but not tonight," he replied in the sweetest tone he could muster. Besides, if we got engaged while in college, I think our parents would be a little upset. We both know they want is to finish college before we make massive life-altering decisions."

Cate frowned slightly.

Troy didn't want to completely sour the mood, so he changed the subject away from the ring finger discussion. "Pops said he stopped by the townhouse in Georgetown the other night."

"Our townhouse?"

He squeezed her thigh. "That's the one. He said there would be a lot of painting when the time arrives to move in. All sorts of projects for a young couple."

"I'll get that place in tip-top shape in no time."

"And here I thought you were just a hot chick with a great rack," Troy said as his eyes glanced down at her chest.

"Don't forget my pear-shaped ass," Cate said before adding, "You pig," playfully.

Troy shrugged. "Hey now, it's not my fault guys are simple creatures. We are hard wired to want hot women with nice figures."

"Yeah, don't I know it."

Just then, Amy stuck her head in the doorway. "You all proper in here?"

Troy sighed, "Yes, Mom, of course, come on in."

"Hope I'm not interrupting," Amy said.

"Your son is just sweet talking me," Cate said.

"Uh oh," Amy replied. "He's not talking about your big boobs again, is he?"

"Mother!" Troy exclaimed.

"Just saying, I know firsthand how those Evans boys can be. One-track minds."

"Uhh, yuk," Troy replied as he stuck his tongue out. "Don't be spilling the beans on your and Dad's...umm...stuff."

"Hate to break the news, but you didn't arrive via a stork, boy," Amy said with an audible laugh.

"Come sit down with us," Cate said as she patted the couch next to her.

"Wish I could, dear, but I've got to turn in. It's a busy day at school tomorrow. Plus, with Matt coming home, I want to do a few things around the house in the morning. I better head off to la-la land."

"Me too," Cate said. "I have to leave by 6 AM so I can be back in Boise on time."

"Your bedroom is all made up, sweetie. If Troy gets any ideas and tries to keep you from getting shut eye, there is a loaded .357 under the pillow."

"Jeez, Mom, like she needs any encouragement along those lines."

"I got my guns right here," Cate replied as she raised her two fists, "These can keep that filthy, rotten, scallywag at bay," she said with a chuckle.

"Thata girl," Amy said as she came over and kissed Cate on the forehead. "Goodnight sweetheart, thanks for coming up to see us."

"I appreciate you having me. Dinner was fabulous, by the way," Cate said.

"I couldn't let Troy serve Hamburger Helper, now, could I?"

"Goodnight, Mom," Troy stood up and hugged his mom tightly.

She playfully pinched his side as she said, "You behave yourself, young man."

"Don't I always?" Troy asked with a sly grin.

"No!" Both women replied in unison.

After Amy left, Cate looked at Troy and then towards the doorway where his mom had stood. "You're really blessed with great parents."

Troy nodded. "I realize that."

"As many times as I've been here, don't think I ever recall either of them giving the other one a hard time or even being snippy with each another. Not once."

"They both told me early on that marriage is hard, but it's one thing in life worth fighting for," Troy paused. "I think they figured things out a long time ago. Mom and Pops always put their marriage ahead of everything else, even me. I think that's the key to their success. Now don't get me wrong, they've always treated me like I was the most special thing they've ever had. But they've worked hard to keep their bond strong. Even after being married for over twenty years, they still have date night once a week, and if Pops misses one or two because of his work travels, they make up those nights."

"That's smart, I don't think enough couples prioritize the little things like that," Cate said.

"I agree, they even go on daily walks, hold hands, and start every morning when they are home having quiet time together. Somehow, between them both working full-time, raising me, and maintaining a small farm, they've been able to keep a spark going that seems to fade for far too many relationships. Hell, they are still frisky as all get out most days, and it's kinda gross. But I'm glad they are like that versus plenty of couples who seem to become more like roommates as time passes instead of lovers. You might not bang like rabbits after the honeymoon phase ends, but a couple best be sure to still bang regularly."

"That was said eloquently," Cate said as she smiled.

"Hey, all I know is I best stay away when their bedroom door is closed."

"Good to know that even when couples get older, they still like to knock some boots."

Troy replied with a hearty laugh. "Hopefully, I've learned from their example on the do's and don'ts of a successful marriage. They've certainly done their best to lead by example."

"They've done you a great service by leading the way. Not every kid gets to have such remarkable parents."

"That's for sure."

They grew quiet and held each other for several minutes.

After a couple minutes, Cate changed the subject. "Seen Paul this week? Is he still following those two guys as they explore the mine? You have said little about it recently."

Troy's response was careful, calculated even. He in no way wanted to keep secrets from Cate, but he knew he could not reveal much. Cate was a rule follower.

Troy did his best to adhere to the rules but believed some rules were meant to be bent, if not broken.

He replied honestly, "Yes, I've seen Paul a few times this week."

"And the two guys he's been following? Any recent developments?"

Here Troy held back some significant pieces of information, "Yes, he is still following them. I went with him earlier in the week. They are up to something, just can't figure out what yet."

"You gonna tell the sheriff? Or your dad?"

"When the time is right," he replied.

Cate studied his expressions. She could read him like a book, "You're holding back something, Troy. I can tell. Your eyes give it away."

He shrugged his shoulders slightly and looked away quickly, diverting his eyes from her.

"Trying to be Mr. Hero and figure it all out on your own?" She asked.

"Something like that," he said reluctantly.

She took her hand and turned his head toward her and looked deep into his eyes. She was not exactly pleased with what she saw. "Ok, I'll give you through the weekend, Mr. Special Agent wannabe. Then we go to the proper authorities. Agreed?"

"What are we going to them with?" He asked.

"With whatever you know," she countered.

"It's not much." He lied. It made him feel terrible.

"It will be enough to get some others involved. It's your choice, bring in Sheriff Barnett or your dad."

Troy nodded slowly.

"It's not up for negotiating Troy Matthew Evans. You have the next few days to come clean."

"Alright," he said reluctantly.

Cate stood up, then grabbed his arm and yanked him up from the couch. "Off to bed," she said. "If you behave, I'll let you spoon for a bit and maybe get a little sugar."

"Giddyup. And what about the .357?" He asked with a smirk.

"It better not be loaded," she deadpanned.

CHAPTER SIXTY

DREXEL

It was late morning when the Suburban pulled into the driveway leading to the log cabin. Waleed stood on the second floor and peered out the window as the black vehicle approached. In less than a minute, he rushed downstairs to greet the four men who approached the front door.

Muhammad Jarah walked in first, and Waleed greeted him eagerly.

"How did it go?" he asked.

"It was messy, but it went fine," Muhammad said with zero emotion evident in his voice. "Just like we planned. It's done."

"And the evidence?"

"We drove about 30 minutes north of here and disposed of everything. The hatchets and other evidence were weighed down and lie on the bottom of Lake Cascade. No one saw anything. We went to an area where there are no houses, only a forest on either side of the lake. There were no fishing boats out there. No witnesses."

"And you planted the items we discussed at the house?"

"Of course. We also left several blood trails quite a long distance into the woods. The authorities will certainly call for reinforcements and spread out in a fruitless search for the perpetrators."

Waleed smiled, "Good. What time will you place the anonymous call?"

"Around two this afternoon. I'll call the state police from a burner phone, and notify them of what took place in Borden."

"What type of response do you expect?"

"Every available law enforcement officer from within 100 miles will converge on that small town," Muhammad said. "Borden, Idaho, will be infamous. Just in time for the six o'clock national news."

"That should buy us at least 24-48 hours," Waleed said.

"At a minimum."

As Waleed stared at Muhammad, he saw a red pigment smeared under his right ear. He pointed at the spot, "You have something under your right ear."

Muhammad rubbed at it with his hand, looked down and replied, "Blood, it flowed freely just as you requested. We cleaned ourselves up, but I must have missed a spot."

Waleed shook his head, "You and your men shower here and change into fresh clothes. Leave your old clothes with Usaim, and he will destroy them and whatever evidence they may contain. Then head to the mine and check the soil. See if it has dried out. If all goes according to plan, we can move the equipment over when night falls."

"And Kadir and Zayan?"

"You will meet them at their place later today. I want all of you at the mine by eight tonight," Waleed instructed in a firm tone.

"What about Mathew Evans, the FBI Special Agent in Charge who lives here in Drexel?"

"My contacts at the Hoover Building say he is still in Washington. He should be no concern of ours," Waleed said.

"Everyone is my concern," Muhammad replied. "In fact, I want to review the files again this afternoon that were compiled on the local police force."

"Ah yes, here they are." Waleed walked over the dining room table and retrieved the three-inch file folder. As he handed it over, he replied, "I looked them over last night, A few of the deputies have military backgrounds, but nothing you couldn't handle if the need arose. It won't though. The team will be in and out of that mine with no one knowing."

"The men with military backgrounds are the ones I need to look at twice. After all, they may surprise us. And I don't like surprises."

"That's right," Waleed said. "One more addition to the file came through yesterday. Apparently, Matt Evans college-age son has an internship with the police force this summer. He starts on Monday."

Waleed retrieved the additional file and handed it to Muhammad. "The boy is named Troy, and he wishes to follow in his father's footsteps and be part of the FBI. The newly formed counterterrorism division if the intel is correct."

As Waleed finished speaking, Muhammad opened the file. His eyes locked onto the picture paper-clipped to the front inside cover and froze. Immediately his mind recognized that face. Those eyes were known to him. But from where?

Waleed recognized the change in the man's expression, "What is it?" He asked slightly alarmed.

Muhammad was quiet for a moment, "I've seen this young man before."

"Where? Here in Drexel?"

Muhammad shook his head now while his mind wandered. Several seconds passed before the memory surfaced, "No, I saw him in the lobby of the Waldorf Astoria hotel in New York City last fall," Muhammad said.

"Are you sure?"

"Absolutely, something about that boy struck me as I saw him that day. He glared at me as..." Muhammed paused for a moment. "His look conveyed the feeling an enemy."

"An enemy? How could you have known he was an enemy?" Waleed asked with a perplexed look on his face.

"I saw it in his eyes," Muhammad said. "A man's core being can be unlocked by the look in his eyes."

"Do you think he will be a problem? I don't expect your team will run into him or any of the police."

"Neither do I," Muhammad said. "And to answer your question, no, the boy should not be a problem. If he gets in our way, I will eliminate him without a second thought."

"Good. Anyway, we are doing this at night for a reason and should be long gone when dawn breaks."

Chapter Sixty-One

Drexel

May 17, 2002

Once dinnertime arrived, Troy made his way up the well-trodden path from the shooting range to the house. Earlier, he left his cell phone on the front porch, and as he picked it up saw he had numerous missed calls. Several of them were from Cate, which was highly unusual. She was not the type to call multiple times unless there was a problem.

As he started to dial her number a call from his father showed up on the screen. "Pops! What up?"

"Where are you, son?" Matt asked.

"Home, just got done doing some shooting down at the range, why?"

"I'm surprised the sheriff didn't pull you into what's going on."

"Huh?" Troy questioned. "Did I miss something?"

"It's all over the news, even back here in D.C.."

"What is?"

"The gruesome discovery in Borden," Matt said.

"I've been away from my phone all afternoon, Pops, so you better fill me in."

For the next five minutes, Matt explained everything he had heard about what took place 30 miles south of Drexel. Borden was a small, sleepy suburb just north of Boise. The events that took place were all the national media covered ever since the bodies were discovered.

When Matt concluded, Troy said, "I can't believe that occurred so close to home."

"I know, things like that just don't happen in Idaho, especially in some quiet place like Borden. I wonder if Cate is involved in the investigation?" Matt asked. "I'm sure the State Police will take the lead on the investigation. My sources tell me that most law enforcement within 100 miles have converged on Borden."

"I was just about to call her when you rang, I had six missed calls from her."

"You better call her back, son."

"Yes sir. And Pops, you gonna be home tonight like you planned?"

Matt sighed audibly, "My meetings are running long, won't be able to make the last commercial flight out after all."

"That sucks, Mom, and I miss you."

"But the director took pity on me and insisted I take his G5 home."

"That's pretty badass," Troy said in a shocked tone.

"Yeah, I was shocked when he offered a few minutes ago. Won't say no to that sweet ride. I'm even giving Pat O'Shea a lift on the way. After we drop him off in Oak Ridge, it should only take four hours to get home."

"Nice, I'll see you later tonight. Love you, Pops."

"Love you too, son, see you soon," Matt replied as the line went dead.

— ◆◇◆ —

Troy stood there for a moment and shook his head at his dad's luck. He then called Cate. She answered on the third ring and sounded upset.

"I've been trying to call you for the last hour!" She said in an exacerbated tone, which was not like her.

Troy could tell she was stressed. "Sorry, babe, my phone was on the porch, and I was out shooting. I just checked it."

"So, you don't have a clue what happened in Borden?" She asked.

"Actually, Pops just called me right before I dialed you. He told me enough. What is the State Police telling you?"

"Telling me? They're not telling me anything. I'm here onsite!"

"You're there at the family's house?"

"I'm looking at the trickle of blood that ran out the front door and down the steps."

"Jesus!" Troy said. "Did you go inside and see the eight bodies?"

There was a pause. Troy could sense Cate was choking up. He could hear it in her breathing. As she fought back the emotions that momentarily overwhelmed her, she replied, "No, they are not letting many people in. Everyone who comes out looks ashen. They all remark on how they have seen nothing like it in all their years of service."

"Dad said it was horrific, two adults and six children," Troy said.

Cate's emotion switched from grief to anger in a moment as she spoke, "These monsters used hatchets...hatchets for God's sake...they chopped up people. Little kids. What kind of sick bastards kill little kids? What the hell is wrong with society today?" The raw emotion and anger in her voice was unlike anything Troy had ever heard.

He knew no words could console her. "The world is filled with some sickos, Cate, that's for sure. When we work for the Bureau, we'll do our best to see that justice is served and those that are wronged get made whole."

Their conversation continued for a few minutes before Cate said she had to go. "They are sending out some more searchers to look for the perpetrators. They found multiple bloody footprints leading into the woods. These idiots were stupid enough to walk through the blood and leave a trail showing which way they escaped. A massive manhunt is about to get underway, officers from all over the place converged here. In fact, I saw Sheriff Barnett and a few of the deputies from Drexel a few minutes ago."

"I saw I had a missed call from him as well. Better call him back now. Be safe Cate. Love you."

"Love you too, babe. I'll call when I can."

⚬

Next, Troy called Sheriff Barnett, the call proved to be brief but informative.

"Officer Hayden is in charge while I'm here, Troy," the sheriff said.

"Donny's a good guy," replied Troy. "Drexel's in good hands."

"I know," said the sheriff. "But he's on his own, I would feel better if you could help keep an eye on things, Troy. We don't know who did this or where they are now, and Drexel is only 30 minutes away."

"I'll be glad to help," Troy said. "I'm catching up with Paul Brighton in a little while."

"You have that badge I dropped off yesterday, right?"

"Yes, sir."

"Well, consider yourself officially deputized," the sheriff said. "You're armed, right?"

"You know me, sheriff, I always roll heavy."

"That's what I like to hear. Bring an extra gun for your buddy Paul since you're meeting up with him. He can go on patrol with you."

"I don't think Paul can hit the broadside of a barn, sheriff."

"Neither can half the criminals," he replied, "That's why they spray and pray."

"Copy that, sir."

"I'll call you late tonight when I head back to Drexel," the sheriff said.

Next, Troy placed a call to Paul. They discussed what had happened and how Paul had even been roped into the local police force. "Great," he replied, "I'm a wonderful shot with a pistol," he said with full sincerity.

Troy just laughed as he changed subjects, "Any activity at the place?"

"Yes, I have the live feed up. In fact, and since you called, it looks like they are headed out. That Muhammad guy is with them," Paul said.

"They're early tonight."

"Both trucks are hauling travel trailers as well. That's new. Something is going down, and I bet it will be tonight."

"Hmm," Troy said as a thought crossed his mind.

"What is it?" Paul asked.

"Just a hunch. I'll share it with you on the ride to Burton State Park. Leaving my house now, and I'll pick you up in ten minutes. Coming with an assload of weapons and ammo."

"You prepping for Armageddon?"

"Hopefully not, just better to be safe than sorry," Troy said as he hung up and rushed into the house to get what he needed.

Chapter Sixty-Two

33,000 FEET OVER BLACKSBURG, VA

Matt rubbed his hand over the expensive Italian leather seat. Smooth to his touch, he reclined the chair back and let out an audible sigh as he looked over at the man who sat on his left. "I could get used to flying like this, buddy. Not sure I can ever go back to flying on a commercial bus."

Pat nodded in agreement, "I hear you, Matt. This is the only way to travel."

"Only one step up from this mode of transportation."

"What's that?" Pat asked.

"Air Force One!" Matt exclaimed.

"Yeah right. Dream on, buddy. The director sure knows how to travel in style, and I sure appreciate the invitation. I feel like a VIP for once."

"Anytime, man."

"You think things will ever calm down?" Pat asked. "You've been burning the candles on both ends for a while."

"Never know, there is always so much going on in the world. Hope I get a few quiet weeks though. I'm seriously thinking of taking a vacation. Maybe I'll take Amy on that second honeymoon I've promised her for years now. Bora Bora or Tahiti sounds good."

"No doubt."

"Any more chatter about those EMP threats?"

"Nothing new, but we hear rumors of nuclear and biological threats often."

"In some ways it's a crazy world to be raising kids," Matt said as he looked out the window to his right and the moonlight sea of clouds that seemed endless.

"I agree, but I'm a glass half full kind of guy. Even though the world has its fair share of wackos, it's an exciting time to be alive. Technology brings many things to your fingertips. Think about it, you'll be across the country in a half dozen hours. It used to take pioneers many months to cross the nation, and the chance of dying along the way was astronomically high."

"You're right, of course," Matt said. "I guess after the last six plus months I'm tired and part of me thinks the world has gone to hell in a handbasket. Mankind feels like it's lost its way, and society is teetering on the edge of a deep abyss."

Pat began to interject when the pilot came over the intercom.

"Making our descent to Oak Ridge, gentlemen. We should be on the ground in twenty minutes," the pilot said.

Pat gathered his belongings.

Matt placed a folder back into his carry-on bag when suddenly his eye caught the large manila folder he still had not opened. He fished it out and looked at it, memories of Preston flooded his mind.

Pat looked over and saw his smile. "What's that?"

"Something that was part of Preston's estate. It was given to me by the attorney after he died."

"Oh yeah? And what's in it?"

"No clue, I never opened it. Every time I thought about opening it, I got distracted."

"Well, rip open that bad boy," Pat said. "Maybe it's the deed to a South Pacific island," he said with a laugh. "You might own Bora Bora."

"Ya right, forget about the deed to an exotic island, it's probably just a tax bill," Matt replied in a joking tone. He tore open the envelope and removed four pieces of paper. "That's odd," he said, "It looks like a handwritten letter. It's Preston's handwriting, that's for sure." Matt looked through the four pages. "The last page is some sort of hand-drawn map. This is quite peculiar."

"What does it say?" Pat asked.

"Let me read it," Matt said. As he read the letter, his expression changed. A startled look soon was replaced by a shocked expression.

Pat was on the edge of his seat. He could tell from his friend's expressions that the handwritten note must be something remarkable. He didn't interrupt but patiently waited for Matt to look up. It took several minutes.

When Matt looked up, the blood drained from his face. Visibly shaken as he made eye contact with Pat and uttered a single word. "Damn!"

"Is damn good or damn bad?"

"Read the damn letter yourself and you tell me," Matt stated as he handed the letter over. His hands shook noticeably as he held out the pages. Matt lowered his head into his hands, not able to grasp the reality of what he had just read. When he looked up after several minutes, Pat glanced back at him with a similar expression.

"I don't think damn is a strong enough word for what I just read," Pat said.

"Tell me about it," Matt said. "I've known Preston for many years. He may have been a politician, but I believe he was the only honest one I ever met. He told some stories that sounded like whoppers, but I know for a fact every one of them was true. If he wrote me this letter to tell me about The Zechariah Option, then it must be real."

"I can't believe there has been a nuclear bomb hidden in an old mine shaft in your hometown for the past 40 years!"

"Neither can I."

"What are you going to do," Pat asked.

"I don't think I have a choice; I have to go home and see if I can find it." Matt's mind raced as he suddenly connected the dots. Knowing what Muhammad Jarah had taken from Aaron Ryker, he felt sick to his stomach. What if Jarah could find the weapon? What would he do with it? His mind went in every direction at once.

He quickly told Pat his fears as the plane made its final approach.

Suddenly Pat yelled towards the cockpit, "Mike!" he screamed.

The co-pilot opened the door when he heard the startled yell. "What is it, Mr. O'Shea?"

"Change of plans, Mike. Tell Carl we need to get to Drexel as fast as possible."

"But we're minutes from being on the ground sir, you're almost home," Mike said.

"Home will have to wait," Pat replied.

"You sure?" Matt asked as he placed his hand on Pat's shoulder.

"Yes, I'm sure."

The co-pilot looked at Matt who nodded in affirmation.

"You heard him Carl, fly it like you stole it," Matt said.

For the next four hours, the two men talked endlessly about The Zechariah Option, the letter, and what it all meant.

Pat shook his head. "I'm no theologian, but I never thought the good book even hinted at the possibility of nuclear weapons."

"When you read the verse in Zechariah, it says their flesh will rot, their eyes will rot in their sockets, and their tongue will rot in their mouth. It sure sounds like something intense. I guess that could result from a nuclear weapon."

"Sure, I guess," Pat said.

"Years ago, I used to go to a Bible study at our church back in Drexel, before my job kept me on the road so much. I know there are cryptic references in the books of Ezekiel and Revelation. Some people say they prove nuclear weapons will be used in the end times. I really never gave too much thought to it, honestly."

Pat held up the handwritten pages from Preston, "Bet you do now!"

"Yes, a bit," Matt said as he shook his head.

After they talked themselves in circles about what could happen and more importantly, what to do next they both agreed they would involve no one else until they knew more.

"Adventure seems to be drawn to you, Matt."

"Truth be told, I just want a quiet place to rest my head for a while."

"No rest for the weary."

"Apparently not until I lay my head down for good," Matt added.

Chapter Sixty-Three

The Harding Mine

Troy and Paul watched the men unload a couple of vehicles from the small trailers each truck pulled. The men made several trips up and down the mountain and repeatedly disappeared into the mineshaft only to reemerge a little while later.

"That vehicle they unloaded looks like a four-wheeler, but it has been heavily modified," Troy said in a low voice.

"What about the other one?" asked Paul.

"Looks like some sort of engine hoist, but it's on wheels."

"Don't see how they would use something like that to transport a load of gold?"

"They wouldn't," Troy agreed. "Something else is going on here, and I'm pretty sure it has nothing to do with gold. That other night when we made our way to the vault door, I wish we could have seen inside that hole they drilled. I bet we wouldn't have seen an ounce of gold."

"Then what's in there?"

Troy frowned, "My gut says some sort of weapon."

"A weapon!" Paul exclaimed. "What type of weapon would be up here buried in an old, abandoned gold mine?"

"Because those guys are terrorists, I would venture to say it's something powerful, a weapon we don't want them to get their hands on," Troy said.

"You mean nuclear?"

Troy shrugged, "Maybe, but I hope to God it's not."

"What are you thinking?" Paul asked.

"I need to see what it is they are trying to remove and somehow get inside that mine shaft."

"Are you crazy?"

Troy smirked, "Like a fox."

Paul sighed. "They'll catch you."

"I'll only go in when they come out, but I need to find a way inside the shaft." Troy removed the earpieces and the two-way radios from his backpack. "We'll need these. The range is two miles, which should be plenty. Once I get inside the shaft, they may not work as well, but this is how we'll have to keep in contact."

"They worked the other night when we tested them. You were near the vault door, and I heard you fine," Paul said.

"Yes, but you were near the entrance, which is not so far away."

"I'll just get closer."

"Can't risk it. If I get caught, you'll need to hightail it into town and contact the sheriff. Get some reinforcements."

For the next few minutes, Troy laid out a plan. Paul didn't like it, but Troy gave him no choice.

Troy wore a tactical vest. The vest held six magazines and one holster, which is where Troy snapped in his nine-millimeter Kimber pistol. While on his right hip he carried a Heckler and Koch .40 Cal handgun. Troy was an expert marksman with both weapons.

"You look ready for war," Paul said as he looked up and down at Troy.

"I'm not going near that mountain unless I'm ready for battle," Troy said as he walked away, "Wish me luck," he said over his shoulder as he headed toward the mine.

Ten minutes later, Troy was about 30 feet from the mine shaft entrance, a large boulder served as his cover. The hillside was littered with numerous boulders, some were small, others as large as a car. Paul served as his eyes and reported where the men were.

For 45 minutes, Troy stayed as still as he could, not making a sound. Finally, all the men had left the shaft, but before Troy could make a move, two of the men returned and went inside the entrance. It was a close call since Troy almost emerged from his hiding place a few seconds early.

Eventually, the last two men came out of the mine and headed down the mountainside where the others were gathered around the trucks. It appeared they were taking a break.

"All clear," Paul said over the radio, which fed into Troy's earpiece. "You have a clear path to the mine."

"Roger that," Troy spoke in a whisper, "If any of them turn back or head to the entrance tell me immediately."

"Understood," Paul said.

Troy left the boulder and successfully reached the opening of the mine shaft. He slipped on his night vision googles and rapidly descended the narrow corridor. Even though his surroundings had a greenish glow, Troy recalled most the details from earlier in the week when he and Paul had explored the tunnel.

Troy moved quickly through the shaft. As he got closer to the vault at the end, his pace quickened as well as his pulse. When he got within a few feet of the sharp left right before the vault door, the two-way radio came alive.

"Troy!" Paul yelled. "A few of the guys left the trucks, and it appears they are headed up the mountainside. You only have a few minutes before they arrive."

"Roger that," Troy acknowledged with no change in his voice. Troy turned the corner and saw the vault door ajar. Before it the modified four-wheeler, while just inside the vault was the thing that looked like an engine hoist.

Beyond the hoist, he saw what it was the men were after. It stopped him dead in his tracks. Troy knew without a doubt that the object before him was a very old nuclear weapon. Without thinking, he clicked his radio on and said,

"Damn, we're screwed. We need backup. I messed up big time and should have brought the cavalry from the get-go."

"What is it? What do you see down there?"

Troy was quiet for a moment before he responded. "The one thing in the world we don't want these nutjobs to get their hands on..."

Paul cut him off, "Well, those nutjobs are almost at the opening of the mine shaft."

"How many of them?"

"Three," Paul said. "What are you going to do?"

Troy knew where he needed to go. He turned and ran up the shaft as he replied to Paul, "I'm gonna get the hell out of here and call for some backup."

—◆◇◆—

In his right ear, Troy heard Paul say, "They just walked into the opening of the shaft, I hope you found a safe place to hide."

"Roger that," Troy said in barely a whisper, "I'm safe for now."

"Stay that way."

Troy had run as quickly and carefully as he could up the shaft to the spot where the cave in had occurred and was now in the parallel shaft. He continued along that tunnel until he was about twenty feet past the spot of the cave in.

He flipped up his night vision goggles and stayed crouched low in complete darkness.

A minute later he heard people approaching. He heard the Farsi roll off their tongues, and he saw a glimmer of light illuminate the tunnel further down from where he was.

As quietly as he could talk, he whispered into the two-way radio, "How about the others?"

Immediately Paul replied, "They are still at the base of the mountain. Only three men entered." It was silent for a moment before Paul added, "How are you getting out?"

"I'm walking right out the entrance," Troy said in a confident tone.

"Good luck with that."

Troy saw three beams of light now in the tunnel ahead of him. The men were having an animated conversation, Troy could pick up several of their words. He heard one of them say, "Less than two hours."

He assumed that was a reference to when they would have the nuclear weapon loaded and be gone.

Troy couldn't let that happen under any circumstances.

The beams of light grew dimmer as the men made their way around the cave-in part and were now back into the shaft that contained the vault. They would be close to the chamber by now.

Troy flipped down the night vision goggles and silently made his way twenty feet down to where the tunnel connected with the other mine shaft. Turning left, he made his way around the rubble and headed towards the entrance.

"I'm almost at the entrance. Is it still clear?" He asked Paul in a hushed tone.

"Yes," Paul said.

A few seconds later, Troy's head peeked out the tunnel, and he drew in a large gulp of fresh air.

CHAPTER SIXTY-FOUR

BOISE

The Gulfstream touched down after midnight, and the plane taxied to the private jet section on the northern end of the Boise Airport. Matt thanked the pilots and made a straight line for the parking garage, where he parked his government issued Tahoe.

Ten minutes later, he and Pat were on Interstate 84 headed west. Matt dialed Troy's number, but it went straight to voicemail. He decided not to call Amy. It was late, and he didn't want to wake her. He checked his voicemail, but there were no messages from Troy.

Pat watched as his friend gripped the steering wheel. "Does he plan on marrying Cate? She seems like quite the catch."

With a smile, Matt eased up on the steering wheel and replied, "Yes, he does, and yes, she is. In fact, Troy won't tell me when or how he plans to propose, but he already has the ring. It was my mother's diamond, and he had it placed in a new platinum setting for Cate. I figure he'll propose before they graduate. Those two are soul mates."

"Like you and Amy?"

"Absolutely. One day they will make Amy and I some cute-as-can-be grand-baby's."

"Grampa means gray hair old man," Pat said in a joking tone.

"Already got it," Matt said as he pointed to the streaks on the side of his head. "Having a boy who thinks he is invincible started my gray hairs a long time ago."

"Takes after you."

"The difference is I have some innate fear within me. Troy has none. That boy would certainly be the one to run into a burning building without a care in the world."

Pat changed the subject, "Are you sure you want to head up to the old mine tonight?"

"Yes," Mat said. "I'd like to look around tonight. Go back first thing in the morning with some equipment and see what we can find. The map Preston drew is specific. It should not be that difficult to find the right mineshaft." He looked over at Pat. "You ok to go there? I know it's been a long trip, and you sure as hell didn't expect to be in Boise tonight."

"Nonsense," Pat said. "I feel like a kid on a scavenger hunt and couldn't go to sleep right now if you drugged me. I'm all in, buddy. Let's try to find this thing and recover it before someone like Muhammad Jarah figures out where it's located. I know Preston's letter said The Zechariah Option was vague, but they've had that letter for over six months. I figure they've been searching like crazy for that nuclear device."

"I hate to think what they would do with it if they found it," Matt said.

Fifteen minutes later, Matt's cell phone rang. They were still about 35 minutes from Drexel. He made good time since his flashing lights were on, traveling 25 mph over the posted speed limit. Also, he knew State Highway 55 like the back of his hand since he traveled it five days a week on average.

Matt didn't recognize the incoming number, but it was pushing 1:00 AM local time, so he answered immediately. "Matt Evans," he said.

"Mr. Evans, thank God you answered," the scared voice on the other end said.

He knew the voice, and his body tensed. "Paul, is everything ok?" Matt feared there must be an issue with Troy.

"No, things are not ok," Paul said in quick gasps.

"Where's Troy? What's happened?"

Pat could only hear one end of the conversation from the passenger's side of the Tahoe, but he knew something appeared seriously wrong.

"Troy is safe for the moment, but he needs you now."

"Where?"

"He's at the old Harding gold mine just north of town, I left him there to come closer into town where I could get a cell signal."

Paul told Matt as much as he knew. Matt listened intently and never interrupted once.

Matt's considered the gravity of the moment as Paul spoke. He knew what had happened in Borden and that most law enforcement officers in the area were still there. When Paul finished, Matt told him to go to his house, he gave him a specific list of what he needed. He told Paul he would call Amy next so that she wouldn't accidentally shoot him when he showed up in the middle of the night.

On the third ring, a groggy Amy answered. Matt spoke quickly and told her the pertinent information. He told her Paul was on his way, and she handled the news better than he expected. His only request was that she not go to the mine. She reluctantly agreed after some intense prodding.

"You'll be my contact if all hell breaks loose. I love you, Amy."

"Bring our son home Matt, I love you too."

———— ◆◇◆ ————

As Matt hung up, he looked over to Pat, who spoke first, "They found it?"

Matt nodded and let out a deep sigh. "Appears so."

"How much time we have?"

"Not sure, but not enough."

Pat frowned, a concerned look clear on his face.

"Does the NNSA have a rapid response team?" Matt asked.

"Several," Pat said. "Closest one is outside Los Angeles. I'll call now, but I can't see how they would get to an area as remote as this in less than a few hours under any circumstances."

Pat dialed the pre-programmed number while Matt placed a call of his own.

It took four calls before Sheriff Barnett finally answered. He was headed back from Borden, and his cell signal kept cutting in and out. Matt gave him few specifics. The sheriff told Matt that several of his deputies were still in Borden. Only Officer Hayden was available. Matt told him where to meet and told him to come, *armed to the teeth*.

It was after 4:00 AM EST as Matt called the number he hoped to never dial in his over 20 years. After authenticating his code, the man on the other end simply said, "What do you need, Special Agent in Charge Evans."

"I need a response team," he replied.

"Where?"

Matt provided the man the location.

"Hostiles?" the man asked.

"Unclear, possibly at least a dozen," Matt said. "Maybe more."

"Armed?"

"Heavily."

"Intent?"

Matt was unsure if he should say the next part. After a moment passed, he decided the hell with it. "Possible WMD but I'm not onsite, so I don't have eyes on the device."

"Hold for a minute," the man replied. An extended pause occurred before the man asked Matt a single word, "Hot?"

He asked Matt for a coded word to know if what Agent Evans replied indicated his answer was given under duress.

Immediately Matt replied, "Comfortable." The reply given when you are making a request of your own free will.

Another moment passed. The man on the other end of the line analyzed the assets he had available. "You're in the middle of nowhere, sir. The tactical team will be at least 90 minutes out, and that is being generous. Will you be able to hold off the hostiles until then?"

"Guess I don't have a choice, do I," Matt replied.

"Not really, but how about local law enforcement?"

"Being assembled."

"This line is dedicated to you now, so call back with whatever you need. Good luck."

"I believe in fate, not luck," Matt said as he disconnected the line.

He looked over at Pat and tried to pull together a plan on the fly with the litany of unknowns that they would face.

Chapter Sixty-Five

Burton State Park

The first thing Matt Evans did when he reached Troy was put his arms around him and give a hard squeeze. Matt never hid his affection from Troy.

"Are you ok?" He asked as he let Troy free from his embrace.

Troy lowered his gaze and replied, "Yes, sir," in a slightly muffled tone.

"What is it?"

Troy made eye contact with his dad before he said, "I made a mistake and tried to be a cowboy. When I should've come clean from the get-go, and maybe this wouldn't be happening."

"Nonsense," Matt said as he hugged his son again. "You did the same thing I would have done. You're a regular chip off the old block."

"I should have told you about Muhammad Jarah," Troy said.

"Learn from the past but live in the present, son. Don't dwell on something you can't change. The past is written, but the future is an open book."

Troy looked around at the men assembled. "Is this everyone?" He asked as his gaze moved from his dad and Pat. Then to Paul, who stood alongside the sheriff and two officers, who arrived right after his dad.

"For the moment," Matt said as he nodded. "The FBI and NNSA are sending tactical teams, but unfortunately for us, neither team will arrive for at least 45 more minutes."

"We don't have that long," Troy said with a concerned look on his face. "The man that Paul works with at Siberdrive pulled up with the large white box truck less than twenty minutes ago. It's parked at the base of the mountain. They have some sort of custom four-wheeler that I believe they are using to move the device. If we don't stop them now, I'm pretty sure they will have it loaded and will be in the wind before anyone arrives."

Matt shook his head and made eye contact with each of the men before him. In less than a minute, he spelled out the plan that he and Pat had discussed on the drive. "Three teams of two men will be our best approach. We spread out and try to take out as many of them as we can. Troy and I will take the center position, Pat and Officer Hayden will flank us to the right, while sheriff, you and Officer Nelson on our left."

"Wait, what do I do?" Paul asked.

"You'll be on our six and move between the three of us and keep us supplied. If any team loses a member, you'll fill in."

"Our six?"

"Behind us, Sherlock," Troy said.

Paul gulped hard as the reality of the moment sank in, "You got it," he said in almost a whisper.

"What if they try to detonate the weapon when the shooting begins?" The sheriff asked.

"I don't think they will be able to," Pat said. "The weapons from the 1960's didn't just have a button to push in order to detonate."

"But..." Officer Hayden said.

"And if they do," Matt said as he crossed himself. "We'll all meet our maker tonight. Better us and the brave people of Drexel than several million citizens in New York or Washington."

"Jesus!" Paul said as his eyes bulged.

"We want Jesus on our side, Paul," Troy said.

"In fact, bow your heads, gentlemen." Matt said as he lowered his own. "We will need some divine intervention tonight if we're to make it out alive."

They all did as instructed.

Matt said a quick prayer. "God, keep us safe tonight, help us acquire our targets and shoot straight. If any of us fall, take mercy upon our humble souls ... Amen!"

The men surrounding him all replied, "Amen," in somber tones. The harsh reality of the situation had set in.

"Ok fellas, let's do this. Eliminate these hostiles and safeguard that weapon at all costs," Matt said.

The men paired up while Paul followed a few paces behind.

Matt placed his arm around his son's shoulder, and they walked through the woods toward the mine.

"You ready for this, son?" Matt said.

"I think so, Pops," Troy replied. "As ready as I'll ever be thanks to everything you taught me."

As they walked, Matt looked into his son's eyes and spoke in a soft yet direct tone, "Taking a life is never easy, son. Pulling the trigger is the simple part. It's after the pull when your true character is revealed."

"These men wish us harm. They'll kill innocent lives with that weapon. Correct?"

"I believe so," Matt said. "If they have their way, millions might perish."

"Then our cause is just."

"It is."

"Then we can't fail. It's as cut and dry as that. We must meet this challenge head on and prevail."

Matt nodded. "That's right."

"And if we capture one of them, what do we do?"

"We need to figure out what their plan is. They must have some attack planned with this nuke, so we need to know what it is."

"How? I mean, what do we do if they won't talk?"

"Use your imagination and whatever you have available to persuade them."

"I won't let you down, Pops."

"You never have Troy. One more thing…"

Troy's eyebrow arched upward, "Yes sir?" he questioned.

"When the time comes to pull that trigger…don't hesitate, and above all don't miss!"

Troy replied in a matter-of-fact tone, "I won't."

They finished the walk in relative silence while Matt glanced over at his son several times. Pride filled his heart seeing the man Troy had become. In silence, he said a prayer and asked that God would spare his son. *And if You must take one of us, I beg of you to take me instead*, he said silently.

About a hundred yards from the base of the mountain, Matt raised his hand and motioned downward. The men got down low to assess the situation. After looking around for a minute and in hushed tones, Matt pointed out that three of the men were down by the white box truck at the base of the mountain.

"Pat and Donny, I need you to take those three out on my signal. I see three more men just outside the opening to the mine shaft. That leaves possibly six men who must be inside. I can only assume they are moving the nuke. Troy and I, as well as the sheriff and Nelson, will lead the assault on those at the shaft entrance. After the men are eliminated at the truck, rejoin us up the mountain. Use the comms I handed out when you need to but otherwise try to maintain radio silence. Understood?"

Pat and Donny nodded as they quietly made their way towards the parked vehicles. Less than five minutes later, they were all in position.

Matt and Troy were crouched low behind two separate boulders about 30 feet from the entrance to the mine shaft. The sheriff and Nelson were in a similar position about 50 feet to their left on slightly higher ground. The number of hostiles standing outside of the shaft opening was now six, that meant possibly three men remained inside. One of them had to be Muhammad Jarah since he was not among the men outside or the ones waiting by the vehicles.

"Do we wait for all of them to come out or take them now?" Troy asked in a whisper.

Matt's mind was racing, "I don't want to shoot with that bomb out in the open. I think it's now or never, son!"

Chapter Sixty-Six

The Harding Mine

The modified four-wheeler worked better than expected. It carried the precious payload to within 20 feet of the opening of the mine. A few times they stopped to clear debris from the wheels, but it had otherwise been a smooth ride from the vault to the entrance.

Muhammad could now see the moonlight illuminating the exit from the subterranean world.

"Wait," he said to Zayan, who drove the vehicle. "I want to verify that we are clear before we bring the weapon out."

Zayan nodded but said nothing. An unknown fear gripped him. Next to him was one of Muhammad's trusted lieutenants, who had hardly muttered two words the entire time Zayan had been around him.

As Muhammad emerged from the shaft entrance, he took in a long drag of clean mountain air. It reminded him of Afghanistan in some ways. He walked over to the six men huddled next to the entrance and spoke.

⸻ ◦ ⸻

Matt and Troy exchanged affirmative nods as Muhammad emerged from the entrance. They both recognized him immediately. Matt mouthed the words "B-I-N-G-O," as he held up his right hand with all five fingers extended. He slowly lowered each finger till only his middle finger was extended. Matt quickly stepped out from behind the large boulder that granted him cover and pulled the trigger on his Glock 23 .40 caliber handgun.

His sight was directly on Muhammad's head, but just as he pulled the trigger another man stepped in front of Muhammad.

The gun recoiled, and the man who stood directly between him and Muhammad had his head blown partially off.

Troy shot at the man closest to him, and his round found its target. The remaining men dove for cover as more rounds flew towards them from Sheriff Barnett and Officer Nelson.

Down at the base of the mountain, Pat and Officer Hayden each had their weapons trained on two of the three men waiting around the vehicles. When the first crack of Matt's weapon was heard, they both fired, hitting their targets cleanly. As they quickly approached the vehicles, they checked the two men on the ground. They were both dead. One shot, one kill. The third man had vanished. Methodically, they searched in and around the vehicles but could not locate the third man.

The sound of bullets on the mountainside reminded them that others were in danger and that they needed to move immediately.

"What do we do?" Donny asked.

Pat shrugged slightly, "I guess we go help the others. Having someone on the run down here isn't good, but we can't stay here. We need to go help the others."

Donny nodded in agreement, and the two men quickly made their way up the side of the mountain away from the vehicles.

Fifty feet away on the hillside, Kadir lay as close to the ground as he could, his body obscured by several large sagebrush plants. He had no clue how he made it away from the vehicles without being spotted, but he silently thanked Allah for his deliverance.

Kadir didn't know what to do next. He could see that the two men had left the vehicles and climbed up the hillside toward the firefight. Kadir felt fear, but he was not a coward. He planned to see the mission completed successfully even if that meant forfeiting his own life. Once the two men were far enough up the mountainside, he pursued them. As he slowly followed them, he decided if either man slowed down, he would catch up and shoot them in the back.

Several miles away, Waleed watched from the back porch of his rental home. He was shocked when the muzzle flashes began. Although his binoculars were the best money could buy, he could not be sure what was taking place or how his men were faring against an unknown enemy. He tried to radio Kadir, but received no reply, only static came through on the channel when he tried to call out to his men. After a brief prayer to Allah, he watched the firefight intently. He felt slightly naked knowing his two trusted bodyguards were at the mine and not by his side. He knew there was nothing he could do but wait to hear from his men.

CHAPTER SIXTY-SEVEN

THE HARDING MINE

Unfortunately, neither Sheriff Barnett nor Officer Nelson stood a chance against the hardened fighters that opposed them.

Muhammad and two of the men moved to the right to get on higher ground. Once they reached cover, they zeroed in on the spot the bullets had been fired from. Muhammad had spent years of his life fighting in terrain just like this. It was second nature to move and dodge flying bullets all around him. Allah had always protected him, and he felt certain his fate would not allow him to die on some rugged mountain hillside in the middle of Idaho.

As Officer Nelson stepped out from behind the eight-foot-high boulder that shielded him to return fire, Muhammad placed the crosshairs on Nelson's head. Two quick retorts with his handgun, and the officer crumpled to the ground with fatal shots to his head.

———◆———

Sheriff Barnett watched Nelson go down and realized the men were hardened fighters, not a ragtag group with no marksmanship skills. After several more exchanges, he got lucky and struck one hostile in the shoulder. The man fell in agony. Although he had hit one of them, Roy knew he needed to fall back and re-group with Matt and the others with Nelson down.

He transferred his handgun to his left hand, turned and made a mad dash down the mountain to what he thought would be safety below. As he ran, he extended his arm behind him and squeezed the trigger as fast as his index finger could pull, emptying his magazine in seconds.

Just when he thought the bullets had stopped, two quick rounds cracked behind him. The first bullet hit him square in the back, knocking the wind out of him. A second later, the next bullet struck his collarbone as he tumbled down the hillside.

Three hundred yards away, Paul watched the events unfold through the night vision goggles he wore. He knew the sheriff was in trouble. Risking his own safety, he ran to the spot where Roy came to rest.

Paul crouched low to help the sheriff wrap his arms around his neck. Using his legs as leverage, Paul struggled to stand as he pulled the injured officer off the ground. Together in more of a shuffle than a walk, they made the arduous hike down the side of the hill to the safety of the tree line away from the gunfight.

⚬

Matt and Troy stood less than ten feet apart but used hand signals to communicate back and forth. The silent way of communicating was something Matt taught Troy at a very young age.

Troy moved closer to his dad and said he was going to get closer to the entrance. He knew two men were still inside with the nuclear weapon, and he wanted to secure the device before one of them did something to it. Matt nodded in agreement and kissed his son on the forehead. "Good luck, son," he said and squeezed his shoulder.

Moving quickly, Troy caught the attention of one hostile, who fired and missed wide to the right. As he ran full steam, Troy raised his weapon and fired three quick rounds at the man. Two of the rounds found their fatal mark.

Troy was now just inside the entrance. He squeezed between two large wooden beams that held up one side of the mine shaft. The thick timbers provided just enough room to keep him temporarily safe.

Inside, everything appeared quiet. Troy knew it was an illusion. Somewhere in there, two men waited for someone to approach. Enough moonlight came through the entrance to illuminate the first ten feet or so of the mine. Troy silently moved deeper into the mine, and about twenty feet from the entrance he came across the four-wheeler, along with the two unaccounted for men.

His right foot brushed against something, and he reached down and picked up a small stone about the size of a tennis ball. With an underhanded throw, he tossed the stone down the shaft. With a distinct clang, the stone bounced off the side of an object hidden in the shadows.

Someone crouched behind the vehicle, stood up and fired five shots towards the entrance. One of the errant shots hit the timber that sheltered Troy, and the splintered wood fragments flew out in every direction. The muzzle flash revealed the man's position. When the shooting stopped, Troy leaned away from the timber, raised his H&K .40 Cal and fired three quick rounds. Two in the chest, one in the head.

***

The dead man crumpled to the ground only a foot from Zayan, who crouched low.

Zayan froze, not sure what to do. As fear encompassed him on all sides, he felt the overwhelming urge to panic. Whoever entered the tunnel must be an expert marksman. Zayan felt certain he didn't stand a chance but would not meet Allah without a fight. With one hand he clutched his nine-millimeter pistol, and with the other hand he removed a bowie knife from his waistband. As he considered his options, he felt sure that stepping outside would mean certain death. He belly crawled slowly further into the shaft and away from the entrance.

***

Troy didn't have time to wait. He hated leaving his dad outside and needed to end this. Quietly, he slipped on his night vision goggles and looked down the tunnel.

It was difficult to see things, but twenty feet away he saw a body lying on the ground. It looked like one of his rounds blew half the man's face off. Next, he saw movement further down the tunnel. Someone appeared to be crawling away from the entrance, heading for the vault.

He made his way after the retreating man as quietly as possible. Troy extended his right hand downward; the handgun pointed directly at the slithering man. His left hand now held his serrated eight-inch Gerber hunting knife.

⸻◆⸻

Zayan heard movement very close. He quickly rolled over onto his back and raised his handgun. Before he could locate the source of the noise, a heavy foot kicked the weapon from his hand. Zayan attempted to stand, but a powerful hand gripped his left wrist, and a steel blade passed through his left arm between his elbow and wrist. Before he could call out in agony, a hand covered his mouth.

Zayan attempted to struggle, but two powerful punches to the face dispelled further attempts.

⸻◆⸻

Troy removed two zip cuffs from his back pocket and bound the man's hands and feet. He had captured someone alive. Now how would he make them speak?

An intense desire made Troy realize he needed to know what these men were planning to do with the nuclear weapon, and he needed to know immediately. Time was precious, and he only could think of one way in order to make the man talk. He sat on the man's chest as he began the interrogation.

Zayan tried to lift his body to push off the man who sat on his sternum, but he did not budge.

After a few seconds of struggle, the man grabbed Zayan by the throat and squeezed as his other hand covered his mouth. Zayan got the hint and stopped resisting.

The mysterious man shrouded in shadows spoke clearly. "I need to know what you were planning to do with the bomb?"

As the firm hand was removed from his mouth, Zayan attempted to call out for help. The hand back over his mouth instantly.

"Wrong answer," the man said as he thrust the Gerber knife under Zayan's clavicle.

Zayan attempted to scream out in pain, but his bellow was muffled by the man's hand. A few seconds later, the hand was replaced by a rag of some sort.

"Look, dude," the man said. "We can do this the easy way or the hard way. I'll be honest, though I don't have time for this. You gonna talk?"

Zayan shook his head, indicating no. The next two stab wounds were in each shoulder, the right and then the left. Zayan had never felt such intense pain in his life. His body quivered uncontrollably and screamed out for relief. No relief came from the pulsating throb shooting out from the stab wounds.

Troy knew the longer he took extracting information from this man, the greater adversity his father and the others faced outside. He had to speed things up.

Once Troy went for the man's belly, he got somewhere. The first stab to the abdomen convinced the man to talk. When he stopped providing details, Troy turned the knife clockwise. He imagined it had to be hell on earth for the man, but he didn't give a damn at that moment. He had an unquenchable desire to know what threat they faced.

Finally, the man recounted all he knew. As the full scope of the attack was revealed, Troy sat upon the man in a state of shock. He had no idea the country would be that vulnerable.

Troy had to tell his dad, and they must secure the weapon at all costs.

The man bled badly, and Troy felt to leave him lying there would be a death sentence. Feeling a degree of pity for the man, he eased him up and led him towards the entrance. Suddenly, the man stumbled and fell to his knees. As Troy looked down, he could just make out the man trying to remove a small caliber weapon from an ankle holster even though his wrists were still bound.

As the man drew the weapon and attempted to raise it, Troy had no choice but to fire one shot into the man's skull. It all happened so fast, and Troy was pissed he didn't examine the man thoroughly.

Outside, Pat and Donny were being hunted. They just didn't realize it yet.

About two-thirds of the way up the mountain, Kadir got close enough to take a shot. He could not allow the two men to join forces with the others and secure the weapon.

Kadir took aim at the man in the police uniform first. His first two shots struck the man directly in the back, which spun the man around. The next three shots finished him.

Officer Hayden died before his body hit the dusty ground.

Pat lunged for cover when the first two shots rang out. He saw Donny go down and then watched the kill shots. He could not tell where the shooter fired from but knew he could very well be the one dead on the ground instead of Donny.

For the next ten minutes, the two men played cat-and-mouse, ducking behind rock formations and exchanging gunfire. One of Pat's shots struck Kadir in the left forearm, but it was not serious, and Kadir controlled the bleeding by wrapping the wound tight.

Pat made a sudden dash from one boulder to another when Kadir got lucky and struck him with a bullet directly in the chest. The round hit the upper portion of the Kevlar vest which saved his life. The force of the round threw him off balance, and when he fell he came down hard against a boulder.

All went black.

Kadir watched the man go down, followed by complete stillness. Foolishly, he did not approach the body. Instead, he turned and made his way towards the mine entrance.

Chapter Sixty-Eight

The Harding Mine

Matt eliminated a man near the entrance as he heard a slew of bullets erupt from within the mine shaft. His heart sunk not knowing if Troy had fallen victim to any of those rounds. He cautiously approached the opening himself and sensed movement to his left. Matt dropped to the ground and rolled to his right, firing bullets in rapid succession, his quick motions took out another hostile.

As he cautiously stood up, a roundhouse kick struck him in the back and caused him to flail forward. Startled by the unexpected strike, his grip weakened and he dropped the weapon to the ground out of reach as he landed hard on his stomach. Matt turned over quickly to see Muhammad Jarah standing directly above him.

"Special Agent Matthew Evans, right?" Muhammad asked with a hiss in his voice. As he stood over Matt, he leveled a weapon at his chest.

"Muhammad, Jarah," Matt said, "You're a hard guy to find." As Matt said the words, he picked his head up off the dirt, and his gaze looked past Muhammad towards the opening of the mine shaft.

Muhammad saw the look and turned his head slightly to see what caught Matt's attention.

That was all the distraction Matt needed. With Muhammad directly above him, Matt swung his leg upward in a swift motion, connecting his hard sole boot with the groin.

Muhammad sucked in as the strike popped him square in the balls as an intense shot of pain permeated the region. A pain no man wants to experience, in a sensitive area they all try to protect. Instinctively, his hands moved towards the area struck as his entire body winced.

Matt used the diversion to reach up with an open palm and swat the gun out of Muhammad's hand. The slap dislodged the weapon from his grip as it skidded across the dirt, landing near Matt's own weapon.

Next, Matt quickly scrambled to his feet as Muhammad doubled over in a look of pain. With his balled fist, Matt struck the stunned man several times directly in the cheekbone.

Muhammad fell backwards as Matt jumped on top of him, delivering a series of vicious punches.

As Matt drew his hand back for another volley of strikes, an immense pain shot through his thigh. His eyes looked towards the source and saw Muhammad's hand encircled the hilt of a knife as he jabbed it further into Matt's soft tissue.

Matt screamed out as Muhammad twisted the knife in a counterclockwise motion. Blood poured from the wound as Matt grabbed Muhammad's hand to pull the blade from his flesh. He succeeded after a firm tug but dropped to his knees as he gripped the wound with both hands to apply pressure and stop the bleeding.

As he dealt with the wound he didn't realize Muhammad rolled away and slowly got to his feet behind him.

Pain still shot through Muhammad's groin as he crouched down below Matt, slid his hand under Matt's jaw and slid his arm all the way through. His hand grabbed his other bicep, and his free hand pushed Matt's head in a forward motion. He squeezed and pulled his shoulders back as he executed a perfect rear naked chokehold.

Matt tried to react, but with blood-covered hands he knew his options were pretty much nonexistent. This wasn't a sparring session with Troy where one of them could tap out. This was a life of death struggle, and Muhammad literally had the upper hand. With seconds Matt felt himself slipping into unconsciousness, he scratched Muhammad's arms, but it proved to be an effort in futility as the blackness of unconsciousness drew him into its all-encompassing grip.

The sound of a single bullet rang out from the shaft. Muhammad looked towards the entrance and sensed movement. He felt certain Matt Evans was unconscious or maybe even dead, so he let the man slump over. Muhammad shuffled over and retrieved his own weapon from the ground. Next, he hobbled towards the entrance to the mine shaft as pain continued to radiate from the kick to his groin area and the punches Matt delivered to his face.

——◄O►——

Troy carefully crept closer to the entrance as he felt the cool mountain air strike his face. He had heard no shots coming from outside for several minutes and wondered if his father was fine.

The cold feel of steel pressed against his neck as he took a step into the open air.

"Drop the weapon, boy," a voice said in heavily accented English.

Troy immediately let the gun fall to the ground at his feet.

"Step out into the moonlight," the voice commanded.

As Troy moved forward into the light, he could make out the face of the person who held a gun to his neck. "Muhammad Jarah," the words slipped off his tongue like a bitter taste.

"Troy Evans," Muhammad replied in an equally incensed tone. "It's been a while since we locked eyes in the lobby of the Waldorf."

"I'll never forget that moment," Troy said.

"Nor I. I knew at that instant you were an enemy and a formidable one at that. Just from the look in your eyes. You have killed many of my men tonight. Good strong fighters. I applaud your resolve. But it ends now."

"I know about the plan," Troy said, hoping to extend his life somehow as he planned a way to distract Muhammad and not get shot. "Zayan told me everything."

"What's that saying you American's have? Ah, that's right, *Dead Men Tell No Tales*."

"Where's my dad?"

"There," Muhammad cocked his head to the right.

Troy turned and saw his dad slumped over a few feet away. He moved towards his father, but Muhammad protested. "Don't do it. Take several steps back."

Troy listened and walked backwards away from Muhammad.

Muhammad pointed the weapon at Troy's skull as his finger applied pressure to the trigger. "Any last words?"

"No. Just a statement," Troy said as he sensed movement behind Muhammad. "When you take your last breath soon, don't expect to see 72 virgins greeting you in paradise."

"That's funny," Muhammad released pressure from the trigger and his mouth curled into a smirk. "I actually concur. The virgin myth is one of the dumber things some religious leaders pontificate to rile up young men for Allah's service. Even if it were true sounds like more work than eternal pleasure." Muhammad paused for a fraction of a second. "Goodbye, Troy. You failed in your mission."

As Muhammad pulled the trigger, his eyes noticed movement. A figure lunged through the air and absorbed the 15-gram slug of lead meant for Troy as the gun recoiled.

Matt Evans last drop of strength expended as he sacrificed himself for his son.

Muhammad pulled the trigger again, but the slide stayed back. Out of bullets, he dropped the magazine and reached for a fresh one, but before his hand could grab one, Troy reacted.

With no time to think, Troy removed the only weapon he had and pulled a knife from its sheath. In one fluid motion, he let it fly directly at Muhammad.

Muhammad dropped the gun as his hands involuntarily grabbed for his neck. The steel handle protruded from his windpipe while the tip of the blade lodged deep into his spinal cord. A fine mist of blood sprayed out before him. With his spine severed, death proved to be instantaneous.

Troy screamed out to his father, scooped him up and placed the limp head on his lap. Blood squirted onto both of them as Muhammad's round found an artery. Troy gripped the wound with both hands and applied pressure, trying to stem the flow of blood but knew in the end the action would be futile. His father had seconds, not minutes, before the loss of blood was too great and he would die in his arms.

Tears flowed from his eyes and landed on his father's face.

"Don't leave me, Dad," he said frantically as his words came out in frantic gasps.

Matt was still conscious, "Not by choice," he struggled to say as blood formed on the corner of his lips and flowed out of his mouth.

"I love you, Dad," Troy said between weeps.

"And I love you too, son," Matt's words came out in a hushed tone.

"Please. Don't go, Pops." Grief turned to rage as Troy felt his father's body slowly convulse. "I'm gonna kill these Islamic bastards, every fucking one of them!"

Matt subtly shook his head slightly. "Your very worst day in life is still an incredible gift." The words came out in only a faint whisper. "Don't squander your life. Seek justice, my son, but don't give yourself over to hate. Remember, vengeance is always the Lord's..." His voice trailed off as his eyes rolled back.

Pops was gone.

Troy sat there in a daze. His father's blood covered him. He pulled the lifeless body close to him as he wept uncontrollably.

⋅◆⋅

Then he heard a noise behind him approaching fast.

Chapter Sixty-Nine

Saint Alphonsus Trauma Center Boise, Idaho

8:00 AM MST

Three full days passed since the events at the Harding Gold Mine.

A half-dozen people were gathered around Troy as he lay in a hospital bed. No one knew when, or if he would wake up.

Troy's eyes felt like lead balloons. His head felt as if it had a cinder block lying directly on top of it. Yet, he could make out the surrounding voices. They were people he cared for, people who loved him unconditionally.

Fighting grogginess, Troy struggled as hard as he could to focus. He did not know how he had ended up in a hospital bed.

His mother was the first to sense movement and stroked his face affectionately as his eyes opened.

With a mouth as dry as sawdust, Troy's first words were, "Water, please?"

Cate approached and brought the cup close to his mouth. The cool water felt wonderful on his dry lips and tongue.

"How long have I been asleep?" He asked after a minute passed. "And where am I?"

"Three days," Cate said. "You're in Boise, at Saint Alphonsus."

"We thought we lost you," his mother added.

Nobody in the room knew what, if anything, Troy remembered from the events at the mine.

"Dad…" The name rolled off his tongue in a draw-out manner as he shifted in the bed and tried to sit up.

His mom gently pushed him back into the bed and cut him off, "Troy, your dad is…"

Troy interjected, "Dead. Yeah, I know, Mom." Tears flowed freely down his face.

Amy cried.

Troy continued between sobs, "I held him in my arms and watched him die. His blood covered me. He died saving me, Mom. Pops threw himself in front of the bullet meant for me."

After a few moments Troy asked, "Who else made it?"

Amy was a mess. She couldn't speak.

Cate choked back the words as she cried as well. "Paul was the only one who was unharmed physically. Mentally he's beat up pretty good. Paul pulled Sheriff Barnett to safety. Roy got shot several times, but he's here in the hospital recuperating on the third floor. Pat made it out as well. Although he was shot and knocked unconscious, the Kevlar jacket saved his life. Officers Nelson and Hayden weren't so fortunate and died during the firefight."

"What's the last thing you remember Troy," Cate asked.

It was all as clear as day to Troy. "I remember holding Pops, watched him die in my arms, helpless to do anything for him. I heard some noise behind me, stood up, and turned. Then, it all went black. What happened after that? How did I end up here?"

"Paul saw everything," Cate said as she squeezed his hand. "After you got up, two men approached and fired at you. While you ran for cover, you returned fire. Paul said you stepped behind a large rock to shield you from their bullets, but you walked backwards a few steps as the men approached. You lost your footing and fell backwards. It was at least 25 feet straight down. When Paul arrived, you were unconscious. He left you where you lay. The doctors said that decision might have prevented a serious spinal injury. In fact, you're lucky just to be alive after the fall you took.

"I don't feel lucky," Troy said, as an angry expression spread over his face.

"You are," Cate said.

"The authorities secured the nuke after I fell?"

Cate looked at him and then looked away suddenly. Unsure what to tell him.

"The nuke," Troy said in a louder voice. "The tactical teams from the FBI or NNSA that arrived retrieved it, right?" He suddenly became irritated when no one answered him.

Cate looked into his icy eyes but said nothing.

Troy grabbed Cate's wrist. "The nuke, where the hell is the nuke?"

She bit her lip at first and then said, "It's gone. The two remaining terrorists left with it. They shot at Paul, and he wasn't unable to stop them."

"My God," Troy uttered.

"But it's ok sweetie," Amy said as he held his other hand. "They know where it is. An operation is going on right now to recover it."

Troy looked from his mom and then back to Cate, "Is Pat involved in the recovery?" he asked.

"Yes, of course," Cate replied.

"I need to talk to him now! He needs all the facts."

"Are you sure that's a good idea?" Amy asked.

"Get him on the phone NOW! It's urgent." Troy screamed the words as his tone shifted dramatically.

Troy was not acting like himself. Both his mom, Amy, and Cate sensed that a very different Troy had awoke from the one they knew and loved so dearly. Neither one knew if it was the head trauma or losing his dad. Maybe a little bit of both.

"Ok," Cate said. She dialed the number, and Pat answered on the third ring.

Everyone in the room could only hear one side of the conversation.

Troy's awake, Cate said.

Yes, he's talking.

He's ok, but upset.

Said he needs to speak with you. Says it's urgent.

"Ok, here he is,"

Cate handed the phone over to Troy.

"You ok buddy?" Pat asked.

"What do you think," Troy said in a sarcastic tone. "Do you guys have eyes on the nuke?"

"Not yet," Pat said. "But we know where it is. A mission just launched to take care of the threat."

Troy tilted his head as his eyes darted back and forth. "Where are you?"

"Los Angeles. The FBI has an operations center here, the NNSA is working with them and various government agencies."

"Los Angeles?" Troy asked in a bewildered tone. "LA wasn't the target. You should be on the East Coast."

"The East Coast? Troy, the nuke is on an oil platform in the Gulf of Mexico. The remaining men from Muhammad's group are planning to load it onto a missile and explode it 100 miles over Lebanon, Kansas, the geographic center of the United States. They're planning on using the EMP blast at that altitude to destroy our entire electrical grid. Throw us back to what life was like in the 600's."

"Like hell they are!" Troy said.

"Troy, I know you took a hard fall, but..."

"Where did you get your intel?" Troy asked it in a way that an adult might scold a misbehaving child.

"NSA picked up some chatter, and we had an anonymous source fill in some gaps. The agencies involved in the recovery feel extremely confident that the missile is on an abandoned oil rig in the Gulf. I'm even looking at satellite photos that show a missile that will be operation within the next few hours. We're taking the entire platform out in less than 30 minutes."

"Your intel's wrong, Pat."

"Says who?"

"Me," Troy answered tersely.

"Look, Troy, I know the loss of your dad..."

Troy cut him off, "Listen to me, Pat. You hit that oil rig and all you will destroy is a clever decoy. Muhammad's group wants you to hit the platform, but the actual target is on the East Coast. You're right, they intend to use the EMP, but it's not being launched with a missile. They are using a balloon. One of those big ass ones they to carry objects high into the atmosphere. Like a weather balloon, only bigger because it has to carry the weapon."

"And you know this how?"

"Because the guy in the mineshaft told me."

Pat became frustrated. "What guy?"

"One of the terrorists. He worked with another guy at Siberdrive named Kadir. The two of them claimed to be British citizens, but they were in town to locate the nuke, that was all. He spilled the beans. Told me all about the decoy site in the Gulf and how the actual launch site is a farm in Pennsylvania."

"And he volunteered this information to you?"

"He didn't volunteer jack shit," Troy said. "The eight-inch hunting knife I twisted inside his gut made him do all the talking."

Amy and Cate recoiled as Troy talked. Neither one of them could believe the words coming out of his mouth. They bore no resemblance to the Troy they both knew and loved.

"Look, Troy, I wish I could believe you, but it just doesn't add up. After this is all over, and we take out that oil rig and secure the nuke, I'm coming to see you. You can tell me everything that occurred, but for now I really must go."

Troy had one last card to play. "Do you know the company that leased the oil rig?"

"We do," Pat said. "Why?"

"So do I," Troy answered.

Pat sat to the right of Marty Thomas, the Director of the FBI, who shrugged his shoulders. *None of what Troy said made any sense,* Pat thought. *Troy couldn't have known any of the details.* "That's not possible," Pat said.

A moment passed, and then Troy calmly said, "M.K.Charlotte, LLC. Opened in Nassau, Bahamas."

In Los Angeles, Pat looked down at the file that lay before him. His mouth dropped open. The call had been on speakerphone. Next to him, the director shook his head in disbelief.

"Damn!" The director replied out loud.

"You still think I'm just some stupid kid with head trauma?" Troy asked angrily. "I know their plan, and it's about damn time you took me seriously and listened to what I have to say if you want to protect our nation."

The director spoke first. "Troy, this is FBI Director Thomas, and we're coming to you. All of us will be in Boise within the hour!"

Pat ended the call. "Shit just got even more real, gentlemen."

The assistant director sat next to his boss. "And what about the platform, Mr. Director?"

"Take it out anyway. Hit it with everything we have just to be safe, but Troy must be telling the truth. There is no way he could know these details unless he extracted information from one of the men at the mine."

"And if the kid is really delusional?"

"I'm hedging my bets that he's not," the director said.

Back in Boise, Troy pulled the sensors off his chest with his free hand and then yanked the IV out of his arm as he stood up to the shock and horror of everyone in the room.

"What do you think you are doing?" Cate asked in a bewildered tone.

Troy looked at her and frowned, "I can't lie around here, you heard them, the director is on his way."

A doctor entered the room and tried to prevent Troy from walking across the room, which was a futile endeavor. "You can't leave in your condition, son."

"Look, Doc," Troy said "You can either get out of my way or you'll be the one needing pain medicine."

The doctor retreated a few steps.

"Good choice. Now where the hell are my clothes?"

CHAPTER SEVENTY

BETHLEHEM, PENNSYLVANIA

Kadir stood on the back porch of the farmhouse and put his hands together to blow warm air into them as a stiff breeze blew from the west. His mind drifted back over the last few stress induced days.

The long drive across the country with a nuclear weapon frayed his nerves. The sight of any police officer on the side of the road put his heart into overdrive. After he left the mine, Kadir knew it would only be a matter of time before someone caught them driving the conspicuous white box truck. Fifty miles outside of Drexel, he secured an alternate vehicle and found a secluded spot to move the weapon from the box truck to the other vehicle. Fortunately, he and the other man who survived the onslaught could use the specialized lifting equipment to transfer the weapon to the Ford F350 4X4. The truck had a hard bed cover, which concealed the weapon perfectly.

The drive proved arduous, over 2,416 miles, which took them over forty hours with stops. They took turns sleeping in the passenger seat. The only time they turned off the truck in order to get gas.

Waleed arrived at the farmhouse outside of Bethlehem, Pennsylvania, before Kadir arrived.

When Kadir pulled up to the farmhouse, one of Waleed's men instructed him to park the truck near the dilapidated red barn in the pasture. With the help of Dr. Ghazini, they unloaded the weapon inside the barn.

Waleed greeted him with a hug and a kiss on the cheek. "You arrived safely and delivered Allah a gift!"

Kadir let out a tired sigh, "I feel like I failed you in Drexel."

"Failed? How so?" Waleed asked.

"We were almost overrun. I don't know how they found us, but they did. And they almost thwarted our plan. It was only by sheer luck the two of us survived and recovered the nuke."

"No luck involved," Waleed said as he moved his arm upward. "It was the will of the prophet."

Kadir shrugged but said nothing in response.

"Come now, you are tired and need to rest. Preparations are being made regarding the nuke. There is nothing else for you to do. In one day's time, the great day will be upon us."

"My job is done?"

"Almost," Waleed said with a warm smile, "One last task I require of you."

"Anything."

"I have a great honor before you," Waleed said as he patted Kadir's shoulder. "You will be the one to stand here on this very porch and watch the weapon rise into the air. You, and only you, will hold the controller that can detonate the weapon if something goes wrong."

"I'm to be a martyr after all?"

"Yes. This is a great honor."

"The highest of honors," Kadir lowered his head. "Allah will welcome me into paradise with open arms."

Waleed nodded. "With arms wide open, my friend. Allah's peace and blessings will be upon you at your time of sacrifice." Waleed walked over, hugged the man who had served him faithfully for many years and kissed him on each cheek before he turned and walked towards the waiting helicopter.

⸺◆⸺

Later that day, Kadir stared out at the lush field before him.

Waleed's helicopter took off thirty minutes before. By now he should be on his private jet and beginning his journey away from the United States with its impending nuclear fallout and catastrophic attack on the electrical grid.

The weather balloon rose from the ground in the distance before Kadir. As the balloon cleared the trees, it looked majestic ascending towards the sky.

As he watched the balloon, the silver box dangled below and reflected rays of sunlight.

Just then, Kadir heard a helicopter in the distance. He wondered if Waleed had returned? Had he decided to stay and perish as well? Or had he changed his mind and sent the helicopter to remove Kadir from harm's way when the weapon exploded?

As the sound got closer, he looked over his right shoulder, believing he could see the helicopter at any moment.

The helicopter sound grew louder. Kadir turned his head between the rising balloon and its magnificent payload and the sound of the approaching aircraft.

As he turned to the right one last time, he saw a large helicopter that had just cleared the trees. His stomach muscles tightened as his gaze focused on the quickly approaching machine.

Chapter Seventy-One

Bethlehem

The flight from Boise to the East Coast felt intense as Troy glanced over at the person who sat across the aisle from him, the director of the FBI.

Troy's first flight on a private jet felt bittersweet as he realized somewhere over the mid-west the director's plane was the last aircraft his father ever flew on. He fought back the strong desire to break down and cry as emotions overwhelmed him. Troy rubbed his fingers along the Italian leather seat and wondered if the seat he now found himself is where his dad sat a handful of nights before. Something inside told him it was, or maybe that desire happened to be a wish.

Troy extracted valuable information from Zayan inside the tunnel in only a few brief minutes, but it wasn't like he gave Troy the address to the farm where they planned to launch the weapon. Tracking down the correct plot of earth required good old fashion investigative work, and fortunately, the United States has the most skilled investigators money could buy.

Troy provided everything he knew as soon as he boarded the plane, and with that information, entire floors of analysts at both Fort Meade and Langley got to work.

Within 60 minutes, forensic analysts discovered that the same day Kadir formed the M.K.Charlotte LLC in the Bahamas, several other LLC's were also created at the same financial institution. The entity Shadow Lab LLC discretely bought an old farm on several hundred acres outside of Bethlehem, Pennsylvania.

Within a few hours, the data gathered by the teams of analysts backed up what Troy explained, and the director of the FBI Director believed the intel he gathered in the tunnel was more likely accurate than not.

The small farm in rural Pennsylvania got its own satellite re-tasked to watch everything happening onsite. The images provided by the satellite appeared troubling to say the least.

When the director's flight landed outside of Philadelphia, a US Navy SEALs Team met them on the tarmac. A quick discussion ensued before the men climbed aboard the helicopter.

The team commander bristled at the idea that civilians would board the Blackhawk helicopter. "No offense, Director Thomas but the kid and the NNSA guy stay put. The chopper is already at capacity with my guys."

"Take two of your men off because they're both going," the Director said in a terse tone.

"Sorry, sir, no disrespect meant, but I don't report to you."

"No," the authoritative voice said from behind all of them, "You report to me, and I say the kid and Pat O'Shea go. You got a problem with that, commander?"

It was a rare sight, but the Commander had a genuine surprised look upon his face as he turned and made eye contact with the man who spoke. He replied, "No, Mr. Secretary, I don't anymore."

"Good," the Secretary of Defense replied as he now stood between Troy and Pat. As he looked at Troy, he lowered his head slightly, "I'm sorry for your loss, Troy, everyone who had the honor of knowing your father respected him."

"Thank you, sir," Troy said.

"If it weren't for your bravery, we wouldn't be here. It's only fitting that you be with the team that gives these terrorists hell and prevents the end of our way of life."

Troy thanked the secretary and then looked over to the director. "Do they have the rifle I requested?"

One of the special agents handed Troy the Remington Model .308. Troy smiled as he looked it over. It had been the first time he smiled all day.

Pat stood next to Troy and patted him on the shoulder, "Climb in, son," he said as he pointed to the open Blackhawk door. "I'll follow you."

They didn't have a moment to spare.

The flight time from outside Philadelphia to Bethlehem was under twenty minutes. Real time intel came in, and they all knew the balloon was prepped to launch within minutes.

Troy sensed the eyes of the frogman inside the helicopter directed at him, and he felt out of place in such a small, enclosed space with the group of distinguished military warriors. However, as they got closer to the farm, a sense of peace radiated from within, even as the aircraft bounced up and down slightly from slight turbulence.

"It's just lifted off," the commander over the comms. Everyone inside the helicopter nodded.

He continued, "Satellite feeds indicate there is a man on the back porch watching the ascent, and he is holding something in his right hand. It may be a manual detonation device, or it could simply be his phone. Only God knows, but once we clear the trees on our approach, that man needs to be eliminated."

The commander tapped his best marksman on the shoulder, "Mike, you smoke him. Understood?"

Mike got his rifle in place and nodded, "He's all mine, commander."

"What do we do now that the balloon has launched?" Troy asked.

"We improvise," the commander said.

"There will probably be an altitude device on the bomb," Pat said. "So even if we shoot the guy on the porch, we can't let that balloon get into the atmosphere or possibly millions of people will die."

"We'll fly this damn bird into the balloon and sacrifice our lives if we have to," the commander said in a monotone voice.

Kadir's body stiffened, and his insides felt absolute terror as he realized that the helicopter hovering overhead was not Waleed's. He knew the only choice was to use the failsafe and blow the nuke. Their plan would fail after all, and only tens of thousands would die in the inferno about to rain down instead of countless millions.

⸺◆⸺

Before the finger could move to the override button, Mike fired a single round from far overhead. The man's head who stood on the porch exploded like a melon as the device he helf fell harmlessly to the ground.

In the field, two of the men fleeing towards the large red barn shot wildly at the helicopter.

Mike didn't miss a beat; he pivoted his body like a machine and put a bead on the first man's head. As he inhaled and held the breath, he fired and the man dropped instantly. The second man continued to fire, and Mike drilled him as well with a shot to the temple. A third man further behind the others turned to run. The fleeing man had no visible weapons, but Mike couldn't take the chance. So, like the other two men, he extinguished another life with a single bullet.

Dr. Ghazini crumpled to the ground in a twisted heap as the bullet blew off the back of his head.

With all the hostiles down, the commander instructed the pilot to go after the balloon.

The commander looked at Pat as they made the rapid ascent, every man's ears popping immediately. "If we shoot down the balloon and the missile hits the ground, will it detonate?"

"It's unlikely to do so," Pat said as he gave a half shrug.

"But you're not 100% sure?"

"No," Pat said. "To my knowledge, no one has ever shot a Cold War era nuke from a weather balloon and let it hit the ground."

The commander frowned. "That B-52 crashed near Goldsboro, North Carolina, in 1961, and the nuke in the payload didn't go off."

Pat nodded. "Right, but that wasn't a bomb hidden in a gold mine shaft for over thirty years in questionable condition."

"Shit," the commander said. "Guess we're about to find out, aren't we?"

Pat raised his eyebrows.

Troy cradled his .308 and raised the weapon as the helicopter ascended to match the elevation of the balloon. Troy put the crosshairs of his scope on the widest part of the balloon. "Pat, if I hit the balloon, it won't explode, right? It will just slow the ascent?"

"So, the expert I spoke with on the plane told me," Pat said.

The commander wasn't thrilled with letting a college kid take a shot at the balloon, but the authorization to do so came directly from the secretary of defense as they stood huddled on the tarmac in Philly. He in turn pulled Mike aside before they boarded the helicopter and whispered, *If the kid misses, you take the shot.*

Troy turned to the commander, "You have any sort of hooking mechanism on this helicopter?"

Perplexed, the commander replied, "Yes, we do. Why?"

"Time to go fishing," Troy said.

With a firm tone, the commander said, "Go for it, kid."

The pilot held back on the stick and got them to within 200 yards of the rising balloon.

Troy steadied himself as best he could, took dead aim at the center of the balloon and fired a single round.

The balloon didn't explode, which caused much relief to the men on board the helicopter. Yet, the round punctured a gaping hole, and the ascent slowed dramatically. The pilot expertly brought the Blackhawk's hook directly above the balloon, and several men who were harnessed to the side of the chopper caught the wires that connect the silver box to the balloon with the hook.

Troy and Mike pumped several more rounds into the balloon, which all but deflated.

Three minutes later, they gently lowered the weapon onto the ground as the SEALs team jumped out and formed a perimeter around the device. Everyone stayed around the weapon and awaited the nuclear retrieval team from the NNSA.

———◆○◆———

With the device secured, the team commander approached Troy, who stood before the nuke as it lay harmlessly on the ground.

The Commander extended his hand, and Troy shook it without question.

"Sorry I gave you shit on the tarmac, son. That was good shooting up there. You can serve with me anytime."

Troy had an enormous grin on his face as he replied, "I just might take you up on that offer, sir."

Chapter Seventy-Two

28,000 FEET IN THE AIR

Even at 28,000 feet in the air, Waleed had eyes on the ground. The closed-circuit cameras placed at the farm in Bethlehem picked up live video. The images of the launch of the nuclear weapon and subsequent failure were beamed through multiple secure, untraceable relays so that he could witness it all happening from a safe altitude moving away from the United States.

Once he saw Kadir gunned down, it was clear the day would not go as planned.

Waleed lowered his head into his hands and cursed the United States. He had the rear of the plane to himself. With the mission an absolute failure, he had no one to comfort him and only had his thoughts.

As the rage welled from within, he questioned what had gone wrong. Why had Allah given him the weapon and then allowed everything to fall apart?

For several minutes he stared at the scene unfolding on the monitor. When he witnessed Matt Evans son Troy emerging from the Blackhawk helicopter after it landed, his rage became verbal. Waleed grabbed the gold lamp that lay next to his suede upholstered seat and with his full force swung the heavy object into the monitor, splintering the screen into tiny glass shards. The violent outburst created quite a large noise that echoed throughout the fuselage.

The two bodyguards rushed in to see their boss visibly upset, his arm shaking.

"Is everything all right, Waleed?" The first one asked in a concerned voice.

Waleed glared back at him with eyes colored crimson as fire, "Damn the American's and especially damn Troy Evans. Mark my words...he will feel my wrath one day!"

Chapter Seventy-Three

Washington D.C.

Immediately after the events in Bethlehem, senior administration leadership brought Troy to Washington for a full debrief. He was forthright, telling the director and several other cabinet level officials every detail all the way back to when he first saw Muhammad Jarah at the Waldorf Astoria.

The President of the United States came to the J. Edgar Hoover Building to meet with Troy personally. Many discussions ensued over the coming days whether to go public with the events. Troy wanted no publicity or fame for what occurred. He only wanted his anonymity.

He got his wish.

The Zechariah Option remained a core secret, and the truth of what occurred was locked away. Very few people would know what really happened in Idaho or in Pennsylvania. The American public would have been shocked to know how close they came to the end of civilization as they knew it.

Troy returned home, at least in physical form, but everything was different after the events at the Harding mine. Not a day went by that he didn't think about his father.

Troy changed after the horrific events at the gold mine, and not necessarily for the better according to those closest to him. The sarcastic, sometimes immature, but always fun-loving Troy was replaced by someone much too serious. He followed the expanding War on Terror nonstop in the media, both on television and in print. Evenings while at home or at school, he sat glued to cable news.

Cate felt the change more than anyone else. For the first several months, she gave him the space he said he needed. After a while, she wondered if the real Troy had died up on that mountainside with his father.

The specialist who examined Troy told both his mom and Cate that traumatic falls can manifest themselves in various ways personality wise. Some people change subtly, while other personalities manifest dramatic changes. Even though many return to normal over time, a new normal is likely for most. The specialist said nobody recovers the same way, and the timetable for true healing can be unpredictable and long.

Still, Cate waited patiently, and she remained hopeful that the day would come when the tough façade Troy presented would fade and the old Troy, the one she had fallen head over heels in love with back in Psychology class their sophomore year, would return.

But that day didn't come...

Chapter Seventy-Four

Boise

Six months passed since the events in Bethlehem, Pennsylvania.

One day in early November, Cate met Troy for dinner after classes and brought up a conversation about their future. He had little to say. In fact, he did his best to change the subject. When she brought up the FBI and the future they had planned, he became almost hostile.

"I don't know," he responded when she asked about a move to Washington after college ended.

"You don't know?" Cate asked, bewildered. "It's all we have talked about for over two years."

"Things change," Troy responded gruffly.

"You used to tell me your love would never change."

"I still love you, Cate," he said, followed by a long pause. "But…"

"But you don't act like you do," she said sternly. "You never want to discuss our future. I can't even recall the last time you mentioned the FBI."

Troy noticeably rolled his eyes.

Cate continued, "I've been understanding Troy. I really have. I've given you time to grieve for your father, but now it's time to live in the present again. All you do is talk about Islamic terrorists and how they need to be stopped at all costs. You watch the news incessantly and read everything you can about the War on Terror."

Troy cut her off, "Look, I lived the War on Terror firsthand. I watched not just Pops, but others die at the hands of these fanatics. If it weren't for me, they would have killed countless American's."

"You're right," Cate replied with sincerity in her cracking voice. "You truly are a hero."

He cut her off in a stern tone. "No. Heroes are the ones who don't come home. I'm no hero, Cate, and I've never wanted to be called one. Pops and the others were the heroes that day." There was silence for a moment before he continued. His voice quieter now, almost as a whisper, "You know what I really want, Cate?"

"Justice," Cate said. She had heard him utter that word countless times since the events had occurred that fateful day.

Troy's eyes narrowed, "Fuck justice...I want my dad back."

Cate softened, "You know that won't ever happen." She reached over, clasped his hand and squeezed it tight. "Babe, why focus on something that's impossible?"

"That's why my fire burns, Cate. I can't let go of the fact that he'll never talk to me again, never impart his wisdom, or ever hug me again and tell me he loves me..." Troy's voice trailed off. He pulled his hand away from Cates in a quick motion.

"It's not fair," Cate said. "You and I both know that. Hell, everybody knows life ain't fair. But you also know your dad would want you to let go of the hatred. He would want you to move on with your life, pick up the pieces and fulfill your destiny."

Troy shook his head in frustration.

Cate continued, "I need you back Troy, I need your humor, your loving embraces, your hope for the future." She cried openly. "What will it take to get that back?"

"Time," he responded. A blank, emotionless expression on his face.

She frowned slightly, troubled by how the conversation had gone. It was not as she had hoped and prayed. "I can give you that," she conceded.

"Good," he replied.

"I love you, Troy Mathew Evans, and always will. I'll give you whatever time you need," she said. "Until then, I'll give you space."

Troy sat there and looked straight ahead as Cate got up and walked out of the restaurant. It was the last time they would spend time together until graduation day.

CHAPTER SEVENTY-FIVE

BOISE

6 MONTHS LATER

Boise State University commencement was held on a Sunday. Besides a few awkward run-ins around campus, Troy and Cate had not gotten together since November. They talked on the phone several times, and even exchanged emails every couple weeks, but not much had changed.

Cate asked if they could meet after the graduation ceremony. They met at the Spirit of the Broncos sculpture in the Quad at the heart of campus.

As usual, Cate looked strikingly beautiful. She had since the moment Troy had first laid eyes on her. He greeted her with a hug, and they sat down next to each other on a bench.

The conversation started pleasantly enough but quickly went downhill when Cate discussed what was going to come next.

"I'm supposed to talk with that recruiter at the FBI tomorrow," she said. "The one your dad introduced me to last year. He mentioned it was only a formality, and my application had already been approved. I'll be getting an offer letter within the week now that my degree has been conferred."

"Glad to hear it, Cate," Troy said. "You'll make one hell of an FBI agent. The counter terrorism division will be better with someone of your caliber on the team." He was sincere in his praise.

"And what about you?" Cate asked, "When do you start?"

Troy remained quiet for a moment as he looked off into the distance. He cleared his throat noticeably before he spoke. "My path has changed, Cate. The events of last year made me look deep within myself and went a different direction."

"Excuse me?" She asked as the shock was evident in her voice.

Troy stayed silent.

She continued, "Being an FBI agent is all you ever wanted. Following your dad has been your life's ambition. You've never spoken of anything else since the first day we met."

Troy looked up and down several times and finally made direct eye contact with Cate. "I can't let go of it, Cate, no matter how hard I try. It fills my waking thoughts and haunts my dreams. It's all encompassing."

"What? What is it you can't let go of?" She asked in a pleading tone.

He looked back down for a moment before he looked up and locked eyes with her once more. He spoke in an eerily quiet voice, "My vengeance."

"I thought vengeance was the Lord's?"

"Not this time," Troy said as he shook his head. "It belongs to me, now."

Cate sat there bewildered, "You killed the guys responsible for your dad's death. Hell, you put your knife through Muhammad Jarah's throat. What else do you hope to achieve? You can't kill him again."

"No, I can't kill him again. But I can kill the others. The ones we fight in the War on Terror."

Her bewilderment turned to frustration, "So you're gonna do what? Join the military or something and be all you can be?"

Troy didn't speak, but he nodded his head, indicating yes.

For several minutes, Cate and Troy just sat there. Her gaze never left his eyes, although he repeatedly looked away.

Troy was clearly uncomfortable.

Finally, she asked, "Army?"

"Yes," he said.

"When do you leave?"

"In the morning."

She knew the words would have no effect, but still she pleaded, "Can I talk you out of this?"

"No," he replied stoically.

Tears flowed down her face, "I can't follow you on this path you're going down, Troy. I made promises to you a long time ago. Promises I still intend to keep. But what you're talking about doing is leading us in two very different directions."

"I understand," he said. "I don't expect you to follow me. This is my burden to bear."

"It doesn't have to be," she pleaded one more time as she reached over and took his hands and held them in hers. They felt cool to the touch. They had always felt warm and comforting in the past.

A few more moments of awkward silence passed.

Troy looked into her eyes and simply said, "I'll always love you, Cate, but this is something I need to pursue. Justice must be served, innocent lives must be protected, retribution must be delivered."

She shook her head, frustration evident on her face. Her body was tense as she released his hands. She tried one final time. "It's either me or your vengeance, Troy. You can't have both."

Troy nodded and in a whisper replied, "I know." For months, he was aware this moment would come. After a few quiet moments, he stood up and looked at the sky. He let the warm sun beat down on his face before he walked away towards the Boise River.

Cate didn't call out, didn't utter a word. She just watched him until he disappeared into the distance.

It broke her heart when he never looked back.

EPILOGUE

MANY YEARS LATER...

A blustery winter day greeted Troy as he returned from another eight-month deployment to Afghanistan. Unlike other soldiers, his return was met with no fanfare. No wife, children, or significant other waited for him. He returned to his simple, sparsely furnished apartment in Clarksville, Tennessee which borders Fort Campbell.

The first weekend passed quickly, Monday arrived back on post at 6 AM. After his early morning physical training (PT) he sat in his office filling out paperwork. The Army has a well-earned reputation for having mountains of paperwork that always must be completed "yesterday". Troy settled into his worn office chair when a loud rap shook at his office door.

"Enter," he instructed without even stopping to look up. No doubt one of his men decided first thing Monday to bitch about one thing or another.

"Captain Evans," a young sergeant assigned to his ODA team peeked his head into the office space.

"Yes, what is it Rogers, I'm up to by eyeballs with paperwork here, what do you need?"

"Actually, I was asked to grab you sir, there is someone to see you, and I was told to get you ASAP."

"So, who is it?" Troy asked.

"A colonel something or another sir, I didn't catch his name. He is waiting for you in the conference room across from the lieutenant colonel's office, sir."

"Jesus, what did you jackasses do this time to get me in trouble? Very well, tell Colonel something or other I will be there in four minutes, I need to hit the head first."

Four minutes later, Troy entered the conference room and came face to face with a man he had never met before. He looked vaguely familiar, but he could not place how he might know him.

Little did Troy know at that moment that man was about to change the course of not only his Army career, but more significantly, his life.

—⟨O⟩—

Captain Evans stood before the colonel. "Sir, you wished to see me?" He asked the unknown superior officer.

The colonel reached out his hand, and Troy took it and returned the firm handshake. "Colonel William S. Marshall, it's a pleasure to finally meet you, Captain Evans. I've heard a lot about you."

"I'd say likewise, but you have me at a disadvantage, sir. You clearly know something about me, but I don't know you. What's this about, Colonel Marshall?" Troy had a moderately perplexed look on his face as he asked the question.

A wry grin formed at the corner of the colonel's lips. "Son, I'm here to offer you a job."

"I have one already, sir," Troy responded in a firm tone.

"Not like what I am about to propose."

Troy arched his back and then leaned forward slightly, "I'm listening, colonel."

"I'm here to recruit you to a brand-new unit nobody has ever heard of, which technically does not exist."

"This is secret squirrel type of stuff?"

"No, son, this is far beyond the silly things soldiers whisper in the chow hall or while they are stuck in the back of a Humvee for God knows how many hours. I'm here to bring you into the fold of The Omega Group!"

———◆O◆———

THE END

———◆O◆———

THE OMEGA GROUP WILL RETURN

— · —

ACKNOWLEDGMENTS

My 6th published work, *DREXEL,* had its beginnings back in 2015 under the working title, The Zechariah Option. I know what you are saying, what a horrible title for a book! Let me take a step back and say the first book I ever completed in 2014 was called Vengeance. A much better title for a thriller. As I crafted that story and the main protagonist, Troy Evans, I had to create his backstory. When I finally put the pieces together and understood why someone would choose the path of vengeance, I had the makings for another novel. After I completed Vengeance and began the arduous process of getting an agent - which went nowhere for almost two years - I began my second novel, The Zechariah Option. Over the next few years, I completed a third novel in the series and still encountered nothing from the publishing industry except rejection and closed doors. At that point, I pivoted, placed the three complete novels to the side and came up with a whole new concept. That fourth book from day one was titled *THE BODY MAN* before I even wrote a single word.

As I created these new characters and a whole new world, a piece of me always thought back to Troy Evans and the three books I created from 2014 to 2017. After a bumpy ride getting published and going with a small publisher, I learned many valuable lessons. When the publisher went out of business and I got the rights back for *THE BODY MAN,* I created my Indie Book Publishing Imprint, **BruNoe Media Publishing**. For those who wonder where the name came from my son is named Bruce and my daughter is Noelle, so I used the first three letters in both of their names, I had my company name, **BruNoe**. See, it's not a mafia inspired name after all.

With my imprint established and a successful series under my belt, I felt confident in going back to the novels I created early on and breathing new life into them since I had learned so much and grew as a wordsmith (at least I hope so). During 2023/2024 I went back to earlier writings, and released the 1st two books in The OMEGA GROUP Series featuring Troy Evans, *Ransomed Daughter* and *Babylon Will Rise*. I reread The Zechariah Option last year and decided to change the story while fixing some of the glaring issues from when I was so new to the writing process. Creating a new title was also on the agenda, and after constructing a long list of possible new titles I can credit my son Bruce with homing in on the title, *DREXEL*, from the choices I presented.

My goal with Troy Evans dates all the way back to 2014 when I wrote Vengeance, and wanted to create a likeable yet relatable character. Troy was never gonna be the alpha male who could get shot, blown up, and tossed from a helicopter all in the first few chapters of a book. Nothing against those characters or the writers who create them, goodness knows I ate up that type of protagonist as a young man, but I wanted to do something different when I created Troy. I hope that comes across in the pages he shows up in with The OMEGA GROUP Series of novels.

⸺◆⸺

Writing is normally a solitary endeavor; however, people help in the overall process from inception to finished product. It's an honor to share in the achievement of publishing books with so many family members, friends, and writing acquaintances who have supported me over the years. I put these words in most my acknowledgments but it's good to remind my kids, readers, and especially myself that, "Life's a Journey, Not a Destination."

Above all, thank you to **I AM** for the gifts you've given me and my family.

Bruce and **Noelle**. I love you both. It's an honor to be your dad, and watch both of you grow into such amazing young people. I can't believe you both started college/high school this past fall, not sure where the time goes but I'm grateful for every moment I get to spend with both of you. As long as I have breath in my lungs, I'll be your fiercest advocate.

My **Mom – Patty** has always been my biggest supporter.

My **Dad – Tom** Not sure I would have cared for reading as much if it wasn't for your influence.

Jackie, **Shawn**, **Meadow**, **(Niece #2)** Love you all.

My brother **Brett,** and his wife **Alli.** Congrats to the newlyweds, keep those date nights sacred, and always be on the lookout for the next adventure.

Aunt Sue. You've always supported me and my dreams.

Grateful for the rest of my **Family**.

DREXEL is dedicated to all those who responded to the terrorist acts on 9/11 and the days that followed. I wondered for years if I could publish a book that had an element of the World Trade Center site as part of its plot especially since so many people lost their lives. Not only on that fateful day, but in the weeks, months, and years to come because of the health complications that arose for those who worked at the site. Hopefully, I handled the situation tastefully and with respect. Even now, over twenty-four years later, there are so many unknowns about that day. And while the internet has propagated wild conspiracy theories, there are some coincidences and unexplained details that make a thriller writer look for connections while wondering if we will ever know the full story of what happened around such a monumental time in our country's history.

Max Council/The Pope one of my first readers and oldest of friends.

TC Thompson/Mr. President From meeting when our sons were in pre-school together to now having freshmen in college, it's been a quick but eventful journey.

Grateful for the **Annual Latina Invitational Golf Trip Crew &** the **Troop 610 Dads**.

I get a lot of joy when including cameos in the pages of my books. For *DREXEL* I included: **Marty Thomas** – A fellow Troop 610 Dad, **Lexi (LeClair) Rines** – Her mom and I have been friends for decades, and **Donny Hayden** – my cousin who I've not seen in ages (sorry cuz but someone has to die in the stories).

Thank you to **Kashif Hussain**, & Col **Steve Thomas** at **Best Thriller Books** for their *SUPREME JUSTICE* reviews. Also, grateful to **James Abt** for the cover reveal.

I read a lot of books as a young man, and two literary giants in particular forged the path I now follow: **Tom Clancy** & **Vince Flynn.** RIP.

More than 10 years into my writing journey and many authors/creators continue to inspire, challenge, and teach me lessons on a regular basis: **Adam Hamdy, Charles Hack, David Darling, Mike Mason, Brad Meltzer, Sam Whitfield, Terrence McCauley, John Guarnieri, Kyle Steele, Jack Carr, Dony Jay, Tony Tata, Jeff Clark, Eric Bass, Ama Adair, Richard Maverick, F.X. Regan, Matthew Leone, Terrance Layhew, Travis Davis, David Buzan, Michael Carlson, Lori Twining, J.B. Stevens, Kyle Mills, Steve Stratton,** and **Dr. Jason Piccolo**

Grateful for all those people who graciously agreed to read *DREXEL* and provide amazing blurbs/reviews and help spread the word.

Appreciate **Marisia Robus** for giving the manuscript a thorough once over and even a final pass before publication.

The awesome covers for *THE BODY MAN, BREACH OF TRUST, BABYLON WILL RISE, SUPREME JUSTICE, and DREXEL* were designed by **Momir Borocki.**

My author cover photo was taken by my talented son, **Bruce Bishop**, check out his Instagram page *@brucebishopphotos* to see his other photo projects.

Blessed to own an Indie Book Publishing Imprint, **BruNoe Media Publishing**, and I'm looking forward to everything it will achieve.

Thank you to everyone who picked up copies of *THE BODY MAN, BREACH OF TRUST, RANSOMED DAUGHTER, BABYLON WILL RISE, SUPREME JUSTICE* and now *DREXEL* since I became a published author in November 2021. It's beyond humbling to know my words are resonating with thousands of readers worldwide. So far, my books have reached over twenty countries and counting! In January 2024, I put my books on the **Kindle Unlimited (KU)** program, which is part of **Amazon**. Since then, my books have had around two and a half million page reads with KU.

If you read my books please take a few minutes and leave an **Amazon** rating and/or review (plus **Goodreads**). It really makes a tremendous difference to myself and all writers. Thank you for the support, I'm grateful you've given me a chance to entertain you with my stories.

Finally, life is a precious gift. You get to choose how you will receive that gift, and what you do with it. Make wise choices. Time is the great thief, don't squander what you've been given from **I AM**.

Onward and upward, my friends,

Eric P. Bishop

December 2025

About the Author

Eric P. Bishop grew up in Connecticut and lived in the South after college. Subsequent moves to the Rockies and the Pacific Northwest occurred before finally heading back East to raise a family.

After many years in corporate America, Eric turned his passion for the written word into reality and chased his dreams of crafting novels.

Eric lives in Western North Carolina with his children, where they explore the great outdoors most weekends, all the while he pursues his next grand adventure. He loves to travel and incorporates what he sees around the world into the stories he crafts.

Visit www.ericpbishop.com to learn more about Eric, his novels, and check out pictures of his amazing journey.

"Life's a journey, not a destination."